AUTUMN
DISINTEGRATION

Also by David Moody from Gollancz:

Hater
Dog Blood
Them or Us

Autumn
Autumn: The City
Autumn: Purification

AUTUMN
DISINTEGRATION

DAVID MOODY

GOLLANCZ

LONDON

The right of David Moody to be identified as the author of this
work has been asserted by him in accordance with the
Copyright, Designs and Patents Act 1988.

First published in Great Britain in 2011 by Gollancz
An imprint of the Orion Publishing Group
Orion House, 5 Upper St Martin's Lane, London WC2H 9EA
An Hachette UK Company

A CIP catalogue record for this book is available
from the British Library

ISBN 978 0 575 09142 9 (Cased)
ISBN 978 0 575 09143 6 (Trade Paperback)

3 5 7 9 10 8 6 4 2

Typeset at the Spartan Press Ltd,
Lymington, Hants

Printed and bound by CPI Group (UK) Ltd,
Croydon, CR0 4YY

The Orion Publishing Group's policy is to use papers
that are natural, renewable and recyclable products and
made from wood grown in sustainable forests. The logging
and manufacturing processes are expected to conform to
the environmental regulations of the country of origin.

www.davidmoody.net

www.orionbooks.co.uk

To the original readers of my 'Infected Books'.
Thanks for waiting.

The Swimmer

They said I should have burned her with the rest of them. When everyone died I cleared this place out room by room, working for hours until every trace of dead flesh had been removed from the building. Except for her – the Swimmer.

I found her a couple of days later, when she'd just started to move. I don't know how I missed her before: poor bitch must have been about to take a dip in the pool when it caught her, and the doors had swung shut, trapping her inside the changing room. When I first found her she was shuffling about in the shadows like those on the other side of the boundary fence, constantly dragging herself from one end of the room to the other, backwards and forward, walking into walls and lockers, tripping over upturned benches and other obstructions. She looked pretty comical crashing around, stupid almost, but I wasn't laughing. I was too scared. I still am.

When the others got here we talked for hours about getting rid of her. Ginnie and Sean were dead against the idea of keeping her inside the building with us, even though there was no way she could get out into any other part of the hotel. Howard and Amir came around to my way of thinking pretty quickly: it made sense to keep watch on her – Christ, those bloody bodies had dragged themselves up onto their feet after they'd been lying dead for days. None of us knew what they might do next. The Swimmer would show us – in a perverse way she's helped us to stay alive. Shut away in the changing room as she is, sheltered from the rest of the dead world outside, we've been able to watch her decay and change. She's shown us how the dead have evolved – what they've become.

The changes have been gradual; sometimes nothing happens for days, then she'll react differently to one of us and we'll know that the hundreds of thousands of bodies on the other side of the fence will soon be doing the same. None of what's happened to the world makes any sense, but what's happening to the dead makes the least sense of all: as they've continued to rot, so their control and coordination has somehow returned. It's like they're starting to think again, and make decisions. Sometime soon I'm sure they'll reach the point where they've decayed to such an extent they can no longer keep moving – but when will that be? More to the point, what will they be capable of by then?

It was a week after the day everyone died when I first realised she was watching me. For a week her movements had been uncoordinated, random – and then suddenly she could see and hear again. Her dark eyes stared back at me whenever I approached. And when Howard's dog barked she reacted too; she lurched towards the window and hammered her hands against the glass as if she was trying to escape. As the days passed her reactions seemed to slow down. They became more deliberate and less instinctive. I realised she was regaining control.

I've spent hours watching her since then. Sometimes it's like I can't take my eyes off her, even though she disgusts me. I'm sure I saw her here before she died; I remember a once-pretty round face, heart-shaped lips, slightly upturned nose and short, dark-brown hair flecked with highlights. Joanna, I think her name was. Her subsequent deterioration has been remarkable. Even in here, where she's protected from the weather and the worst of the insects, I'm astonished at how quickly she has been reduced to a grotesque shadow of the person she once was. The colour of her flesh has changed from the white-pink of life to a cold blue-grey. Her skin has shrivelled in places and slipped in others. There are bags under her bulging eyes where her mottled flesh has sagged. Her body is almost turning itself inside out. Gravity has dragged her rotting guts down and now they're dripping out between her unsteady legs. Even from the other side of the door I can smell the stench of her decay.

It's almost two months since this nightmare began. Recently the Swimmer's behaviour has changed again. Perhaps it's my imagination, but she seems more aware than ever now – not just more aware of me and the others but more *self-aware* too. I don't know if she has any memory of who she used to be, or if she understands what she has become, but whatever she does or doesn't know, a couple of days ago I swear I caught her trying to open the door. I found her leaning up against it, banging her right hand down on the handle repeatedly. She eventually noticed me standing at the window and stopped. She looked at me for a few seconds, then she stumbled back into the shadows. If she'd run at the glass I'd have been less concerned, but she didn't: she actually moved away. She saw that I was watching her and she tried to hide.

Yesterday afternoon, for a short time, she stood in the middle of the room looking back at me through the window. I couldn't take my eyes off her grotesque face and I found myself wondering again who she might have been before she died. Does she see me and remember what she once was, or does she see me as a threat? Am I her enemy?

I've begun to hate her. She's one corpse in a world filled with millions, but because she's in here with us, I've begun to focus all my pain and frustration directly on her. Sometimes I feel like she's taunting me, and it's all I can do not to destroy her. Yesterday when she was watching me I stood on the other side of the door with an axe in my hands for what felt like for ever. I wanted so badly to cut her down to nothing, batter her into memory.

But I know I can't harm her; we still need her.

1

Webb kicked his way through the litter behind the counter of the petrol station kiosk. Even though they'd been here several times before and had cleared the place out, he hoped he'd find one last packet of cigarettes, something that he'd missed last time, or a previously overlooked bottle of drink, maybe – it was always worth a look. Christ, what he'd give for a can of lager right now.

What was that? He could hear an engine – no, more than that, he could hear *three* engines: the bike and both the vans. Bloody hell, they were going without him! The fucking idiots were leaving him behind— *No time to think*. He scrambled back over the counter, plunged through the mess of twisted metal and broken glass where the entrance door used to be and ran out into the middle of the forecourt.

'Wait!' he screamed. Had they not heard him when he told them he was going back to check the kiosk again? He caught a glimpse of the roof of the Transit van as it raced back towards the flats, a momentary flash of sunlight on metal which was gone in a second, but it was enough to leave him in no doubt that he was now completely alone. Alone, that was, apart from a fractious mob of more than two hundred dead bodies fast closing in on him. The whine of the engines faded away into echoes, and all Webb could hear was his own panting. He covered his mouth, desperate to stifle the noise but knowing it was already too late.

What are my options? he asked himself. *Can't go back into the store – the back door's blocked. They'll follow me in and I'll be trapped.*

He looked around the forecourt and caught sight of the

green-and-yellow-liveried tanker they'd been siphoning fuel from. Could he climb on top of it, maybe wait until something else distracted them? It might well work, but it would take time, and although the sky was clear immediately above him, it'd been filling with threatening grey rainclouds all afternoon. And it would be dark soon. He didn't relish the prospect of being stranded on top of the tanker all night, soaked through and surrounded by rotting flesh.

So that left only one option: he'd have to run.

Webb surveyed the opposition and gripped his weapon tight. His baseball bat had four six-inch nails hammered through its end, making it a rudimentary but undeniably effective modern-day variation on the mediaeval mace. It might've been basic, but over the weeks he'd used it to get rid of literally hundreds of these vile, germ-infested bastards, and he was thankful for it.

Vast swathes of disintegrating corpses were advancing from all sides, so it didn't matter which direction he chose. He yanked the loose helmet off the withered head of a dead motorcyclist lying at his feet and spun around like an Olympic hammer thrower before letting go of the helmet. It flew towards the store, smashing through what was left of the front window and filling the air with ugly noise. The nearest of the shambling cadavers turned and began to shuffle towards the building, their movements in turn attracting more and more of the dumb fuckers, who followed like sheep, buying him a few precious seconds' breathing space. Webb held his position as the crowd surged predictably, then ran the other way.

He could still just about hear the bike in the distance; its powerful engine was louder than the two vans combined and he knew he'd probably be able to hear it until it reached the flats, which were only just over a mile away. If the streets were clear he'd probably be able to run there in ten minutes – the problem was, the streets were never clear any more. Between here and home there were thousands upon thousands of corpses, crammed together shoulder to shoulder, and one of the nearest had just lifted its bony arms and begun lurching forward in his direction. With a grunt of effort he lifted the baseball bat and swung it into the creature's chest, sweeping it off its already unsteady feet. Another swing, this time in the opposite direction, and two more swaying corpses were hacked down.

Three gone, he thought to himself as he started running again, *just a few thousand more to go.*

Christ, he hated the smell of these bloody things. The stench was always there now, hanging in the air like an ever-present fug, but it was a thousand times worse at close quarters. He dropped his shoulder and charged into the middle of the crowd straight ahead. Most of the bodies were too slow to react and they toppled like dominos, each one causing more of them to fall. Webb kept moving, leaping over their slow, grabbing hands as he held his weapon out in front of him like a battering ram, using its rounded end to smash them out of the way. A sudden unexpected gap in the crowd opened up as the repulsive remains of a forty-eight-day-dead traffic warden still dressed in the rotting remnants of its black uniform threw itself angrily at him, moving with a sudden burst of unexpected speed and ferocity. Webb had seen more and more of them attacking like this recently and he didn't like it. The faster ones scared the hell out of him, although he'd never admit it to any of the others. He couldn't understand how something which had been dead for weeks could be getting stronger. For a split-second he looked up into what was left of the traffic warden's hideously decomposed face before swinging the baseball bat around again and burying the points of two six-inch nails deep in the side of its skull.

Shit! It was stuck! He'd hit the body with such force that the sharp metal spikes were wedged tight into the bony skull and he couldn't get his weapon free. He yanked hard, but succeeded only in pulling the thrashing body to the ground. It lay squirming at his feet as more and more of them closed in on him. He could almost feel their fingers on his back now; he imagined them clawing and scratching him while he was trying to free the nails from the body's skull. *Stay calm*, Webb thought to himself, struggling to keep himself from panicking. *They're dead. I'm alive. I can do this . . .*

He stamped his boot down across the throat of the writhing corpse. The dead traffic warden, now flat on its back with its arms and legs flailing wildly, glared up at him with a single dark eye. The other had been gouged out of its socket by the force of the baseball bat. Moving with frantic speed, Webb began twisting the bat backwards and forwards, all the time keeping the pressure on the corpse under his foot. As the other corpses congregated around him, getting closer with every passing moment, Webb yanked the bat from side to side and around and around in a desperate attempt to sever the head. Long-dead flesh, muscle and cartilage began to tear and brittle bone snapped and as the final few troublesome connecting sinews gave way and the body finally lay still, he stomped angrily on its neck. He took a deep breath of the germ-filled air, lifted the bat (with dead head still attached) and swung it out in front of him as he started running again.

Now, as Webb forced himself to keep moving, pushing his way through an almost impenetrable forest of cadavers, he recalled the conversation between Hollis and Lorna on their way out to the petrol station, less than an hour earlier. Hollis always annoyed him, but he knew Hollis'd been right when he told Lorna, 'If you're surrounded, do anything but stop. Stand still and you'll have a hundred of them onto you in seconds. Keep moving, and they can't get you. You've got speed, strength and control on your side; you can be gone before they've even realised you're there.' Webb was trying not to panic as he wondered how the hell he was supposed to 'keep moving' when suddenly all he could see in front of him was a brick wall. He changed direction and dived to his left. *Just keep moving*, he told himself again, willing his already tired legs to keep working. Another swipe of the baseball bat (and still-impaled head) knocked another trio of bodies off their feet, and those immediately behind fell over the fallen corpses in their hopelessly uncoordinated attempts to get to Webb.

Stupid fuckers, he thought as he pushed another pair of them away before dropping his shoulder once again and bulldozing through a pile of them, clearing the way for him to scramble up a slippery grassy bank towards the road. He cursed as he reached the top, shook himself and started to sprint again. His muscles were burning with effort now.

The wide carriageway ahead was packed solid with corpses. *Maybe it's not as bad as it looks*, he tried to reassure himself as he barged past the nearest few. The dead had such a lack of colour about them that it was sometimes difficult to make out any detail. Weeks of decomposition had eliminated many of their distinguishing features; different skin colourings and individualistic markings – freckles, tattoos, scars – had all been bleached away by decay, so that the endless crowds now appeared to have mutated into a single dead 'race'. Their ragged clothing was so stained with dirt, blood, mould and seepage that now they all looked as if they were wearing a kind of grey-green uniform. The upshot of all this, Webb decided as he threw a pretty decent punch at another one which had shown a little control and lashed out at him with gnarled, twisted hands, was that he couldn't tell whether there were a hundred of them up ahead or a thousand.

Just keep moving.

Webb found himself in a narrow sliver of space with just enough room to swing the baseball bat again. He struck out in an arc and made contact with the neck of an advancing dead pensioner, hitting it with sufficient force to throw the skeletal frame up into the air like a ragdoll; it also loosened the traffic warden's impaled head, and Webb's second swing was enough to dislodge the decapitated head completely. He watched in amazement, thinking to himself, *That's just about the most bizarre home run I'll ever score!* as the head went spinning high up into the grey sky above the massive crowd. He followed its flight until it crashed back down to earth, when a sudden surge of bodies forced him into action again.

Keep moving . . .

The ground beneath his feet was unexpectedly slippery; when he looked down he saw that he was ankle-deep in a foul-smelling slurry of human remains. A mixture of nerves and adrenalin helped him keep his stomach under control, rather than reacting to the gross stench of the bloody mire. He knew that this appalling mud-slide of rotting flesh and dismembered body parts was, perversely, a good sign: this gruesome wake had been left by the bike and two vans which had abandoned him. They'd made their base in a block of flats just over the next ridge, and this grisly trail was leading him home, if he could just keep his footing . . .

No sooner had Webb had that thought than another unexpected rush of movement from the restless crowd caused him to trip and he landed on his backside, deep in the obnoxious mess. Webb gave silent, heartfelt thanks for the heavy motorcycle leathers he wore whenever he was outside. All around him an endless number of cadavers ceaselessly strived to get closer to him, slipping and scrambling over the remains of their brethren.

Webb struggled to get back on his feet as the soles of his boots kept sliding in the noisome muck. At last he managed to get onto all fours (doing everything he could to avoid looking down and seeing exactly what his knees and gloved hands were sinking into) before using the baseball bat for support and forcing himself back up. Panting heavily, he threw himself into the next wave of bodies, heading towards the top of the hill.

It wasn't far now: he just had to get over the rise and down the other side, then take the narrow track which snaked around the dilapidated garages behind the flats. Christ, what he'd give to be back there now. Thankfully, the frantic physical exertion was taking the edge off his fear – he didn't have time to be scared. Instead, he had to concentrate on moving forward, smashing his way past body after body after body: something which used to be a school teacher, another which had once been a chef, a car mechanic, a librarian, personal trainer . . . but whatever these hideous things had once been didn't matter any more. He didn't give any of them even a split-second's thought before destroying them with as much force as he could muster. He was getting tired now; the muscles in his neck and shoulders were aching, but he couldn't stop yet.

God, this hill is taking for ever, he thought, but even though gravity and the slippery slope had slowed him down, and at the same time the corpses seemed to be hurling themselves at him with unprecedented force, he'd almost made it. As he finally neared the top, he thought, *Maybe the other side will be clear and I'll be able to take a bit of a breather?*

Webb didn't stop running when he reached the summit but made the most of the velocity he'd finally achieved to power down the steep descent on the other side. Still holding the baseball bat out in front of him, he ploughed into an even deeper sea of constantly shifting undead flesh, silently repeating his mantra to himself over and over: *Just keep moving. Just keep moving . . .*

The huge crowd which now engulfed him was almost completely silent. These creatures didn't speak or moan or groan; the only sounds came from their heavy feet dragging along the ground, and the constant buzzing of the millions of insects which were gorging themselves on a never-ending supply of decaying flesh – and Webb's own laboured breathing. But just for a moment, he was sure he could hear something else. He swung the bat into the chest of a peculiarly lopsided corpse, then stopped when he heard the sound in the distance again: it was an engine.

Thank God, he thought, *they've finally realised they left me behind; they've come back for me!* With renewed energy he threw himself forward yet again, knocking a half-dozen scrambling bodies down like skittles.

The noise was definitely getting closer. He could make out two engines this time – the bike and one of the vans, perhaps – and they were fast approaching. There was a change in the behaviour and direction of the foetid crowd around him: suddenly he was no longer the sole focus of attention as many bodies turned and started to stagger away from him.

He was desperate to let the others know exactly where he was – if he didn't, there was a good chance they'd drive straight into the middle of the crowd looking for him, and might even run him over – he stopped using the baseball bat as a weapon and instead shoved it into the air above his head as a marker.

'Over here!' he screamed at the top of his voice as he anxiously barged through the dead, fighting past them as if he was the sole passenger trying to get off a train that everyone else wanted to get on to. He heard the van and bike stop.

'We can see you,' Hollis' distinctive voice yelled back. 'Now get your fucking head down and get over here!'

Webb knew what was coming next. They'd had to do this kind of thing before, after all. He immediately dropped to the ground and started crawling furiously away on his hands and knees. Speed was suddenly more important than ever now; he had to get as close as he could to the others before—

—a sudden searing blast of light and heat tore through the crowd a matter of yards behind him. He kept moving forward, ignoring the pain in his knees and wrists, as the bodies all around him began to converge on the area into which Hollis had just hurled a crude, but effective, petrol bomb. They'd discovered the cadavers were attracted to the sudden burst of light and heat – the stupid things tried to get as close to the epicentre of the blast as they could, oblivious to the fact that when they succeeded, they burned. Webb could already smell the corpses nearest to the petrol bomb; they were smouldering nicely.

Now the crowd had thinned sufficiently for Webb to risk getting up and running again. He could see the van and the bike waiting behind the gutted remains of a burned-out coach, parked at such an angle that the dead weren't able to get too close. He pushed through the final few figures and slipped between the side of the coach and the front of the van. Hollis lobbed another two bombs directly over his head and watched them detonate deep in the heart of the maggot-ridden mob.

'Idiot,' Jas, the bike-rider, snarled.

'I told Lorna I was going back in,' Webb said.

'We'll argue about it later, let's just get out of here,' Jas sighed wearily as he climbed back onto his machine, then, as Webb moved towards him, 'Piss off! You're not getting on here like that. Look at the state of you – you're covered in all kinds of shit.'

Webb looked down at his blood and gore-soaked leathers. With a grimace he bent down and picked a piece of scalp, complete with a clump of lank brown hair, out of a crease in his trousers and tossed it away with a look of disgust.

'You're not coming in here either,' Hollis snapped, looking him up and down. 'You'll have to hold onto the back of the Transit.'

He was too tired to argue. He picked up his trusty baseball bat and climbed wearily up onto the footplate at the back of the van.

Jas pulled up alongside him and shouted over the roar of the bike, 'And when we get back you make sure you wash yourself down before you take one step inside. I don't want to be stepping through your shit all night!'

Webb didn't respond. He tightened his grip on the bars of the roof-rack as they began to move away and looked back over his shoulder, watching the smoke rise up from the burning crowds. One of the dead, its clothes and hair aflame, had broken free and staggered after the van like the last firework on Bonfire night, dropping to the ground only after its last remaining muscles had burned away to nothing.

Is that the best you can do? Webb mumbled to himself. *Is that all you've got left?*

2

Webb was cold and tired and angry. He stormed up to the third floor and headed straight for the communal flat where most of the small group spent much of their time. He barged into the living room, almost tripping over Anita, who was asleep on the floor. She had her head on a cushion and her legs stretched out just in front of the door. Her grubby velour tracksuit was almost the same colour as the carpet.

'You left me,' he yelled when he found Lorna, 'you bloody well left me!'

Lorna was sitting on the threadbare sofa in the corner of the room. She barely lifted her eyes from her magazine.

Anita groaned at him to shut up.

'Yeah,' Lorna mumbled, her voice devoid of any sincerity, 'really sorry about that, Webb.'

'You stupid bitch,' he shouted, her lack of concern only increasing his anger, 'I could have been killed!'

'Now there's a thought.'

'Did you not even *notice* I wasn't there? Did you not realise the seat next to you was *empty*?'

Lorna sighed and finally lowered her magazine. 'Sorry, Webb,' she said, her voice now dripping with sincerity, 'the truth is I *did* notice that you hadn't made it back. The problem was, *I* was trying to drive a van filled with cans of petrol through a crowd of dead bodies. I could either turn back to get you and risk being blown to kingdom come, or I could just keep going. We both managed to get home in one piece, didn't we? I'd say I made the right decision—'

'You bitch,' he yelled, 'you wouldn't be so cocky if it was *you* who'd been left behind. If I'd been in the van—'

'Two things to say to that,' she interrupted, pointing her finger at him. 'One, *I* wouldn't have gone mooching around for fags when I'd been given a job to do, and two, *you* can't drive.'

'You always have to bring that up, don't you? You've got a problem because I—'

'No, *you've* got the problem; *I* couldn't care less if you could drive two cars at the same time. I just think you need to start—'

'Will you two shut up arguing?' Caron demanded as she entered the room carrying a pile of recently looted clothing. 'You're like a couple of kids – for crying out loud, look out of the window, will you? The whole world's dead and all you ever do is fight with each other.'

'We don't have to look out the window, Caron,' Lorna sighed. 'We've just been outside, remember?'

'And we're all very grateful,' Caron replied calmly, refusing to allow herself to be drawn into the same pointless argument they had on a regular basis. 'Thank you, both of you. Now will you please stop fighting and start trying to get on with each other.'

'Yes, Mum,' Webb mumbled.

Insensitive prick, Lorna thought. Caron had been a mother – up until the day she'd spent almost an hour trying to resuscitate her seventeen-year-old son Matthew, oblivious to the fact that the rest of the world outside her front door had just dropped dead as well. Still, she thought, at least Caron's trying to come to terms with what's happened, which was more than could be said for some of the others. She glanced over at Ellie, who was sitting in an armchair beside the door cradling a plastic doll which was never going to be any kind of a replacement for the seven-month-old daughter who had died in her arms that first morning of the nightmare. Everyone knew it was wrong, but Lorna couldn't bring herself to say anything. Webb watched her too, scowling at the way she talked to the damn thing, and how she tucked it into her anorak and kept checking it was warm, planting kisses on its cold plastic cheek. He thought she was a nutter. He might have a point.

Caron dumped the pile of clothes on the arm of the sofa and gazed out of the window. This was one of the few apartments in the block which was still fully glazed; most of the others had either been smashed by vandals or boarded up long before the infection made vandals a thing of the past. She found it hard to believe she'd actually ended up here – she'd driven past these flats hundreds of times before the world had fallen apart: this estate was the last place on the planet she'd ever wanted to live. The three grotesque concrete constructions had both dominated and blighted the local landscape for decades; the decision to demolish the dilapidated two-winged buildings which had once housed hundreds of underprivileged families had been announced by the housing authority more than a year ago, but thanks no doubt to pointless local government bureaucracy, bickering and red tape, they'd only got as far as taking down one and a half towers before the whole country – maybe even the whole world, for all they knew – had been reduced to ruin. They could have packed up and moved on to somewhere better, but they hadn't. Most of the others had been content to stay – after all, she thought, this was probably as good as they were used to – and she hadn't the nerve to break out alone.

Webb left the room again as quickly and angrily as he'd entered, cursing under his breath. He slammed the door behind him and the sound echoed around the flat like a gunshot. Caron cringed. Ellie held her doll closer, soothing her. Lorna shook her head and continued to read her magazine.

Caron looked out over the dead world outside, beyond the ever-shifting (and ever-growing) sea of bodies on the other side of the blockade of cars and rubble at the foot of the hill and into the far distance. She found herself doing this a dozen times a day, pretty much every time she looked out of the window. She traced her route home along the once-familiar suburban roads which were now barely recognisable. From her elevated position she could see Wilmington Avenue, and from there she counted the rooftops until her eyes settled upon number thirty-two, *her* house. Her precious home, which she'd tended for years, and where her dead son still lay on his back in the middle of the kitchen floor – at least that was where she hoped he was. She didn't allow herself to think about the alternative; she couldn't cope with the thought of her boy endlessly dragging himself through the streets like the rest of those vile creatures out there.

Her breath was misting up the cold glass in front of her face. She wiped it clear and caught her own reflection. She looked so old and haggard today, her grey-blonde hair limp and lifeless. She'd have killed for a hot bath and some pampering. She still had plenty of make-up and beauty products in her room, but what was the point?

'So how was it today?'

'Same as usual,' Lorna grunted, still flicking through her magazine.

'The neighbours seem a little more restless,' Caron said. She still couldn't bring herself to call them bodies or corpses, let alone any of the thoughtless, disrespectful expressions the others used. At least none of them used the 'Z' word. It was easier just to refer to them as the neighbours; then, in her mind at least, she could shut the door and close the curtains on them and forget they existed, just like she'd done with that awful man Gary Ross, who'd lived and died over the road from her in Wilmington Avenue.

'Some of them were a bit wild,' Lorna answered at last, after Caron kept watching her, waiting for a proper response. 'There was nothing we couldn't handle.'

'So what happened with him?'

'Who, Webb?' she replied, looking up momentarily. 'Just what I said: he decided he'd go off looting, so I decided to teach him a lesson. I'm sick of the rest of us having to risk our necks because of him. Bloke's a bloody idiot.'

'It sounds like he was nearly a dead idiot.'

'Maybe. He always makes things sound worse than they are. Anyway, it serves him right.'

Caron closed her eyes and leant against the glass. What had she ever done to deserve being trapped in this horrible place, surrounded by these horrible people? She looked out of the window again and focused once more on the grey slate roof of her house. She squinted, trying to block out the thousands of cadavers, wishing she could just make them disappear.

Wilmington Avenue was five minutes' drive by car, but number thirty-two and the world she'd left behind felt a million miles away.

3

On a fifth-floor balcony three men stood together drinking beer and watching the dead. A three-quarters-full moon hanging high in the empty sky above them provided the only illumination.

'Is that a corpse?' Stokes asked, pointing down into the shadows below.

Hollis peered into the darkness, momentarily concerned; the figure was moving with far too much coordination and control. After a moment he relaxed. 'Nah,' he yawned, 'it's Harte.'

Hollis watched as the tall man walked over to the left side of the building and looked through the motley collection of buckets, bathtubs, wheelbarrows and paddling pools the group had left outside to gather rainwater. He filled a jug from what looked like a large plastic plant-pot, then wandered back inside. For a moment everything was still again.

'So what exactly happened with Webb today?' Stokes asked, disturbing the silence.

'He's a liability,' Hollis said quietly, leaning over the metal railings.

'He's a fucking idiot,' Jas said from just behind him.

Stokes shuffled forward, manoeuvring his sizeable bulk around the limited space on the balcony so he could reach another beer. He snapped back the ring-pull and held the can out in front of him as the gassy froth bubbled up and dribbled over the edge. He wiped his hand dry on his threadbare cardigan, took a long swig, then bustled himself back into his original position next to Hollis. 'He's just a kid, that's all,' he said, stifling a belch. 'He's all right.'

'He's got to learn to keep himself under control, not let himself get distracted,' Jas sighed. 'We've all got to be smarter when we're out there.' He stamped on an empty can, flattening it under his boot with a satisfying crunch, then picked it up and pushed his way to the front of the balcony between Stokes and Hollis. He flicked his wrist and hurled the can out into the darkness like a Frisbee, watching the moonlight light its curved path downwards until it clattered against a half-demolished wall near the remains of the second block of flats. The sharp, unexpected sound caused a noticeable ripple of inquisitive movement within the ranks of the nearby dead. As Jas stared out into the night he thought he could see a sudden momentary swell of interest amongst the tightly packed corpses on the other side of the wall of rubble and wrecked cars they'd erected to keep the hordes at bay.

'We've just got to be sensible,' Hollis said, 'just keep doing what we're doing until they've rotted away to nothing. We're not prisoners here – we can keep going out and getting what we need when we need it. We're the ones in charge here, after all. Those things will only ever be able to get to us if we let them.'

'Webb's the one who's going to get someone killed – maybe we should leave him here next time,' Jas suggested.

'He's a bit of a loose cannon,' Stokes agreed, but added, 'don't write him off – he just needs to learn how to keep himself under control, that's all.'

'I've seen dead bodies in the streets with more control than him,' Jas grumbled as he stomped on another empty can.

'Don't joke about it,' Hollis said, leaning over to one side as the second crushed can flew past his ear. 'Did you see that one today?'

'Which one?'

'The one with the branch.'

'What are you talking about?' Stokes asked, confused.

Hollis explained, 'It was just after we'd filled the first van.

One of the dead came marching out through the middle of the crowd dragging half a bloody tree behind it.'

'Must have got itself caught up,' Jas suggested, sounding only half-interested.

'That's what I thought,' he continued, 'but I was watching it, and—'

'And what?'

Hollis paused, as if he wasn't entirely sure what he was trying to say. 'And I swear it was trying to pick it up and use it.'

'Use it for what?'

'A weapon, I guess. Maybe it was planning on attacking us with it.'

'You're worried about being attacked by a corpse carrying a branch?' Stokes said, smirking. 'Christ, mate, you're going soft! There's thousands of them out there, and they're all ready to gouge your bloody eyes out. I don't think we need to lose any sleep over one who thinks it's going to kill you with a bit of tree!'

Christ, Hollis thought, *Stokes can be a pain in the backside at times. Talk about being an insensitive, uneducated prick.* 'You are a fucking idiot,' he cursed, amazed that he was even having to spell out his concerns, 'it's not *what* it was carrying that bothers me; it's the fact it was carrying anything at all. Have you seen any of them carry anything before now?'

'No, but—'

'Exactly! The last thing we want is for them to start picking stuff up and starting to—'

'Are you sure it was carrying the branch?' Jas interrupted.

'I was only looking at it for a few seconds,' he admitted, 'and there were loads of them around us—'

'—so don't get wound up about it. It was probably nothing – like I said, maybe it just got caught up—'

'Maybe, but what if—?'

'Never mind *what if*,' Stokes snapped, 'let's just concentrate on what we know they're capable of, shall we?'

23

'And what's that?' Jas asked.

'Fuck-all!' he laughed. His bellowing voice echoed around the desolate estate, bouncing off the walls of the empty buildings.

'What I think,' Webb suddenly announced from the darkness behind them, 'is that we should go out there tomorrow and start burning them again. And this time we should keep at it until there's nothing left of any of them.'

'You're a bloody pyromaniac, Webb – you're the reason we had to go out there to get more fuel today in the first place,' Hollis reminded him.

'It's got to be worth it to get rid of a few hundred of them though, hasn't it?'

'Problem is, you don't get rid of *hundreds* of them, do you? How many was it you managed last time?'

'Fuck off,' Webb said, helping himself to the last can of beer. 'At least I'm trying to do something.'

'Seven, wasn't it?' Stokes laughed, leaning across and flicking up the peak of Webb's ubiquitous baseball cap. 'He takes two cans full of petrol right down to the edge of the crowd and he only manages to get rid of seven of them! You've got to try hard to be that useless!'

'It wasn't my fault,' he started angrily, pulling his cap back down, 'the wind changed direction before I could—'

'Funniest thing I've seen since all this started,' Stokes howled, 'you running away from that fire with all those bodies just standing there watching you! Bloody priceless!'

'At least I stopped them getting any closer,' Webb said grumpily.

'No, you didn't,' Hollis said quietly. 'They stopped getting closer long before you started with your party tricks. It's been days since any of them tried to get over the barrier.'

'Why is that?' Jas asked, suddenly more serious. 'Why do you think they're holding back?'

'They're waiting for Webb to go back out there,' Stokes said, still laughing. 'They're waiting for you to entertain them, mate. Or maybe they want you to light another fire to keep them warm!'

'Fuck you, Stokes.' Webb slumped against the wall and swigged his beer.

'I thought you were going to show us how to keep him under control,' Hollis said quietly.

'I am,' Stokes whispered back. 'He needs putting in his place. If we tell him he did a great job getting rid of seven of them, he'll be back out there tomorrow morning trying to do it again, just like he's the fucking Terminator or something.'

Hollis could see Stokes' point of view, but he wasn't convinced. He thought perhaps Stokes continually put Webb down for no other reason other than to make himself feel better.

'No one answered my question,' Jas said.

'What question?' Stokes mumbled.

'Why do you think they're holding back?'

'Who?'

'The bodies, you moron.'

'Well, it ain't because of Webb!'

Hollis stared out at the vast crowd of corpses. In the low light the thousands of individual figures merged together to form a single unending mass of decaying flesh. 'No way of knowing for sure, is there?' he finally admitted.

'But what do you think?' Jas pushed. 'What's your gut feeling?'

'That they're either too scared to come any closer, or they're biding their time.'

'Biding their time?' Stokes protested. 'What the hell are you talking about?'

'Maybe they're waiting for us to drop our guard? Maybe they're waiting for us to come out into the open so they can make their move and attack. They've got us outnumbered by more than a thousand to one, after all.'

'Bullshit,' Stokes said, 'they're not waiting for us.'

'Like I said, we should just go out there in the morning and get rid of the whole fucking lot of them,' Webb shouted from the shadows. 'And if we can't get rid of them, then we should just keep pushing them back until there's at least a mile between the nearest one of them and me.'

4

'Where are we going again?' sighed Driver, picking a lump of dried food out of his untidy beard and flicking it under the table.

Hollis held his head in his hands for a moment, then jabbed his finger down onto the map. 'Kingsway Road,' he growled, 'halfway down, going towards town, just before you get to the station. Haven't you been listening?'

'That's the old twenty-three route,' Driver answered, suddenly marginally more animated. 'I know where you mean now.'

'Thank God for that.' He made momentary eye-contact with Harte, who shared his concerns about Driver – Christ, they didn't even know his real name, did they? The man'd turned up at the flats in the bus he'd been driving when the infection had first struck. He'd picked up several other survivors along the way, but he had been disturbingly vague about what had happened to him. Lorna had been one of his passengers, and she had told Hollis she'd found a woman's carcase wedged under one of the seats. The smell of the decomposing grandmother had been strong enough for her to notice long before she'd managed to find her booted foot sticking out from under one of the front seats. Apparently Driver had been driving around with her rotting in the front of his bus for days, and he hadn't even noticed.

He'd been less than forthcoming with any personal details, so in the end they'd decided on the unimaginative label of 'Driver', partly because he still wore his uniform, but mainly because of his pre-apocalypse job. Good job they'd not had to adopt the same naming-strategy for the rest of them,

Hollis thought to himself with a wry smile. Jas could probably have got away with 'Security', and Harte would have quite suited 'Teacher'. Caron might have been quietly pleased to have been given the moniker of 'Housewife' – although he'd have bet good money that whinging, repressed Gordon, the warehouse manager, would probably have insisted they call her 'Homemaker' in a pointless effort to be politically correct. He decided he would have christened Webb 'Young Offender' and Stokes would be 'Failed Store Manager and Alcoholic'. Ellie, Lorna and Anita didn't have many distinguishing traits; by rights they would have all been labelled 'Unemployed' – and that, he decided, would have just been confusing. He didn't like to group Lorna with the other two girls, even though they were of a similar age and background. He liked her. She had more about her than the rest of them.

'What's the name of this place we're looking for again?' Harte asked, leaning over the map to get a better view. Caron looked at the business phone directory in her lap and ran her finger down the page.

'Shaylor's,' she answered once she'd found the right advert, 'wholesale cash and carry for retailers. More than twenty thousand lines, including a wide range of fresh and frozen food, groceries, beers, wines, spirits, tobacco and non-food items.'

'Sounds perfect,' Stokes chipped in. 'Maybe we should move in there. It'd be a hell of a lot easier than going out looting all the time.'

Jas, sitting across the table, shook his head. 'Have you been down the Kingsway Road recently?'

'You know I haven't.'

'It'll probably be crawling with corpses.'

'Isn't everywhere?'

'Can't we find anywhere safer?' Gordon piped up from his usual position by the window. 'Do we really need to risk going so deep into town just to get booze and cigarettes?'

'Last time I checked *you* weren't risking anything, Gord,' Stokes said. 'How long's it been since you last went out?'

'I've got problems with my hip; you know I have,' he answered quickly, rattling off his stock excuse. 'Seriously, I'd just hold you all up and slow you down. I've been on the waiting list for a replacement for more than two years, you know.'

'Well, you're not going to get your operation now, are you, mate? You might as well get used to the pain and start pulling your weight.'

'Let it go,' Hollis sighed. He was tired of having to act like everyone's dad, and he wasn't in the mood to referee yet another slanging match – and to tell the truth, he didn't particularly want to risk being out in the open with someone as useless as Gordon anyway. Five-foot-nothing, skinny as a rake, little piggy eyes – he seemed almost to enjoy the role of perennial victim.

'Sounds good,' Ellie said, sitting on the windowsill, cradling her doll and kicking her legs. Wearing shorts and trainers and with her hair tied up in bunches, she looked half her age today. 'Get me some fags, will you? Me and Anita are down to our last couple of packs.'

'Cigarettes are bad for you – think about your baby,' Stokes smirked.

Webb bit his lip and looked away, trying not to laugh.

'Where is Anita, anyway?' Jas asked, glancing around the room.

'In bed,' Ellie answered.

'In bed?' he repeated. 'Bloody hell, it's like a holiday camp here. What's she doing in bed?'

'She says she feels sick – she thinks it's something she's eaten,' Ellie said.

'I reckon it's just another one of her excuses, lazy cow,' Stokes said, putting into words what just about everyone else was thinking. Anita always managed to find a way of getting out of doing – well, practically anything.

The bickering continued around him, but Hollis did his best to shut out the constant, pointless racket and concentrated on the map spread across the table. They'd been systematically working their way through all the large supermarkets and stores on this side of town. Once they'd cleared a store out, stripping it of anything that might conceivably be of use in the future, they put a cross through it on the master map and moved onto the next. The strategy had worked well so far, but with every supply trip the danger was increasing. Their missions outside were taking longer, and thorough planning was necessary – but the problem was, Hollis thought, with this shower of tossers the risks were dramatically increasing too. He knew he could count on Jas, Stokes (despite his obvious faults), Lorna and Harte to a lesser extent, but as for the rest of them . . .

'I said, when are we going to do it?' Stokes asked, slapping his hand down on the table when he didn't get an answer, making Hollis jump.

'What?'

'Do we go now, or leave it until later?' Stokes asked again.

'We should just get it done,' Hollis replied. 'Let's get out of here, get back and then have a bloody good drink.'

5

Jas ran his hands over his freshly shaved head then pulled on his leather motorcycle gloves and pushed his Honda out of the front lobby of the flats. He wheeled it over to where the other vehicles were waiting. Hollis acknowledged him as Harte climbed onto the back of the bike to ride pillion. Lorna was sitting next to Hollis in the Transit, the larger of the two vans. She looked pensive, and was chewing her lip nervously, quite unaware that he was staring at her. He often found himself watching her – even now, quietly worried, she had a spark about her. She might be about to head out into the grim, unpredictable ruin of their world, but still she remained remarkably positive; she was wearing a trace of make-up, and she'd tied her hair up neatly. He'd noticed that she did something different with her hair almost every day; it said something about her that she still took pride in her appearance. He, on the other hand, hadn't brushed his teeth for more than a week, and despite the fact they'd looted ample amounts of clothing, he couldn't remember when he'd last changed his grubby jeans. It just didn't seem to matter any more.

The hydraulic hiss of the doors of the bus opening on the other side of the car park distracted Hollis and he turned as Driver let Stokes and Webb on board. Before disappearing inside Webb glanced along the length of the bizarre-looking vehicle. It had started out just like any other double-decker bus, but over the weeks the group had fortified it to the best of their limited abilities. Now barbed wire was spooled along both sides, to make it as difficult as possible for the dead to reach the survivors inside. Sheet-metal had been shaped and bolted to its otherwise flat front to form a rudimentary plough, perfect for cutting through the inescapable crowds which gathered around them whenever they left the relative safety of the flats.

The air which was so eerily quiet most of the time now was suddenly filled with noise as, one by one, the engines were started. Lorna shuffled forward in her seat, raised her binoculars and scanned the grey sea of cadavers. Even from this distance she could see that they were already beginning to react to the rumble of the machines.

It was the geography of the area around the flats that had made the ugly concrete building a surprisingly effective base. They'd no doubt have found more luxury and comfort elsewhere, but security remained their prime concern, and the longer they'd stayed here, the less inclined they were to leave. Their building was perched three-quarters of the way up a steep hill, which made it difficult for the bodies to get close. Occasionally some of the less damaged or decayed cadavers were able to drag themselves through the desolation to get closer to the survivors, but they were easy pickings when they did. Webb in particular seemed to take great pleasure in destroying them, although Jas, Harte and Hollis were always ready to take their turn. Behind their building, a multitude of streets led through the rest of the maze-like housing estate which had also been awaiting demolition, before everything had ended. Many of the houses had been boarded up, and there was a wealth of materials which the group had used to build makeshift road blocks, leaving only the most inaccessible roads clear for them to get in and out themselves – and making it all but impossible for even the most determined of corpses to reach them easily. They had become entrenched.

No one was sure how much of a difference it made any more, but it had become standard practice to create a distraction whenever anyone left the flats. Regardless of how much control the bodies had begun to exhibit, they could still be fooled. Fire had proved to be one of the best diversions; a little heat, light and noise was usually enough to take the pressure off whoever was heading out into the open.

'Ready?' Ellie yelled from Hollis' right, and he gave her a leather-gloved thumbs-up. On his signal she ran over to where Caron and Gordon were standing and started working. Hollis wiped sweat from his brow; Christ, he was hot. One of the worst things about going outside – apart from the unwanted attention of the rotting remains of the local population – was the regulation uniform they had decided to adopt: biker leathers, wetsuits, over-trousers – anything that might protect them from the slimy, germ-ridden decay which was gradually coating every square inch of the world outside.

Ellie lit a petrol-soaked rag and tossed it through the open window of a silver BMW. A puddle of fuel on the driver's seat and in the footwell immediately burst into flame. Moving quickly with sudden purpose, she ran around to the back of the car and, with the other two, began to push it away from the flats. They could hear the crackle and pop of the fire taking hold inside, and dirty black smoke was already beginning to belch out through the window.

'Come on,' Gordon grunted, his face flushed red with effort and his dodgy hip feeling like it was about to pop out of his pelvis. Ellie took a couple of steps back, then launched herself at the BMW again, finally feeling its wheels beginning to turn. It picked up some speed and, its interior now completely ablaze, rolled down the hill with increasing velocity until it had completely run away from the three people who'd been pushing it.

Breathless, Ellie stood with her hands on her hips and watched as it raced down the slope, bobbing up into the air as it hit the kerb, then juddering along a little further until it thudded into the barrier.

'Could have done with that being a little more dramatic,' Hollis grumbled, disappointed. 'I guess it'll have to do.'

'It should be okay,' Lorna said, watching through the binoculars as bodies swarmed around the part of the barrier closest to the burning car. Worryingly, she was sure that one or two of them were actually trying to climb over the blockade to get closer to the flames.

'We'll just need to make sure we—' Hollis began before his sentence was abruptly cut short as the quarter-full fuel tank of the burning Beemer exploded in an incandescent mushroom of flame, showering the ground with shrapnel. The sudden burst of energy caused huge numbers of diseased creatures to surge towards the epicentre of the blast. 'That's better,' he said to himself, and slammed his foot down on the accelerator.

'Here we go,' Driver announced to his two passengers in his monotonous, emotionless drawl. 'Hold tight, then.' He checked his mirrors and indicated before pulling out.

Stokes and Webb held onto the handrail inside the bus as if they were rush-hour commuters on their way to work.

Jas paused for a moment before following, watching the bodies swarming around the burning car. Many had been drawn to the flames, some had been crushed in the confusion and others had found themselves close enough to the heat to be set alight. But now he noticed others had changed direction; he was positive he could see six or seven of them actually trying to move *away* from the burning wreck – almost as if the damn things had realised the fire was nothing more than an unsubtle decoy.

He flinched as Harte tapped his shoulder and shouted, 'Come on,' his voice muffled by his helmet. Jas flicked his own visor down and powered after the bus.

6

'Almost there,' Lorna said, glancing up from the map she was gripping tightly in her hand. The windscreen of the van was covered in an opaque film of grease and dripping gore and she couldn't see much up ahead. Hollis had tried using the wipers, but all they did was to make the problem worse, smearing the foul muck from side to side, a gruesome rainbow arc of rot. He squirted screenwash again, managing to clear just enough of the glass to be able to see through.

'Turn left and we're on the Kingsway Road,' Lorna announced, not quite hiding the relief in her voice.

Hollis swerved around a tight corner, then put his foot down again. The Kingsway Road stretched out in front of them. Apart from the fact it was crowded with the dead, it didn't look anything like he remembered.

'What next?' he asked, and Lorna looked down at her notes again. She felt like the co-driver in a surreal nightmare rally, but she knew her assistance was vital: the never-ending waves of bodies made it virtually impossible to navigate by sight alone any more. On previous missions they had found the bodies were frequently packed so tightly together that it was almost impossible to see where the road ended and the kerb began.

'Keep going for half a mile,' she told Hollis. 'We go through a set of lights, then Shaylor's should be on our right.'

'*Should* be on our right?' he queried.

'*Will* be on our right,' she corrected herself, jumping at a sudden thump as a dismembered arm (or it might even have been half a leg) spiralled up from a ruckus in the crowd ahead of them and thudded against the windscreen. The bloody stain it left was a sudden splash of crimson-red in the midst of all the putrid yellow-greys and browny-greens.

'Nice,' Hollis mumbled, 'they're virtually falling apart now.'

'Just wish they'd hurry up and get on with it.'

Hollis looked into his rear-view mirror but couldn't see anything clearly. 'Are the others still behind us?'

Lorna turned and peered down the length of the empty Transit. She struggled to focus (the ride was increasingly uneven as they powered through and over the dead) before finally catching sight of the bright lights of Jas' bike between the crisscrossing corpses. Further back still, she could see Driver's bus, continuing to trundle sedately through the carnage. It was so big and heavy that it could move at a more pedestrian pace; it didn't matter at what speed Driver drove, nothing was going to stop him.

Harte was transfixed by his surroundings. Everything looked so different from when he was last here: both instantly familiar and yet completely different, like looking at the world he remembered through a filter of grime. He held onto the back of the bike as Jas jolted the Honda up over the kerb and mounted the pavement, skilfully weaving through a gap between an overturned hotdog stand and the front of a furniture store, then leaning the bike the other way to avoid the grabbing hands of a corpse. Until now, Harte hadn't seen as many of them this morning as he'd expected – they'd passed hundreds, not thousands. His theory was that the dead had gradually spread out like blood on tissue paper. But this godforsaken place had always been heaving with too many people – he'd taught at a school just a few miles away, and he'd always done everything he could to avoid coming here. Kingsway Road ran right through some of the poorest parts of town, and today the squalor and ruin here looked uncomfortably familiar. He could still see some of the pitiful residents of this densely populated hellhole, trapped behind the doors and windows of the buildings they were passing. Some of them were still moving, as if they were about to find some miracle escape route which had eluded them for the last couple of months. Others were standing slumped against the windows, pointlessly pounding their fists against the filthy glass.

Less than fifty yards in front, the Transit had slowed down. Lorna wound down her window, stuck out her hand and pointed to the right, Jas' cue to take the lead. He accelerated and roared past towards Shaylor's. The group of survivors might be volatile, frequently argumentative and even down-right unhelpful, but when it came to a mission, they could be surprisingly well-organised. They had developed a well-rehearsed routine for times such as this. The van dropped back, leaving Jas to get closer and suss out the building they were planning to loot.

After dodging a small group of cadavers which had lurched perilously close, Jas rode across the wide car park at the front of the building at speed. Harte spotted a signpost marked 'Deliveries' – perfect. He tapped Jas on the shoulder and pointed, and Jas accelerated along a straight length of road, no more than one hundred yards long, that stretched all the way along the side of the building down to a fenced-off loading bay. He turned a tight circle and rode back the way he'd just come, gestured for the others to follow and returned to the bay. Hollis skidded around the corner after him, while a short distance behind, Webb and Stokes held on for dear life as they approached the turning in the bus. The swarming bodies suddenly felt like the least of their worries – how the hell was Driver going to get the bus around the corner and along the gap between the side of the building and the fence?

'Bloody hell, are you going to get this thing down there?' Webb asked.

Driver grinned confidently, checked his mirrors and gently swung the bus around to the right to follow the others down the track. 'We'll be fine,' he said calmly. 'This is a delivery

bay, isn't it? So they got lorries down here, didn't they?'
He carefully shunted his massive vehicle a few feet further
forward, then hard-locked the steering wheel. He took his
time – he'd spent his life driving according to timetables and
regulations, and he wasn't about to start hurrying now, not
for anyone or anything. With a total lack of urgency – or any
visible emotion – he continued to inch forward, constantly
checking the mirrors to be sure the furthest forward corner
of the bus didn't clip the fence. He was oblivious to other
distractions – to Stokes and Webb, mumbling incessantly
behind him, to the endless stream of cadavers which had
caught up with the bus and were now hammering on the
back, to the rattle of the coils of barbed-wire which were
being scraped off the sides of the vehicle by the tall fence on
one side and the brick wall on the other. Where it fell, it
immediately entangled many of the bodies, and their flesh,
already ravaged by decay, was lacerated, stripped from their
bones by the countless, razor-sharp metal barbs.

Hollis had turned the van full-circle as soon as he'd
reached the loading area and now parked, the engine still
running, face-to-face with the oncoming bus.

'You get out,' he told Lorna. 'I'll plug the gap.'

They had practised this move before. Lorna grabbed her
weapon (a claw-hammer), jumped out of the Transit and
ran across the tarmac towards Harte and Jas. Hollis gripped
the steering wheel tightly as the bus negotiated the narrow
entrance and thundered past him. The moment his view was
clear, he powered forward again, hurtling back down the
narrow alleyway and annihilating the few pathetic carcasses
which had somehow managed to avoid the barbed-wire.
When he had almost reached the front of the building he
slammed on the brakes, and the wet remains of several more
bodies slid to the ground, dislodged by the sudden stop. The
track was a foot wider on either side than the van, maybe a
little more, so Hollis steered to the right and edged forward
again until he had managed to wedge the vehicle across the

full width of the road, preventing any more of the dead from getting through and disrupting their precious looting time.

He gave himself a thumbs-up and scrambled over the back of his seat and into the back of the van. It was a matter of seconds to open the back door and climb out, then he was sprinting down the track towards the others.

'Watch yourself,' he heard Harte shout as a solitary body slipped out from behind a rat-infested wheelie-bin in the furthest corner of the enclosed area. He watched it as it moved towards them with inexplicable intent. Just two months ago it had been a night worker here at the warehouse; a happily married father of four. Now it was a pitiful bloodstained shell of a human being. A fall on the first day after reanimation had shattered the bones in its right arm, leaving the useless limb hanging heavily at its side, swinging like a pendulum with every uncoordinated movement.

'I'll do it,' Lorna volunteered, striding towards the body with confidence, but found herself taking a step back, unaccountably shocked as it lurched angrily towards her, its broken arm flapping. Then she pulled herself together and moved forward again, raising the hammer and caving in its head with one hefty blow. The corpse dropped motionless at her feet and the contents of its shattered skull slowly leaked out over the ground, glistening in the sunlight. She nonchalantly shook the hammer to get rid of any gunk and returned to the others.

'We ready then, ladies?' Jas asked as Stokes and Webb finally emerged from the bus. Driver remained in his cab, door closed, reading his newspaper.

Everyone carried with them their weapon of choice. Hollis and Jas both had machetes; Webb his trusty spiked baseball bat, Harte carried a hand-axe and Stokes, bizarrely, had a garden spade.

'Let's just get on and do it, shall we?' Stokes said. 'I need a drink.'

Jas led the way. He pushed the door open and waited for a

second before entering the dark building. He held his breath and listened; there was nothing at first, then he could hear the sound of something moving close by: shuffling footsteps, maybe. As he took another step forward, he heard a clattering and crashing just ahead of him. So there were several bodies here at least, though it was impossible to tell how many yet.

'Anything?' Harte yelled from outside.

'There's something in here,' Jas replied, inching forward slowly. 'Can't see very much . . .'

'Be careful, mate.'

Sensing movement in the darkness to his right, Jas looked around quickly and with a single well-aimed flash of his blade, sliced through the neck of a cadaver which had been about to attack. It fell at his feet and he stepped over it to reach a second door. He could definitely hear movement on the other side. He banged his fist against the wood and almost immediately felt something thump back against it in angry response. Taking another deep breath, he pushed it open and shoved back the body that immediately launched itself at him from the gloom. He slashed through the corpse's neck, then propped the second door open with the fire extinguisher standing next to it and began banging the machete on the metal canister, making as much noise as he could.

'Come and get us,' he shouted, and his voice echoed through the vast mausoleum-like building.

There was an almost instant reaction to his words as, from the shadows all around, cadavers began to appear, all gravitating towards him. He quickly backed out through the open door.

'Any idea how many?' Lorna asked.

'Nah,' he replied, 'couldn't see much.' He cleared his throat and shouted through the door, 'Come on you fuckers! Get a move on! Get yourselves out here! We're wasting time!'

The first two bodies which appeared were almost fighting with each other to get out of the door first: a dead security guard, trying to push past the awkward bulk of a badly decayed but still grossly overweight female shopper. The shopper's slobbering mass prevailed and as it heaved itself forward it sent the smaller corpse crashing to the ground and trampled mindlessly over it as it moved towards the survivors.

'Fuck me,' said Stokes, 'look at the size of that thing!'

The group stood together in silence and watched the body as it waddled towards them. Its massively distended, discoloured belly hung heavy over the top of a pair of brown-stained leggings, and little shockwaves ran through its curiously lumpy flesh with every ungainly step it took. Huge, pendulous breasts swung down like bags of grain, almost reaching its waist, a tear in its shapeless T-shirt revealing dark-veined skin like blue cheese. For a moment no one moved, everyone waiting for someone else to take the lead and dispatch the enormous cadaver. The appearance of another six bodies from the building in quick succession forced them all into action.

'Watch yourselves,' Hollis warned as his colleagues lifted their weapons and began to attack. Harte was first to strike, grunting with satisfaction as he sank the blade of his axe into the neck of the body of a teenage girl. The force of the strike knocked it to the ground, and as it reached up for him he hauled it back onto its feet, then yanked the axe free and swung it down again at its now lopsided head, this time managing to hit the back of its neck and almost completely cut through its spinal cord. The body went suddenly limp and slumped against him and he tossed it away as if he was throwing out a bag of rubbish. He stepped back, almost falling over the legs of the huge corpse which Stokes was now doing his best to destroy by ramming his shovel repeatedly into the creature's grotesquely swollen stomach. Although he was slicing through its flesh and splattering its rancid guts everywhere with every strike, the damn thing continued to fight, its arms and legs thrashing.

'Go for its head, you moron,' Harte suggested, looking around for his next target, but Stokes was too engrossed in his work to hear him.

Lorna dragged another body into the space in the middle of the tarmac, spun it around and slammed it down on its back. Keeping a tight grip on its neck, she dropped down onto its exposed rib-cage, feeling bones crack and rotten flesh slide beneath her leather-clad knees. With her gloved left hand she grabbed hold of the corpse's chin and shoved its face over to the side before smacking the hammer down onto its temple, causing enough damage to its putrefying brain to immediately and permanently incapacitate it.

But still more of the hellish things were dragging themselves out of the darkness and into the open, drawn out of hiding by the racket outside. In the time that Harte and Lorna had taken to deal with one body each, Jas and Hollis had both disposed of several more and now the two men were stepping cautiously through the bloody carnage, dragging the dismembered remains of their kills out of the way and dumping them against the back fence. Hollis was watching Stokes struggling with his obese victim when he was distracted by a sudden yelp of surprise from Webb.

'What's the problem?' Hollis yelled, but he could see: the idiot had somehow managed to get himself backed into a corner by two of the dead, and although he was swinging his baseball bat wildly, he wasn't making contact with either of them – it looked almost as if they were deliberately keeping their distance.

'Nothing,' he shouted back breathlessly, 'I'm all right.'

'We don't have time for this,' Jas said angrily as he marched across the loading bay and grabbed hold of one of the bodies by its shoulder, dragging it to the ground, where it kicked and flailed furiously. Without a flicker of emotion he raised his machete and chopped down just above the creature's vacant eyes, hitting it with such force that the blade sliced right through the skull, taking the top of its head off like an egg. Taking advantage of the distraction, Webb angrily shoved the remaining corpse against the fence, stepped back and swung his bat around, burying the spikes in its face.

'I *said* I was *all right*,' he said as he yanked the bat free and let the body drop to the ground.

'You two finished?' asked Lorna.

Jas looked around. The only person still fighting was Stokes, who continued to struggle with the massive corpse by the entrance. The body's arms and legs continued to move wildly, even as Stokes was shredding its grossly oversized torso with his shovel. Much of the surrounding area – and his own legs – had been drenched by a layer of dark-brown gore.

'You fucking idiot,' Webb spat as he stormed past Stokes and stamped down hard on the face of the hideous aberration, crushing its features under his boot. It immediately lay still.

Jas was waiting by the door into the building again, peering inside and banging his fist on a metal storage cabinet. The noise rang through the entire building and echoed around the loading bay and surrounding area outside.

'Any more of them?' asked Hollis, standing just behind him and peering over his shoulder.

'Probably – there are bound to be a few of them stuck in there.'

As Hollis pushed past and disappeared inside he found himself struggling to see much in the low light. The others followed as he weaved his way along a gloomy passageway, pushing open doors which had remained closed for more than six weeks, until they reached the main section of the warehouse. Grimy skylights let in just enough light to illuminate the vast space. They were immediately aware of movement around them, but the shop floor was so huge that most of the creatures were still some distance away.

Hollis marched purposefully towards the nearest of the bodies and raised his machete, knowing they were all that stood between him and a decent-sized stash of food, liquor and other vital supplies.

'Fuck me,' Webb laughed as Harte dragged a heavy trolley through to the back of the store, 'just look at all that!' He stared at the boxes of cigarettes, crates of beer and bottles of drink piled up on the trolley with eyes as wide as a child's on Christmas morning.

'Instead of just looking at it,' Harte said, panting, 'you could try helping.'

Webb grinned widely and moved around to the back to help Harte push. Groaning with effort, the two men managed to guide the unresponsive trolley down an aisle strewn with rubbish and the skeletal remains of several shop staff, through a pair of swinging double doors which led out into the loading area. As they hauled it towards the waiting bus they could see Hollis and Lorna were already unloading another similarly filled trolley. Stokes was standing a little way back, leaning against the side of the bus, trying to convince the others that he was, in some strange way, helping.

Hollis picked up a tray of food, but he stopped and looked at Harte. 'You might want to try getting something we actually need while you're in there,' he said as Harte staggered towards him carrying more beer.

'There's plenty of room,' he replied indignantly.

'Don't forget about the others – not everyone drinks, you know.'

'We are thinking about the others: look,' Webb smirked, holding up a bumper-sized pack of disposable nappies. 'For Ellie's plastic baby!'

Stokes let out a roar of laughter, but Hollis was not impressed. 'You know what I mean.'

'There's plenty of room,' Harte said again, clearly irritated. 'When those lazy bastards actually come out here and start taking risks like we do every week, then I'll start giving what they need a little more consideration. Until then, we'll get the essentials, but I need booze – Stokes and I are having a competition to see whose liver rots first.'

'He's got a point,' Lorna said quietly as she slipped past and dumped the food she'd been carrying.

'I know,' Hollis admitted.

'There's *loads* of clothes and bedding back there,' Jas said as he stumbled towards them, his arms laden with bags. 'They've got *everything* in this place!'

'Then we should get everything,' Stokes suggested, still keeping his distance from the workers, 'and quick. The local population are starting to show quite an interest.'

'What?' Lorna asked, immediately concerned. 'Where?'

He pointed towards the back fence. There was a hole where several wooden slats had broken and when Lorna crouched down and peered through the gap she could see Stokes was right: there was a mass of rotting, unsteady legs on the other side of the fence. Hollis jogged back to where he'd left the Transit parked at the other end of the track. There was a large crowd of corpses gathering outside the front of the store too.

'Many?' Stokes asked when he returned.

'Enough,' he answered, picking up more food. 'We should get this lot shifted and get home.'

7

It was just after three in the afternoon, but it felt much later. The sun was beginning to lazily sink below the horizon, drenching the flats with hazy, warm orange light. The unexpected brightness combined with the heat indoors was almost enough to give the illusion of an August afternoon, instead of the post-apocalyptic late-October twilight it really was.

The frenzied activity of earlier in the day had slowed to a virtual standstill. When the scavenging party had returned, each person had taken a little treasure for themselves – food or drink, clean bedding, fresh clothes – and then scattered to their individual private places throughout the building. Jas sat alone in the corner of his room, looking at the remains of the best meal he'd eaten in weeks, which was scattered over the dirty carpet. It had all been cold, processed, high-sugar nutrition-free crap, but right now he didn't care: it tasted great, and it had filled his stomach, and that, he decided, was all that mattered. He couldn't remember how long it had been since he'd last felt this full.

The room was becoming dark save for a few shards of waning sunlight which squeezed through the narrow window just above his head, illuminating strips of peeling wallpaper. Despite its shabby appearance, Jas liked the isolation of this particular flat. He thought one day he might make an effort, drag some furniture in here, but until he could summon up the interest and the energy, he was happy to relax on an inflatable camping mattress. He yawned and stretched and rubbed his eyes. The efforts of the morning had quite worn him out. It was – what? More than six weeks on? And yet he was still finding it almost impossible to get used to this stop-start, stop-start existence. Life either ran at a snail's pace or hurtled along at breakneck speed, and there didn't seem to be any in-between. And the truth was, he preferred it when things were moving quickly. He found it easier to lurch from crisis to crisis than to sit alone in empty rooms like this and think, because thinking, he'd discovered, inevitably meant remembering, and that still hurt as much as it had on the first day. He slipped his hand into the inside pocket of his jacket and pulled out his wallet, which he carried everywhere with him, even though he had no need for it any more. He took out the last remaining photograph of his wife and children, which was sandwiched between useless credit cards and re-dundant bank notes. There they were: Prisha, Seti and Annia, still beautiful despite the horizontal crease in the picture which ran across their smiling faces. And just behind them, sitting with her arms around them all, was his Harj. God, how he missed her.

'Bloody hell!' a voice yelled suddenly from one of the other flats nearby, distracting him from his darkening thoughts. It sounded like Driver or Gordon – although, come to think of it, he didn't think he'd ever heard Driver shout or show any enthusiasm for anything – and it sounded like it had come from the shared apartment. Jas jumped to his feet and ran towards the source of the scream, tucking the photo back into his wallet as he moved. What had happened now? If he had to guess, he'd say it was probably a fight, most likely Webb and Lorna, at each other's throats again.

Jas burst into the shared flat—

—and immediately stopped and screwed his face up in disgust as the stench hit him like a punch in the face.

Anita was leaning over the side of the sofa, retching wildly. On the pale yellow carpet beside her was a puddle of vomit the colour and consistency of red wine. Most of the others were now standing around the edges of the room, their backs pressed against the walls, as far as they could get from the foul-smelling mess on the floor. Only Caron was brave enough to get any closer, but even she was forced to scuttle quickly out of the way as Anita lunged forward and threw up again. The sound of her heaving followed by the splatter and stench of fresh vomit made the bile rise in Jas' own throat and he struggled not to be sick himself. He backed out of the door he'd just come through, desperate to get some fresh air.

'Can somebody get me something to clean this up with?' Caron asked as she started to scrub at the floor with a strip of sick-soaked rag. No one moved until she looked round and snapped, 'Guys – come on!', and the tone of her voice finally prompted Gordon to start looking through some of the boxes of supplies which had been collected earlier.

As Anita began to retch again, Jas took the opportunity to get out, but as he stepped back out into the corridor he walked straight into Harte, who was coming the other way.

'What's going on in there?' he asked, concerned.

'Anita's chucking up,' Jas answered. 'She must've eaten something dodgy.'

'Something we brought back with us?'

'How am I supposed to know? Go and have a look for yourself if you're that interested,' he sighed, grimacing. His own stomach was still churning.

'No thanks,' he replied, gingerly peering around the edge of the door. 'She's probably just gorged herself like the rest of us. I'm not feeling too good myself . . .'

'What's all the noise?' Webb shouted, appearing at the end of the corridor with a can of lager in one hand and three more in the other. 'Jesus, what's that smell?'

'Anita's sick,' Harte replied, and watched as Webb stopped and considered his options. It didn't take him long to decide what to do next.

'Fucking stinks in here,' he said over his shoulder as he turned and walked away again.

8

Webb clattered down, spinning quickly around the turn of each flight of stairs. He was desperate to get out of the drab concrete building – having spent some time outside earlier today, he felt more confined by his grey-walled surroundings than ever, and the putrid stench of Anita's vomit just now had been the final straw. If he'd been able to drive he might even have risked getting into a car and disappearing for a while. Sometimes there wasn't much to choose between spending the evening with the dead outside or the morbid, miserable fuckers inside. The last thing he wanted was to sit there and listen to their tedious conversation, going around and around in circles, until someone got upset or started a fight, which was, inevitably, what happened. He felt trapped. The whole world was empty, and he was free to leave at any time, but he still felt trapped.

In the shadows of the block of flats, near the area where they collected rainwater, Webb kept his pride and joy. To the others it was just another car, but to him it represented escape – maybe not much of an escape, given that he couldn't drive it, but it was a place where he could be alone. It might not have been what he'd have *chosen*, not if he'd had more of a choice, and he knew his mates would have laughed at him if they'd seen the custard-coloured, old-style Nissan Micra, but right now it was pretty damn good from his point of view, because it was his sanctuary. He'd tried driving from time to time and had got as far as kangaroo-hopping up and down outside the flats, doing enough to keep the battery alive. Stokes had offered to teach him, but the thought of being trapped in this little yellow box with that fat bastard didn't appeal. Besides, there was plenty of time.

Webb climbed in, shut the door and turned the key in the ignition, just far enough so that he could switch on the CD player. A CD clicked and whirred in the player and after a few moments of silence, the inside of the car was filled with the relentless *thump, thump, thump* of high-speed dance music, played so deafeningly loud that it made the windows and door panels rattle and vibrate.

Webb pushed himself back into the driver's seat and pulled his cap down over his eyes, hoping for a while that the beer and the noise would enable him to fool himself into believing this was a normal night in a normal world.

After three and a half cans of lager and more than an hour's sleep, Webb woke up in darkness. The CD had finished, and everything was silent save for a high-pitched ringing in his ears. He felt a bit nauseous, so he took another swig from the can in his hand to make himself feel better. He looked out through the windscreen, and for a moment he was sure he could see movement up ahead. Who was it? It was rare for any of the others to come out looking for him after dark.

He struggled with the controls until he eventually managed to switch on the headlamps, on full beam. There, just a few yards in front of him, dragging itself forward on clumsy feet, was a single rotting body. He guessed it had somehow managed to break free from the crowds below, though God knew how it had managed to find a way over the blockade. He'd only seen a handful of them climb this far up the hill before. The repulsive creature's movements were painfully slow, and yet it had an undeniable air of determination about it. It had altered direction and sped up slightly when he'd switched on the lights.

Curious, Webb got out of the car and went around to the boot in search of a weapon. He'd stupidly left his baseball bat inside, figuring the less he took out with him, the more beer he could carry. He grabbed the short metal handle of the jack and walked over to the swaying cadaver, which was still illuminated by the light from the car. He stopped a short distance away and waited for it to haul itself closer.

'Come on then,' he said, loud enough to attract the corpse's attention. The monstrosity obliged, reacting to his voice by taking another few awkward steps forward until it was little more than a yard away. Webb lifted the metal bar, ready to smash in what was left of its face.

And then it stopped.

The corpse was standing face-to-face with Webb. *What the hell was it doing?* he thought. He'd never seen one of them stop like that before; they *always* kept moving, even when there was nowhere for them to go. For a few seconds he stared deep into the black, emotionless pits of its eyes. It had been male (he could tell from what was left of its clothing) and it had been of similar height and build to him when it had died. But its bottom lip was swollen and split down to its chin, revealing a gaping black hole, and a few remaining yellow tombstone teeth inside, which jutted out at unnatural angles. Its disfigured face was unrecognisable, *but who knows*, he thought, maybe I even knew this person? Perhaps this was all that remained of someone he used to hang out with or maybe it was—

—the creature threw itself at Webb, abruptly ending the bizarre stand-off. it grabbed at his face with clawed hands held high, and he responded with a single, well-aimed swipe of the metal bar to the side of its head, strong enough to knock it down to its knees. His second swipe did more damage, the third and fourth even more, until little of the head remained left save for a mass of bloody pulp and shattered fragments of skull and jaw. Breathless, Webb looked around anxiously, worried that more bodies might have managed to follow this one up the hill.

There was nothing. Everything was clear.

9

Both Stokes and Webb were up unusually early the following morning.

'Where are you two going?' Jas asked as they began to walk down the hill away from the flats. He shielded his eyes from the early morning sun which was shining on the ruins of the dead city in the distance. He always felt nervous when Webb and Stokes went off together like this.

'Therapy,' Stokes answered, sounding surprisingly cheerful. 'Webb's feeling a little tense today so I thought it might do him good to take out his frustrations on a few of our friends down below.'

They kept moving, forcing Jas to shout to make his next question heard. 'And what exactly is it you're going to do?'

'Still smells indoors,' Stokes said, being deliberately vague. He held up a plastic bag bulging with food and drink. 'We thought we'd have breakfast outside this morning.'

'Nosy bastard,' Webb grumbled as Jas continued shouting after them. They both ignored him and carried on down the hill.

'Ah, don't worry about him,' Stokes said. 'He's just trying to let us know he's in charge. Him and Hollis are like a pair of bloody mother hens. They nag me more than my old missus ever did!'

Webb smirked as he swung his baseball bat around, loosening his shoulders ready for the fight. This would make him feel better.

Stokes glanced back over his shoulder. Jas had disappeared – *Probably gone back inside to moan about us to the others*, he thought.

In front of them, the bottom of the hill looked like a series of interconnected bomb-sites. Hardly anything remained of the lowest block of flats, and over time the bodies had managed to encroach on most of the uneven land where the building had originally stood. The second building had been midway through its demolition when the sudden apocalypse had abruptly halted work. One wing had already been completely levelled, the other reduced to a windowless, skeletal frame. The whole area had been enclosed by a wire-mesh fence to keep vandals at bay. There were two large diggers on site, and once the group had worked out how to drive them, the powerful machines had been invaluable in shifting tons of debris – building rubble, broken cars and other wreckage – to construct an ugly but effective barricade between the ruins of the first two buildings. It might have been a bit uneven, but it had successfully kept the ever-growing mass of corpses at bay for weeks now.

Webb and Stokes reached the wire-mesh enclosure and Stokes lifted a loose section of the fence for Webb to duck under. Once he was through, he held it up for Stokes to do likewise, and together they walked out into the centre of the large patch of waste ground that was now littered with piles of masonry and sprouting weeds. They'd been using this area as a training ground: a place where Webb could flex his muscles and the older man could flex his vocal cords. Webb fancied himself a champion. Stokes fancied himself as his coach.

'How many you going for today?' he asked.

Webb stared out through the wire-mesh fence at the hordes of bodies held a short distance away.

'I'll start with five,' he said, adding with a grin, 'though the way I feel, I could get rid of the whole fucking lot of them.'

'Just see how you get on,' Stokes suggested, perching himself on a pile of crumbling brickwork and opening his first can of beer of the day. 'Take your time, lad. There's no rush.'

Webb continued to look deep into the endless mass of loathsome figures, eyeing up potential opponents, even though he knew it didn't really matter which monstrosity he plucked from the crowd; after all, one maggot-ridden piece of decaying shit was much the same as the next. He ran forward, peeled back a previously prepared section of the wire fence, scrambled through the hole he'd made and then jogged out towards the corpses. He climbed up onto the dented bonnet of an old black taxi, then reached down and grabbed the nearest body by the shoulders. It weighed virtually nothing and he hefted its withered frame and chucked it over the taxi and back towards the hole in the fence through which he'd just emerged. It landed in an undignified heap in the dust, arms and legs akimbo, but almost immediately it dragged itself up to its feet and began to stagger back in his direction. He paid it little attention, instead concentrating on plucking more creatures from the crowd. Many hands reached up into the air as if volunteering for slaughter, but he ignored them as he quickly hauled another four cadavers over onto the other side of the blockade. He jumped down off the taxi's bonnet and herded them back towards his 'arena'. For the most part they conveniently followed him, and as soon as they were close enough to the gap he shoved each of them through. If they tried to retaliate or resist, he simply threw them to the ground and kicked them through to the other side of the fence.

'Fuck me, look at that one!' Stokes laughed as Webb forced the last one in. 'It's got no arms!' he cried, howling with laughter. He pointed at the remains of a middle-aged woman stumbling back towards Webb as he closed and secured the fence. The pitiful carcase had somehow managed to lose both arms, one at the shoulder and the other just below the elbow, and the longer stump twitched angrily as Stokes said, 'Christ, Webb, fighting a dead woman with no arms? You really know how to pick them, you bloody idiot!'

'Piss off,' Webb snapped as he sized up his opponents. He

picked up his baseball bat and watched the five wretched shells as they slowly lumbered across the wasteland towards him. Their already unsteady gait was worsened by the uneven ground beneath their decaying feet and several of them fell over as they moved towards him, hitting the dirt with force, but immediately hauling themselves back up again. Not a flicker of emotion showed on their faces, no matter how many times they crashed to the ground.

Stokes watched closely as he slugged back his beer, lifting his legs out of the way as one of the creatures stumbled uncomfortably near. 'Take your time,' he instructed, stifling a gassy belch. He lowered his voice when the body that had just passed him turned back and shuffled towards him again, saying quietly, 'Nothing clever, son. Just take your time, do it right.'

Webb wasn't paying much attention. He'd already chosen his first victim and now he advanced quickly towards a six-week-dead fireman. It looked vaguely comical in its oversized protective jacket – it might have fitted once, but weeks of emaciation had reduced the size of the body considerably and it now looked more like a child who'd been wearing a jacket from a dressing-up box. Its helmet had slipped off its shrunken head and now hung around the neck by the strap.

With a sudden roar of exertion Webb swung his baseball bat around and thumped it up into the dead fireman's chin. The force of the impact flung the body up into the air and it crashed down at the feet of another shambling corpse.

Webb rushed towards the two of them with predatory speed and planted his boot on the chest of the body on the ground while swinging a wild punch at the other creature. More through luck than judgement he caught it square in the face with maximum force. His leather-gloved hand sank deep into its flesh and he quickly pulled it back again and shook it clean as the faceless cadaver crumbled.

'Not bad, eh?' he grinned breathlessly as he lifted his boot and stamped on the head of the fireman on the ground. Two down.

'Not bad at all,' Stokes agreed, enjoying the show. 'Watch out, here she comes!'

Webb spun around to see the armless aberration shuffling closer. It had a lopsided walk and an unusually melancholic expression fixed on its frozen face. Unusually, save for its almost translucent skin and myriad dark purple veins, the torso looked relatively untouched by decay and Webb found himself staring at its surprisingly pert bouncing breasts as it lumbered towards him. When it got close enough he rammed the rounded end of the baseball bat forward, hitting it right between the eyes and sending it sprawling back. He lashed out viciously again, and the second blow split the paper-thin skin stretched tight across its forehead. A third smack briefly exposed bare bone before Webb lifted the bat and hammered it down, splitting its skull and permanently stopping it.

'Too easy,' he said, wiping his brow, and without stopping he marched on towards the fourth carcase. This time he used the long shaft of the bat to attack, smashing it into the monster's right arm with a satisfying thud, then swapping hands and swinging it in the opposite direction, hitting the left side with enough force to shatter bone.

The body continued to advance, not able to understand why it suddenly couldn't use its arms, and Webb allowed it to get a little closer than usual – after all, what was the worst it could do? Stumble into him? Finally he shoved it away and swung the bat around again, this time smashing its pelvis. He'd already done more than enough damage to completely disable it but he continued to attack, and the corpse found itself on its back, looking up at the sun, unable to move. Webb continued to land more brutal blows on its ribs and legs, but he took care not to damage it above the shoulders. Once he was certain it was incapacitated, he stepped back and stared at his handiwork. The cadaver's head still moved constantly, just as curious as it had been minutes ago, but completely unable to work out why it couldn't get up.

Webb decided to leave it where it was. Rather than end its miserable existence, he would allow it to watch him. He liked an audience.

Now for the last one. He sized up his final opponent.

'What are you waiting for?' Stokes shouted.

'Watch this,' Webb yelled back, and ran towards the final corpse, swinging the baseball bat. He timed his strike to the head perfectly; weak flesh tore and withered sinews snapped and the partially decapitated head flopped to one side as the creature staggered backwards, then collapsed on the ground, flat on its stomach. The head was still looking up.

'Nice one,' Stokes said, throwing away his empty beer can and giving Webb a slow handclap. 'Here you go, get this down you.' He threw an unopened can over to him and opened another for himself.

Webb drank thirstily. 'I'm going to do a few more,' he said between gulps.

'Might as well,' Stokes agreed. 'Nothing else to do.'

The adrenalin from the satisfying – if one-sided – fight was coursing through his veins. Webb finished his can, then scrambled back out through the wire-mesh fence and unceremoniously snatched four more corpses from the edge of the heaving crowd. As before, he rammed them back through the hole in the fence.

'Take your time,' Stokes suggested, standing on the pile of rubble now so that he could get a better view. 'Fifty points for a kill, double if you do it with one hit.'

Webb grinned as he picked up his weapon again. 'Easy. Watch this.'

His next victim was hunched forward like an old crone. It was so physically deteriorated that it was impossible to be sure how old it had been when it had died – but six or sixty, it didn't really matter; it only had seconds left now. Using the cadaver's top-heavy gait to his advantage, Webb lifted the baseball bat high and brought it down hard on the back of its skull as if he was trying to hammer it into the ground.

The corpse fell face-down in the dust, twitched for an instant, then lay still.

'One hundred points!' Stokes announced. 'Good lad!'

Webb gave a bow, then turned and moved towards his next victim, ready to repeat the manoeuvre and double his score. Maybe he'd knock this one's head clean off its shoulders, he thought – but a sudden flurry of movement from another body on his right caught him off-guard, and though he spun around to defend himself, he was too late. He lost his balance and tripped over a pile of broken bricks as the corpse of a boiler-suited rubbish man grabbed hold of him. Stunned by the unexpected attack, he struggled to shake the creature off, watching in disbelief as the horrifically decayed monstrosity sank its few remaining yellowed teeth into the leather sleeve of his jacket.

'Jesus Christ,' Stokes shouted, knocking his beer over as he jumped down from his own pile of bricks. Although he usually did all that he could to avoid physical contact with the dead, he immediately grabbed the corpse, yanked it off Webb and threw it to the ground.

Webb pulled himself to his feet and unleashed a furious attack on the body, kicking its face repeatedly with his steel-toed boots. 'Damn fucking thing,' he seethed, 'you stupid *fucking* thing!'

The bloody body on the ground stopped moving almost instantly and Webb turned to deal with the remaining two corpses. Bizarrely, it looked like they were actually trying to move away from him. He ran at the first, grabbed it by a handful of its greasy hair and slammed its face down hard into a mound of broken concrete and twisted metal. This time he felt none of the usual satisfaction, just fear.

A short distance away, Stokes was gingerly pushing the last body away from him as he tried to summon up the courage to attack. He might be full of words, but he wasn't usually big on action, and he couldn't begin to match Webb's ferocity.

Webb grabbed a length of narrow-gauge copper pipe which was sticking out of the rubble at his feet. 'Get out of the way!' he screamed at Stokes as he ran towards the corpse and Stokes obediently did as he was told, leaving the last body standing alone, swaying unsteadily. Webb speared it with his makeshift lance, sinking the pipe so deep into its chest cavity that it burst out through the other side, pushing out the decayed innards that slopped down to puddle on the ground behind it. Unbalanced, its legs gave way and he made certain of the kill with a single stomp of his boot on its emotionless face.

'Did that thing actually bite you?' Stokes asked, standing over the fallen rubbish collector, and Webb gave a nervous nod of the head before turning and running back up the hill towards the flats. Stokes followed close behind with un-characteristic speed.

10

'It *bit* me!' Webb yelled as he flew into the communal living room, his voice close to breaking. 'The fucking thing *bit* me!'

Hollis and Gordon were playing cards and Gordon looked up from the table momentarily, but then looked back down again, uninterested. Driver was asleep in an armchair with his newspaper draped over his face. Lorna had headphones in and was listening to music.

Only Ellie showed any interest in Webb's drama. 'What bit you?' she asked as she changed her doll's nappy.

'One of those fucking things out there!' he cried, his voice shaking.

'One of what things?' She wasn't really listening.

'One of the bodies bit me!'

This time Hollis glanced up from his cards. Was Webb on something? None of them bothered taking drugs any more, mainly because they couldn't find any – but maybe he had found something in the warehouse yesterday? Or perhaps he was still drunk from last night?

Stokes' sudden appearance in the doorway derailed his train of thought.

'It's true,' he gasped, red-faced and fighting for breath, 'one of them bit him!'

'Did it cut you?' Ellie asked.

Webb, still panting for breath, shook his head. He held up his arm and pointed with his other hand to show the place. 'It just grabbed hold of me, here, and bit me,' he explained. 'Thank *God* it couldn't get through my jacket.'

'So what's the problem then?' Ellie asked, bemused. If he wasn't hurt, what was he so upset about?

'The *problem*, you stupid bitch, is that it *bit* him,' Stokes yelled, wondering how they'd ever got landed with someone so thick.

Ellie shrugged off the insult; she'd been called much worse recently. 'Are they going to start trying to eat us now?' she asked. 'I think you've watched too many crap films,' she added, putting the doll over her shoulder then getting up and walking around the room, gently patting its back.

'Are you sure it bit you?' Hollis asked, finally putting down his cards. They weren't going to get any peace until Webb had had his say.

'Of course I'm sure, you fucking idiot!' he screamed, his normally cocky voice filled with genuine panic and fear. 'It had its *teeth* wrapped around my fucking arm!'

'But did it really bite you? Are you sure you didn't just put your arm in its mouth?'

'Are you having a laugh?' Stokes said in disbelief. 'It *bit* him. What don't you understand? The bloody thing *bit* him.'

Hollis looked at him for a moment longer, then picked up his cards again. 'It didn't really though, did it? Why would it? Think about it – as far as we know they don't eat, so it wasn't trying to take a chunk out of you because it was hungry, was it?'

'It *bit* me,' Webb snarled, his fear now giving way to anger.

'Put anything in their mouths and chances are they'll bite down on it. It's an instinctive reaction, isn't it? Just the same as walking or—'

'It *fucking bit me!*' Webb's voice was so loud now that everyone stopped what they were doing. Even Driver moved his newspaper slightly so that he could see what was happening. Jas and Caron appeared from the flat next door. Only Anita, who hadn't yet managed to get out of bed that morning, was absent.

'What's the matter?' Caron asked, concerned.

'Calm down,' Hollis warned Webb, who looked like he was poised to erupt again.

'Calm down?' Stokes gasped, having finally got his breath back. '*Calm down?* For Christ's sake, man, just listen to yourself, will you? One of those things out there tried to take a chunk out of his arm and you're telling him to calm down? Can't you see what—?'

'It was just an instinctive reaction,' Hollis sighed.

'You weren't even there!' Stokes yelled at him.

'But like I said, they don't eat,' he protested. 'They're not controlled enough to be able to attack like that – like Ellie said, this isn't some stupid horror film; you're not going to become one of them because you've had contact with infected blood or anything like that.'

'How the fuck do you know?' Stokes growled.

Hollis rolled up his sleeve to reveal a seven-inch-long zigzag cut running along his forearm from his elbow to his wrist. The cut had been deep, but it was beginning to scab over and heal. 'One of them did this to me last week.'

'How?' Jas asked from the other side of the room. 'You told me you did it trying to move a car.'

Hollis shook his head. 'No, I said it happened while I was moving a car. I got scratched, that's all – just a lucky hit from a body that had lost a lot of flesh on one of its hands. It caught me with a sharp edge of bone.'

'Did you clean it up?' Caron quickly asked, her motherly instincts coming to the fore again.

Hollis sighed. Did she really think he was that stupid? 'Of course I cleaned it up. Look, this really isn't anything like the films you used to watch or the books you used to read: those things out there, they're just dead bodies. They're not flesh-eating monsters. They don't want our brains or anything like that.'

'No, but they *do* attack us, and they are getting smarter,' Lorna said, and in an instant the focus of everyone in the room switched to her. 'I don't know how or why, but they are definitely getting smarter, aren't they?'

'What's she talking about?' Gordon asked nervously. He turned around and repeated his question directly to her. 'What are you talking about?'

'If you'd actually bothered to come outside with us, if you'd ever done something remotely useful, you'd know exactly what I was talking about,' she said.

'My hip—' he began, immediately making his usual excuse.

'Fuck you and your hip,' Webb said angrily, 'you fucking waster.'

Gordon looked down and shuffled his cards again. He'd never been able to handle confrontation.

'Is that right?' Caron asked, her voice suddenly unsure. 'Are they really getting smarter?'

'Not all of them,' Harte answered, 'but some do seem to be.'

'And did it really bite him?'

Hollis made eye-contact with Caron and shook his head, the movement subtle enough for Webb not to see.

'I don't think it's anything to worry about,' Lorna continued. 'It doesn't matter how hard or fast they come at you, they're still falling apart. It'll still take a shit-load of them to cause you any problems.'

'What, a shit-load like the fifty thousand or so we've got camped out at the bottom of the hill?' Stokes grumbled unhelpfully.

'You know what I mean.'

'But what if they get up here?' Gordon asked anxiously.

'They're not going to get up here,' Harte answered quickly.

'Who says?' Webb snapped.

Driver removed the paper from his face and sat up in his seat. Gordon put down his cards. Caron moved further into the room.

'Shut up, Webb,' Hollis said, 'you're just winding everybody up. For the last time, that thing *didn't* bite you, and none of them are going to get up here. Okay?'

'One of them did last night,' Webb said calmly.

'What?'

'While I was out in the car,' he explained, 'one of them managed to get almost all the way up here.'

'So? It must have just got lucky.'

'What happened to it?' wondered Ellie, looking nervously out of the window.

'I beat the shit out of it, that's what happened,' he replied.

'So one of them managed to get over the barrier,' said Hollis, 'so what? The rest of them haven't – they're still stuck down there.'

'At the moment,' Stokes said.

Hollis looked up at the ceiling in despair. 'For crying out loud, will you please stop trying to wind everyone up? We're safe here. Nothing's changed.'

'You reckon?' Stokes said softly.

'Yes, I do,' Hollis said firmly.

'Hollis is right,' Lorna agreed, 'we're safe here. We just need to keep a close watch on things, so if something does happen, then we'll be able to deal with it straightaway.'

'I'm ready,' Webb said purposefully, a mask of machismo hiding the mounting fear he was feeling. 'I'll fucking *deal* with them.'

'I know you will,' Lorna said quietly, 'and that scares me more than the bodies do.'

11

'Pass it,' Harte screamed at Webb, who looked up and kicked the ball wide to Jas, who made a diving run forward and booted it straight at Stokes, in goal. The ball hit his wide belly with a loud slap and bounced away and he ran towards it and kicked it back across the car park.

Harte scuttled after it furiously. He was taking the game far too seriously. It took him back to when teaching football skills to the kids at school was all he had to worry about.

'You won't get anything past me,' Stokes boasted, watching him disappear.

'That's because you fill the fucking goal,' Webb laughed.

'Cheeky bastard!'

Harte reappeared and curled the ball to Jas on the wing; Jas dummied and swerved around Webb, who ran at him at speed.

'That's out,' Webb screamed. 'You're off the pitch – we said the line was level with the front of the van—'

'Piss off, Webb,' he gasped as he sprinted towards the goal. Stokes readied himself for the shot. Did he shoot high or aim low, try and swerve it around the side, or just kick it straight at him? Jas lined himself up for the shot, only for Webb to slide along the tarmac and take his legs out from under him. The ball rolled away, Webb chasing after it furiously.

'Go on, Webb,' Harte yelled, 'shoot!'

'You little bastard,' Jas seethed, running at Webb again, grabbing his shoulders and hauling him down. Webb stuck his foot out and managed to get in a shot before he fell. The ball bobbled up in front of Stokes, who ran forward and booted it away again. It soared over Harte's head and bounced down the hill.

Jas and Webb stood face-to-face in the middle of the pitch. 'You do that to me again and I'll—'

'You'll what?' Webb jeered. 'You'll let me get past again?'

'You little shit,' he said, lunging forward and grabbing hold of Webb's collar.

Webb squirmed, but he couldn't get away. 'Go on then,' he said, still writhing, 'hit me—'

'You blokes are pathetic,' shouted Ellie, pushing a pram across the car park. 'Doesn't matter what else is happening, there's nothing like football to bring you closer to each other, eh? Bloody pathetic.'

Jas let go of Webb and pushed him away. They continued to stare at each other for a second, neither prepared to be the one who backed down, until Harte broke the deadlock by pushing his way between them both to fetch the ball. He grinned at them both. He'd separated hundreds of stand-offs like this in the playground at school.

'Sort yourselves out, boys,' he shouted as he ran down towards the bodies.

Sliding tackles and bad challenges were forgotten as quickly as the final score of the ill-tempered kick-around. Although it was virtually dark, the footballers and Ellie, their sole spectator, remained outside. Webb sat on the bonnet of his Micra, his legs dangling down. The others sat on the filthy red corduroy three-piece suite they'd dragged out of a damp ground-floor flat several weeks earlier. Ellie was sandwiched between Harte and Jas on the sofa on one side of the car; Stokes sat slumped in an armchair on the other.

'So what are you suggesting?' Jas asked.

'Hollis reckons they're not a problem,' Stokes said, his teeth chattering with the cold, 'but I think they are. Like someone said, you're okay if you're up against one of them, but we've got thousands down there.'

'We could move on,' Ellie suggested, zipping up her track-suit top while she bounced her doll on her knee. 'Find somewhere else.'

'No point,' Stokes said quickly. 'It's going to be the same wherever we go, isn't it?'

'So what are you thinking?' Jas asked again.

Stokes paused before answering, 'Webb and I have been talking about this. We think we should try a little crowd-control.'

'Haven't we been here before? Didn't you try and wipe them all out once before?' she laughed sarcastically.

'Piss off,' he hissed. 'The wind changed direction. It wasn't my fault—'

'Crowd-control?' Jas said, ignoring their bickering.

'We think we should try and push them back a little bit.'

'And how exactly are we going to do that?'

'A bit of brute force and coordination,' Stokes said. 'We'll take our time, torch the ones at the very front, then use the diggers to shunt the barrier back.'

'And you think that'll work? Problem solved?'

'Not quite, but problem reduced at any rate.'

Jas slumped back in his seat, looked into the distance and gave serious consideration to what he'd just heard. He couldn't see much; the rest of the world was drenched in an impenetrable shroud of never-ending darkness but, given the scale of the problem they faced at the bottom of the hill, he decided that was probably a good thing. 'It's a hell of a job you're planning,' he finally said, sniffing and wiping a drip from the end of his nose. 'It's going to take time.'

'We've got plenty of that,' Harte said quickly. 'No one's saying it's all got to be done by this time tomorrow, are they? But I do think it's worth giving it a go.'

'Why now?' Jas asked. 'We've been here for weeks and—'

'Because they're changing, aren't they?' Stokes interrupted. 'You heard what happened when we were out there earlier.'

'One of them *bit* me, for fuck's sake,' Webb interrupted

energetically as if it was breaking news, although it was all he'd been talking about since it had happened.

'Look, are you sure you're not getting this a little out of proportion?' Jas wondered. 'Hollis said that—'

'I'm sick of hearing about what Hollis says,' Webb snapped. 'He's full of shit. He thinks he's everyone's dad and you know what he's like; he never wants to do anything until he's got no choice. If we sit and wait for him to make a decision we'll have corpses knocking on the front door before he's even agreed there's a problem.'

'So are they really changing?' Ellie asked.

'Go down and have a look,' Webb sneered.

'We know they are,' Stokes said, 'and the longer we leave it, the worse it's going to get. We need to get in there now and sort them out before they're capable of fighting back. We should get down there tomorrow and get rid of as many of them as we can.'

12

'I didn't think you wanted to play,' Harte said to Hollis as he followed him out of the lobby and walked across the car park.

Hollis covered his mouth and stifled a yawn. He'd given up wearing a watch several weeks ago, but he guessed it was sometime around six in the morning, maybe even as late as seven. It was a cold, wet and miserable day, but at least the long overdue rain was finally filling the buckets, pots and pans they'd left outside to gather water.

'I don't. I'll be keeping an eye on you silly bastards from the window,' he said quietly as he filled a jug from the puddle of rainwater at the bottom of a plastic paddling pool. 'For the record, I don't know if this is going to work, but I guess it's probably worth a try.'

Harte was a little surprised that Hollis sounded so positive. He pulled on a motorcycle helmet and ambled across the car park to where Jas stood checking the bike. Hollis looked at them both, dressed in near-identical leathers. Harte, tall and spindly, towered over the broad-chested Jas. They couldn't have looked much more different – they were both capable enough, but this morning he thought they looked like a bad comedy double act.

Jas looked up as Harte approached. 'You ready for this?' he asked. He sounded subdued.

'Suppose,' Harte mumbled, adjusting the straps of a small rucksack which he then hoisted onto his back. 'Let's just get it done, shall we?'

Last night it had sounded like a sensible plan, but now, standing here in the cold light of morning, in full view of the endless devastation that was all that was left of their world, they were beginning to wonder exactly what they'd agreed to. The plan was for them to go out and create a distraction in a bid to reduce some of the pressure at the front of the crowd, but Jas suddenly felt less like a decoy and more like bait.

Forcing himself to move, Jas turned his back on the huge expanse of rotting flesh stretching out below him and climbed on the bike. He started the engine, the spitting roar of the powerful machine disturbing the uneasy silence, and Harte picked up the can of fuel he'd prepared and got on behind him, hanging onto the back of the bike with his free hand as they drove away.

Stokes and Webb watched the bike disappear from the dubious comfort of the now rain-soaked sofa where they'd sat and talked last night. 'We should make a start,' Webb suggested. 'Get down there and get ready.'

Stokes opened a can of lager. 'Plenty of time for that, son,' he said. 'Plenty of time.'

Jas weaved around the back of the building, cutting between the piles of rubble and swerving around mountainous heaps of rubbish which had been discarded by the survivors during their incarceration here. He drove the bike through a narrow alleyway shortcut, then powered across an empty rectangular yard lined on either side with lock-ups and garages, through a gap in a chain-link fence and up a steep grass verge to the road, all without coming across a single body. Mind you, there were always fewer of them on this side; the steepness of the hill and the maze-like layout of the dilapidated housing estate meant that the dead were naturally channelled down towards the foot, rather than gathering in numbers up here behind the flats.

The plan this morning was simple: get far enough away from their base to be safe, yet close enough to create a distraction that would attract the attention of some of the huge crowds gathered around the bottom of the hill – they all agreed their work was likely to be easier if the corpses were looking in the opposite direction when they mounted their main attack. Navigating through the dead world was becoming more and more of a problem for Jas, particularly at high speed, but he didn't want to drive any slower, despite the relative absence of dead bodies on this particular stretch of road. He knew that he'd be able to get past any of the bodies foolish enough to get in his way at this speed; if he reduced his speed at all, the corpses would have a chance, albeit a slight one, of knocking him off-balance.

He hoped Harte was maintaining his one-handed grip on the bike as the powerful machine dipped from side to side, Jas steering skilfully around the occasional wandering cadaver and other random obstructions. He'd been here many times before, but the myriad streets all looked broadly the same, and as the world decayed, so everything was becoming less defined.

Jas zoomed down a long tree-lined road and finally spotted his landmark; they drove parallel with a long drystone wall which ran the length of a massive reservoir, then passed the silent remains of a once-thriving college. Even now, weeks after they had died, the imprisoned corpses of students pressed their decayed faces against the windows when they heard the bike approaching, looking for release from their dormitory and lecture room tombs.

Now Jas knew exactly where he was, and where he wanted to be. He'd ridden in a large loop which had taken them right around the back of the immense crowd at the bottom of the hill. Two sharp left-hand turns in quick succession, and they were almost there.

He looked up: he could see the block of flats above them in the distance, a dark, imposing structure silhouetted against the ominous grey sky. Although their distance from home was unsettling, he was reassured by the fact that, seen from here, the building looked rather like an impenetrable fortress.

As Jas turned left again, Harte felt his shoulder nearly wrenched out of its socket by the force of the bike dipping to the side. They stopped, and he flicked up the visor of his helmet. 'What's the matter?' he asked, looking anxiously around. He could already see several twisted figures emerging from the shadows on either side of the road.

'Need to work out how we're going to get out of here,' Jas replied, his voice muffled.

'Don't you think we should have thought about that before we came out?' He stared at a creature which was limping closer to them. A huge chunk of flesh was missing from its torso, almost as if something huge had taken a bite out of its right-hand side. It wore a pair of soiled pyjama-bottoms and slippers, and with every awkward movement, more of its putrefied guts spilled out of the hole in its chest.

'Are you listening to me?' Jas asked angrily.

Harte cursed himself for being so distracted by the monstrosity he'd been watching and the glistening trail of guts it had left on the road. 'Sorry,' he mumbled. 'What were you saying?'

'We'll go around the back,' he yelled driving a little further forward, then stopping midway down what had once been an ordinary suburban street, lined either side with unremarkable semi-detached houses. He looked up to make sure he could still see the flats (no point creating a distraction that can't be seen from up there, he thought) then gestured towards the nearest house. More bodies were hauling themselves towards them now; one group of three looked like they were actually moving together.

'Open that gate!' he ordered, pointing to the narrow passageway which ran down the side of the house.

Harte immediately jumped off the bike and ran down the driveway, pausing only to barge a particularly unsteady body out of the way, sending it tripping over onto the tarmac. He tried to force the wooden gate open, but it wouldn't move.

'It's locked,' he shouted to Jas, who had driven down the drive after him.

'Of course it's locked, you idiot!' he shouted back. 'Just climb over and get the bloody thing open!'

Inquisitive bodies were beginning to swarm down the driveway now, almost completely blocking the way out. Still holding onto the fuel-can, Harte hauled himself up over the top of the tall gate and crashed down into the passageway on the other side. He immediately picked himself up, turned around and slid the bolt across.

As soon as the gate was open Jas drove towards him, barely giving him a chance to get out of the way. Once he was through, Harte ran back and pushed the gate shut again, slamming it in the rotting face of a pregnant cadaver. The creature's distended belly, filled with the partially developed remains of its dead child, slapped against the wood like meat on a butcher's slab.

'Now what?' Harte asked, returning to Jas, who'd parked his bike on a patio. Weeds were already sprouting between the slabs they stood on.

'Now we move on foot,' he said. 'We'll cut through a few more gardens, then do it. That should disorientate them – and once we start the fire, they'll lose track of where we are. It'll give us a better chance of getting back out.'

Harte didn't argue. He followed Jas deeper into the long garden, moving away from the back of the house and looking for a way through into the next door property. Jas found a broken fence panel two-thirds of the way down and pushed it over and clambered through to the other side. Harte stayed close, running across the second garden and checking back over his shoulder to make sure he could remember where they'd started out from.

'Bloody hell,' Jas cursed as he crawled through a gap in a laurel hedge into the third garden, then stood up and walked straight into the dead arms of something which, from the look of its blood and paint-stained overalls, might have been a builder or decorator when it had been alive. It had been on the right side of the garden at exactly the wrong time for Jas. It managed to grab hold of him with its clumsy, outstretched arms and when he pushed it away it stumbled back, then pivoted around on barely coordinated legs and lurched towards him again.

'I've got it,' Harte said, and Jas stepped out of the way as he plunged a garden fork through the creature's face, one prong drilling through the side of its cheek and into the roof of its mouth, another gouging an eye then sinking deep into what was left of its brain.

'Cheers,' Jas grunted, stepping over the now-motionless body and continuing through into garden number four. In no time he'd managed to get through gardens five, six and seven, but Harte, still struggling to get across garden six (he was nowhere near as fast) yelled for him to stop.

'Come on,' he wheezed as he clambered over the final low fence, 'surely this'll do?'

Jas stopped and looked around, his hands on his hips. He cleared his throat and spat a lump of phlegm into a fish pond beside him and his spit settled on the surface, barely even causing a ripple in the murky water. He could just make out a few shards of orange and white in amongst the grey-green water, all that remained of someone's pet goldfish.

Harte was already walking towards the house, moving around the edge of a large, circular children's trampoline. The centre of the trampoline sagged a little where a puddle of rainwater had gathered over the weeks. He climbed four low steps up to another patio, then paused at the back door.

Jas joined him and peered in through the dirty kitchen window. 'Can't see anything in there,' he said after a moment, not really aware that he had started to whisper.

Harte tried the door; it was stiff, but a hearty shove with his shoulder was enough to get it moving and he pushed it fully open and stepped into the house. The building was filled with the suffocating and disturbingly familiar stench of death. His concern was not how many bodies he'd find inside, however, just how many were moving.

Now speed was vital. The two men didn't need to discuss the routine. Instead they immediately began moving quickly, Jas checking downstairs while Harte worked through upstairs, briefly looking into every room and ready to react if anything moved, grabbing anything they thought might be of use later. Apart from two motionless bodies curled up in bed together, the building was empty.

'All clear,' Harte shouted as he ran back down the stairs. 'Couple of stiffs up there, that's all – nothing moving.' He paused for a moment to look out of a small window beside the front door. He was a little shocked to see that there were an uncomfortably large number of bodies milling about in the road outside now, and most of them were gravitating towards the house they'd first entered. The numbers were nothing they couldn't handle, but still, it was something they could have done without.

He found Jas in the dining room, piling furniture up against one wall. He had pushed a long rectangular dining table over onto its side and was stacking chairs up against it. As Harte watched he pulled down the curtains and began to stuff them into the gaps between the upturned wooden chair legs.

'Where's the fuel, Harte?' he asked as he worked, and Harte disappeared into the kitchen again, leaving him alone. Jas ran around to the other side of the upturned table to look for more to burn, but he stopped immediately when he saw it – how he hadn't noticed it before, he didn't know. Slumped in the corner of the room under the bay window was the curled-up body of a child, two years old, three at most when it had died. Just for a moment the defenceless little husk of a child was all that Jas could think about. It had died lying on its back, its tiny hand held across its face, almost as if it had been trying to hide from whatever it was that was killing it.

'What's the matter?' Harte asked as he came back into the

room and found him standing over the corpse on the carpet. He threw down a pile of coats he'd grabbed from the hallway and started to pack them around the table and chairs.

Jas continued to stare at the child; the little boy looked about the same age as his girl Annia had been when she'd— *Don't do this*, he thought to himself, *please don't do this*. He could feel the pain of the family he'd lost welling up inside him. Most of the time he managed to keep this suppressed, but like everyone else there were moments when he was caught off-guard. He couldn't allow himself to break down, not here, not now . . . He had to forget about everything he'd lost and—

'Jas!' Harte snapped, 'now's *not* the time. Come on, mate, get a fucking wiggle on, will you?'

But Jas didn't move. The last time he'd seen his children alive they'd been at home in their house, which was just like the one in which they were standing now. He hadn't been back there since he'd lost them – were they still there, lying motionless like this poor little creature, or were they moving about? Was Annia up on her feet, staggering around aimlessly, tirelessly? Were the kids alone or had—?

—a corpse slammed against the window directly in front of him, bringing a sudden, thankful release from his increasingly dark thoughts. He turned around and acknowledged Harte. 'Sorry, mate,' he mumbled, 'I just—'

'Doesn't matter,' Harte said quickly, trying to avoid getting involved in another awkward conversation. He unscrewed the fuel can and began to empty its contents over the pile of material and furniture. Jas pushed past him as the acrid smell of petrol filled the air and ran back to the kitchen, Harte following more slowly shuffled out backwards, carefully spilling a trail of petrol behind him. Once the can was empty he kicked it across the kitchen floor and it clattered noisily on the hard tiles.

'Keep still,' Jas mumbled as he ferreted around in the rucksack on Harte's back for the box of matches. As soon as he had them they both barged out through the back door, and Harte didn't stop until he was on the far side of the trampoline again. He shielded his eyes from the light drizzle and watched as Jas crouched down in the doorway.

Jas didn't allow himself to think about the body of the child again, but struck the match. The vapour in the air caught light immediately and he turned and ran.

By the time the two men had worked their way back through the seven gardens and were ready to get on the bike, the house down the road was well and truly ablaze. The crackling, spitting flames, the noise, the belching black smoke and the dancing lights were enough to distract virtually all of the bodies out in the street. Jas and Harte were away before the dead had even realised they were there.

13

'They're coming,' said Stokes. 'I can hear them.'

'About bloody time,' grumbled Webb. He watched the house in the near distance burning, incandescent orange against the dull grey of everything else. 'We might as well get started.'

'Give it a few more minutes,' Hollis suggested. 'Go in too fast and they'll forget about the fire and turn back at you.'

'Doesn't bother me,' Webb sneered. 'I've been looking forward to this. Bring it on.' Pumped full of adrenalin, he marched down the hill, ignoring Hollis' warning. He glanced back as the motorbike finally returned, watching it sweep around the front of the building behind him, then turned back to the crowd in front. Their distraction seemed to be working. From here, halfway down the slope, he could see that the fire had spread along the terrace, and as the size of the blaze had increased, so more and more bodies were being drawn to it. Although many thousands remained pressed up against their rubble barrier, at the back of the huge gathering, hundreds more were beginning to peel away and stumble towards the heat and light.

He stood and watched the dead crowds below while he waited for the others.

To her surprise, Lorna found that Webb was right for once. The thought of destroying as many of the dead masses as they were able to was strangely appealing. As she walked down towards the foot of the hill with Hollis, Harte and Stokes at her side, all of them dressed in their standard-issue biker leathers, she decided that she too was in need of what he called 'therapy'.

'So, is there a plan?' Jas asked as he caught up with the others.

'Of sorts,' Hollis replied. He'd originally planned to stay indoors, to have nothing to do with this massacre, but the thought of Webb, armed to the hilt, having free reign outside was enough of a concern to force him outside too.

'And?' Jas pressed.

'Lorna's going to use one of the diggers to start shifting part of the barrier back,' he explained.

'And we're going to get rid of every single one of those fucking things that manages to get through,' Webb finished as they finally reached him. The others lined up in silence alongside him and squared up to their decaying foe. Most of their usual encounters with the dead happened at speed, with the living doing their utmost to destroy any corpses they came upon in the shortest time possible. Here, however, the rules of engagement were suddenly very different. Standing just a short distance away, looking across the no man's land of the barrier, they had the opportunity to study their horrific opponents. The bodies were continually moving, writhing and surging forwards and back, but they weren't going anywhere. After six weeks their grotesque appearance had become less immediately shocking, but being face-to-face with thousands upon thousands of them like this was an unnerving prospect for even the most hardened fighter. There were just so bloody many of them.

Harte found himself wondering whether he and Jas should have torched several streets full of houses, or even the whole town, to distract the apparently endless crowds. Their small fire seemed painfully insignificant as a distraction now.

Webb moved further forward, only stopping when he was less than two yards away from the nearest cadaver. He locked onto one particular creature and stared deep into its ravaged face. It was hard to believe that it had once been human: not a single inch of unblemished skin remained. Gross yellow, pus-like fluids had seeped from every visible orifice. Its ill-fitting skin appeared mummified and hard in some places, unnaturally pliable in others. And the damn thing's jaw moved continually. Was it getting ready to sink its teeth into him? He wasn't going to give it the chance. *As soon as this one gets through*, he decided, *I'm going to rip its fucking head off.*

'You sure you're okay with that thing?' Jas shouted to Lorna, who had climbed up into the cab of the larger of two yellow diggers. Truth was, he wasn't concerned with Lorna's ability to drive it – he knew she'd done it before – it was more that he felt unaccountably nervous; he'd had wanted that seat for himself.

'Been practising,' she answered quickly, annoyed that he'd questioned her ability. For several weeks now she'd been messing around with all of the various machines they'd found lying around the partially demolished second block of flats, not just the diggers. At first her interest had been a way to alleviate her boredom, however temporarily, but now she was glad to have found a practical use for her new-found skill.

'Shift this one,' Webb shouted to her, slapping his hand against the wing of a small Mazda. 'Don't want to give them too much space to get through, do we?'

'He's good, isn't he?' Harte laughed sarcastically. 'Got it all planned out in that tiny brain of his, he has!'

'Fuck you,' Webb spat. 'Your problem is you're too—'

No one heard what he said next as Lorna started the digger's engine, then Hollis pulled the rip-cord on the chain-saw he was carrying.

Webb shut up and focused on the task at hand, holding his baseball bat ready in one hand and an axe in the other. The bodies on the other side of the low wall of twisted metal and concrete were reacting to the noise, surging forward. It looked remarkably like they were beginning to get riled.

Lorna accelerated slowly and the digger moved forwards.

She lowered the heavy scoop, cringing as the metal scraped along the uneven ground, then raised it slightly and punched it into the door of the blue Mazda, shoving the vehicle back. From her position in the cab it was difficult to see how far the car had moved. She gave another hard shunt and the car popped out of the barrier almost completely, leaving a gap on either side of it.

—and then they came—

Driven forward by their unnatural anger and by the weight of many thousands more bodies pressing behind them, the corpses at the front of the crowd began to ooze through the holes in the barrier on either end of the little blue Mazda which had helped to keep them at bay for so long. They spilled forward like oily sludge.

As Lorna reversed the digger and readied herself to try and block the gaps she'd left by shoving the next section of the barrier forward, Hollis reacted. He covered his face with his protective plastic visor, raised the spinning chainsaw and marched purposefully towards the advancing dead. The first of them walked face-first straight into the chainsaw's power-ful churning teeth and most of its head disintegrated on impact. Hollis continued to hold the blade out in front of him and dealt the exact same fate to a second body that was lurching too close behind.

Webb stood back and watched, transfixed by the waterfall of crimson-brown gore which was soaking the ground like red rain around Hollis and the pile of body parts mounting at the other man's feet, until one of the cadavers lunged to the side and slipped past Hollis, moving towards Webb and forcing the young man into action. He dispatched it with a single axe-blow to the forehead, the blade leaving a deep, dark groove between its eyes. The satisfying crack and splin-ter of the creature's skull was reassuring.

Lorna pushed the next car back as she had the first, taking care this time to make sure she plugged any gaps. There were still corpses pushing their way through the opening on the other side of the first car, so she decided she'd deal with that problem next.

Stokes, finding himself uncomfortably close to the fighting for once, had scuttled back out of the way and was heading for the smaller digger. He started the engine and slowly drove it back towards the front line, making a slight detour to crush a single corpse which had somehow managed to sneak past the others. Although he now felt safe, protected by the cab and the height of the vehicle, from his elevated position the size of the job ahead of them looked even more daunting. He quickly counted the number of dead heads, some now lying on their own in the mud looking like unwholesome footballs, he estimated that in the few minutes since the barrier had been breached, the survivors had destroyed somewhere in the region of ten to fifteen corpses, though it was difficult to estimate with any real degree of accuracy because of the continual frenzied movement all around him, But however many of them they'd managed to get rid of so far, it was just a drop in the ocean compared with the many, many thousands more lining up to take their place. It was going to take *hours* to make any kind of meaningful dent in their numbers. Not for the first time Stokes found himself silently questioning what they were doing, wondering if this really was as bloody stupid an idea as it suddenly appeared?

'Pile 'em up over there,' Hollis yelled, struggling to make himself heard over the combined noise of the fighting, the digger engines and his chainsaw. He gestured wildly towards an area of land close to the fenced enclosure, Webb's training ground, where Webb claimed he'd been bitten yesterday.

Stokes moved towards the mass of fallen bodies, trying to familiarise himself with the controls of the digger, and once satisfied that he'd worked out how to move the shovel properly, he clumsily scooped a bucket full of dead flesh (some still twitching), turned around and drove it over towards the area Hollis had pointed to. He tipped the shovel, emptying its contents onto the rough ground with a reassuring splatter –

but even now, as the last dregs dripped off the metal shovel, some of the dismembered creatures he'd scooped up were continuing to move. His stomach churned as he watched the head and half-torso of a cadaver which had been hacked in two by the chainsaw just below its nipples reach out with its one good arm and try desperately to drag itself away.

Lorna moved another car, closing one gap but inadvertently opening another. The digger's shovel had become entangled with the door of the car and she struggled to knock it free, concentrating on the mechanical claw and trying to ignore the wave of corpses which now surrounded her, all of them pointlessly fighting to get even closer. A sudden flash of light overhead distracted her momentarily and she looked up to see Harte hurling petrol bombs into the front of the crowd. He was obviously trying to disrupt them, take out enough of them so that she could shunt the barrier back. The bombs flew through the grey sky above them in beautiful arcs of spiralling flame before smashing down into the bodies and exploding.

Hollis noticed the crowd growing around the digger and marched towards it. They were preoccupied with the machine, and disposing of them was a simple matter. The noise from the digger was drowning out the powerful grind of his weapon, so he simply held up the chainsaw and walked into them, carving them up before they'd even realised he was there.

Lorna looked down and acknowledged him with a thumbs-up, then suddenly pointed behind him in warning; he spun around to see a group of three corpses moving towards him. They attacked at the same time, surging at him with flailing limbs. He lashed out with the chainsaw, effortlessly cutting down the nearest two, and then ran towards the third (which, incredibly, now appeared to be retreating, although obviously it couldn't have been doing that *consciously*) and, with a flick of his wrist, sliced a jagged diagonal cut across its bony chest. The body fell to the ground, legs going one way, head and shoulders the other.

Just inches away from Hollis, Webb smashed his axe into the ravaged face of a body which reminded him of a social worker who had once been assigned to him. He was concentrating on the satisfying splintering of the creature's skull, quite unaware that the digger being driven by Stokes was close behind, until Hollis grabbed him by the shoulder and yanked him out of the way. Webb turned to attack, but then lowered his weapons when he saw that there was no danger. They stepped back to allow Stokes to collect another scoop full of bloody remains.

'You having fun?' Hollis yelled over the noise.

Webb grinned. 'You?' he asked back as he shook a lump of flesh off the end of his baseball bat and readied himself for his next victim.

As perverse as it felt, Hollis was enjoying himself too. 'Wonderful,' he grunted.

'They're fucking stupid,' Webb laughed as he swung the bat at the head of another corpse and sent it flying into the side of Lorna's digger. 'Look at them – they're just lining up to be wiped out!'

'Is that what you think?' Hollis asked.

''course it is,' he answered.

'You're really dumb at times, Webb,' he said as he lifted his chainsaw and readied himself to move forward again. 'It might look that way, but just watch them – more to the point, watch yourself.'

'Why?'

'Because if you look closely,' he continued, pausing to cut another body in two from its groin up to its neck, 'you'll see that some of them are actually trying to coordinate themselves in their attack.'

Webb laughed out loud at Hollis' comment, but he found himself watching the next cadaver more closely. It was slow and weak, but Christ, Hollis was right! It was definitely moving with very real intent. He expected it just to leap straight at him aggressively, but it didn't. Instead, it watched him with dull, unblinking eyes for a second or two, and then, as if choosing its moment, it suddenly lifted its skeletal arms and, increasing its speed, rushed at him

Whether it had been a considered attack or not, Webb destroyed it with a dismissive thump from the baseball bat to the side of its head.

After hours of constant fighting it was time to stop. Lorna dropped a big old Mondeo onto its roof, dumping it diagonally across the bonnet of a Toyota she'd placed previously, plugging the last remaining gap and finally stemming the flow of bodies. Webb, Hollis and Harte were all exhausted, and soaked in mud, blood and gore, but working together they quickly disposed of the last few cadavers before dropping their weapons and shaking their limbs out, trying to get some feeling back.

Stokes was long gone. Jas moved in and cleared the area with the smaller digger, dropping the larger body parts onto the smouldering pyre they'd started, then scraping the metal shovel along the ground and dumping the last scoop full of once-human slurry over the other side of the wall of cars and rubble, onto the heads of the unsuspecting crowd.

Job done, he switched off the engine and climbed out of the cab. Without the constant mechanical drone of the two machines the world was suddenly, eerily, quiet – so quiet that the loudest sound remaining was the trickle of liquefied flesh dripping from the metal scoop behind him.

Webb was the first to break the silence. Still buzzing with excitement from the kill, he babbled breathlessly as they began to walk back up the hill, ' So how many do you reckon then?'

'What?' Lorna said, looking blank.

'How many did we get rid of?' Webb asked, 'couple of hundred, maybe?'

'Something like that,' Harte replied, shaking something unpleasant from his right glove.

'Christ, but I'm tired,' Jas sighed wearily.

'I could do more,' Webb continued.

'Be my guest,' Hollis said, grimacing. 'You carry on.'

'I could spend all day getting rid of those bloody things. There's nothing better than wiping out a load of them when you're all pissed off and wound-up,' Webb chattered on, oblivious to the others' lack of interest.

'Most of us seem to be pissed off and wound-up all the time,' Harte said after a bit. 'I've felt like that since this all started.'

'Well, at least we're doing something positive now,' Webb said firmly. 'We're taking a stand, letting them know who's in charge—' He shut up when he realised that Hollis had stopped walking. He turned around to look back at him.

'Problem?' Harte asked, concerned. Hollis was gazing back down the hill towards the crowd. Thick smoke was still rising from the smouldering heap of charred flesh by the diggers and drifting out over the heads of the dead.

'Look what we did today,' Webb said excitedly, gesturing towards the pyre. 'Look how many of them we got rid of—'

'That's exactly what I am looking at,' Hollis said.

'And?' Webb pushed

'That,' Hollis said, 'took six of us a few hours to clear.'

'So what's your point? We did it, didn't we?'

'That's my point exactly,' Hollis explained. 'It took six of us the best part of a day and a shitload of fuel and effort just to take out a hundred or so bodies. Bloody hell, Webb! Look down there, properly: there are *hundreds of thousands* of them! How long's that going to take? We haven't cleared even one per cent of the dead yet – we haven't even scratched the surface.'

'You're a miserable fucker,' Webb snarled, getting annoyed. 'Tell me you didn't feel good when you stood down there and ripped those fucking things apart.'

'I'm not denying that,' Hollis said.

'So what's your problem?' Webb really didn't understand.

'There're too many of them, that's all. We're never going to get rid of all of them, are we?'

'No one said we were trying to do that,' Harte said, trying to calm the rising tensions.

'Wiping the floor with a few dozen stiffs might make you feel like you've done something worthwhile,' Hollis continued, 'but listen, do me a favour: let's not pretend it's going to change the world, shall we? I don't want to spend all day every day down there fighting. There's got to be more to life than that.'

'Has there?' Webb said. 'Seems to me this is just about all we've got left.'

Hollis sighed and carried on up the hill, leaving the others standing there, staring in silence at the insignificant grey scar they'd left on the landscape below.

14

Hollis and Lorna sat at the bottom of a dark staircase, their faces illuminated by the flickering light from half a dozen candles. Gordon stood in a doorway opposite, his arms folded. It was late, but although they were all tired, no one wanted to sleep. Stokes, Harte and Webb were standing out on the balcony at the front of one of the flats on the floor below, making plans to continue their cull at first light. Their muffled voices echoed around the building.

'I like your hair,' Hollis said unexpectedly.

Lorna looked up and managed a quick smile before looking down again. She didn't like it when he commented on her hair – she didn't dress her hair for anyone but herself, and when Hollis paid her a compliment it made her feel like she was being chatted up by her uncle. She didn't tell him, though. She didn't want to upset him when he was just trying to be nice.

'Thanks,' she mumbled, hoping that would be the end of the conversation, she wasn't so lucky; he wasn't going to let it go.

'You always make an effort,' he said admiringly. 'You always look good.'

'Why shouldn't I?'

'No reason,' he quickly back-pedalled, worried he'd offended her. 'I'm down to one shave a week myself.'

'Just because I feel like shit doesn't mean I have to look like shit, does it?'

'Sorry,' he said, 'I didn't mean that you should . . .'

He tailed off, and Gordon looked away, feeling embarrassed for Hollis. He was relieved when Caron appeared at the top of the staircase, carrying another candle. She carefully made her way down to the others.

'How's she doing?' Hollis asked, his whispered words echoing in the silence.

Caron had spent the evening sitting with Anita. She shook her head and sat down. 'Not good,' she replied, her quiet voice sounding weary. 'She's worse than ever tonight.'

'What is it?' Lorna asked, though she knew full well that Caron knew as little as she did. 'Is she still being sick?'

'She's got nothing left in her stomach to throw up,' Caron answered. 'She hasn't eaten anything today, or had anything to drink – not even water. I did try, but she couldn't.'

'I don't like this,' Gordon said nervously. 'It's like a tropical disease or something. It's come from the bodies, it must have. There are flies and maggots and germs out there, and—'

'Shut up, Gord,' Hollis said, silencing him. 'You're not helping.'

'But it could spread – we could all end up catching it. For all we know she might—'

'I mean it,' Hollis snapped, a warning tone in his voice. 'So just shut up, will you, Gord?'

'I read something in a magazine once, about outbreaks of disease after natural disasters,' Caron said, cutting across them both. 'I can't remember exactly what it said – I think someone did a study after an earthquake or something like that, when there were lots of bodies lying around . . .'

'And?' Lorna pressed.

'I didn't pay much attention to it at the time,' she admitted; 'I didn't think I needed to. It wasn't the kind of article I usually read—'

'So do you remember *anything* useful?'

'I think it said most germs were spread through direct contact with the bodies, or through contaminated water – they weren't airborne, I don't think.'

94

'That's just perfect,' Lorna moaned. 'We've just spent most of the day ankle-deep in their shite.'

'Yeah,' Hollis said quickly, 'but it wasn't on our *skin*, was it? That's why we wear the suits, right? And all of it got washed off, didn't it? And we collect rainwater, don't we, so we should be okay.'

'Yes, but—'

'But nothing. I doubt if any of us have caught anything.'

'How do you know?' Gordon said, clearly agitated. 'Anita has – so how did she get it? She hasn't been outside for ages. She's been drinking the same water we have.'

'She might have had it before she got here,' Hollis replied, clutching at straws. 'Maybe it's something that takes a few weeks to show itself – or she could have just got unlucky and eaten something that was contaminated.'

'I don't like this,' Gordon grumbled. 'What if we catch it off her?'

'Then we'll just have to deal with it, won't we,' Hollis said firmly.

'And how are we supposed to do that?'

'We'll try and get her some drugs, keep her isolated,' he said after a moment. 'That's probably all we can do for now.'

'But what if that doesn't work?'

'For Christ's sake, what exactly do you expect me to do about it? Do you want me to go down to the edge of the crowd and see if any of the dead bodies used to be a doctor? Bloody hell, Gordon, just get a grip!'

'He does have a point though,' Lorna said quietly. 'We can't just let her lie up there like this, can we?'

Hollis stood up and paced away along the corridor, then he stopped and walked back. He stopped a short distance away. The light from the candles was just strong enough to catch the outline of his tired face. 'Maybe a couple of us should go out tomorrow and try to find her some drugs,' he suggested again. 'Hopefully some antibiotics will do the trick.'

'And if it doesn't?' Gordon shouted after him as he turned and walked away again.

'We'll cross that bridge when we come to it,' his fading voice replied as he disappeared into the darkness.

15

The early morning sun unexpectedly broke through the layer of dull grey cloud which was smothering the land. Hollis was waiting in front of the flats for Lorna. Down below them, the cull had begun again. It wasn't yet seven, but neither the early hour nor the previous day's exertions had put any sort of damper on Jas, Webb, Stokes and Harte's enthusiastic desire to obliterate more bodies. This morning, to Hollis' great surprise, Gordon too had found himself an ill-fitting set of biker leathers and had joined the others at the edge of the crowd. He finally seemed to have overcome his pathetic inhibitions; today, with or without a dodgy hip, he was facing the bodies head-on. Either that or Gordon found the prospect of waiting inside the flats even more nerve-wracking than fighting the corpses outside; every conversation Hollis had overheard since waking up had been about Anita and her worsening condition.

A wash of golden sunlight dappled the heads of thousands of writhing bodies at the foot of the hill. He wasn't sure why, but the one-sided battle below him looked different to yesterday; more ferocious – maybe it was just a different perspective, but when he'd been dealing with the bodies yesterday at close quarters, he was sure they hadn't been as violent and animated as these were today . . . Or maybe it was just because people like Gordon and Stokes were less experienced, less capable when it came to hand-to-hand combat?

Or could it be the bodies themselves? Were they more animated because of what had happened yesterday? Of course it was impossible, but it almost looked as if the dead were scared this morning, or somehow angrier, or pissed off and ready to retaliate after yesterday's slaughter, or—

'You ready?' Lorna asked, startling him.

He turned around and saw that she was standing just behind him; he grunted, and climbed into the grime-splattered Ford Transit van he usually drove. He and Lorna had taken it upon themselves to go out searching for drugs – if they didn't do it, she'd pointed out, no other fucker would; they were all too busy playing hero by killing dead people.

'So where to?' he asked as she climbed in next to him and slammed the door shut. She knew the area far better than he did. He looked across at her. Her face was clear of make-up, her eyes bright. Her hair was scraped back in a tight ponytail. She looked serious, focused.

'There are three pharmacies near here,' she replied quickly. 'Let's head for the one at the bottom of Bail Hill first – that was a pretty big one, so there should be plenty of stuff there. Um, have you got any idea what we're looking for?' she added as he started the engine.

'Not really,' he replied as he drove towards the maze of garages behind the flats. 'I suggest we just get in there and empty the contents of the shelves into the back of the van. We'll work out what we've got when we get back.'

Hollis pulled up outside the pharmacy, leaving the van parked on the pavement, as close to the front door as he could get. 'Five minutes,' he told Lorna, 'and then we're out of here.'

Lorna quickly disappeared inside and he paused for a second before following, stopping just long enough to look up and down the road and see what effect their arrival had had. He counted ten creatures crawling slowly towards them from either direction. No doubt there'd be hundreds by the time they were finished.

Lorna was already working when he got inside, sweeping entire shelves clear with her arm and catching the contents in wire shopping baskets; she'd already filled three in the brief time she'd been there.

Hollis grabbed them and ran them back out to the van. There were twice as many bodies as before now, maybe more. Christ, they were going to have to be quick.

'How are we supposed to know what any of this stuff is and what it does?' Lorna shouted across the shop as he returned. 'Maybe there's a book or something we could take?'

'Doubt it,' he said, grabbing the next two baskets and heading for the door again. 'They'd have had it all on computer, wouldn't they?'

'I suppose – but there might be something, though. It's worth having a look.'

He placed the baskets into the back of the van and as he shut the door again, decided there were too many bodies now, and they were getting close. Too close.

'We're out of time,' he shouted, collecting what would be the final baskets. 'Come on, Lorna; we need to get gone.'

Lorna was pulling open a heavy white door next to where she'd been working. She presumed it led to an office, or maybe another drugs store. Perhaps she'd find some information in there which would help her to—

—a body lunged out from the shadows into the light, missing Lorna and throwing itself at Hollis, who was standing in front of it, completely unprepared. The corpse, wearing the once-white coat of a pharmacist which was now yellow with seepage, hurtled towards him with unexpected venom. It had been trapped behind the door for more than fifty days, and its sudden release seemed somehow to energise and invigorate it. Though its weight was insignificant, its velocity was enough to knock Hollis over and he fell backwards, smashing the side of his head against the wooden counter. The pain was excruciating.

Lorna looked around, panicking, and spotted a fire extinguisher next to the door. She grabbed it from its bracket on the wall and brought it crashing down on the back of the cadaver's skull with a sickening crunch. As it collapsed on top of Hollis, black clots of blood and other foul-smelling gunk dribbled out of its mouth and nose. He kicked it off of him and scrambled away desperately, horribly aware of the germs which might be thriving in the gruesome liquids which were dripping all over him.

Finally free, he dragged himself back up onto his feet, gagging in disgust as the remains of the pharmacist slid onto the floor. He angrily put his boot through its face.

'Fucking thing,' he cursed, gingerly touching his left ear. When he drew back his fingers he saw blood.

'Let's go,' Lorna said, picking up another basket and carrying it towards the door, but she came to an abrupt halt when she saw that the entire width of the glass frontage of the pharmacy was now a solid wall of dead flesh. The whole mass reacted violently as she approached, parts of the crowd recoiling away from her, while others appeared to be pushing harder against the dirty windows, as if they were trying to get to her through the glass.

'Bloody hell,' Hollis moaned under his breath. 'How the hell are we going to do this?' They were used to being hounded by huge crowds of corpses wherever they went, but this felt different. Had they spooked themselves, talking about the bodies getting smarter, or were some of the creatures on the other side of the glass really demonstrating conscious, controlled behaviour? It felt horribly like they were waiting for the two survivors to come out into the open. It was almost as if they knew they'd have to leave the safety of the pharmacy sooner or later.

'Are we going to stand here waiting for Christmas or are we going home?' Lorna asked, trying to hide her mounting unease.

'No such thing as Christmas any more,' he replied. 'Ready?'

'Think so,' she mumbled, sounding far from sure.

'Get closer to the door.'

Without questioning him she moved forward. The bodies were just inches away from her now, separated only by a single sheet of glass. One of them was pushing at the door and Lorna heaved a sigh of relief when she realised it was pushing the hinged side; it was never going to get the door open that way. But its intent was clear.

Hollis disappeared back into the shop and picked up the bloodied fire extinguisher Lorna had used moments earlier. Still wincing with the pain behind his ear, he lifted the red metal canister above his head and threw it at the section of window furthest from the door. It thumped against the toughened glass, cracking it, but not breaking through, before it dropped to the ground with a sonorous thump and rolled into a display rack. Many of the bodies immediately turned and began to shuffle nearer to the noise. Hollis picked up the extinguisher again and this time slammed it into the glass like a battering ram. The glass shattered, huge, jagged shards falling out of the metal frame, and the dead immediately began to force their way inside, ignoring the daggers of broken glass which sliced their feet to ribbons. Without stopping to look at the results of his actions Hollis ran over to Lorna, pulled the door open and pushed her through. She threw the basket of medicines she'd been holding into the crowd, sending packets and bottles flying, and with the bulk of the crowd pouring through the broken window, they forced their way through the rest of the bodies. Hollis dropped his shoulder and barged into them as Lorna crouched down and wormed her way through their legs. She managed to scramble into the van first and turned around to see what she could do to help Hollis.

Hollis was surprised by the dogged resistance of the dead. Most of the creatures had fallen for his ploy; they were still jostling to get into the shop through the smashed window. But there were plenty of others standing firm; though they were still weak, as clumsy and uncoordinated as ever, they were undeniably more determined than they ever had been before. He was struggling with one particularly aggressive cadaver which had a huge black hole in its face where its right eye should have been, until Lorna managed to grab hold of him around his chest and yank him back into the van.

She peered around him to see that many more bodies had turned away from the window and were shuffling towards them again. They needed to go.

'What the hell are you doing?' Hollis jabbered nervously as he fell back into his seat. He knocked another rancid figure back onto the street and slammed the door shut. It was dark inside the van, but they could see emotionless faces pressed up against every window.

'We really need to go,' Lorna replied, peering through the bodies to see the pharmacy quickly filling with dead flesh. 'We need to get out of here.'

He started the engine and the noise had an immediate effect, causing the still growing crowd to become even more animated. He shuddered and drove forward, dragging several of the rotting shells beneath the wheels of the Transit and churning them into the ground. Lorna turned around in her seat and watched as part of the crowd lethargically marched after them, like a mob rampaging in slow motion.

16

A frantic, unscheduled stop at a well-sheltered medical centre north of the flats they'd forgotten about till now allowed Hollis and Lorna to collect more drugs and to pick up several medical journals and reference books. They didn't know if the information would make any difference, but just having it made them feel marginally better. The only medical training Caron had ever had was a basic first-aid course at work some twenty years ago. She gratefully took everything that was offered to her and shut herself away in the flat next to Anita's. She found descriptions of all sorts of conditions and diseases which Anita might have been suffering from, but next to nothing in the way of real guidance or treatment advice. Just after midday Hollis appeared in the doorway of the flat, carrying with him some more drugs, which he'd found rolling around in the back of the van.

'Any good?' he asked hopefully.

Caron put down the text book she'd been reading and rubbed her tired eyes. 'Not really,' she admitted.

'How's she doing?'

'No better.'

'Is she still being sick? Has she eaten anything?'

She shook her head. 'She's not doing anything. Her temperature's sky-high and she's barely conscious. That's probably for the best . . .'

'Have you managed to find anything that might help?'

She looked around the room at the piles of drugs surrounding her. 'I've got no idea what I'm looking for,' she answered honestly, 'and even if I could find the name of a drug which might help, how am I supposed to know what it looks like? I wouldn't even know if it was a pill in a packet or a medicine in a bottle.'

'Point taken,' Hollis said quietly as he walked across the room and stood at the window. 'Do you know what I think?'

'I know what I think,' she interrupted abruptly, 'I think I should just force as much of this stuff as I can down the poor cow's throat and put her out of her bloody misery. Honestly, Greg, is it even worth her getting better?'

Hollis didn't answer. He was staring out of the window trying to remember the last time anyone had called him by his first name. Natalie used to call him Greg, and his mum and dad, and Mark, and all the others he'd lost.

'What the hell is that idiot doing now?' he said suddenly, glad of the distraction.

'Which idiot?' Caron asked, standing up and walking over to him. 'There's more than one around here.'

'Webb – just look at the stupid little bastard!'

Webb was walking precariously along the uneven top of the barrier of cars and rubble which was somehow still succeeding in keeping the dead at bay. As he walked, he was emptying the contents of a fuel can over the heads of the carcases which were incessantly grabbing at his feet.

'He scares me when he starts playing with fire,' Caron admitted, her voice low.

'He scares me whenever I see him.'

As they watched, Gordon passed another can of fuel up to Webb, who immediately began tipping it out over the crowd, drenching some cadavers which had already been soaked once.

'Careful with that stuff,' Hollis muttered under his breath. 'He'll set fire to himself if he doesn't watch what he's doing.'

'I'm not bothered about that – I just don't want him to use up all our fuel! I'm the sucker who'll end up out there fetching more.'

They watched as Webb finished emptying the second can,

then jumped down to stand with the others a short distance back from the corpses. There was no denying the fact that they had worked hard again this morning: they had already reclaimed an area of land almost as big as the patch they'd taken the whole of yesterday to recover, but their methods were becoming more haphazard and less effective as time progressed. The diggers which had previously been used to carefully move one car or lump of masonry at a time now sat redundant a little way back. It was clear from Webb's actions that anything resembling safety or planning had been forgotten; the group outside now were in the business of finding shortcuts. Now it was all about destroying the maximum number of corpses with the minimum amount of effort.

'I can't watch,' Caron said, turning away, but then looking back when curiosity got the better of her. Hollis stared intently as Stokes, Jas, Gordon and Webb scuttled away to a safe distance leaving Harte on his own trying to light the limp rag fuse of a petrol bomb with what looked like a frustratingly unreliable cigarette lighter. A sudden flash of orange appeared which made him jump back with surprise. Realising that the rag was finally alight, he hurled it towards the wall of cars and it ricocheted off the roof of a beaten-up 4 × 4 before exploding into flames. A chain-reaction spread instantly across the petrol-soaked crowd as an arc of fire raced to the right and left and back out over the decaying hordes.

Harte ran for cover.

'Looks like it worked,' Caron said, relaxing again as the people down below congratulated each other, laughing and pointing as the bodies burned.

'Thank God for that,' Hollis sighed. 'They're lucky it's not them that's on fire. If the wind had caught the fumes like last time they'd—'

A sudden explosion tore through the air outside. Hollis stared out of the window, trying to work out what had just happened. It didn't take long for him to spot the hearse (complete with coffin and body), which had been blown up into the air. The long vehicle flipped over and over, until the charred chassis clattered back down to the ground several yards behind the spot it had originally occupied, crushing scores more unsuspecting corpses.

Outside, the survivors had run for cover.

'Bloody hell,' grinned Stokes, 'that was close. You could have been standing on top of that, Webb.'

'I was standing right on top of it a couple of minutes ago,' he replied, subdued. 'Good job Harte took his time getting the fuse lit.'

'Piss off,' Harte snapped. 'It was your lighter that slowed things down, nothing to do with me.'

'Guys, I think we've got a problem here,' Jas said ominously, taking a few tentative steps forward and peering through the heavy cloud of dense black smoke which was drifting low across the scene from the burning bodies and the blazing hearse. He shielded his eyes and looked down into the gap in the barrier where the hearse had originally been. The flames there had died down and now he could see movement.

'What is it?' Gordon asked nervously, careful not to get too close to the barrier. At first Jas didn't answer but just pointed at the wide gap which had appeared in their defences. A mass of furious bodies was beginning to scramble through, and they were moving remarkably quickly.

'Block it up!' Jas screamed, his voice suddenly hoarse with panic. 'Block the fucking hole up!'

Webb and Stokes peered into the haze, still not sure what was happening, but Harte, immediately realising the danger, sprang into action, sprinting over to the nearest of the two diggers and hauling himself up into the cab. He started the heavy machine and as he rumbled towards the lumbering bodies, he was trying to work out how best to stem the flow of dead flesh pouring through the ruptured barricade.

Webb suddenly lurched into action, swinging his nail-skewered baseball bat around with scant regard for his own

– or anyone else's – safety. Even Gordon was forced to fight, battering a single crippled creature to the ground with a bloodied fencepost, then standing over it and repeatedly slamming the wooden post into its face, continuing long after it had stopped moving.

Stokes scampered out of the way and climbed into the other digger, hand on the ignition, ready to get involved only if he had absolutely no alternative.

Harte blasted the digger's horn and Jas, still fighting furiously, looked up in time to step back out of the way as the vehicle moved towards him, rolling relentlessly over the dead and squashing them into the mud. On the other side of the breached barrier, a short distance into the advancing crowd, he could see another wrecked vehicle, a Land Rover, which he could use to block the hole left by the still-burning hearse. He accelerated, carving a deep and bloody furrow through the sea of cadavers as he made his way out through the gap and into the crowd. He concentrated on the car just ahead, doing his best to block out the fact that now, for the first time, he was completely surrounded by corpses on every side. Shutting out the noise of their constant, tireless hammering on the sides of the digger, he stretched out the vehicle's scoop and smashed it down through the roof of the Land Rover, punching a hole. He slammed the digger into reverse and powered back, slipping out through the gap again, then steering carefully over to the right so he could wedge the car across the breach.

All around the digger the chaos continued, though the smoke and constant movement made it almost impossible to see what was happening clearly. Looking down from the flats, Hollis estimated that more than fifty corpses had managed to push their way through the barrier before Harte had managed to block the gap. Around half that number had already been destroyed, most obliterated by the digger.

'I should go down there,' he muttered, but Caron put a hand on his arm, stopping him.

'They can take care of themselves,' she said. 'They made the mess; let them clear it up. Little idiots – if they'd just slow down and think before they—'

Her voice trailed away to nothing as she watched the fighting continue. Several cadavers had managed to surround Gordon; through bad luck or inexperience, he'd somehow allowed himself to be cornered and now his back was pressed up against a section of wire-mesh fence. He cowered as the dead approached, and even from that distance Caron and Hollis could see how badly he was shaking.

'Get out of the way!' Jas shouted, noticing the other man was trapped. 'Move!'

Terrified, Gordon looked for a way out, but he was too slow. He was about to drop to his knees and try crawling away through the mud when the bodies attacked – not lethargically, like the survivors were used to, but surprisingly controlled and inexplicably coordinated. It was almost as if they were working together.

'Get down!' Jas screamed again, running towards Gordon. He unsheathed the machete he'd been carrying on his belt and began to lash out, sinking the blade into the small of the back of the first of them, cutting deep into its already partially exposed spinal cord. He yanked it free and immediately struck out at the next nearest corpse, which was smaller than the first, almost disarmingly child-like. He looked away as he slammed the blade down onto the top of its head, parting what remained of its lank hair and splitting its skull. Now that he found himself facing only one opponent again, Gordon managed to force himself back into action. He fumbled around for the fencepost he'd been using as a bludgeon, then picked it up and swung it into the side of the third corpse's body, smashing its pelvis and giving it a far more serious hip problem than the one he himself suffered from. It collapsed into a puddle of bloody rainwater.

'You okay, Gord?' Jas asked, wiping his blade clean on the back of a slumped body lying next to him.

Gordon was standing over the corpse he'd just crippled, pounding its face with the fencepost. 'Fine,' he said between angry grunts of effort, 'nothing to worry about.'

Stokes watched from the safety of the stationary digger as Webb continued to hack down those cadavers unfortunate enough to find themselves within striking range of his baseball bat. Jas too had returned to the fray and was chopping at the remaining figures which lumbered towards him. Harte continued to operate the other digger, stretching the articulated arm out over pockets of attacking corpses, then dropping the heavy metal scoop on their unsuspecting heads, crushing them instantly. Stokes might have found their slapstick demise funny if he hadn't been so bloody terrified.

'Looks like they've got everything under control now,' Caron said optimistically.

'I know, but I really don't like this.'

'What's the problem?' she asked. From where she was standing the survivors on the ground seemed to be doing well. The sudden surge of dead flesh through the barrier had been stopped, and those which had made it through were being destroyed quickly, and with very little effort, from what she could see.

'Watch him,' Hollis answered, pointing at Gordon again. 'He's not used to this. He's not as quick as the others.'

He was right. Rather than move towards the corpses, bringing the attack to them, Gordon was holding back, waiting for them to come to him. Perhaps he was hoping that someone else would take action before he had to. Whatever the reason, it was causing him problems, as four decayed figures started closing in on him at once.

'Look!'

With remarkable coordination the four bodies suddenly increased their pace and launched themselves at Gordon. At the last possible moment he lifted his fencepost and skewered the creature immediately in front of him through the abdomen, then he swung the post (with the limp body still impaled on it) from side to side, knocking two more of the foul figures clean off their clumsy feet.

To Caron's intense relief, Jas returned to Gordon's side to help him finish off his rotting assailants.

'Did you see them?' Hollis asked.

'Yes, but—'

'Did you see the bodies?' he asked again. 'Did you see what they were doing? The fucking things were moving together like pack animals.'

'That's impossible—'

'It might very well be impossible, but so's the fact that they're dead and still moving,' he said. 'Look, they're working together! It's like they're starting to realise they're no match for us on their own. The damn things have started to fight in packs!'

17

'You okay, Webb?' Hollis asked as the two men met on their way to the communal lounge. It was just before nine in the morning, much later than most of them usually dragged themselves out of bed, but the effort of the previous two days' fighting had exhausted everyone and an early, relatively undisturbed night had followed.

Webb's eyes were glazed and he still looked half-asleep. 'Slept like a fucking log,' he answered with his usual lack of tact, 'but I'm still fucking knackered.'

'You were out there for a long time yesterday. Those things might be falling apart, but they still take some getting rid of when they're coming at you.'

'Didn't see you out there much.'

'I didn't feel like it,' he replied. 'I smacked my head when I was out with Lorna yesterday morning – it still hurts.'

'You know,' Webb said, gradually becoming more animated as they walked, 'someone needs to go out there and tell those things that they're *dead*. You should have seen how they were going for us – I swear they're getting faster. I mean, they're still slow compared to you and me, but they're quicker than they used to be.'

'You're right,' Hollis agreed. 'It makes no sense, but you're right. We've just got to be careful and not take any chances. It's like—'

'And one of them bit me!' Webb interrupted. 'Don't forget that! Fucking thing tried to take a chunk out of my arm!'

'Yeah, you've already mentioned that.'

'We just need to keep doing what we're doing. If we can get rid of a load of them every day, then we can keep pushing them back, and if we can do that we'll— Christ, can you smell that?'

The two men were nearing the door of the flat, and Hollis too suddenly smelled food being cooked. He couldn't tell what it was, but that didn't matter: he was starving, and the appetising aroma was making his mouth water and his belly growl. Stokes appeared from the other direction, moving with more speed than he had for weeks, still getting dressed. The powerful smell was like an alarm call. Stokes only ever moved this quickly when his life was on the line or there was food on the table.

'Morning, boys,' he grinned cheerfully. 'Smells like grub's up!'

Stokes and Webb barged into the crowded flat and Hollis followed close behind. Harte and Lorna were in the small galley kitchen, cooking on portable gas-rings. Driver sat in the corner, rereading the same two month-old newspaper as usual. Jas and Gordon stood at the window. Only Caron, Ellie and Anita were missing.

Jas looked back over his shoulder to see who had arrived.

'Morning,' Hollis said as he walked over.

'Morning,' Gordon mumbled.

'What are you looking at?'

Jas sighed dejectedly. 'The bodies, same as always. I was just trying to see if we actually achieved anything yesterday.'

Hollis peered over his shoulder. The morning had started off misty, but the sun was beginning to burn away the haze and they could now see as far as the foot of the hill, where the battles with the dead had taken place over the last two days. There was a definite scar of dark discolouration – the butchered and burned bodies – but it was hard to see from this distance how much land had actually been reclaimed. The reason for Jas' lack of enthusiasm, however, was painfully obvious: no matter how much ground they'd gained, there was still an incalculable amount of work left to be done. Hollis lifted his eyes beyond the barrier and looked deeper into the crowd of corpses. It looked as large as ever, maybe even bigger. There must have been tens of thousands of bodies left to destroy, and for every single one they'd hacked down, it looked like hundreds more had flooded in to take its place.

'Going to take a little while, isn't it?' he said wryly.

'Going to take for ever,' Gordon agreed, leaning his head against the glass.

'Is it worth the effort?' Hollis asked, but no one answered.

'I busted my balls yesterday,' Jas complained, 'and risked my neck – and for what? All that work wasn't worth shit.'

'Of course it was,' Webb shouted across the room as he waited for his food. 'Look how many of them we got rid of.'

'Yeah, but look how many are left.'

'Thousands,' Gordon said quietly. 'Millions even.'

'Less than yesterday though,' Webb continued, grabbing a plate and filling his mouth with breakfast. 'And we ain't got to get rid of the lot of them, just enough so's we can push what's left back some more.'

'Forget it,' Hollis announced, 'it's not working. Don't go back out there today.'

'Has that bang on the head knocked you stupid?' Webb asked. ''course we're going back out!'

'What else are we going to do?' Stokes added, helping himself to food. 'If we're not out there killing them, all we'll be doing is sitting in here watching them.'

'I haven't actually seen you take one of them out yet,' Jas sneered.

'Piss off,' Stokes spat, sending a spray of partially chewed food splattering over the kitchen worktop.

'Watch what you're doing,' Lorna protested, screwing up her face in disgust. She wiped away his greasy spittle with a damp cloth.

'At least I'm out there,' Stokes protested, picking up his plate and carrying it over to the window towards Jas. 'There're some folk here who've done nothing to help. At least I'm out there.'

'Okay, okay . . .'

'Look at him,' Stokes ranted, pointing accusingly at Driver. 'The lazy bastard sits and reads the same bloody newspaper, all day every day. We have to force him to do anything useful.'

Driver glanced up from his paper, but he didn't react.

'You've made your point, okay,' Jas sighed, 'so now shut up.'

But Stokes ignored him, and still talking through a mouthful of food, he snarled, 'And there's Caron – can't remember the last time she went out and did anything worthwhile, can you? She spends all her bloody time with Anita – and she's another one, too. Christ, how much looking after does one stupid woman need? It's just another fucking excuse if you ask me.'

'Well, maybe I'll be able to do more to help now,' Caron said, and everyone turned to look at her as she walked into the room. She looked drained, her face ashen.

'What do you mean?' Harte asked.

Caron slumped into the nearest chair and dropped her head.

'What do you mean?' he asked again, crouching down in front of her. 'What's happened, Caron?'

Caron cleared her throat and wiped the tears from her eyes. 'She's dead,' she whispered. 'Anita's dead.'

'You're joking,' Stokes said stupidly.

'Like she'd joke about that, you fucking idiot,' Harte snapped angrily.

Hollis turned back to look out of the window, trying to absorb what he'd heard. Even when the world was so full of death, this unexpected loss was almost impossible to accept. He could hear people talking, some crying, but he kept his emotions locked tight inside. He didn't want them to see that he was completely fucking terrified that whatever had killed Anita might still be hanging in the very same air he was breathing now. *The next breath of air I take in*, he thought, *might be the one that kills me*. He could see the reflections of the others behind him in the glass; were they all thinking exactly the same thing? *I might already have it. We all might. And there's fuck-all any of us can do about it*, he thought.

18

He had to get out. It was always hard, being trapped inside with all the others, but it was worse than ever this morning. He understood why, of course, but that didn't make it any easier. Webb walked down the hill towards the fenced-off area where he'd previously fought with the dead for sport. He didn't feel like fighting today. He still had his baseball bat with him, of course, but today it was for protection only. He knew he was dumb and insensitive a lot of the time, but he'd taken the news of Anita's death as badly as anyone. He might not be the sharpest tool in the box, but even he'd quickly realised that what had killed her could probably kill him too. He could cope with thousands of decaying bodies, but this was something else altogether, a germ or a virus that was invisible and undetectable, something he couldn't punch, kick or smash into oblivion.

He'd left the others talking about the body. They were arguing about what they should do with it, but none of them, himself included, wanted to go anywhere near the corpse. Stokes had been arguing that Caron should deal with Anita, because she'd already spent so much time in the same flat; chances were she already had the germ inside her. Caron argued that they'd all got as much chance as each other of catching it – and that just scared everyone even more. When Gordon said they needed to do something quick, just in case she got up again and started walking around, Harte told him to shut up and get a grip and then Gordon became hysterical, ranting on about how Harte didn't know that wasn't going to happen, and how they couldn't afford to take any chances. Harte chucked an axe at him and told him to go to her flat and chop her body into pieces if he was so worried, and Gordon had threatened to attack Harte before he went anywhere near Anita's body and—

—and that was when Webb had got up and walked out.

He'd been sitting cross-legged in the dust for almost fifteen minutes when he realised he hadn't even looked at the dead today. He laughed sourly, thinking it said something about both his state of mind and the state of what was left of his world that a sea of tens of thousands of reanimated cadavers no longer interested him. He picked up a stone and threw it lazily towards the featureless mass of flesh, smirking to himself when it clattered against an old car door and the resulting sound caused a sudden ripple of animation on the other side of the barrier.

He threw another stone, then another, taking some sort of morose pleasure in making the corpses dance to his tune. Feeling marginally more interested, he got to his feet and walked closer, pausing to swing at a small rock, using his baseball bat like a golf club. The bodies trapped just in front of him were reacting angrily to his presence. They were slamming themselves against the blockade now, shuffling back, then throwing themselves forward again to get maximum impetus.

'Look at you,' he shouted, oblivious to the pointlessness of addressing the dead, 'you're all fucking pathetic.' He looked at the wall of putrefied faces, which stared back. He glared at one in particular which reminded him of his older sister. It was wearing the soiled shreds of a revealing pink summer dress, and the stupid fucking thing still had a fucking ribbon in its hair! *For Christ's sake*, he thought, *after everything that corpse must have gone through and it's still managed to keep its fucking hair tied up!* That reminded him of his sister, the silly bitch. She'd been arrested after a fight in a club once; she'd put some poor bastard in hospital. He'd watched the police shove her in the back of their van – and as they'd driven her away to the cells, he'd seen her checking her make-up in her reflection in the window, stupid cow.

Then Webb began to think about everyone else who had been a part of his life before the world had been turned upside-down, and he swung his baseball bat and thumped it into the side of the nearest car. The shockwave rippled back through the crowd like a pebble dropped into water and he hit the car door again, now actively *wanting* the dead to react. How many of these dumb, stinking pieces of shit were the same dumb, stinking pieces of shit who used to give him a hard time and make his life difficult? He hit the door a third time and the metallic clang ricocheted around his empty world. *How many of these things have ever given me grief or caused me pain or—*

Webb was suddenly aware of movement to his right. *What the fuck?*

Bodies – there were *bodies*, on *his* side of the blockade. Momentarily stunned, the first one was almost upon him before he was able to react. He swung the bat into its groin, sending it flying, just as another one lunged. He jabbed the end of the bat into its face, knocking it back into two more. What the hell was going on here – where were they coming from? Yet another body hurled itself forward, its arms reaching out for him, and he grabbed it by the collar and dragged it over onto its back then stamped on its emaciated face until it was still.

But there were more of them coming, too many—

Now absolutely terrified, Webb turned and ran from a crowd of almost twenty cadavers, which turned and slowly lumbered after him. Through a momentary gap between their constantly shifting shapes he thought he saw more climbing over the barrier, but that was impossible, wasn't it? He ran further up the hill, the slothful dead no match for his speed, then turned back and looked again.

His eyes hadn't deceived him: the bodies were dragging themselves up and over the blockade. Helped up by the countless corpses crushed under their rotting feet and by the relentless pressure of others constantly pushing them forwards, the damn things were managing to clamber over the cars and rubble and now they were heading straight for him.

Webb turned back to the flats once more and scrambled up the hill as fast as he could manage, screaming, 'Help!' at the top of his voice, though he didn't know if anyone could hear him. 'Get out here, now!'

Hollis, Harte, Lorna, Jas and Gordon were already on their way down towards the surging bodies before Webb had even made it back to the flats. They thundered past him, leaving him standing alone at the top of the slope. He stopped to catch his breath before heading back down after them.

'Did you see them?' he started to say to Stokes, who was pounding after the others at his usual slow pace.

'We all saw,' he answered quickly. 'It's your fault for winding them up, you fucking jerk!'

'What?' he protested. 'But I didn't do anything—'

His pointless words of denial were wasted; Stokes was already out of earshot. Still panting, Webb ran back down the hill. In the distance he could see that Harte and Lorna had reached the diggers.

'Just push them back,' Jas shouted. He pointed deep into the growing crowd. 'They're getting through over there – build the wall up!'

Lorna was the first to get her digger started. She drove it across the uneven ground at full speed, heading straight for the mass of bodies which were still spilling over the top of the barrier. It didn't look quite as bad from down here – when they'd first spotted the breach from their high vantage point in the flats above, there had appeared to be hundreds of figures pouring over. In reality there were far fewer, but that was academic – one corpse on the wrong side of the barrier was one too many. Scoop down, she thundered into the centre of the crowd, forcing many of the advancing grotesques up into the air and back over the blockade – until she collided with the very car they were managing to clamber over. The sudden shock jolted her back in her seat.

'Block it up,' Hollis shouted to Harte, gesturing at the place where the dead were managing to get over. It was hard to see clearly through the continual, frantic movement, it looked like they were dragging themselves over the crumpled bonnet of a black Vauxhall Vectra. Once he was sure that Harte had heard him he returned his attention to those foul aberrations which had already crossed over. It wasn't long before he was dispatching them with his machete.

Harte turned the digger around and moved away from the corpses. Behind him Lorna was now driving furiously from side to side, obliterating hordes of the dead with every pass. He drove towards a pile of rubble, collected a huge shovelfull and trundled it back to the barrier. It looked like they were beginning to regain control. Lorna had quickly dealt with a great mass of corpses, leaving Jas, Gordon, Webb and Stokes to wipe up the few that had managed to get away.

Hollis, unusually, was standing a little way back from the centre of the chaos. The dismembered remains of a blood-soaked police officer was twitching at his booted feet.

With a loud warning blast on the horn, Harte powered forward and stopped just short of the blockade (ploughing down six more cadavers on the way). He lifted the digger's articulated arm and dropped several tons of masonry onto the front of the black Vectra. Once the dust settled, it was immediately clear that he'd hit the spot perfectly. The dead were shut out again.

Harte felt a sense of smug satisfaction when he jumped down from the cab and saw that when he'd dropped the rubble, he'd also managed to crush a handful of bodies just as they'd been about to get across. Still-flailing arms and legs were jutting out from the confusion at awkward angles. The head of a trapped corpse, wedged at the shoulders between the bonnet of the Vectra and a block of concrete, watched him until he ended its unnatural existence with a well-aimed punch to the face.

'Come on, you fuckers!' Webb screamed at the top of his voice, fighting to make himself heard over the noise of Lorna's digger and the chainsaw which Jas was using. Suddenly pumped full of adrenalin again, he braced himself as yet another body hurled itself at him, its decayed face and gnarled lips almost seeming to sneer. He shoved it back towards Jas, who sliced it in half with a single swipe, the whirring chainsaw blade sliding through its torso like a hot knife through butter.

Two more foul bodies edged towards Jas, who shoved the chainsaw into the face of the nearest, angling the whirring blade away and down, and wincing in disgust as a thick spray of blood and rotten flesh soaked the ground. The other body of the pair seemed to have a little more sense – if that was at all possible. It suddenly veered to the left, evading the next swipe of the chainsaw, and turned its head back to watch Jas over its shoulder as it moved awkwardly away.

It never even noticed as it staggered straight into the path of Lorna in the digger.

'One behind you, Gordon,' Jas yelled.

Gordon spun around and waited nervously for the dishevelled remains of an elderly woman to attack. He gripped his axe tightly, wishing he could fight with the confidence and speed of the others. He felt hopelessly inadequate, despite the obvious strength advantage he had over the corpses, but the monstrous thing was upon him now and he had no alternative but to take action. Go for the head, he silently repeated to himself, remembering what the others had told him, and he swung the axe around and smashed it into the side of the corpse's face, shattering its cheekbone and splitting its ear in half. He wrenched the sunken blade free then panicked as the creature continued to stagger forwards, completely unperturbed by his blow. He swung the axe again, this time wedging it deep into the body's neck, and this time it took one more stumbling step closer, then dropped to the ground in front of him, dark crimson gore slowly dribbling out of its open wounds.

As quickly and as unexpectedly as it had started, the teeming movement on the survivors' side of the barrier wound down to nothing. The diggers and the chainsaw were silenced. On the other side of the barrier the bodies continued to surge forward, aftershocks of movement running through the huge crowd in response to the carnage and noise.

Everyone looked around until they were all satisfied that the job was done. Then, one by one, they began to move back towards the flats. Lorna walked over to Hollis when she noticed he wasn't following them.

'Is there a problem?' she asked, anxiously surveying the scene, worried that he'd spotted something the rest of them had missed.

He looked away. 'Doesn't matter,' he murmured.

'What is it?' she pressed, concerned.

Hollis angrily kicked the corpse lying at his feet. 'This thing caught me off-guard,' he reluctantly admitted. 'I didn't even know it was there until it got hold of me.'

'So? You sorted it out, didn't you?'

'Yes, but—'

'But what?' she pressed. It was obvious there was something he wasn't telling her.

'I didn't hear it coming,' he admitted.

'So what? I'm not surprised – what with the diggers and the chainsaw and Webb's mouth it's no wonder you didn't—'

He was shaking his head. She stopped talking. 'It's not that,' he said. 'Remember when we were out yesterday morning, you let that body out in the pharmacy and it went for me? I hit my head when I went down.'

'I know. Is that why you're—?'

'I've damaged my ear,' he said, his voice suddenly unusually emotional. 'I can't hear a fucking thing on my left side, and that's why this fucking thing nearly had me.' He kicked the corpse at his feet again, sending its bloodied head skidding across the ground like a football, then walked away from her and began to march up the hill.

19

'So what are we going to do?' Harte asked, slumping in a chair and holding his head in his hands. Four hours had passed since the bodies first breached the barrier, and since then they'd broken through three more times, smaller advances which had been quickly contained. 'Those damn things out there are *learning*! They're *copying* each other, for Christ's sake!'

'The obvious answer is to try and make the barrier stronger,' Hollis replied, 'but I don't think that's going to help.'

'Of course it's going to help, you prick. How can it not help?'

'I don't think we're looking at the problem the right way.'

'What are you talking about?' Harte grunted. He wasn't in the mood for riddles.

'Thing is,' Hollis explained, 'I don't think it matters *how* they got over the barrier, or if they're going to do it again. I think we need to be working out *why* they're doing it.'

'That's bloody obvious,' Lorna interrupted, 'it was Webb. We saw you standing out there, throwing stones at them.'

Hollis shook his head dejectedly. 'That's not it,' he sighed. 'Mind you, it didn't help.'

'So what then?' she snapped.

'I don't think it's just because of what you were doing today, Webb. I think they were reacting to what we've all been doing down there this week.'

'I still don't understand,' said Harte.

'For the last two days we've been pushing them around and smashing them up and burning them, a few hundred at a time.'

'So?'

'So, they're running scared – except they can't run, because there're too many of them and they can't get away. The only option they've got left—'

'—is to fight,' Jas said, finishing his sentence for him.

'Exactly. Webb, they reacted like that when you got down there today because they thought you were about to start laying into them again. And they're climbing over the barrier now because they know that they can. They've seen others doing it.'

'You've got to be fucking kidding me,' Stokes laughed from the other side of the room. 'Is anyone actually falling for this bullshit?'

'Well, think about it,' Hollis continued. 'They're adapting to what's happening around them. It makes sense.'

'None of this makes sense,' Gordon said.

'So what are we going to do about it?' asked Harte. 'I hear what you're saying, but can't we just build up the barrier and sit tight?'

'That's what I think,' Stokes said.

'First off, how? We don't have enough stuff to build it up with, and anyway, I don't think we can risk doing it. You saw what effect Webb going down there had on them this morning. If we start throwing our weight around again, even if we're not directly attacking them, we're going to push them over the edge and we'll end up with a full-scale pitch invasion.'

'So what are our alternatives? Sit here and do nothing?'

'There's no way I'm just going to just sit in here, waiting for them to give up and keel over,' Webb protested. 'No way am I going to spend all my time shut up in this fucking building, waiting. There's a fucking corpse in here too, don't forget.'

'No one's forgotten, Webb,' Hollis sighed. 'I know it's not ideal, but it's either that or leave – pack up and get out of here.'

Webb turned and looked out of the window. He didn't want to make eye-contact with anyone. He didn't know which was worse, the idea of staying put, or the prospect of heading out for good. The flats might be cold and uncomfortable, and right on the edge of the biggest cesspit of rotting human remains imaginable, but they'd been relatively safe here until now. None of them had any idea what they'd find elsewhere.

'There's something else you need to know,' Caron said, standing in the doorway. Everyone looked around. No one knew how long she'd been there.

'What's that?' Hollis asked, immediately concerned.

'It's Ellie. She's sick.'

'What do you mean?' he asked anxiously, horribly afraid that he knew the answer to his question already. 'Is she—?'

'Same as Anita,' she answered abruptly. 'She said she felt sick last night, but I didn't think much of it then – but today her symptoms are just the same.'

'This thing's going to wipe out the whole fucking lot of us,' Stokes said, putting into words what everyone else was thinking.

20

Late afternoon. Another wave of bodies had managed to scramble over the barrier. Between them Harte, Jas, Stokes and Webb had fought back the ninety or so cadavers which had forced their way over during the fifth breach and had worked quickly to strengthen the compromised blockade at the weak point. Stokes and Webb had been left outside to mop up the last few which had escaped the initial cull.

'Five left, I think,' Stokes wheezed as he moved towards the remaining corpses. Webb shielded his eyes and surveyed the area around them. The setting sun was framed in a narrow strip of clear sky between the horizon and a band of heavy grey cloud. The brilliant orange disc drenched the world in light, casting long, eerie shadows across the rubble. He soon saw the bodies that Stokes had spotted, trapped between a skip and a pile of masonry. One of them had fallen and become wedged in the way of the others. He swung his spiked baseball bat up onto his shoulder and headed down after Stokes. Tonight, more than ever, he was in need of therapy.

Stokes was already fighting by the time Webb reached the dead, doing all the damage he could to the trapped corpse with a chisel and a lump hammer he'd found in a toolbox in the back of a car and was now using as a makeshift dagger and mace. It was an indication of how the day's events had altered the individual survivors, that a man as lazy as Stokes, who was normally reluctant to fight, had, through sudden necessity, become remarkably aggressive. He yanked the fallen corpse up onto its feet and dragged it out of the way, immediately allowing the remaining bodies to move again.

'Let's get this done and get back inside,' he suggested. 'I've had enough for one day. I need a drink.'

Webb nodded, wearily watching the bodies hauling themselves onwards. – *Mind you, probably for the best*, he decided as he chose which of the creatures he'd go for first.

Panting with effort, Stokes shoved the lone figure away then readied himself for its attack. It moved closer, lunging unsteadily because of a broken right tibia which was jutting out from an angry wound in its leg. Stokes gripped his weapons tight, expecting the cadaver to throw itself at him, like so many others had already done today. But instead it held back, rocking clumsily on its feet, almost as if it was sussing out its opposition – if it was actually capable of seeing anything through those dark, unfocused eyes. Stokes, already anxious, felt even more uneasy. He decided to take the initiative, thrusting forward with the chisel and swinging the lump hammer at the foul thing's head. He caught its chin, wrenching its jaw bone out of its socket and leaving it dangling. Part of him wished he'd started fighting like this earlier, because Webb was definitely right: getting rid of these abominations so aggressively was strangely therapeutic. It made him feel alive. It reinforced the fact that he was so much better than these useless lumps of decaying gristle and putrid flesh.

'How're you doing, Webb?' he yelled as the body fell at his feet. He stamped on its chest, feeling a huge wave of satisfaction as its ribs cracked beneath his boot.

'All right,' Webb replied from a short distance away. He'd already got rid of one body and had incapacitated another which was on its knees just behind him. He'd broken both of its ankles and smashed its pelvis and though it could no longer stand, still it tried desperately to reach out for him, clawing wildly at the air. He ignored it and instead concentrated on another corpse, which he'd just shoved face-down in the dirt. He repeatedly slammed the baseball bat down onto its back, ripping its flesh apart and sending coagulated blood and slimy rotting flesh flying.

Stokes looked around for his next victim. Oddly, the fifth body looked as if it was trying to keep out of sight. As it moved behind the large yellow skip, Stokes went around the other way to meet it and dragged it back out into the open. He threw it to the ground, dropped down on its exposed ribcage and hammered the chisel through its left eye.

Webb was still attacking the same corpse – he'd long since incapacitated it, but the urge to batter it into oblivion was strong; he felt like it was helping him deal with the all-consuming fear that'd overcome him when Anita had died and Ellie got taken ill.

Stokes noticed the cadaver behind Webb was still moving and he strode towards it purposefully, ready to put it out of its misery.

Webb, concentrating on the carcase on the ground but suddenly aware of another figure approaching at speed, turned into the sun and swung his baseball bat around with massive force.

Stokes let out a screech as it hit him square in the chest, the nails piercing skin and muscle and puncturing his lungs. He dropped to his knees, clutching his wounds.

'What the—?' he whispered, stunned, as the pain rolled over him like a wave.

Webb's legs turned to jelly as he realised what he'd done. 'Christ! I'm so sorry, Stokes,' he stammered pathetically, 'I swear I didn't mean to— I didn't know it was you . . . I just—'

'It really hurts,' Stokes groaned, tears of agony running down his face. He looked at his hands and saw that they were soaked with blood. His jacket and shirt were drenched too. 'Go and get the others,' he wheezed. 'Get Caron—'

Webb crouched down next to him. What the hell was he going to do? He reached out his hand but stopped before he touched him.

Stokes looked at him again, his eyes wide with shock, then slumped over onto his side heavily. He managed a few more laboured, gurgling breaths, and then he stopped. Everything was silent, save for the corpse scrambling around in the dust just out of reach.

'Stokes,' Webb said, getting as close to the other man's face as he could without touching him, 'Stokes, come on! Don't die—'

He reached out his hand again, this time forcing himself to touch Stokes' shoulder. He shook it, but there was no response. *He can't be dead. He just can't be . . .*

The creature behind him had managed to drag itself far enough forward to reach Webb's boot and as he touched it with outstretched fingers, Webb turned and grabbed the corpse by the shoulders and threw it several yards away into the dust. He didn't even notice when it flopped back over onto its chest and began to drag itself towards him again. He was concentrating instead on Stokes, who still hadn't moved. *Jesus Christ*, Webb thought, his panic mounting, *what have I done? It was an accident – it was all his fault; if the stupid idiot hadn't crept up on me like that it never would have happened. They'll understand, won't they? They'll know I didn't do it on purpose . . .*

For a few desperate seconds longer he weighed up his limited options – turn and run, or go back and face the others. Much as he would have liked to just quietly disappear, one look at the thousands of corpses gathered around the flats was enough to tell him he'd never get away in one piece. If he'd been able to drive, then maybe things would have been different, but he couldn't. He was stuck here, with the consequences of his own actions.

'What's the matter with you?' Hollis asked as Webb burst into the communal flat. Bloody Webb, why did his heart always sink when he saw him?

'They got him,' he gasped.

'What are you talking about? Who got who?'
'Stokes. They got him!'
'Who got him?' he repeated.
'The bodies. He's *dead*.'

21

'I'm going,' Harte announced, his face pressed against the window. 'They're coming over the barrier again. Fuck this, I'm going.'

His words were met with silence as the rest of the survivors thought about what they'd heard. Several others had reached the same decision individually, but no one had yet found the courage to stand up and say as much. Harte wasn't courageous either; he was entirely motivated by fear.

'Are you sure there's no other option?' Caron asked. The room was dark. She couldn't see how anyone else had reacted.

'I'll listen to anything anyone else has got to say,' Harte replied anxiously, 'but I can't see any other way forward. For Christ's sake, Anita's dead upstairs, Stokes is dead down there and the bodies are climbing over the barrier again. You tell me if there's any better option than getting the hell out of here.'

Silence.

'We could go down there in the morning and clear them out again,' Jas suggested. 'I'm not going out there tonight.'

'How many will be down there by then? I've seen half a dozen get over in the last couple of minutes. At that rate that's almost a hundred an hour. There'll be a thousand of them by the time the sun comes up.'

Hollis got up and walked over to the window. Harte was right; in the pale moonlight outside he could see that the corpses had found another weak point in their increasingly ineffective blockade and once over, they were scrambling across the open ground like cockroaches scuttling across a dirty kitchen floor.

'But is it going to be any different anywhere else?' Gordon asked. He was sitting on the floor in the furthest corner of the room, knees pulled up close to his chest. 'It's not going to be any better, is it?'

'Couldn't be any worse,' Lorna mumbled.

'Don't count on it,' Jas said quickly. 'We thought we were doing well here.'

'I don't understand what's happened,' Caron said. 'Why's it all gone so wrong so quickly?'

'Bad luck,' Hollis answered.

'It's a bit more than bad luck, you fucking idiot,' Harte said nervously.

'We couldn't have planned for any of this,' he continued.

'No one could have planned for anything that's happened since September.'

'I know that, but we thought we'd be able to sit this out here, didn't we? I thought we'd be okay here until they'd decayed away to nothing – and maybe we still would have been, if Anita hadn't got sick.'

'But why now? Caron asked. 'Why are they climbing over the barrier today?'

'Because they're scared,' Jas replied. 'Because they've seen us down there beating the shit out of several hundred of them at a time, and we've scared them. They can't get away because there are so many of them, so they're fighting back like caged animals. What's left of their brains is telling them to get us before we get them.'

'Do you really believe that?'

'I do,' Hollis said quickly. 'Jas is right. We've brought this on ourselves.'

'So is there any point in leaving?'

'Well, yes,' he responded with almost irritating bluntness, 'of course there is. Anita's dead and Ellie's dying – if we stay here, there's a strong chance more of us will go the same way.'

'But like I said,' Gordon whined from the corner, 'aren't we just going to end up in just as bad a mess somewhere else? Wherever we go, we'll end up with another bloody huge crowd of them gathered around us.'

'Maybe, but it probably won't be as big a crowd as we've got here. It's taken more than a month for this many of them to drag themselves over here. It's going to take time for things to get this bad if we're starting again from scratch, isn't it?'

'Yes, but—'

'You've seen what kind of a state they're in, haven't you? So, logically, by the time we get to this stage again with these kind of numbers, the bodies should be pretty much incapable of harming us, no matter how many of them there are.'

'I'm sold,' Lorna said quietly. 'What you're saying makes sense to me. I'm going.'

'But right now,' Caron protested, 'this is all irrelevant.'

'Is it?' Lorna asked. 'Why?'

'Because we can't go anywhere with Ellie the way she is.'

'Yes, we can,' Harte quickly replied.

'We can't just leave her here—'

'Yes, we can,' he said again. 'We can't take her with us, can we? That kind of defeats the object, doesn't it? If we take her, we take whatever she's got with us, don't we?'

'But we can't just leave her,' Caron repeated, sounding shocked.

'Are you sure she's got the same thing that killed Anita?' Jas asked.

'Her symptoms are the same, and she's been getting worse as quickly as Anita did.'

'So she's probably going to die, isn't she?'

Although she knew the answer, Caron didn't want to say it, in case it made it the truth. 'She might not,' she stammered awkwardly. 'Anita might have had some other medical problem that we didn't know about. She might have—'

137

'I think she's going to die,' Hollis said, 'and a few more of us probably will too if we don't leave here now.'

'But you can't just abandon her!'

'Does she say anything when you walk into her flat?' Jas asked.

'No, but—'

'Does she sit up in bed? Does she look at you and talk to you? Does she even know you're in there with her?'

'Sometimes. Most of the time she's asleep or—'

'By the time we're ready to leave here that poor cow won't have a clue what's going on. She won't know if she's on her own or if we're all in the room with her. More to the point, she won't give a shit.'

'We can't just leave her here to die – it's inhuman!'

'Then maybe we should put her out of her misery?' Hollis suggested. 'If what's going to happen to her really is inevitable, speeding it up is only going to help.'

'Christ, she's not a dog,' Caron screamed, crying now. 'You can't just put her down.'

'I'll do it,' Harte said, surprising the others. 'Give her some dignity—'

'*Dignity?*' she yelled in disbelief. 'Where's the *dignity* in being murdered?'

'There's more dignity in dying quickly and quietly at the hands of one of us than there is lying in a dirty flat, surrounded by thousands of dead bodies and in so much pain that you lose your mind.'

'No one's trying to force you to do anything, Caron,' Jas said, his voice a little calmer, quieter and less emotional than the others. 'All we're saying is that we can't afford to take Ellie with us. If you want to stay here and nurse her, than that's up to you.'

Caron stared angrily into the darkness, her mind filled with so many painful thoughts and impossible decisions that she couldn't make sense of any of it.

'When did you last check on her?' Lorna asked, but Caron

didn't answer. She tried asking another question. 'Have you seen her this evening? Did you go up there after the bodies first got through this morning?'

'I haven't seen her for hours,' Caron eventually replied, having to force herself to spit the words out. 'I haven't seen her since early this morning.'

'Why not? I thought you'd—'

'I'm too scared,' she admitted. 'I don't want to go in there any more after what happened to Anita, all right? I don't want to catch what she's got.'

'Then there's your answer,' Harte said under his breath as Caron's sobbing filled the room.

'The longer we leave this, the worse it's going to get,' Jas said. 'If the germs don't get us, then those bastards outside will. Look what they did to Stokes.'

'Poor bastard didn't know they were there until they'd got him,' Webb said from where he'd been sitting on the floor next to the arm of the sofa. He swallowed hard and hoped that the others were sufficiently wrapped up with their own problems not to notice his sudden nervousness.

'You're right,' Hollis agreed. 'We've all seen it. Their behaviour is changing. They're more aggressive, and they're working together.'

'So where would we go?' Gordon asked, begrudgingly beginning to accept that leaving now looked like their only option.

Silence.

'In the summer,' Driver suddenly announced, 'I used to drive the 222 out of Catsgrove.'

'Fuck me, Driver,' Harte gasped. 'I didn't even know you were in here!'

'He's always in here,' Lorna muttered angrily. 'Lazy bastard never goes anywhere else.'

'What were you saying?' Hollis asked, trying to pick out Driver in the darkness.

'I used to drive the 222,' he repeated. 'Day trips to the coast.'

'What? You want to go to the seaside? You're a fucking idiot,' Webb cursed.

'On the A197 out of town,' he continued, unfazed, 'you pass this bloody huge exhibition centre. Make a good place to go, that would. Out in the country. Loads of space. Nothing else for miles.'

The room was suddenly completely silent. Even Caron had stopped crying to listen to Driver and think about his suggestion.

Hollis couldn't help wondering why Driver'd waited until now to decide to speak up. Whatever the reason, he was glad that he finally had.

22

After a sleepless night and an hour spent collecting her belongings from her flat, Caron climbed the stairs to the room where Ellie lay. Her nervousness increased with each step she took. She couldn't believe she'd allowed herself to be coerced into doing this. She clutched a polythene bag full of drugs in her hand, though she didn't know if she'd be able to use them. She didn't even know if she'd be able to go into Ellie's room this morning. The stench had been appalling when she'd last checked on her. She'd made a half-hearted attempt to clean her up, but the mess had been too much. Hollis had pointed out that the poor girl was bound to be long past the point of caring now – it would have caused her more distress lugging her around so they could clean her than to leaving her lying in her own shit, and though she hated to admit it, she could see he was right.

The cold wind blew through an empty window frame, gusting into her face like a slap across the cheek. She walked down the final long, dark corridor and reached the door to Ellie's flat. She was too scared to go in, too scared to stand outside and too scared to go back downstairs without having seen her. She could hear the others out in the car park, loading their supplies into the bus and one of the vans. She didn't want to leave, but she definitely didn't want to stay either. When she'd looked out of the window first thing this morning the barrier at the foot of the hill had all but disappeared, obscured from view by the hundreds of bodies which had managed to drag themselves across during the long hours of the night just ended. Only the steep slope had so far prevented them from getting any further.

Closing her eyes and struggling to hold her nerve, Caron cautiously pushed the door open and looked inside, but there was no movement, and no sound. She tiptoed into the flat and peered through the bedroom door. Still no movement – but, Lord, the smell was even worse than she remembered: the stagnant stench of sweat, vomit and excretion mixing with the ever-present wafts of death and decay drifting in from outside. Was Ellie dead? She wasn't moving. Maybe it would be better for her – for all concerned – if she'd gone in her sleep. Caron took a few steps further into the bedroom, the drugs gripped tightly in one hand, a handkerchief held over her mouth and nose with the other.

'Ellie,' she whispered lightly. 'Ellie, honey, are you awake?'

Ellie still wasn't moving. Caron crept a little closer, not wanting to get too near. Her foot accidentally caught Ellie's doll, sending it spinning across the floor, and she cringed at the noise. She squinted into the darkness until she could make out Ellie, lying on her side with her back to the door. She'd thrown off the covers. Caron still couldn't see any movement. Was Ellie breathing? Maybe she should try and touch her, check for a pulse or—

'Jesus!' she screamed with surprise as Ellie threw herself over onto her back with a sudden, painful groan of effort. Caron's first thought was one of disappointment that she was still alive, and then massive guilt that she'd actually wished the girl dead, though she wasn't sure whether it was because she'd hoped Ellie had been put out of her misery, or whether it was because she didn't want to have to do it for her.

Ellie groaned again and mumbled something unintelligible. Without realising she was doing it, Caron backed away.

'I'll get you some water,' she whispered, her eyes filled with stinging tears. She went through into Ellie's living room and found a half-empty plastic water bottle sitting on a windowsill. Though she didn't want to take her eyes off the girl's bedroom door, she looked down and pulled out a handful of capsules from her bag, which she broke apart and emptied into the water, then shook the bottle. For half a second she considered drinking it herself. She wasn't able to look after anyone any more – she'd lost her son, then Anita, and now Ellie . . . What kind of a mother had she turned out to be? Would she be any better at killing them? But no, that was stupid. She couldn't allow herself to think like that. She looked at the bottle in her hand and wondered whether it would actually have any effect at all – or would it just make Ellie even sicker?

Despite being high up, she could hear the others outside again, and that forced her into action. She wasn't sure exactly what she did want any more but she definitely knew she didn't want to be left here. With nervous determination she walked purposefully into Ellie's room and found her lying motionless on her back, naked and soaked with sweat, staring up at the ceiling with wide, vacant eyes.

'Ellie, sweetheart,' she said quietly, gingerly putting her hand on the girl's cold shoulder and shaking her slightly, 'take this; it'll make you feel better.'

She raised the water bottle to Ellie's chapped lips, but she couldn't make the girl drink. In desperation she began to pour it into her mouth, but most of it just ran down her cheek and onto the already drenched bedding. She didn't even react to the temperature of the water. Ellie was as good as dead already.

The easiest option – the *cowardly* option – was to put the bottle in her hand and leave. With tears running down her face, that was exactly what Caron did.

23

The barrier at the base of the hill had disappeared now, swallowed up by a slow-moving but unstoppable tide of cold, dead flesh. Thousands of restless bodies, pushed relentlessly forward by thousands more, had surged silently over the blockade of vehicles and rubble throughout the night. The stronger cadavers, those which had somehow avoided suffering any major physical damage, now crushed their weaker brethren beneath their feet. The foetid remains of countless fallen figures had been compressed into a thick pad of rotting matter, allowing other corpses to trample over them and use them like an access ramp to scramble up and over the barrier. It didn't appear to matter whether they were being driven by curiosity, fear, instinct or hate; the only thing that did matter was that they were moving ever closer to the living. And as Hollis and Harte had already noticed, the compromised barrier not only allowed bodies in, it also acted like a valve, preventing those creatures inside from getting back out. Although none of them had, as yet, managed to climb the hill, it was inevitable that they eventually would. Staying put and doing nothing was no longer an option.

Driver folded up his tattered newspaper and shoved it into the gap behind the steering wheel of the bus. He leant out of his cab and watched as Jas and Harte struggled to load up the last few bags and boxes. They were breathing heavily, out of breath from the effort of stowing Jas' Honda in the back of the Transit van – he'd just decided he'd be safer travelling on four wheels with the others.

'You could get off your backside and help if you wanted to,' Harte sneered sarcastically.

'You've almost done it now,' Driver mumbled.

'Thanks for nothing,' he said as he stormed back off the bus. Harte's bad mood was made worse by the discovery that even though they had managed to pack everything they had into the bus and one van, there was still plenty of space to spare. They'd even decided to leave the other van behind. It was unreliable and had an oil leak, and they really didn't need it – but Harte suddenly felt hopelessly ill-prepared for life away from the flats.

Hollis was walking away from the building which had been their home since the world collapsed, his arm around Caron's shoulder. Gordon followed close behind, looking typically awkward and uncomfortable.

Jas moved to one side to let the three of them onto the bus. He waited for Caron and Gordon to disappear upstairs before asking Hollis, 'What happened in there?'

'I don't know,' he replied abruptly, 'and I don't want to ask. Are we ready to go?'

'I think so.'

'Do you reckon she did it?' Harte whispered.

'Did what?'

'Finished her off?'

'Christ, you're an insensitive prick,' Hollis said. 'For Ellie's sake I hope she did.'

'I'm not insensitive,' Harte protested. 'I just want to know what happened.'

'Doesn't matter what she—' Jas began.

'Just leave it,' Hollis interrupted. 'We need to get going. Are you ready?' he asked, looking at Driver, who nodded wordlessly. Hollis got off the bus and jogged over to the Transit van where Lorna and Webb were waiting for him. He climbed in and started the engine, keen to get moving.

'I reckon we should torch this place before we go,' Webb suggested, sitting in the back of the van behind the other two.

'What good's that going to do?' Lorna asked.

'You're a fucking pyromaniac,' Hollis said grimly.

'I'm not, I just think—'

'No, you *don't*,' Lorna yelled at him angrily, sounding unexpectedly furious, 'and that's the problem. You don't *think* at all. You just bulldoze and bullshit your way through everything. Ellie is dying in there, and we're leaving her behind. Isn't that enough for you? Do you want to make sure you finish the job off by burning her to death? Christ, do you know what I—'

'Will you both just shut up,' Hollis shouted, slamming his fist down on the steering wheel. 'You're for ever bickering like a pair of fucking five-year-olds. Just shut up!'

He swung the Transit around in a wide circle and as he waited for Driver to line himself up behind he took one last look at the dead, who were now beginning to creep slowly up the hill. Then he peered up at the towering grey block of flats, the closest thing he'd had to a home since they'd all lost everything, weeks ago. It was so strange: he felt worse about leaving this place today than he had when he'd last walked out of his house, the day his world had fallen apart, back in September. Staying there had never been an option – it had been full of memories, of people and places, everything he'd lost. For a while though, this horrible, damp estate had given them all some security, a base from which they could try and rebuild their lives.

That was all gone now. Lorna and Webb were still arguing as he put his foot down and drove away.

Gordon pressed his face up against the glass, feeling his whole body shake as the bus rattled through the carnage on the roads leading away from the flats. He was sitting on the back seat of the top deck. Caron sat opposite, her back to him, staring out of the window on the other side. Harte was three seats in front, Jas another five seats ahead of him, as spread out as the limited confines of the transport would allow. Gordon used to travel by bus regularly; he had always considered it an unwritten rule to put as much distance as you could between yourself and any strangers. Today, however, everyone kept their distance to avoid sharing their fears and concerns. A couple of days ago everything had been relatively okay. How had it all gone so wrong so quickly? Gordon glanced over at Caron. What was she thinking? She still had a plastic bag full of pills gripped tightly in her hand. Who were they for – had she not given any to Ellie? Did she intend taking them herself? Surely things couldn't be that bad, could they?

Driver swerved left then right to avoid the blackened remains of another bus, which was straddling the carriageway. Dead passengers were visible inside, trying endlessly to get out. Driver's own passengers were momentarily thrown into the air as the cumbersome vehicle clattered up the kerb then back down again. Gordon was thrown to the side and banged his head against the glass. Rubbing the bump, he closed his eyes and tried to concentrate on the sound of the engine. Unexpectedly, for just the slightest of seconds, everything felt reassuringly familiar, and for a moment he allowed himself to believe that instead of driving away from the silent, rotting remains of the city where he'd lived all his life, he was actually on his way home from work. He tried to convince himself that if he opened his eyes he'd see the comforting, familiar sights of his daily commute again. Any moment now the bus would slow down, then it would grind to a stop as they joined the snaking queue of traffic escaping the city centre. If he looked outside, he'd see hundreds of people, all making their way back home like him. Another fifteen minutes' drive and he'd reach his stop. A ten-minute walk after that and he'd be home. What would Janice be cooking for him tonight? A piece of fish, or maybe a pork chop with chips? His mouth began watering at the thought of it. Christ, he hoped she hadn't been experimenting – he always hated it when she cooked her 'exotic' dinners – he didn't like pasta or rice or curries, but he always forced himself to eat it. Maybe he'd have to do his usual trick, take the dog for a long walk tonight, giving him a chance to grab a burger from the place on the corner and eat it on his way through the park . . .

Gordon opened his eyes and stared out at the dead world around him. Drained of colour, raped by disease and disintegrating almost as he watched, it bore little resemblance to the place in his imagination. The remains of his fellow commuters were scattered about on the ground, kicked all over the place by these horrific creatures which were still dragging themselves through the streets, weeks after they'd ostensibly died. And Janice, his long-suffering wife of twenty-three years, was still suffering too. She was condemned to spend the rest of for ever trapped in their living room, behind the door he'd boarded up after she'd got up and started moving again.

24

The van stopped suddenly. Driver, following too close behind, slammed on his brakes to avoid crashing into the back of it.

'What's the matter?' Caron asked anxiously, getting up from her seat and running to the front where Jas was already standing at the window. They'd been on the move for less than an hour. The road they'd been following had meandered through open countryside for a time but they'd now reached Cudsford, an unremarkable town nestled between two larger but equally uninteresting towns, the first relatively built-up area they'd come across. On balance they'd decided it was easier and quicker to drive straight through rather than skirt all the way around and add miles to their journey.

'Doesn't look like anything major,' Jas said, looking down onto the street below. 'There's a van blocking the road, that's all.'

Harte was already on his way down the stairs, hand-axe at the ready, just in case. Jas followed, pausing to pick up the chainsaw from where he'd dumped it on the lower deck, next to the door. By the time he stepped out onto the street, Webb, Hollis and Lorna were already out and surveying the scene. A single corpse staggered out from behind the crashed van, tripped in the gutter and fell at Webb's feet. He smashed its skull with his spiked baseball bat, as nonchalantly as if he were swatting a fly.

'Well?' Harte asked, keeping his voice low. Hollis pointed at the front of the blue-liveried van which had thumped into the front of an office block, leaving its rear-end jutting out into the road. That's what was blocking their way through.

The dead driver (which was still trying to get out from behind the wheel) slammed its decaying face up against the glass as they moved closer.

'Problem is,' Hollis explained, ignoring the corpse's frantic movements, 'it looks like it's wedged in good and proper.' He leant over the front of the van and looked up. The impact had brought the low canopy of a porch crashing down onto its roof. There were visible cracks running up the face of the building and the glass in many of the first floor windows had smashed. 'There's a chance if we move it that we'll bring the whole lot down.'

'So?' Webb grunted, returning his attention to the crash.

'So we could end up blocking the road even more instead of clearing it,' he replied, wishing that he wasn't stuck out in the middle of nowhere with someone as dense as Webb.

'I think it'll be all right,' Harte said, carefully stepping under the canopy and looking up to try and assess the damage. 'I don't think there's any other way of shifting—'

A sudden movement from Lorna distracted him and he turned to see her rush across to the other side of the road and start grappling with the bloody figure which threw itself at her. She grabbed its scrawny neck, forcing it back against the nearest wall and cracking its skull, then beating it repeatedly with the claw-hammer she'd been carrying. Sometimes she scared herself with her own brutality.

She looked further down the street. The damn thing hadn't been alone.

'Get a move on,' she whispered, counting at least seven more bodies heading in their direction. 'They're coming.'

Webb, his appetite for violence clearly undiminished despite the events of the last twenty-four hours, ran forward to head off the approaching dead, swinging the baseball bat wildly through the air. He thumped it into the face of the cadaver nearest to him, catching it perfectly and laughing out loud as it tripped blindly back, like an uncoordinated drunk, into two more bodies and knocking them both over. He ran towards them with predatory speed, determined to finish them all off before they could pick themselves back up.

'So what do we do?' Jas asked hurriedly. Even more bodies were closing in now. 'Move this thing, or turn around and find another way through?'

'Driver's never going to get the bus turned around here. He'll have to back it out—' Hollis stopped when he heard the bus suddenly begin to move.

Jas started up his chainsaw and ran back towards the huge vehicle as the nearest figures, leading an uncomfortably large crowd of corpses, began to stumble and surge past it on either side. He held the chainsaw at waist-height and waded into them, moving the churning blade from side to side, scything down the creatures almost as if they were trees being felled. The road beneath his feet was suddenly awash with gore and the remains of the limbs he was slicing off the bodies that were still foolishly stumbling towards him.

The bus accelerated and Jas realised that Driver was shunting it forward and angling it across the street to fully block the width of the thoroughfare and prevent any more of the dead from getting closer.

Caron, standing next to Gordon at the back of the bus, looked down in disbelief as the entire street behind them quickly became clogged with dead flesh. She hadn't been this close to the ambulatory cadavers for weeks and she was terrified, both of their appearance and their sudden vast numbers. Physically they were grotesque: they had deteriorated to an incredible extent and their decaying bodies were literally falling apart in front of her. But at the same time, they were continuing to move with unquestionable intent. When she'd last been this close to them they'd been not long dead. Now their faces were hideously scarred and mutated, barely recognisable as human. Gordon was rambling incessantly, making endless excuses about why he should stay up here with her, how he probably would just get in the way out there, but Caron wasn't listening. She hadn't realised how strong and secure the flats had been. *All that's separating me from them now*, she anxiously thought, *is this bus.*

Out on the street, Harte yanked open the door of the crashed van and recoiled from the stench in the cab. He found himself gagging as he grappled with the driver's corpse trapped inside. It threw its withered arms at him and he battered them away with the axe, trying to get the right angle to use the weapon properly in the confined space. At last he managed to grab the squirming cadaver and undo its seatbelt. His gloved hand easily wrapped around its bony wrist and with an almighty heave he yanked it out into the open. Its right foot caught between the gearstick and handbrake and Harte desperately tugged at the struggling creature finally pulling with enough force to rip the foot off at the ankle. As soon as the corpse was free he slammed its face into the pavement until it stopped moving.

Harte paused for a moment to catch his breath, then he climbed up into the van and settled himself behind the wheel. The seat felt sticky beneath him, but he tried hard to ignore that. He reached down and unhooked the dismembered foot from under the pedals and threw it out of the window.

He automatically adjusted the rear-view and wing-mirrors – and in them he saw that the number of bodies hauling themselves down the street towards the survivors had increased massively. Driver had used his bus to block the road one way, but a relentless deluge of flesh was now approaching from the other direction, channelled by the tall buildings on either side. He could see Jas a couple of yards ahead of Lorna and Webb, carving up as many of them as he could reach with the brutally efficient chainsaw, and the other two were standing shoulder to shoulder, mopping up any of the figures that managed to get past.

Harte jumped when Hollis yelled, 'Get it started!' and hammered on the back of the van. He turned the key in the ignition, willing the engine to fire, but it groaned and whined and wouldn't start.

'Careful, don't flood it,' Hollis warned.

Harte tried again, turning the key once more, this time pumping the accelerator pedal with his foot, not knowing if that would help or make the problem worse. This time the engine almost caught. 'Come on!' he shouted in frustration, slamming his hand against the steering wheel angrily, and tried again—

—and the engine suddenly spluttered into life. Harte gunned the engine, trying to keep it turning over, and the delivery van's exhaust started belching dirty clouds of fumes into the street. In the heat of the moment he forgot everything Hollis had said about being careful and driving slowly and instead slammed it into reverse and hit the accelerator pedal. As he careened back, steering hard round to keep the van on the pavement, he peered out of the windscreen at the canopy at the front of the damaged building, praying it would hold.

It didn't: the sides of the porch collapsed inwards, littering the ground with rubble – but thankfully, the front of the building remained intact.

Harte drove up onto the pavement, leaving the road clear, and parked.

'Come on, we need to get out of here,' Hollis shouted as he climbed out of the van. 'This isn't looking good.' He pointed at Lorna, Webb and Jas, who were just about managing to hold back the tide of the dead. Though they remained in control for the moment, the dead masses were herding towards them, and their numbers were increasing. The three survivors had been laying about themselves with a will and in the ten minutes it had taken Harte to move the van they had reduced more than fifty corpses to little more than a bloody pile of unrecognisable body parts, but easily twice as many again were still stumbling inexorably towards them, and more would undoubtedly follow when the next fifty had been hacked down, then more and more . . .

Harte ran back to the bus, distracted momentarily by a body which appeared to come from out of nowhere, dropping face-down onto the street just in front of him and disintegrating on impact like bad fruit. He recoiled in disgust as foul substances splashed up at him from the splattered remains on the tarmac. He looked up at the office block beside him, bewildered. The sudden, constant noise and movement out in the street had alerted the corpses which had been trapped inside the building but which were now finding a way out through the gap left by the van he'd shifted. Drawn out of the shadows by the sound of the chaos outside, the stupid creatures were plummeting out from the first floor like lemmings. Ignorant of the danger and desperate to get closer to the living, the damn things were literally falling out of the sky around him – and just as he realised what was happening, another one crashed to the street nearby. Its head had somehow been protected from the fall, but its body was badly damaged – but as if completely unaware how broken it was, it tried to pull itself along the ground towards him with its one remaining good arm.

'That's it. We're going,' he announced to Driver, who didn't need any further instruction. The bus driver straightened his vehicle again and as he moved it forward, stumbling corpses began to slip through on either side, their speed increased by the pressure of others pushing from behind.

A short way up ahead, Hollis drove the Transit up to where the others were still fighting. Lorna climbed in quickly, shouting across at Webb and Jas for them to follow, and Webb ran back the moment he heard her – and then stopped when he realised that Jas was still out there, isolated from everything else that was happening by the noise of his weapon. He ran forward again and grabbed his shoulder, stumbling back as Jas spun around and lunged at him, his chainsaw blade whirring angrily—

—and at the last possible second he realised it was Webb and yanked the blade back. 'What the fuck do you think you're doing?' he screamed furiously as unchallenged corpses began to hurl themselves at him. 'I could have killed you, you stupid—!'

But he shut up when he saw what was happening behind him: the cadavers, suddenly able to get through again, were streaming ever closer, and he and Webb were about to be sandwiched between two advancing walls of dead flesh.

'Get in!' Lorna screamed, her voice so loud that it hurt, and as Jas and Webb jumped in the back, bodies slammed against the van, just missing them. One of them, half of its face eaten away by rot or rodents, glared at her with its one remaining eye and hammered against her window with greasy fists. She turned away from it in disgust, but there were more equally hideous dead faces staring back through every available square inch of glass. Hollis drove forward, knocking the monsters away like skittles as he powered through the crowd. He was hugely relieved that they had decided to move before the corpses had been able to bunch up tight; already the entire street – which had been empty just minutes earlier – was now teeming with hundreds of cadavers.

'What the hell just happened?' Jas breathlessly asked from the back. 'That was so *fast*.'

'I guess that's the reception we're going to get wherever we go now,' Hollis answered, clutching the steering wheel tight as they juddered through the seething crowd.

'Ten minutes,' Jas said, as if he couldn't quite believe what had happened. 'We couldn't have been out there any longer than ten minutes—'

'If we're all that's left,' Lorna said quietly, 'then this will keep happening. Back at the flats there were thousands of them gathered in that one place because they knew we were there. Out here they're running wild.'

25

The rural roads they were using now were relatively clear, once they'd outrun the last of the rotting population of Cudsford. There were hardly any bodies on this side of the town, in stark contrast to their encounter a few miles back, and there were considerably fewer wrecked vehicles than they'd seen in a long time. Though there were still plenty of the tell-tale signs of the devastation which had blighted the country, Hollis realised he had to look a little harder to see them. Weeds were sprouting everywhere; it wouldn't be long before buildings, abandoned vehicles and dead bodies alike would be completely swallowed up by the encroaching vegetation and absorbed back into the landscape.

'Where's the bus?' Jas asked suddenly, anxiously looking over his shoulder.

Hollis had been enjoying the rare freedom of the open road and had been driving too fast. He slowed down, not quite daring to stop, despite the relative lack of bodies around them, and after a few seconds the lumbering, blood-splattered bus came back into view. 'Here they are,' he announced, hoping he'd successfully hidden the sudden fear which had gripped him when the rear-view mirror had shown nothing but empty road behind him.

The wide, tree-lined road curved to the left around the foot of a large hill. Several hundred yards ahead was a traffic island, signposted with names which didn't mean anything. Hollis searched for something familiar – he thought he could remember the route to the exhibition centre Driver had talked about, but like everyone else, his nerves were shattered. He needed reassurance.

'Any ideas?' he asked hopefully.

'Second exit,' Lorna replied, though she sounded nervous and unsure, and Hollis gave her a thumbs-up and steered the Transit around the roundabout.

They all flinched as he ploughed into a lone body which had foolishly tripped into his path.

'Oi, mate, I need a piss,' Jas said, banging on the side of the van.

'What do you want me to do about it?' Hollis snapped.

'Well, you could stop the van and let me out,' he answered, annoyed. 'I'm not going to do it in here.'

'And I'm not going to stop!'

'Don't be stupid, Hollis, I'm bloody desperate,' Jas said, crossing his legs uncomfortably.

'You've got to stop,' Webb chipped in. 'Come on, I need to go too.'

'You'll have to piss in a bottle and throw it out of the window,' Hollis said crossly. 'I'm not stopping. Look what happened back there—'

'That was different and you know it,' Jas said. 'That was the middle of a *town*, for Christ's sake. There's nothing around here.'

'You reckon? Look over there.' He pointed to an area of land over to the right of another roundabout, where a number of corpses were gathered outside what looked like a petrol station and service area. It looked like they were milling around between the pumps and outbuildings, but as soon as they heard the noise of the engines, the ragtag group immediately turned and began to move towards the road.

'So what?' Webb protested. 'There's fifteen of them, twenty at most – bloody hell, Hollis, back at the flats any one of us would've sorted that number out on our own.'

'Yes, but we're not at the flats now, are we?'

'A corpse is a corpse; doesn't matter where it is.'

'I know that, but we don't know the area. Things are different when we don't know the area.'

'It's all *fields*, for fuck's sake,' Webb said, gesturing out of the window. 'There's nothing *to* know.'

'Look what happened earlier,' Hollis said defensively. 'You don't want to be caught out by a hundred of them while you're standing out there with your dick in your hands, do you?'

'Come on, Hollis, stop making excuses. Just stop the van for a minute so we can have a piss, will you?' Webb was trying not to lose his temper; the more he thought about it, the more he was *desperate* to go.

'No!' Hollis shouted, and put his foot down. Making a point, he accelerated towards the first of the group of cadavers from the service station, which had staggered out into the road, swerved into them and raced away down the long, straight road, leaving the bus trundling after them in the distance.

'You fucking jerk,' Webb hissed. 'Just because you're scared, you think that gives you the right to make the rest of us suffer. You know what I hate most about you?'

'I don't give a shit what you think about me, Webb, so just shut up!' Hollis ordered, determined to silence the whining little idiot in the back. He swung the van around a sharp right-hand turn, going so fast that two of the wheels left the ground, then crashed heavily back down. 'Jesus Christ,' he cursed, slamming on the brakes and bringing the speeding vehicle to a sudden, lurching halt just inches away from the side of a lorry which had been left blocking the full width of the road. Behind him Driver had accelerated to catch up and was now struggling to stop the bus in time.

Jas curled his head into his arms and braced himself for impact, silently cursing Hollis' stupidity, but there was no collision other than a bloody thump where a lone corpse that had stumbled out in front of the fast-moving bus was thrown into the air and hit the back of the van. He watched as it slid slowly down the glass, and by the time it had dropped to the ground the bus behind had come to a halt. He could see the relief on Driver's normally expressionless face.

'Oh, that's just bloody perfect,' Lorna moaned, looking at the obstruction in front of them. 'What the hell are we supposed to do now?'

As if they'd been waiting for just this moment, decayed figures immediately began to converge on the two vehicles, flinging themselves forward and hammering on the metal sides.

'Now do you believe me?' Hollis shouted, turning around to face Webb and Jas in the back. 'You see, according to your logic there shouldn't be any bodies around here – but look, there are loads of the damn things – do either of you want to go for your piss now?'

He was right: inexplicably, yet again they were being surrounded by the swarming dead. Jas didn't have time to look for explanations, nor did he want to prolong the argument with Hollis. The sooner he got this mess sorted, he decided, the sooner he could empty his bladder. He moved quickly, grabbing a crowbar – he decided he didn't want to risk the noise from the chainsaw again – and climbing out of the van. He slammed the door shut behind him and swung his fist at the nearest body, knocking it into the back of the Transit, then battered the head of another corpse into a bloody pulp with the crowbar. As more of the pitiful creatures lurched after him, he ran past them towards the cab of the crashed lorry. Before they'd even managed to swing around after him he'd scrambled up onto the bonnet and from there clambered onto the roof.

'Can you shift it?' Hollis shouted from the van, leaning out of the window and pushing a furious cadaver away with one hand. 'Is there any way around?'

Something definitely wasn't right: hordes of bodies were clamouring around the vehicles, reaching up for Jas, trying to get to Hollis and Lorna, banging incessantly on Driver's bus. It had taken no more than a couple of minutes for the stretch

162

of road they'd just driven along to become a seething mass of baying corpses – and from on top of the lorry he could see there were hundreds more coming towards them. Where were they coming from – and how many more were there? And more importantly, how would they get away if he couldn't get this bloody lorry shifted? They'd have to move quickly if they wanted to—

Hang on a second, he thought as realisation suddenly dawned. *The ground on the other side of the lorry is clear. Absolutely empty. Not a single damn corpse anywhere to be seen.*

The lorry had stopped in such a position that it had blocked the entire width of the carriageway. Its bonnet was pushed up close to a brick wall, and its back end overlapped with the side of another delivery lorry, making it impossible for anything to get past. He dropped to his knees and pressed his face against the filthy windscreen, confirming his suspicion: there was no body, dead or moving, in the cab. No driver. This lorry hadn't crashed here, he realised, the bloody thing had been parked! Suddenly revitalised, he jumped down onto the clear side and pulled himself up into the cab. Christ, whoever had done this had even left the keys in the ignition! He'd never driven anything of this size before, but he had to act fast and do what he could. He started it up, cringing inwardly as the machine shuddered into life and the throaty roar of its powerful engine drowned out every other sound. More through luck than judgement he managed to select a reverse gear and sent the lorry juddering and kangaroo-jumping back, steering hard to swerve its tail around the other vehicle.

As soon as the gap was big enough Hollis drove the van through, and Driver followed close behind. As the bus squeezed through, so did some thirty bodies.

Jas searched anxiously for a forward gear now, aware that every second he wasted allowed more and more of the dead to flood through after the survivors. With a huge sigh of relief he felt the gearstick crunch into place and the lorry lurched forward again, stopping just inches short of the wall, crushing another handful of figures which had managed to get halfway through before he'd blocked up the gap again. Jas stopped the engine and sat there with his head in his hands, panting with exhaustion, feeling as if he'd just run a marathon.

By the time Jas climbed out of the lorry, the job of destroying the cadavers which had made it through the gap was well in hand. Webb, Lorna and Harte were standing in a rough triangle, attacking the bodies with a variety of weapons, whatever they'd managed to lay their hands on.

As Jas watched the corpses, he began to wonder if the dead were deliberately taunting the survivors. It looked almost as if some were deliberately standing back and waiting, while others seemed to be moving together in groups of two or three. Of course they couldn't be working together . . .

Hollis had stayed in the van, and now he started driving in a tight circle, doing all he could to wipe out as many of the dead as possible without hitting any of the others. Gordon had finally plucked up enough courage to emerge from the bus, and realising what Hollis was doing, offered himself up as bait. He walked towards a relatively fast-moving long-dead shell of a man, and as he caught the attention of the repellent body, it stumbled around and reached for him—

—and he stepped smartly backwards out of the way and watched with smug satisfaction as the van drove over it, smashing it into oblivion.

Lorna shoved the grotesque remains of what might have been a schoolteacher back into the path of the van. The tattered rags of the dead woman's blouse revealed her exposed torso. Her greenish skin was severely lacerated, and what remained of her intestines hung down like a bizarre adornment to her outfit. The van ploughed into her at speed, the force of impact hurling her high into the air. Lorna spun around, shielding her face from the dead woman's splatter, then ducked out of the way as Webb swung his baseball bat into the chest of the last corpse standing, sweeping it up and smashing it back against the brick wall. He yanked out his weapon and the body dropped to the ground.

Driver and Hollis stopped their respective vehicles and suddenly everything was quiet again – except for a muffled thumping and banging, the noise of countless dead hands hammering against the other side of the lorry.

'What the hell's going on here?' Jas asked, wiping sweat from his brow and unzipping the front of his heavy leather jacket slightly.

'What do you mean?' Lorna replied.

'Look around you.'

Lorna did as he said. Until now it had been difficult to see anything through the mass of constantly shifting bodies, but now she saw that she was standing next to a set of traffic lights. There were signposts, and yellow-hatched markings on the road, and . . .

And she realised that this had once been a busy crossroads, with the road they'd been following continuing through the junction, and turnings to the right and left. But apart from the remains of the corpses they'd just disposed of, the area was completely clear. Lorna kept looking around; she couldn't understand it. Every road she'd seen had been lit-tered in wrecked cars and bodies. Surely this road would have been equally busy at that moment when everyone had died back in September? She looked further, and saw that all the other exits had been similarly blocked off with vehicles. It looked as if the entire junction had been cleared, and if that was the case . . .

'Which way now, then?' Gordon asked as he carefully wiped his boots on the overgrown grass.

'Don't know,' Hollis answered, looking around for in-spiration. 'Whoever did this must be around here somewhere. They wouldn't have gone to all this effort if they were just going to—'

He was interrupted by the sudden slam of a door and the rumble of an engine starting. They all looked around, and Harte pointed as a vehicle up ahead – a long white-and-blue coach – slowly began to move out of the way. 'There's our answer!' he said with a grin.

26

Hollis waited impatiently behind the wheel of the van as the driver of the coach moved out of the way. As the cumbersome vehicle trundled slowly and very carefully backwards, it revealed the entrance to a narrow, previously unseen road. A solitary figure stood a short distance back up the track and waved his arms, beckoning them towards him, and once he was sure they'd seen him, he began to jog away, occasionally looking back over his shoulder to make sure they were following. Behind them the driver of the coach parked it back into its original position across the width of the road, then got out and climbed onto a bicycle which he had obviously parked by the tall hedgerow. He pedalled furiously after the bus and the van.

'Where the hell are we going now?' Jas asked, standing at the front of the bus next to Driver's cab. Virtually impenetrable hedges lined either side of the road, preventing them from seeing anything other than what was immediately ahead and behind them.

'The Bromwell Hotel,' Gordon answered, standing at his shoulder, holding onto the handrail as the bus lurched from side to side. 'I thought it looked familiar.'

'How on earth do you know that?'

Gordon pointed towards a purple sign set into the trees just ahead of them where the road forked. Ornate white writing proudly proclaimed The Bromwell Hotel, and an arrow directed them to the right. The person they'd been following had already jogged away in that direction.

'I came here a few Christmases ago for an office party,' he answered, his voice suddenly sounding flat and unenthusiastic as he remembered the occasion. 'It was a bloody terrible night. I didn't recognise the place until now – I mean, I thought we might be close, but not this close . . .'

'So what's it like, this hotel?' Jas wondered, glancing back at him.

Gordon shrugged. 'Okay, I suppose. Decent enough place. The facilities were good, but the food was vile. It was all that horrible nouvelle cuisine stuff – a little pile of this, a dribble of that, a *froth* of the other . . . Didn't fill me up. I had to stop for a kebab on the way home. You want turkey and all the trimmings at Christmas, don't you, not a few scraps of meat and a bloody vegetable puree.'

'Fuck me!' Harte gasped, ignoring him and pushing past to get a better view. 'Look at the state of it. Fucking brilliant!'

The bus, followed closely by the van, slowly drove around the final bend in the road. The hedgerow on their right gradually tapered in height and then disappeared altogether, revealing a large car park and, beyond that, an open expanse of grass. Ahead of them now was the hotel itself. The fairly modern, off-white building was, in comparison to the grim concrete surroundings they had left this morning, an unexpected paradise. There was space to move around outside. The windows all had glass which hadn't been smashed. The grounds appeared clear of all rubble and dead flesh. This place was an oasis of normality.

'Jesus, this is fantastic,' Gordon said, all memories of his disastrous office party now completely forgotten. 'How many people do you think are here?'

'Don't know,' Jas replied, grinning. 'There must be a fair few of them, at least. There's plenty of space, and the way they'd got the entrance hidden back there was genius. I think we've landed on our feet here, lads!'

The lone runner, who had just about managed to keep ahead of the vehicles, finally slowed when he reached the steps at the front of the hotel. He bent over double, his hands on his knees, and breathed in deeply, the effort of the sudden sprint obviously taking its toll, but he looked up as the bus and van both stopped and quickly emptied. Jas and Harte walked over to him – but both found themselves tongue-tied, neither immediately able to think of what to say. These people were the first new survivors they'd seen for months. This man looked as well as could be expected. He wore jeans and a loose fitting jumper, and his short dark hair was neatly combed. It looked almost as if the apocalypse had passed him by unnoticed.

Gordon broke the uncomfortable stalemate. 'I'm Gordon,' he announced, moving towards the other man with his hand outstretched.

The runner wiped his hand on his trousers before reciprocating. 'Amir,' he replied quietly, standing up straight and shaking. 'Where did you all come from? Was it your helicopter?'

'Helicopter?' Hollis asked, confused. 'What helicopter?'

'Christ,' Harte said, 'this gets better by the minute.'

'We've heard it a few times now,' Amir explained, 'a couple of times earlier this week, and again this morning. We've been trying to attract their attention. I just assumed they'd seen us and you were with them.'

'We don't know anything about a helicopter,' Jas interrupted. 'Christ, we didn't even know about you until we nearly drove into your lorry back there. Bloody hell! That must mean there are even more people left alive.'

'Well, they might not have found you yet, but we have,' Hollis said.

The man riding the bike finally caught up. He jumped off, letting the bike clatter over onto its side, then walked purposefully forward and shook Hollis by the hand. He too appeared clean and well-presented. More formal than his companion, under a thin sweater he wore a slightly grubby white shirt, buttoned up to the top. His trousers were tucked into his socks. 'I'm Martin Priest,' he said, shaking furiously.

'Greg Hollis.'

'It's good to meet you, Greg – it's good to meet *all* of you. It really is so good.' He brushed a wisp of unkempt hair from his narrow, bearded face and then took off his glasses and cleaned them on his sweater.

Harte started to smirk at the man's appearance, then looked down at his own wardrobe: a curious mismatch of biker leathers, ski-wear and other incongruous garments. *There's something about the end of the world*, he thought, *that makes everyone dress like complete fucking idiots.*

Lorna stood a little way from the others and looked around, her eyes wide with a combination of surprise, tiredness and relief. The hotel looked safe and welcoming, its faux-Mediterranean appearance out-of-place and yet somehow still reassuring and familiar. The car park had just a handful of vehicles parked here and there.

Harte had noticed that too. 'I guess this wasn't the most popular of hotels, judging by how many cars are left.'

'More than half the rooms were occupied when it happened,' Martin said. 'There were more cars than this when we started.'

'So what have you done with them all?'

'We used them to block the roads and entrances. They've been useful.'

'How come everything's so —' Lorna began to ask before losing herself in her question.

'Clear?' suggested Martin.

'Empty?' added Amir.

'Quiet?' said Gordon.

'No, it's more than that . . .'

'What have you done with all the fucking bodies?' Webb grunted, successfully putting Lorna's feelings into words with surprising perception and his trademark lack of tact. 'You got rid of them all?'

'We couldn't actually do that,' Martin answered. 'I don't know what it's like where you've come from, but there are far too many of them around here for that.'

'So where are they?' Lorna asked.

'The grounds of the hotel are completely enclosed,' he explained. 'We blocked up the entrances like you saw back there, then tricked them into going elsewhere.'

'Martin used to work here,' Amir added.

'Believe me, I know every inch of these grounds. Before all this happened I was chief groundsman and—'

'What do you mean, tricked them?' Hollis asked, cutting across him.

'Well, they're not the brightest of sparks, are they? It doesn't take much to distract them.'

'So what did you do?' he pressed, intrigued.

'Did you see the fork in the road just now? The road runs right the way around the western edge of the grounds,' he explained, gesturing with his arm. 'Over there and to the north is a golf course, a full eighteen holes-worth of empty space. We've blocked the other end of the road to stop them getting through and made a few gaps in the fence around the golf course to let them onto the greens.'

'And how's that helped?' Gordon wondered.

'You know what those golfers are like,' he said with a smile.

'Were like,' Gordon corrected.

'They've got – *had* – more money than sense, half of them,' he continued. 'They built themselves a lovely club-house, beautiful place. Huge, it is. There's a track leads from the road right around to the kitchens at the back of the building.'

'Get to the fucking point,' Webb grumbled impatiently.

'The point is: we can get inside the building and they can't.'

'I still don't understand how that makes any difference,' Lorna said, obviously unimpressed.

'It's simple, really. I play music to them, and they think we're in the club-house.'

'You play music?' Gordon said in disbelief. 'Are you serious?'

'I don't stand there with a guitar serenading them, if that's what you're thinking. We set up a couple of portable generators and I leave CDs playing on repeat until the fuel runs out. They think we're sitting in the club-house, so they crowd around it and stay away from here. Because there are so many of them and so few ways onto the golf course, once they get through the holes in the fence, it's almost impossible for them to get back. Might sound a little unusual, but it works.'

'There's no doubting that,' Jas muttered under his breath.

'I have to go up there two or three times a day to change the music and refill the generators, but—'

'Sorry, but can we get inside?' Caron asked nervously, hiding under the hood of a heavy winter coat and wrapping her arms around herself. 'I don't care if there aren't any of them around; I don't like standing out in the open.'

Martin picked up his bike and led the way to the front of the hotel complex. He took them inside, up some low stone steps and through a wide glass door with arched windows either side into a long, open-plan reception area where Lorna collapsed onto a dusty brown leather sofa. She gazed around at her surroundings, still unable to take it all in.

'You okay?' Hollis asked, concerned.

She looked at him and smiled. 'I'm just trying to get my head around everything. I never thought we'd find anywhere like this.'

'If you could all just check in at reception,' Martin laughed as he leant his bike up against the side of the ornate wooden desk, 'I'll get your keys and have someone take you up to your rooms!'

Amir shook his head and sighed. 'Silly bastard's been waiting to say that to someone since we first got here!'

Harte looked around anxiously. He could hear something. It was a *clack-clack-clacking* sound, coming towards them along a corridor on their right. It didn't sound human, but it was moving much too quickly to be one of the dead. He instinctively looked around for a weapon, but immediately relaxed when the source of the sound appeared: a scruffy black-and-white dog with short, wiry fur wearing a tatty red collar poked its head through the doorway and ran out, its claws tapping against the terracotta floor tiles as it moved. It stopped and cocked its head to one side, then looked back over its shoulder at the sound of more footsteps, heavier this time, and much slower.

A tall, stocky red-faced man who was hopelessly out of breath entered the room and grabbed hold of the dog's collar. 'Wow!' he said, looking with disbelief at the size of the crowd gathered in reception.

'This is Howard Reece,' Martin said, and Howard grinned.

'Good to see you all,' he wheezed, relaxing and letting go of the dog.

It bounded over to Lorna and began to sniff at her dirty, bloodstained trousers and boots. She leant down and stroked its head. 'What a beautiful dog,' she said, ruffling its short fur. 'What's its name?'

'I just call her Dog,' Howard replied.

'Original,' Jas said sarcastically.

'She doesn't care,' Howard said with a wry smile. 'She just attached herself to me when all this started, and now I can't get rid of her.'

'You love her,' Amir said, 'don't pretend otherwise. You spend more time with that bloody dog than you do the rest of us.'

'She's good to have around,' Martin interjected. 'She's got a good nose on her. She sniffs out the dead for us.' At Lorna's look, he explained, 'They freak her out, send her wild.'

'They freak us all out,' Harte mumbled.

'But she catches their scent earlier than we do; she lets us know when they're close.'

'But what about her barking? Isn't that a risk?'

'She's not stupid,' Howard said as the dog padded back over to him and sat down at his feet. 'She had a couple of close calls early on, when they first started to react to us. She knows not to make any noise, but she lets you know when they're near. You can see it in her face and the way she moves.'

'Bullshit,' Webb said.

The dog cocked her head and looked at him.

'So where's everyone else?' Jas asked, keen to get on to the more important issues.

'In the restaurant,' Amir answered. 'Follow me.'

He led the group across the reception area and into a corridor directly opposite the one from which Howard and his dog had just appeared. In silence they walked along a wall full of windows which looked out onto an enclosed court-yard, half-paved, half-lawn. Hollis noticed a sign on the wall at the foot of a glass-fronted staircase which pointed to 'West Wing – Rooms 1-42'. He assumed that the similar-looking part of the complex on the directly opposite side of the courtyard – an identical staircase at either end, three floors, many equally-spaced windows – was the east wing, and that it almost certainly had a comparable number of rooms to the west. He looked up at the mass of rectangular windows he could see from ground level. *Christ*, he thought, *there must be eighty rooms. If just a quarter of them are occupied then we've more than doubled our number.* He remembered the disorientation, the desperation and cold fear he'd felt on the day everyone had died, and how much easier everything had felt when he'd finally found other survivors. *The more people I'm with*, he'd long since decided, *the easier the ride should be.* The potential of using the hotel as a long-term base was immediately apparent, as it obviously had been for everyone else who had ended up here. It was strong, safe and secure, and a damn sight more comfortable than the flats where he'd spent almost all of his time since the infection had first struck. Proper beds, space to move around freely, kitchens, and no bodies . . .

'Swimming pool,' Jas said, grinning, as they passed another sign on the wall.

'Out of action,' Martin immediately told him. 'I'll show you around properly later.'

'All this space,' Caron mused, looking across the courtyard at the three-storey block of bedrooms, trying to decide where she wanted her room to be. This was more like it. She'd become used to living her life surrounded by rubbish, but the hotel looked to be relatively well-kept – sure, it was dusty, and there was a faintly stale smell, and she doubted it was a three-star hotel, let alone the four-star properties she was used to, but the floors were clean and the rooms she'd seen so far were tidy. If she really was condemned to spend the rest of her days scavenging alongside these people, at least it was beginning to look like she'd be able to separate herself from them from time to time. Imagine that – the luxury of being able to close the door behind her and shut everyone else out! She was sick of trying (and failing) to look after people, cleaning up for them, sorting out their pointless, petty squabbles. Maybe now she could just stop, and spend some time looking after herself.

At the end of the corridor a sudden sharp right turn led the group along the furthest and shortest edge of the rectangular courtyard, parallel with the reception area they'd originally entered. They passed an empty meeting room and a bar. The rows of half-full optics behind the wooden counter caught the attention of several of the new arrivals and Webb attempted to make a quick detour, but he was jostled back on course by Harte. They followed Amir through a set of swinging double doors into a restaurant. Two people – a middle-aged woman wearing plain, practical clothes with a face framed by a mass of lightly curled auburn hair, and a tall, thin, much younger man dressed in jeans and a hoodie – immediately got up from where they'd been sitting slouched around a table playing cards and walked towards them.

'Ginnie and Sean,' Amir announced.

Harte acknowledged them with a nod and looked hopefully around the large empty room. 'So where are the others?' he asked.

'There are no others,' Martin replied. 'Just the five of us.'

'And a dog,' Webb added unhelpfully.

'That's all?' Jas said, surprised. 'Just five?'

'Yes,' he answered. 'I was working here when it happened and Howard found me a couple of days later. We found Ginnie and Amir when we were out looking for supplies, and Sean found us when he heard us driving around.'

'So that's it?'

Martin appeared perplexed. 'You sound disappointed.'

'I am,' he admitted. 'This place is great – I thought there'd be loads of people here.'

'Well, to be honest we haven't exactly been broadcasting the fact that we are here; we don't want those things out there to start dragging themselves back over to us.'

'But what about when you go out? Have you not looked for anyone else?'

'We don't go out,' he answered abruptly. 'It's too dangerous. We'll go back out there when the time's right.'

'You need food, though.'

'We've got enough.'

'But how do you get—?'

'We manage. We don't need to go outside, or make any noise, or do anything that might risk what we've got here,' Martin said, sounding both aggressive and defensive at the same time.

'We do have one other resident,' Howard said cryptically. 'I think we should tell them about her, Martin – we don't want them stumbling into her in the dark, do we?'

Hollis felt the hairs on the back of his neck stand on end.

'You're right,' said Martin, his voice a little calmer. 'Come this way. I'll introduce you to the Swimmer.'

27

Hollis and Harte followed Martin back into the hotel corridors. Howard's dog walked alongside them, constantly sniffing at the air.

'You've got the pool, a gym and a small sauna room down here,' Martin explained, 'though none of it's any use without power, I'm afraid. We hardly ever come up here, actually – only to see *her*.'

'I don't like the sound of this,' Harte admitted, his voice low. His head was rapidly filling with all kinds of unsavoury thoughts – necrophilia, torture, some other kind of weird perversion he hadn't even thought of. He was beginning to get a little frightened by whatever they were about to find going on in the shadowy depths of the hotel.

'Dog usually follows when anyone comes down here,' Martin continued. 'She thinks she's protecting us – not that we need it, of course.' He stopped walking as the cream-walled windowless corridor began to curve away to the right. The smell here was noticeably worse and the light levels were uncomfortably low. He beckoned them further forward and gestured towards a narrow rectangular window set in the wall. He peered cautiously through the glass.

'What's going on?' Hollis demanded, his nerves getting the better of him.

Martin scowled and lifted his finger to his lips.

The dog padded forward, clearly agitated. They could see what Howard meant now – the animal was pacing up and down below the window, snarling, but not making a noise.

'Does that mean there's a body in there?' Hollis whispered, and when Martin beckoned, he stepped up to the glass and found himself looking into a dark office, illuminated only the shards of light that trickled through a grimy skylight. Something was moving in the furthest corner of the room; he couldn't make it out at first, but when it shifted again he saw that it was a corpse. It had once been female, perhaps a little shorter than he was, with short blonde hair. It was wearing only a swimming costume, now discoloured after weeks of putrefaction.

Harte shoved him to one side so that he could look in too, but the sudden movement agitated the corpse, which lunged forward with surprising speed and threw itself at the glass with huge aggression, slamming against the window and leaving a smeary, face-shaped stain. It took a few stumbling steps backwards, then stopped and stood swaying on its unsteady feet, staring at Harte with dull black eyes.

'She likes you!' Hollis smirked, watching with equal amounts of fascination and disgust as the cadaver stumbled back into the shadows. He felt a wave of sadness, perhaps even pity, for the abhorrent creature. Why had she been at the hotel, on holiday, or business? Had she been here alone, or were the bodies of her family nearby? He found it strange that he was suddenly asking himself so many questions about this one particular carcase when he'd seen thousands upon thousands before and not given a damn about any of them. Had he come across this poor bitch outside he probably wouldn't have wasted another thought on her – he'd have gone straight for her head with whatever weapon he'd had and he'd have beaten her until she stopped moving. Maybe it was because she was isolated and trapped here, because he could watch her without fear of attack . . . As she moved away he noticed that she had a tattoo on her right shoulder blade, just next to the strap of her swimming costume. Her skin had an unnatural, mottled green tone, but he could just make out the faded outline of Winnie-the-Pooh. He hadn't expected that. Seeing the tattoo increased the strength of his confusing feelings – it had reminded him that the animated lump of dead flesh in front of him had once been a living, breathing human being like him, with friends, family, likes, dislikes, passions and vices. Now look at it . . .

'She was a guest here,' Martin said quietly, gently forcing his way between Harte and Hollis. 'I saw her the day before it all happened. Good-looking girl, she was.'

'So how did you get her in there?' Harte asked.

'I didn't,' he replied, 'she got herself trapped. The changing rooms are on the other side of this office. Poor cow must have been getting ready to swim when it killed her. She must have been bloody terrified, and dragged herself in here looking for help. It was most likely the last conscious thing she did.'

Hollis and Harte continued to stare at the pitiful creature in the shadows. Her movements were slow, but they looked definite and considered. She was more coordinated than many of the bodies they'd come across previously; although there had been some which had exhibited a similar level of control, they'd never had the opportunity to study any of them at such close quarters and without fear of attack.

'So why is she here?' wondered Harte. 'Why haven't you got rid of her? Have you got a thing for dead women in swimming costumes?'

Martin ignored the jibe. 'She's protected in here. She's useful.'

'Useful? How exactly?'

'She's like a human barometer.'

'What the hell are you talking about?'

'You know what a barometer is, don't you?'

'Of course I do,' Harte said quickly, offended, 'but what's a dead body got to do with the weather?'

'Absolutely nothing,' Martin said. 'It's not about the weather, it's about their behaviour.'

'You can study them without going outside,' Hollis said. 'You can see what they're doing without getting too close.'

'Exactly.'

'But what would you want to study them for?' Harte

grunted ignorantly. 'You're never going to find a cure, or a reason why it happened, or—'

'No, nothing like that,' Martin interrupted, beginning to lose his patience. 'That girl in there is protected from the elements. She's still decaying, but there's nothing in there to speed up the decay like wind or rain. That means—'

'—that she's probably stronger and in better condition than most of the corpses outside,' Hollis said, beginning to understand.

'Maybe she's not stronger, but she's certainly in better physical shape than most of them.'

'So what you've got in there is the worst-case scenario?'

'Something like that. By watching her and how she reacts, we can get an idea of how the rest of them are going to respond next time we have to go outside. We can see what they're going to start doing even before they've started doing it!'

'So what have you learnt?' Harte asked, still not taking his eyes off the corpse.

'That they're becoming more violent, and they're starting to make decisions.'

'Is that all? We could have told you that.'

'And they think we're a threat.'

'And?'

'And we're not going outside again until we absolutely have to. We're going to make our supplies last and sit this thing out.'

28

Ginnie, Sean and Amir volunteered to help Gordon, Webb and Caron unload the supplies from the back of the bus. There was a lack of coordination, with the six of them all trying to get in and out of the bus and hotel doors together, and frequent bottle-necks formed. After working hard (by his low standards) for almost half an hour, Webb took advantage of one such delay to disappear for a smoke, stopping only to grab a four-pack of beer from a cardboard box he'd been keeping a very close eye on. Sean noticed him leaving and followed him around the side of the building, out of view of the others. He found Webb sitting on a low wall, opening a can of beer and lighting a cigarette.

'Fuck me,' he cursed as Sean suddenly appeared, 'you scared the shit out of me!'

'Sorry, mate,' Sean said apologetically, brushing his overlong fringe out of his face.

'Thought you were one of the others, come to find out why I'm skiving.'

He shook his head. 'Nah, I just felt like having a break and it looked like you'd had the same idea.'

'Smoke?'

'No, thanks. I'll have a beer though.' Webb threw a can over to him. 'Cheers,' he said, swigging it back. It was the first beer he'd had in a couple of weeks, ever since they'd run out, and God, it tasted damn good.

'So how have things been here?' Webb asked after a moment.

'Boring,' Sean replied.

'Boring!?' he repeated, surprised. 'You've got to be fucking kidding me! It's the end of the fucking world! There are millions of dead bodies out there trying to rip us apart, how can it be boring?'

'Do you see any bodies here?' he said, sitting down next to Webb.

'Fair point, but you must have had to deal with some of them? Christ, we've been surrounded by thousands of the fucking things for weeks.'

'I got here before they really started to turn,' he explained. 'We've seen Martin's pet corpse and how she's changed, and we've seen others fighting from the window, but we've just stayed put.'

'For nearly two months?'

'Something like that.'

Webb couldn't believe what he was hearing. Next to him, Sean shivered with cold. He was dressed in a thin hooded fleece, T-shirt, jeans and trainers. Webb, in comparison, was still wearing his heavy boots and blood-soaked biker leathers. He looked like he'd been fighting the dead for weeks on end, without a moment's rest. Sean looked like he'd just got home from college.

'I don't know how you've done it, mate. I'd have gone out of my fucking mind,' Webb said.

'It's not the bodies that get to me,' Sean quickly said, glad to finally have a chance to say what he thought, 'it's that lot in there. They're so fucking cautious. It's "sit here", "do this", "don't make a noise", "keep your head down" . . . I'm fucking sick of it.'

'I know what you mean. This lot's just as bad. Fucking Hollis reckons he's everyone's dad, and that Jas thinks he's a hard-nut just 'cause he used to be in security.'

'At least they involve you.'

'Yeah, right. Anyway, can't you just walk?'

'What?'

'Can't you just get out of here for a bit? I did it when we

were back at the flats. I used to go and sit in my car, or I'd find a few bodies to beat up.'

'You went *looking* for them?'

'Sometimes – it was pretty easy where we were. I'd get a hold of a few of them and batter the fuckers until there was nothing left but a pile of blood and bones.'

'I don't know if I could do that.'

'Don't be so fucking soft! Of course you could. It's not difficult. The bloody things are already dead – as long as you don't do anything stupid you'll be fine.'

'But they killed one of your people, didn't they? I heard someone say the bodies killed a man.'

Webb took another swig of beer and looked out towards the horizon, avoiding eye-contact. 'That's right,' he answered, not wanting to say anything else about Stokes' death, but feeling obliged to keep talking to cover his tracks. 'I was with him when it happened, poor bastard.'

'So is that why you're here?'

'I suppose – that and the germs.'

'Germs?'

'A couple of the girls got sick and died. We got away before anyone else got ill.'

'Shit, I didn't realise . . .'

'And you're telling me you're bored?'

Sean looked down at his feet, feeling suddenly foolish and naïve. He couldn't deny his frustration, nor how the relentless and increasingly intense claustrophobia was getting to him. He'd risk putting his neck on the line just to get away for a while. Christ, what he'd have given to have seen some of the action Webb had described. 'They sit around at night and play cards, for fuck's sake,' he moaned. 'I tell you, it's like being on a day trip to the end of the world with your fucking grandparents!'

'What about when you go out for supplies?'

'You're kidding, aren't you? We don't. They *won't*.'

'What d'you mean?'

'What do you think I mean? You've already heard Martin; he goes mental if you even mention it.'

'So how long's it been since you last left here?'

'I haven't. I got here less than a week after it started, and I haven't been anywhere since. I'm going out of my fucking mind.'

'So just go!'

Sean didn't say anything for a few moments. He drank more of his beer, got up, walked away and then stopped and turned back to face Webb. 'I can't,' he reluctantly admitted.

'Why? Scared of what the folks will say?'

'No, it's not that.'

'I tell you, mate, the whole fucking world is out there for the taking. If all you're going to do is sit here and moan about it, you might as well roll over and end it right now.'

ight o'clock. It was pitch-black outside, and silent. The
entire group sat around tables in the restaurant and ate
while Howard's dog prowled up and down, sniffing the air
hungrily and grabbing at the few scraps that happened to fall
her way. There wasn't much going to waste: those who had
been living in the hotel were starving, surviving on meagre
rations to eke out the supplies in the kitchen, but it was
nothing compared to the relative riches the others had
brought with them.

'I never used to like tomatoes,' Ginnie said excitedly as she
helped herself to another serving of chopped, canned tomatoes, 'but my God, this tastes good!'

Caron and Hollis exchanged glances across the table.
What had these people been eating? Caron asked the question.

'Not much,' Howard replied, just visible in the candlelight
at the other end of the table. 'I reckon I've lost a couple of
stone.' He lifted up his baggy sweater to reveal an equally
baggy T-shirt. 'Few more stones to go yet, mind,' he added,
patting his still-wide belly.

'I don't understand why you haven't just gone out for
supplies,' Harte said. 'There's a town just down the road;
you could have been there and back in a couple of hours. And
you've got those lorries too – if you filled one of them you'd
have had enough to last you weeks, months even.'

'We just haven't wanted to risk going out there,' Martin
answered. 'Okay, so we've gone a bit hungry, but none of us
are starving, and we've all been safe, so far at least. I know
what I'd rather have.'

'I'd have risked it,' Sean said from a table a short distance away where he was sitting with Webb and Jas.

'We all agreed, Sean,' Martin sighed. 'There were only five of us here. We'd have been taking too much of a chance.'

'*You* all agreed,' he protested. 'I don't remember getting to have much of a say. You'd decided before I even knew you were having a discussion.'

'It was for the best, Sean. Come on, son, everything's worked out okay, hasn't it?'

Sean grunted and carried on eating. He found it a little easier to stay calm and not lose his temper now that he wasn't so hungry. Christ, it was good to taste so many different flavours again – it might be all tins and packaged convenience food, but it was more than he'd had in a long time. And *beer*! Although the lager made the cold night feel colder still, the numbing effect of the alcohol was worth it.

'There are more of us here now,' Amir said quietly. 'That kind of changes things, doesn't it?'

'Does it?' Martin asked, thoughtfully chewing.

'Of course it does. Now there're more than twice as many of us, maybe we could risk going out?'

'We don't need to. They've brought plenty of stuff with them.'

'You think?' Jas interrupted. 'We brought as much with us as we could, but it's not going to last for ever. It seems to me we've got no choice but to go out at some point.'

'You don't understand. It's not as easy as that.'

'I do understand – I understand perfectly well. I understand that if we're all going to stay here, then we're going to need a lot more food than we've got at present, and I also understand the bodies a lot better than you do too. We've dealt with thousands of them at a time.'

'But it's not as black and white as you're making it sound,' Martin protested. 'Our safety relies on them not knowing we're here. If you go out there and start throwing your weight

around, you'll attract their attention and before you know
it—'

'I think we're talking about one trip outside to begin with
– surely that's not going to have too much of an effect if you
keep playing your music to them?'

'They're starting to work things out,' Hollis warned. 'You
can't just assume that—'

'There's no need to go outside,' Martin repeated, his voice
tense but still low. 'We just need to show some self-control, a
little discipline. Make the food that we've already got here
last—'

'One trip out and one busload of supplies will make all the
difference,' Jas sighed wearily, already growing tired of
the conversation. At the mention of his bus Driver stirred in
the corner. Jas glanced across at him. He was fast asleep with
his paper over his face, backside on one chair, feet propped
up on another. He'd barely even eaten anything.

'Jas is right,' Harte agreed. 'The risks are small, but the
potential rewards are huge. We could set ourselves up here
for months.'

'Oh, so we're definitely staying, are we?' Lorna asked,
disgruntled. She'd been following the conversation with no
real interest. After spending the best part of two months
trapped with these men she'd begun to find their relentless
arguments and indecision incredibly tedious, and it was
beginning to look like the people here were no better. Put
more than two men in a room together and make a suggestion, she'd long ago discovered, and they'd spend hours
debating the most obvious points before finally deciding you
were right all along and claiming they'd had the idea in the
first place. She was sick and tired of the way they felt obliged
to take charge, then blundered their way through every situation trying to convince themselves – and everyone else – that
they knew what they were doing. 'Not that I have a problem
with staying here,' she explained, 'it just would have been
nice to have been consulted, that's all.'

'No one's decided anything,' Hollis said.

'You see,' Sean interrupted angrily, 'that's exactly what I'm talking about. They're doing to her exactly what you do to me all the time: you think you always know what's best and I can't stand it.'

'Keep the noise down, Sean,' Martin warned, cringing at the volume of his voice.

'No one's decided anything,' Hollis repeated.

'I have,' Caron said quietly. 'I don't know about the rest of you, but I think I'll be staying here.' The faces in the room all turned to look in her direction. 'I don't mind going without much food until those things outside have disappeared. I'd rather starve and be safe, and if we're away from the bodies, then there's less change of anyone else catching whatever it was that killed Ellie and Anita. We've got space here, and I can have my own room with four strong walls and windows which aren't smashed and—'

'Ellie and Anita?' Ginnie asked.

'They caught some kind of germ from the bodies,' Hollis explained dismissively.

'All the more reason to stay inside,' Martin quickly interjected.

'Are you sure it was from the bodies?' Ginnie wondered anxiously. 'There's no chance you could have brought it here with you, is there? I try and keep this place clean the best I can but the last thing we need is—'

'They caught it from the bodies,' Hollis said firmly, 'They must have. And if there are fewer bodies here, then there's little chance of anyone catching anything.'

'Caron's right,' Gordon agreed, yawning. 'We'll struggle to find anywhere better than this. And the fact that you've kept the bodies at bay so far is an added bonus. The safety's got to be worth a little discomfort.'

'You're just too scared to go outside, Gord,' Webb said. 'It's got nothing to do with the bodies or how much food there is.'

'We'll keep watching the Swimmer,' Martin said. 'If she looks like she's going to start causing problems, then we'll know it's time to change our plans.'

'The bodies are falling apart. They're going to become less of a problem, not more,' Ginnie said, helping herself to more food.

'Don't count on it,' Harte started to say, but Webb interrupted him.

'One of them bit me,' he said, suddenly animated, 'and they killed Stokes.'

'Christ, change the bloody record, will you?' Hollis sighed.

'Well, you all do what you want, but I'm staying put,' Caron said again, standing her ground admirably. 'You can all go back outside if you want to. I've got a suitcase full of books, a comfortable bed and all the time in the world.'

'What you've done here is incredible, and I think we'd be stupid not to stay,' Hollis agreed, 'but I also think we need to get out and get supplies. It's like Jas said, one properly coordinated trip out there and we could set ourselves up for weeks, maybe even months. Just think about it: safety *and* comfort.'

'But it's taken weeks to get the bodies away from here,' Howard protested. 'You're just going to bring them straight back again.'

'Sure, we'll excite a few hundred of them, but once we're back we'll batten down the hatches and sit and wait for them to disappear. Martin can keep playing his music to them and within a couple of days no one will be any the wiser.'

'Makes sense. I'm in,' Amir volunteered, surprising the other residents of the hotel.

'And me,' Sean agreed quickly before anyone else had a chance to speak.

30

Martin stood at the back of the kitchens, sheltering from the wind behind an overflowing waste bin. He tucked his trousers into his socks, pulled on a hat, zipped up his warmest coat and dragged his bike out of the passageway where he stored it. The world was reassuringly dull and gloomy, and he was pleased: he liked it like that. It was early morning and no one else had yet emerged from the individual bedrooms they'd claimed as their own late last night. His breath condensed in icy clouds around his face as he straddled the bike and listened. *There it is. Thank God for that*, he thought. He could just about hear it in the distance. He always found it easier to do this when the music was still playing. With his heart thumping in his chest and his mouth dry with nerves, he began to pedal away from the hotel.

He'd ridden this route so many times now that he'd carved a muddy furrow across the once well-tended lawns at the back of the main building, right the way over to the boundary fence. Slowing down as he reached the edge of the estate, he edged his front wheel forward through the gap he'd made, looked up and down the empty road on the other side, then pushed through and began pedalling again. It was easier now that the ground beneath his wheels was solid and even. He could move quickly and with much less effort, and he felt relatively safe, shielded from the rest of the world and the risk of attack by the thick, virtually impenetrable hedgerows on either side of the road. He could occasionally see them moving on the golf course through the gaps between the branches – those stupid, staggering, aimless creatures – but he remained invisible to them. They'd blocked both ends of the road with cars belonging to dead hotel guests and nothing was going to get through.

He could clearly hear the music now, a beautiful, lilting tune carried gently on the air, underscored by the steady belching *thump-thump-thump* of the generator. Only one of the CD players was still playing; the fuel must have already run out in the generator powering the other machine, he decided. Good job he'd got access to plenty more from the various vehicles abandoned locally. He and Howard had built up a store close to the back of the clubhouse; it would be enough, he hoped, for several trips a day for a few more weeks at least. *I have to keep the music playing*, he told himself as he filled two fuel cans. *It's vital.*

Up ahead, Martin could now see the turning in the track which led to the back of the clubhouse and his heart started to race again. Christ, he hated being this close to the dead. He didn't want to look at them, didn't want eye-contact for even a split-second, and yet at the same time he had to keep watching. He had to stay alert and on guard, although he didn't know what he'd do if he found himself face to face with any of them. Clearing the hotel of stiff bodies before they'd got up and started moving again had been one thing, but dealing with the obnoxious creatures they had subsequently become was a different matter altogether.

Martin was grateful he'd found this sheltered way inside. It was fenced off, hidden from the rest of the building: a tradesmen's entrance into the clubhouse for those who couldn't afford to walk through the front door. It had allowed deliveries to be made and refuse to be collected without the over-privileged club members being disturbed by the staff. Today it allowed him to get inside without being seen. How he loved walking through the clubhouse once he was there. For too long this place had been the exclusive retreat of the overpaid and underworked, and he felt a deep, smug satisfaction knowing that he'd survived when the golf club members, no matter how rich they'd been, had almost certainly all died. Martin had always loved the outdoors, and he had never been able to understand why so many acres of beautiful land had been reserved for a select few to traipse around hitting little balls into holes. He used to hate golfers with almost as much venom as he now hated the dead.

He stood at the bottom of the staircase and listened to the stirring classical music blasting out from the floor above. The illumination downstairs was negligible – all of the windows had been blocked up and the doors shut and barred to prevent the corpses from catching sight of him whenever he was there. More importantly, it stopped him from having to look at them. He knew they were out there – hundreds of them, probably thousands, their rotting faces pressed hard against the sides of the building, hammering continually on the walls with leaden hands.

He took a deep breath and quickly climbed the mud-splattered but luxuriously carpeted stairs, carrying the cans of fuel past the expensively framed portraits of numerous dead golf captains to the meeting room where he'd set up the first CD player. It was cold and damp in the large room, for he'd got all of the windows propped wide open, to spread the noise and fumes as far as possible. Working quickly, he refuelled the still-warm generator and fired it up again, drawing comfort from the constant chugging noise. Once power had been restored he moved over to the CD player which he'd left sat on a table just far enough inside to be sheltered from the wind and rain. With cold hands he re-started the disc, checked the volume was at maximum and switched it to repeat.

Martin stepped back as the music began to blare out from the speakers, the volume cranked to such a deafening level that they rattled and the sound crackled with distortion. It didn't matter; as long as it was loud enough to attract the dead and keep them here he didn't care what it sounded like. For a moment longer he stopped and listened to the music – the first track of a country music compilation CD he used to listen to in his car. Sean had joked that his taste in music would probably drive the dead away rather than draw them closer. Cheeky little bastard.

Moving faster now, he ran across the landing to the administrator's office, where he'd left the second CD player sitting on a windowsill. He repeated his well-rehearsed refuelling operation and leant back against the wall once the music began to play again, feeling protected by the screeching cacophony of noise which now filled the entire building. By itself, each CD was, in his humble opinion, a masterpiece. Played together, with the accompaniment of the generator, they sounded ear-splittingly awful.

Should he look?

Some days it was easy; other days he didn't want to do it. He wasn't sure today. He had been feeling a little more confident since the others had arrived yesterday, but at the same time their spontaneity and bravado made him feel uneasy. At least if he looked outside today he'd have an idea of the size of crowd that had gathered out on the golf course. He hadn't wanted to look for a week or so, maybe longer . . . in fact, now he thought about it, he couldn't remember when he'd last done any sort of real check. Mostly he preferred to try and convince himself that all he'd see out there would be the well-tended greens and freshly mown, rolling fairways. Maybe he should just have a quick look this morning . . .

'Been far?' Hollis asked Martin as he wheeled his bike back through the kitchens.

'Jesus Christ,' he gasped, grabbing onto a stainless steel worktop for support, 'you scared the hell out of me. What are you doing down here at this time of morning?'

'More to the point,' Hollis said, standing up and walking closer so that he didn't have to shout, 'what are you doing out on a bloody bicycle at this hour?'

'I told you yesterday,' he replied, his composure returning, 'playing music. First refuelling trip of the day.'

'Many of them about out there?'

'Enough. I didn't hang around to do a headcount – I can't stand the sight of them.'

'You and me both. So is it working?'

'It does appear to be. I guess the fact that there aren't any here indicates that it is.'

'Fair point. It's a good plan, actually.'

'I think so.'

'You've managed to channel them away and keep them at a distance.'

'Keeping them at a distance is just about the best we can do, I think. There are too many to try doing anything else.'

'Try telling that to Webb.'

'What?'

'He's a bit of a loose cannon, is our Webb. Where we've just come from we had crowds right around the front of the building. He seemed to think he had to get rid of them all, or at least enough to be able to push them back.'

'That's never going to work, though, is it?'

'I suppose not. I thought it might for a while. Most of us got involved when he first suggested it, but it was obvious pretty quickly that it wasn't going to happen. It would have taken us years.'

'All you're doing is winding them up. You're just showing them where you are and inviting them to come and pay you a visit.'

'Like I said, try telling Webb.'

'Your friend's not very bright, is he?'

'He's not very bright and he's definitely not my friend,' Hollis said, looking around at the empty racks and shelves. 'I'll tell you something though, Martin, at the risk of sounding like a broken record, we do need to get out of here and get supplies. We're going to sit here and starve if we don't.'

Martin's heart sank. *Not again*, he thought. Since the others had arrived yesterday, and after the conversation they'd had last night, he'd thought about little else. As much as he didn't want to admit it, he knew that Hollis was right. For the sake of a few hours out in the open they could improve their situation here dramatically. The thought of having to survive on the pitiful scraps they had left in the hotel stores was depressing. Last night they'd eaten something resembling a proper meal. Sure, none of it was fresh and it had been thrown together, but it was the best food he'd had for weeks. It was amazing: some decent food, some new company, a few glasses of wine and a long-overdue cigarette had, for a while, made him feel re-energised, almost human again.

'You're right,' he grudgingly admitted at last. 'I know you're right . . .'

31

Caron sat on the end of her bed and held her head in her hands. She was exhausted. It didn't make sense: the most comfortable bed she'd had in almost two months, the safest surroundings, fresh faces, no crowds of dead bodies, and yet she still hadn't been able to sleep. The truth was she couldn't clear her head enough to switch off, not even for a few precious minutes. Every time she closed her eyes she pictured Ellie, Anita, her son Matthew, or any of the others she'd let down recently.

Caron's room was the first on the second floor of the west wing. Its corner position afforded her an impressive view to the front and side of the hotel. She stood up and walked to the window, keen to benefit from the limited heat of the sun which had just begun to peek out through a layer of heavy cloud. The carpet felt unexpectedly warm and soft under her feet. She couldn't remember the last time she'd been able to walk around barefoot. The uninterrupted view outside went for miles back in the direction from which they'd arrived yesterday. She couldn't see anything recognisable, just hills and fields and open space.

She tried to look even further into the distance, right out towards the horizon. Somewhere out there, she thought sadly, was the dilapidated block of flats they'd left behind, and inside it, the sick girl they'd abandoned. She knew that Ellie had been dying, and that there was nothing more she could have done to help her, but had she really deserved to be left alone like that? Had she even been alone? Had those godforsaken monstrosities which so tirelessly dragged themselves along the streets somehow managed to force their way even further up the hill and into the building? Had they found her and torn her limb from limb, ripping her to pieces as they had done Stokes? Even worse, what if she'd recovered from her illness? Imagine that, finally coming out of her fever and finding herself alone, with no way of following the others – not even knowing in which direction they'd gone. Whatever had happened to Ellie (and she hoped for her sake that she'd died a quick and relatively painless death), Caron felt like shit.

She turned away from the window and entered the small bathroom on the other side of the room. She switched the light on instinctively, despite knowing full well that the electricity had been off for weeks. She flicked the switch down again, feeling unnecessarily foolish and angry, and shoved the door open as wide as it would go, hoping that the sunlight would stretch far enough across the room to reach the bathroom. The sink and the mirror above it were partially illuminated by the daylight. She wiped the dust-covered glass clean with an equally dusty towel which had been left draped over the edge of the bath by a long-dead housekeeper, and stared at her own reflection. Christ, she looked old this morning. Perhaps it was the poor light, or maybe it was the fact that she no longer used the creams and lotions and make-up that she'd lavished on her skin for years? Or maybe it was just because her life had become an unbearable nightmare? Whatever the reason, she dumped the towel angrily in the sink and went back and lay down on the bed.

Caron's stomach was knotted tight with nerves. She'd felt like this before, a couple of years back, when she'd discovered that her husband had been sleeping with Sue Richards, the receptionist from the doctor's surgery. It hadn't been his deceit or lies which had hurt her – in fact their sex-life had already deteriorated to such an extent that it was something of a relief that he'd found himself an alternative channel to vent his pent-up sexual frustrations. Instead,

Caron had struggled with keeping the secret and maintaining the façade of a happy marriage, after she and Bob had decided it would be better for all concerned (particularly Matthew) if they just pretended his little indiscretion (actually, *numerous* little indiscretions, if truth be told) hadn't happened at all.

She remembered how much she'd hated sleeping in the same bed as Bob, so much did she despise him. She hated him touching her – he made her skin crawl – and she hated forcing herself to speak civilly to him when all she wanted to do was scream in his face and tell him to fuck off and die.

What was strange was that she should feel so similar today. As she buried her face in her pillow she decided it was because, like her dead husband Bob, all these people wanted her to pretend to be someone she wasn't. They all thought she was capable of things which, in reality, she couldn't do. Ellie and Anita had thought she'd help them. Matthew had believed she would always look after him . . .

So this is it, she thought to herself, rolling over again and looking up at the ceiling, *this is my best chance – my* last *chance – to make something of what's left. So do I take it, or is it time to give up and admit defeat?* It was a difficult decision. Her instinct was to continue to fight, to try to survive, but her brain was saying something else entirely. Was there any point in fighting if there was no longer anything worth surviving for? If the events of the last few days were anything to go by, then probably not. But here, out in the middle of nowhere in this unexpected oasis of corpse-free space and silence, there was the slightest chance that things might actually prove to be different. Yesterday evening Ginnie had said how nice it would be to finally have someone to help her in the kitchen, 'looking after the boys'. She used to be a cleaner, apparently, and now she appeared to spend much of her time pointlessly scrubbing at floors and wiping down surfaces. Caron had baulked at that; she'd told Ginnie she was sick of playing mother-hen all the time – if she wanted to keep doing it, then more fool her.

And that, she decided, *is the decision I ultimately have to make: do I try and survive to make things easier for everyone else, or for myself?* Without consciously thinking about it, she'd arranged on the bedside table a symbolic representation of her ultimate choice. On one side was a bottle of cognac and a trashy romance novel, on the other the bag of pills she'd brought with her from the flats, enough to kill a horse.

Tired, irritated and unable to get comfortable, Caron got up again and walked back over to the window. She could see people outside now: there was Howard Reece, walking his dog across the overgrown lawns on the far side of the car park. She could see Harte and Jas, peering in through the windows at the swimming pool, then pulling open a door and disappearing inside. It certainly looked as if the others were going to give their new surroundings a chance. I'll *do the same*, she decided. *I'll give it a couple of days and see how things are going. If it looks like everything's going to work out, I'll keep drinking the booze and reading the books. If I wind up just facing the same old problems, then maybe I'll have to think again.*

32

'The problem is,' Jas sighed, 'you need power to use most of this stuff.'

Harte continued to walk around the collection of gym equipment at the side of the pool. It was just far enough away from the water to avoid the worst of the stench; they'd tried to clear it by propping open the outside doors. This place would have been lovely in the summer, he thought as he gazed around through the cobwebs. He'd never been much of a fan of exercise, but the prospect of finally having something constructive to do with his time was appealing. Providing they could get enough food and nutrition to re-place whatever energy they used up whilst working out, the benefits of using the gym equipment were obvious. As well as keeping them in shape (or, in the case of most of them, *getting* them into shape) the physical exertion would also undoubtedly allow them to release some of their frustrations. Webb could continue with his 'therapy' sessions without having to round up decaying corpses and batter the hell out of them.

'The weights are all right though, aren't they?' he said.

Jas looked up and nodded. He'd been wiping the dust off a screen attached to the front of some kind of rowing machine. 'The weights are fine,' he replied. 'I used to do a lot of weight-training. I can show you a few exercises that'll help.'

'I don't want to end up looking like a bloody bodybuilder,' Harte immediately protested. 'All the muscle turns to fat as soon as you stop training, doesn't it?'

Jas grinned. 'You've got to get the muscle first, mate!' he laughed. 'Have you got any idea how much they had to eat to get like that? And then there's the bulking-up foods and the steroids and—'

'Okay, okay, I get the picture.'

'We just need to do enough to keep ourselves in shape, just in case.'

'In case what?'

Jas shrugged. 'You know the score. If it's not the bodies, there are a few people in here who look like they're ready to kick off.'

'Such as?'

'Such as Webb.'

'Oh, him,' Harte said. 'I don't need much strength to keep him in check. The kid's a bloody idiot – you shout at him loudly enough and you can see his lips start to quiver. I tell you, mate, when I was teaching I came across hundreds of kids like Webb. They're all talk and no action. He's no threat.'

'You sure about that?'

'As sure as I can be.'

'And how sure's that?'

Harte didn't answer. Instead he started looking at another piece of training equipment. It looked more like a mediaeval torture device than anything that might actually have been designed to do some good. 'What's this do?' he asked.

Jas didn't answer for a moment, then said, his voice low and deadly serious, 'Just watch yourself around Webb. I've seen him in action and I don't like it. I've watched him when he thinks no one's been looking. I've seen him do some things . . .'

'Like what?'

Jas stopped talking and walked past Harte until he was standing at the edge of the pool. He looked into the murky water. *We'd need to drain the pool*, he decided. The glass doors, roof and walls made the place like a greenhouse. 'It doesn't matter now,' he said eventually. 'Just be careful, that's all. He's got himself a new friend now; we need to make sure he doesn't get carried away and start showing off.'

'Sean? That kid seems okay – he seems pretty sensible.'

'He's like a coiled spring,' Jas said. 'The poor sod's been trapped in here with a bunch of old bastards who are scared of their own shadows. By the look of the dust in here he hasn't been using the gym to let off steam, so he's got to be full of frigging teenage angst and hormones. I tell you, he'll be itching for a chance to get out of here and see some action to prove he's a man.'

'Looks like a strip of piss to me,' Harte grunted. 'I can't see him fighting his way out of a bloody paper bag.'

'You always keep your eye on the quiet ones.'

'Whatever.'

'I mean it, Harte. Don't let him get carried away. If you see him getting out of control, jump on him, hard. If he starts looking up to Webb and seeing him as a role model, then we're going to have all kinds of problems to—'

Jas stopped, interrupted by a sudden crashing noise.

'What the hell was that?' Harte asked anxiously, following Jas as he disappeared back out through the nearest door and ran along the corridor. Howard's dog pelted towards them from the opposite direction, followed by her owner, and stopped beneath the window of the small office where Martin's 'pet' corpse was kept. She looked up and snarled, but didn't make a sound.

Jas peered through the glass. He could see the Swimmer scrambling about on the floor, slowly picking herself back up.

'Problem?' Howard asked, breathlessly.

'The stupid thing fell over,' Jas answered. 'It looks like it knocked itself into a locker.'

'Was that all it was?' Harte asked, his heart pounding. He looked over Jas' shoulder. In the dappled light from the skylight he could see a metal locker lying on the ground. He was sure it hadn't been there yesterday. He couldn't see the corpse.

Howard leaned down and ruffled the dog's fur. 'She hates that bloody thing, don't you, girl,' he said, stroking Dog's head. The animal didn't move. 'She gets all defensive when it starts making noise.'

'You sure that was all it was?' Harte asked again, his whispered voice barely audible. 'Where is it?'

'Over there,' Jas replied, pointing towards a corner of the room.

Harte squinted into the gloom, following his finger, but he couldn't see anything. Then, just for a fraction of a second, he caught sight of an arm, swinging clumsily behind a metal storage rack. 'It probably heard us while we were by the pool. Fucking thing's hiding now!'

Feeling slightly braver, he took a step closer and pressed his face against the window. Now that his eyes were becoming accustomed to the light he could clearly see the outline of the side of the corpse. For a moment he could have sworn it was looking back at him.

'None of us like having that thing around,' Howard mumbled. 'I think Martin's getting too attached to it. I just tolerate it because I know that when this one's rotted down to nothing and it can't get up again, it'll be safe to go back outside.'

'How can you tell what condition it's in if it spends all its time hiding in the dark?' Harte asked. 'Maybe we should force it out into the open so we can see exactly what it's up to.'

'What do you want it to do?' Jas sighed. 'A bloody tap-dance routine?'

'Stupid fucking thing,' Harte said. He lifted his fist and hammered on the thick safety glass. 'Come out where we can see you, you stupid fucking thing!'

'Give it a rest,' Howard said. 'Keep the noise down.'

Harte ignored him, and carried on hammering.

'Harte,' Jas said angrily, 'cut it out!'

'Not until it comes out – what's the point of having a pet you can't see?'

The corpse suddenly lurched forward and threw itself across the room, slamming into the window. The impact sent it recoiling back into the shadows again.

Harte nearly jumped back across the corridor with surprise. 'Christ,' he said, trying unsuccessfully to appear calm and unfazed.

The Swimmer dragged itself back to the window and stared out, its dull eyes constantly moving from face to face.

'What the hell are you doing?' Martin asked, rushing towards them like an over-protective parent. He pushed his way closer to the glass, and Jas noticed that the trapped corpse almost appeared to relax when it saw him. It immediately backed off and returned to the shadows. Had it recognised Martin, or had he just imagined that?

'*We're* not doing anything,' Harte replied, sounding like a guilty child who'd just been caught doing something he shouldn't.

'Leave her alone,' Martin said, seething with anger and turning on the other men. 'She's important. The day she finally drops is the day we're free to go outside again. We *need* her. We've managed perfectly well here so far, and we don't need cretins like you lot coming along and screwing it all up. Understand?'

Harte didn't say anything – Martin didn't give him a chance; before he could open his mouth the groundsman had turned his back on them and stormed away along the corridor.

33

'**Y**ou must have got rid of one of them?'
   'No, nothing.'
   'Christ, it's been almost two months and you haven't even fought one? You haven't got your hands dirty once?'
   'No, I told you – look, I'm not proud of it; I wish I *could*'ve been out there instead of being stuck in here, but you've seen what they're like. You've seen what I'm up against. This lot are scared of their own shadows.'
   'It does you good to get rid of a few of them from time to time. Me and Stokes, we used to call it therapy.'
   'Therapy?'
   'Good for the mind and good for the body. You should try it.'
   'Maybe I will—'
   'Come on then.'
   'What? Now?'
   'Why not? You scared?'
   'No, it's just that I don't think we should—'
   'Come *on*, you fucking wimp.'

Webb and Sean sprinted down the twisting track which led away from the front of the hotel, glancing anxiously over their shoulders to make sure they hadn't been seen. It would be easier if they could get away without the others knowing – they'd just ask stupid, pointless questions. They wouldn't understand; they'd try to stop them. But Webb knew what he was doing; this was *important*. Sean was surely going to have to fight eventually, so better that he got used to it now, rather than freeze up when it really mattered. More to the point,

Webb didn't want to find himself fighting side by side with a bloody amateur.

'Slow down,' Sean moaned, 'I've got stitch.' He was nervous and overheated, and he was struggling with the sudden exertion after weeks of sitting around doing very little. Webb had also insisted he put on as many layers of clothing as he could find, and he was feeling increasingly uncomfortable.

Webb grinned at him without any sympathy. 'Not chickening out on me, are you?'

'No, it's just that—'

'Come on,' he shouted, running towards the coach which blocked the end of the road, 'get a move on!'

Sean watched as Webb athletically pulled himself up the side of the coach using the wing mirror, then scrambled over the roof and lowered himself down the other side. With considerably more effort and less success he followed, clambering clumsily over the vehicle then half-jumping, half-falling to land next to Webb in the middle of the desolate road junction where the survivors had fought yesterday. The carnage was incredible. He'd never seen anything like it. The carpet of blood and gore and dismembered remains which covered the ground was grotesque – and yet he couldn't take his eyes off it. He'd seen some sights since everyone had fallen and died weeks back, but nothing like this . . .

Sean also found himself watching Webb who casually kicked his way through the mayhem, using his nail-skewered baseball bat weapon to sweep decaying guts and smashed bones out of the way. The violence he had imagined beyond the hotel walls suddenly felt uncomfortably close and real.

'Okay then,' Webb announced, his voice cocksure, 'let's get started.'

Sean tried to say something, and realised that he couldn't. His mouth was dry with nerves, and he started shaking as Webb jogged across to the far side of the junction. He climbed up onto the roof of the cab of another lorry and knelt down, watching the dead on the other side as they immediately started swarming towards him. Using his spiked baseball bat like a bizarre fishing rod, he hooked the back of one of the nearest corpses and dragged it up out of the crowd. Its emaciated weight was negligible and lifting it was easy. He stood up and paused momentarily to steady himself as it threatened to slip off the nails which had become wedged between the bones of its neck and shoulder. Webb yanked the cadaver a little higher until its swaying feet were hanging above the heads of the other corpses, then flipped it over and threw it down onto the other side of the lorry. It landed unceremoniously in the road close to where Sean was standing and immediately began to drag itself up onto its feet.

Sean backed away nervously.

'Don't be so fucking useless,' Webb said as he jumped back down and speared the back of the creature again. 'There's nothing to worry about. One of them on its own won't hurt you.'

Sean took a single tentative step towards the hideous remains of the man writhing angrily on the end of Webb's bat. He was transfixed by its grotesque appearance. Could this thing have ever been human? The discoloured skin on its face was ripped and pockmarked. All manner of stuff had matted the patchy beard which covered its chin and the curly dark hair drooping over its forehead. Its mouth hung open and its jaw was moving up and down constantly, giving the impression that the damn thing was chewing or mumbling, or both. As he neared the corpse it lifted its arms and began to lash them through the air, trying to reach out for him, though it was held firmly in check by Webb.

'Are you sure about this?' Sean asked, starting to move backwards again.

'Completely,' Webb replied. He twisted the bat around, wrenching it free from the creature's neck. Suddenly finding itself able to move without restriction again, the body lunged forward with surprising speed, almost immediately colliding with Sean, who was desperately slow to react. As the obnoxious creature crashed into him he lifted his arms and shoved it away, feeling his gloved hands sink into its rotten flesh. Unbalanced, it tripped over its own clumsy feet and fell to the ground again, slamming face-first into the tarmac.

Sean felt an unexpected rush of power, immediately silencing his earlier nerves. 'Fuck,' he mumbled as the figure began to pick itself up again.

'See,' Webb said, 'just like I told you. They're useless by themselves. There's nothing to worry about.'

The cadaver stood upright, swaying unsteadily. It tipped awkwardly to the right, allowing the remains of its bowels to slip through a gaping hole in its abdomen and land on the tarmac with a nauseating splatter.

Sean put his hand over his mouth and gagged. He closed his eyes and desperately tried not to vomit.

'Can't do this,' he said, his mouth watering, about to throw up.

'Yes, you can,' Webb immediately told him. 'Thing is, mate, you ain't got any choice.'

'What?' he mumbled uselessly, still looking at the glistening puddle of decayed guts in the middle of the road.

Webb threw his bloodied baseball bat along the ground towards the other man, then ran over to the far side of the junction, putting the maximum distance between himself and the advancing corpse. 'Next time you face one of these,' he shouted to Sean, 'you might be on your own. You might not have anyone else to bail you out. You might have to get rid of it before it gets rid of you.'

'But I don't know what to do,' he stammered. 'I don't know if I can—'

'You just hit it,' Webb yelled, getting annoyed. 'Just hit the fucking thing as hard as you can, and if it gets up you hit it again. Keep hitting it 'til it stops moving.'

The body slipped in its own entrails and stumbled. Sean jumped back again, but then stopped, Webb's words ringing around his head. What if he was right? What if he did find himself face-to-face with one of these things out in the open? He swallowed hard, then ran forward and shoved the cadaver away. It managed to keep its balance – just – and immediately began moving back towards him. His confidence increasing, Sean shoved it back once more, then again, then again, but the stinking, maggot-ridden aberration in front of him wouldn't give up.

'That's it,' Webb shouted in encouragement. 'Keep going!'

Another brutal shove sent the corpse slamming back into the side of one of the lorries blocking the junction exits.

Feeling more confident, Sean stood his ground as it bounced back and came towards him, and this time he thrust it back much harder, suddenly revelling in the unexpected satisfaction of the one-sided fight. After weeks of being stifled, he could understand why Webb thought of this as therapy. Problem was, what did he do next?

'What now?' he asked, feeling nervous again.

'Finish it,' Webb replied.

'How?'

'The bat.'

He looked over his shoulder. The baseball bat was on the ground, a short distance behind him. Giving the body another hard shove to keep it at bay, he ran to pick up the bat and turned back around to face his dead opponent. The weapon felt comfortable in his hands, reassuringly natural. As the cadaver began to stagger forward again he swung the bat, almost two months of pent-up anger, pain, frustration, fear and grief adding to the strength of his attack. He felt the bat slice through the air, heard it whistle as it flew past his ear, then felt it smash into the body, lifting it clean off its feet. An unexpected shock ran through his arms as the end of the bat drove straight through the dead man and thudded into the side of the lorry, the nails sinking deep into the metal. He dropped his hands. The weapon remained stuck in the lorry door.

'Fuck me,' Webb said, getting closer again. 'Good shot, mate.'

Panting, Sean looked up and admired his handiwork. The remains of the bearded man were pinned to the lorry. The bat had pierced its throat, almost flattening it. The creature's feet were swinging inches off the floor. With a satisfied grunt he pulled the bat free and the bloody carcase dropped to the ground.

'So how're you feeling now?' Webb asked.

'Get me another.'

34

Bloodied and exhausted, Webb and Sean returned to the hotel hours later to find the rest of the group gathered in the Steelbrooke Suite, a large, bright conference room with floor-to-ceiling windows along two sides, overlooking the grounds and the boundary fence.

The two men stashed their soiled clothing in an empty bedroom before joining the others, hoping like naughty schoolchildren to hide the evidence of their excursion. They needn't have bothered. Hardly anyone even looked up when they arrived.

'Where've you been?' Harte asked, only slightly interested.

'Exercising,' Webb replied before Sean could say anything which might incriminate them. He walked towards the back of the room where Hollis, Lorna, Martin and Gordon sat looking at a map of the area. He stopped first at another table, upon which a pile of food had been left. He helped himself to a bar of chocolate, threw one across the room to Sean, then began cramming it into his mouth.

'Take it easy,' Martin complained as he immediately picked up a second bar and unwrapped it.

'Why?' Webb protested, his mouth full, showering the map in chocolate and spittle. 'There's plenty left.'

'We've only got one more box left in the stores,' Ginnie piped up from where she sat nearby, sewing a pair of trousers.

'I'm not talking about what's in here,' he explained. He pointed out of the window. 'I'm talking about out there.'

'I'm working on them, Webb. Give me time,' Hollis told him.

Webb looked down at the map. 'Where's this then?' he asked, still chewing.

'You are here,' Hollis answered, tapping his finger on the top right corner of the page.

'So what's here?' Webb wondered, drawing a large circle in the air above the map. 'Anywhere worth going?'

'Bromwell,' Gordon volunteered, pointing out the small town a few miles to the east.

'So that's where we're heading?'

'We're not sure yet,' Martin quickly interrupted. 'That's what we were talking about, but no decisions have been made.'

'Well, I'm sure,' Harte said from across the room. 'Forget all this bullshit, that's where I'm going.'

'And that's what bothers me.'

'What's that supposed to mean?'

'You know exactly what I mean. I saw how you were with the Swimmer this morning. If you go out there making as much of a disturbance, you'll end up bringing thousands of bodies back here with you.'

'Whatever,' Harte mumbled, far from interested.

'We are going to make some noise,' Hollis said. 'It's inevitable.'

'Yes, but I don't think you understand how dangerous that might be.'

'I don't think *you've* got any idea how dangerous it might be,' Harte said, obviously annoyed. 'How would you know? You haven't been out for weeks.'

'That's right, and we've done perfectly well so far. I'm starting to think we should just delay this, and see how long we can last with what we've got.'

'But there isn't enough food,' Harte sighed.

'You're right,' Martin agreed, 'but there is *some* food. If we ration ourselves properly we could make it last for a while. Then when we do leave here the bodies will be weaker.'

'And so would we,' he protested. 'Why the hell should we

214

ration anything? Christ, we're probably the only living people for hundreds of miles. There's never going to be a queue at the fucking supermarket, is there?'

'No, but—'

'You're out of your damn mind if you just want to sit in here and do nothing. I've already said this: half a day's effort now and a little risk will make the difference between us living like beggars or living like kings.'

The strength of Harte's outburst surprised the others, even those who had spent the last few weeks living with him.

'Nicely put,' Hollis said after a moment.

'Well, I'm not going back out there,' Caron mumbled from behind the pages of one of her books. 'I'd rather starve and be safe.'

'Me too,' Ginnie agreed.

'I'm going,' Sean said defiantly. 'I'm sick of sitting here doing nothing. This isn't living, this is just existing. We're no better off in here than those poor bastards out there. Christ, they'll have a better quality of life than us if we stay locked inside this bloody hotel any longer.'

'Do you have any idea how stupid a comment that was?' Martin complained, belittling Sean and trying – unsuccessfully – to put him in his place.

'Oh, piss off!'

'Don't you dare use that kind of language with me—'

'You see,' Webb interrupted, 'that's half the problem here. You're not his fucking parents, you know.'

'We're looking out for him.'

'Yeah, well it's all going to come to nothing if you starve to death,' Harte said, silencing the argument.

Hollis rubbed his eyes and wearily looked up from the map again. 'The way I see it,' he began, 'is we don't have enough food to last. We need to get more, and I'd rather go out there now than wait until I'm half-starved. We've got a town just a few miles from here which has probably been left untouched.

If we can get there and fill the bus, that'll do us. Harte's right, half a day's effort will make a massive difference to all of us.'

'I *know* that,' Martin reluctantly agreed, 'but I just—'

'No one has to go outside if they don't want to,' Harte continued.

'I'm going,' Sean quickly said again, desperate to secure his place.

Harte glanced up at him then carried on speaking. 'As long as there are enough of us, then we should be fine. We'll get in, get what we need and get out. We've done this loads of times before, you know. We'll not be just making it up as we go; we have a system.'

'I know you're right,' Martin said again, his voice suddenly sounding a little frightened, 'but just be *quiet*. For Jesus Christ's sake, *be quiet*. Make as little noise as you can.'

35

The brightness of the early afternoon belied the low temperature. The sky was clear, an uninterrupted blue, and the sun was high above the red-tiled roof of the hotel. Despite pushing to go out for supplies sooner rather than later, last-minute nerves and tiredness had combined to delay the planned trip until the morning. Now most of the group found themselves outdoors, relaxing in the fresh air and enjoying the luxury of being able to spend time out in the open. It wasn't long before the football had been found.

'Shoot, you idiot!' Jas yelled at Harte, who'd just dribbled the ball between Webb's legs and now had a clear shot at goal. Sean waited on the goal line, trying to guess which way he needed to dive.

'I've got him,' shouted Amir, sprinting towards Harte, ready to throw himself at the ball. Aware that he was there, Harte waited until the last possible second, then sold him a dummy, flicked the ball a couple of feet to his right, lined his shot up and blasted the ball at Sean. To his credit Sean moved in the right direction. He just managed to touch the ball with outstretched fingers, but only succeeded in deflecting it into the corner of the goal he was defending.

'You're fucking useless,' Webb screamed across the makeshift pitch. 'What are you playing at?'

Dejected, Sean dropped his head and jogged after the ball. He picked it up and booted it back into play. The sun was in his eyes and he sliced it off the side of his foot, sending it bouncing over the boundary fence, right over the road and onto the golf course.

'Sorry,' he whined.

'You jerk,' Webb yelled. 'You complete fucking *jerk*. What did you do that for?'

'It was an accident.'

'You can go and get it!' Jas joked, a wide grin on his face. 'Listen, don't worry about it, mate. We'll get another one tomorrow.'

'You never know, they might throw it back!' Harte laughed, his mind filling with images of dead bodies playing football across the road. 'I can see it now. There're bound to be a few of them that—'

'What's the matter?' Amir asked anxiously, unnerved by the way he'd suddenly stopped talking.

'Shh,' Harte said, lifting his finger to his lips and looking up. 'Listen.'

'What?' Webb demanded.

'The helicopter,' Amir said, spinning around and scanning the skies. 'It's back.'

'Where?'

'There!' he said excitedly, pointing up into the distance.

'Is it the same one you saw before?' wondered Jas.

'I think so,' Amir replied, following the flight of the machine through the air. It looked to be a little closer today than it had been when they'd seen it previously. He allowed himself to dream that the pilot had seen them. *Perhaps he's just scouting around trying to find somewhere safe to land?* he wondered.

Martin, Hollis and Ginnie had rushed outside. 'How many times have you seen it now, Martin?' Hollis asked.

'This is the fifth, I think,' he answered, standing on tip-toes to try and keep track of the tiny aircraft as it flew further away.

'And which way has it been going?'

'Alternate directions each day.'

'So it's flying between two sites?'

'Maybe – there's no way of knowing for sure, but that's the likely answer.'

'We've just got to hope it comes back again, and work out a way of making ourselves more visible.'

'I don't know how – I don't want to do anything that's going to bring the bodies back.'

'We might have to. We might not have any choice.'

A handful of people remained out in the open long after the helicopter had disappeared, desperately hoping it might return. Hollis and Caron sat together on a wooden bench at the front of the hotel, watching as Howard played with his dog. He threw a rubber toy as far away from the building as he could, and the little dog sprinted after it, skidding in the long grass, almost running too fast to stop. She grabbed the toy in her teeth and ran back, dropping it obediently at Howard's feet and waiting expectantly for him to throw it again. He hurled it up into the air and watched as it dropped back down.

'Doesn't she ever get bored of this game?' Hollis asked.

'No,' Howard replied, rubbing his hands to keep them warm, 'but I do. I don't mind though. She doesn't get enough exercise. It's not like I can take her out for a walk or anything like that.'

'Shame,' Caron said, shielding her eyes from the sun and looking into the distance. 'All this beautiful countryside and we're stuck here.'

The dog returned, dropped the toy and looked up again hopefully. Howard sighed with effort, but still he stooped down, picked it up and threw it again, this time hurling it further than he had previously, out towards the hedgerow. The dog sprinted away at full pelt, covering almost half the distance before the toy had hit the ground.

'Nice throw,' Hollis commented. Howard massaged his suddenly aching shoulder and cursed under his breath. 'I've had enough,' he announced. 'I'm going in.' He turned and began to walk back towards the entrance door.

Caron stood up to follow him, but Hollis didn't move.

'What's the matter?' she asked. He was still staring out towards the hedgerow which enclosed the hotel grounds. He stood up slowly and shielded his eyes from the sun. Then, when he still couldn't see properly, he stood on the bench. 'Greg, what's the matter?' Caron asked again.

'Where's the dog?'

Howard stopped walking and turned around. His first instinct was to call out, but that would be stupid. *Any second now*, he thought, *and she'll come thundering back, her toy clamped tight between her teeth*. Maybe she hadn't found it. Perhaps it had become stuck in a tree or in the hedge? Still no sign. Hollis jumped down from the bench and began to jog across the grass. Howard was close behind.

'Be careful,' Caron urged, her stomach suddenly knotted with nerves.

Hollis ran up over a slight rise and then stopped. He could see the dog. She was standing perfectly still, her ears pricked up.

'What's the matter with her?' he asked.

'That's not good,' Howard replied ominously. 'See how she's standing? That's what she does when they're near.'

The two men continued cautiously towards the hedge. The dog hardly moved. Her ears twitched and she sniffed and turned her head momentarily as they approached, but otherwise she remained completely still. Hollis noticed that her teeth were bared. She was snarling, but not making a sound.

'Must be on the other side of the road,' he whispered. 'I take it from this reaction that they don't usually come down this far?'

'We've not seen them here for a long time,' Howard replied.

Hollis edged closer to the boundary. Iron railings ran around the perimeter of the hotel. Over the years they had been swallowed up by thick laurel hedging. Beyond that was the road and, on the other side, the golf course, itself enclosed by another hedgerow. Despite the distance, he could see flashes of movement through the mass of twisted branches. He could see three or four bodies, maybe more. Their awkward, stumbling gait gave them away.

'What's brought them back?'

Howard looked at him incredulously. Did he really not understand? Christ, from what he'd seen Hollis was supposed to be one of the more intelligent of the new arrivals. Did he have to spell it out to him? 'You noisy bastards,' he whispered angrily. 'Them being here is the direct result of the noise you lot made when you got here yesterday, and your friends playing football earlier. Now just imagine how much damage you'll probably do when you go out again tomorrow.'

Hollis began to walk back towards the hotel. 'Two hedges, metal railings and a road,' he said. 'They won't get through. I don't care how many of them there are, they'll disappear again in time.'

'You reckon?'

Hollis kept walking.

Howard crouched down next to his dog, held her head in his hands and blew gently into her face, distracting her. 'Come on girl,' he said quietly, grabbing her collar and leading her away, 'it's all right.'

36

A long evening doing nothing, a relatively good night's sleep, the most substantial breakfast they could muster from their dwindling reserves, and they were finally ready to move. Eight o'clock in the morning saw Hollis, Harte, Jas, Webb, Lorna, Amir and Sean preparing themselves to head into town. They climbed onto the battered bus as Driver started the engine. Jas watched him intently. What was this unkempt and increasingly insular man thinking? Did Driver feel as nervous as Jas himself did? Could he taste bile in his mouth, and were his guts churning with nerves too? As he slumped into the nearest seat he couldn't help wondering why he felt so damn uneasy this morning. As the doors closed and the bus began to move he put it down to the fact that the hotel had, unexpectedly, provided them with the most isolation they'd yet had from the nightmare world outside, and yet here they were, already on their way back out into the chaos again.

Driver edged his huge vehicle slowly along the track, past the fork in the road and back down to the junction. Howard, Gordon and Ginnie were waiting for them there – somebody had to move the vehicles to let them through and, as that job was considerably safer than venturing into Bromwell, Howard and Ginnie had reluctantly volunteered. Gordon, as the most experienced fighter remaining at the hotel, was there to mop up those few (he hoped) random corpses which managed to slip through as the bus drove out. He stood on one side of the junction, nervously swinging an axe in one hand and a crowbar in the other. He was dressed in as much protective clothing as he'd been able to find, enough to keep him safe from the germs and any slimy slugs of decaying flesh that an encounter with the dead might throw up into the air. He didn't care how ridiculous he looked in the fisherman's waders, safety goggles and bright yellow construction worker's hard hat.

'Ready?' Ginnie shouted from behind the wheel of the coach, fighting to make herself heard over the rattle of the engine and, for once, not worrying about the volume of her voice. Driver acknowledged her with a thumbs-up and stared straight ahead as the coach began to move to the side. He inched slowly forward before increasing his speed and driving out into the middle of the deserted road junction. He stopped to give Howard a chance to pull himself up into the driver's seat of the lorry blocking the exit they planned to use. With Dog in tow he settled into the cab and immediately peered down at the mass of bodies on the other side. There were too many to count. It might not have been the biggest crowd he'd ever seen, but there were too many all the same. His hands suddenly trembling with nerves, he started the engine and waited for Driver to pull the bus closer. The dead began to thump and push against the exposed side of the vehicle. The dog sat in the passenger seat and silently snarled at them, her nostrils full of the stench of rotting flesh.

The lorry Howard was driving spanned the gap between a six-foot-tall brick wall ahead and another lorry just behind. As the bus began to move towards him he slowly reversed.

'Get as near as you can,' Hollis said to Driver, standing next to him at the front of the bus like a passenger waiting for the next stop. 'You want to try and push as many of them back and out of the way as you can, try and stop them getting through.'

'Thanks, I'd worked that bit out for myself,' Driver grumbled. He tightened his grip on the steering wheel and nudged forward as soon as there was room for him to move. Bodies began to pour through the gap, most of them immediately dragged down beneath the bus or mashed by the impromptu snowplough they'd bolted to its front weeks earlier. Driver accelerated, slicing through the crowd with ease. Hollis looked over his shoulder along the length of the bus and through the window at the back he could see Howard immediately shunting his own lorry forward again, blocking the road and preventing any more cadavers from getting through.

'Well, that wasn't too bad,' Harte said, relieved, standing just a little way behind Hollis and watching the rotting world rushing by through the windows on either side.

'There were nowhere near as many of them as I thought there would be. Must be Martin's music,' Hollis admitted. 'Give him his due, I thought he was off his head, but maybe not.'

'Crazy bugger says he's been playing music to them every day for more than a month,' he laughed. 'The damn things are probably sick of it!'

Hollis turned to look ahead as the first buildings of the town of Bromwell loomed on the horizon.

Incredibly, just three bodies had managed to drag themselves safely through the gap and into the blockaded road junction while the lorry had been out of position. All the rest had been crushed by the bus. Gordon, feeling far less confident now the others had gone, stood rooted to the spot, waiting for the first of them to get close enough to attack.

'You okay, Gordon?' Ginnie shouted from the relative safety of the coach. The bodies were instinctively moving in her direction now, distracted by the noise of the engine and her voice. He wanted to stop them getting any closer. He liked Ginnie. The way she fussed constantly reminded him of how Janice used to be, and that unexpected familiarity, no matter how tenuous, was welcome. He took a deep breath and swallowed hard. Time to fight.

Running forward, he swung the axe into the side of the nearest cadaver's neck, wedging it deep into its putrid flesh, just below its ear. The body, a stocky, awkward creature with only one arm and one eye, was overbalanced by the speed and force of Gordon's strike. He dragged it over onto the ground and plunged the end of the crowbar into its exposed temple. A few seconds of twitching and kicking, then it lay still and he yanked out his blood-soaked weapon, suddenly feeling like a gladiator, and turned to look for the next kill.

The body of a nurse was stumbling precariously close to the side of the coach. Gordon spun it around and, with another savage swing of the axe, ripped through the front of its throat, cutting so much weak flesh away that its head flopped back and dangled over its shoulders, now looking behind. The corpse, unbalanced, dropped to its knees and Gordon delivered another killer blow with the blade, this time decapitating it and sending its head rolling away along the ground until it eventually became wedged under the coach.

Howard's dog suddenly shot past Gordon, the unexpected speed and movement making his pulse race. He'd lost sight of that third body momentarily, but as he spun around, looking for it, he saw the dog had come to his aid, jumping up and wrapping its teeth around the forearm of what remained of a young garage mechanic. The animal was too strong for the corpse and pulled it over. As it fell flat on its face, Dog scurried back towards Howard (who was keeping a safe distance, skirting around the edge of the junction and avoiding the violence). Now feeling more confident, Gordon strode over to the creature struggling to pick itself up off the ground. It managed to lock its arms and raise its head and shoulders and it looked up at him. He stared back, studying what was left of its face. It had very little hair, and a gold hoop earring in its right ear – though the ear itself was almost completely detached, clinging to the side of its head by nothing more than a few slender strips of cartilage. The creature managed to lift its decaying bulk a little higher, startling Gordon and forcing him to take a few steps back, but he stopped. The pathetic lump of flesh at his feet was no threat to him, or anyone else. It straightened its arms again and lifted its torso. Just above the breast pocket of its blood and oil-stained overalls, the name 'Kevin' had been embroidered. Strange to think that Kevin had once had a life and a home and a family and friends and— And so what? Gordon finally realised that today, almost sixty days after the world had been irrevocably changed for ever, Kevin and every other corpse that still walked the face of the planet no longer mattered.

He sank the crowbar deep into its half-open right eye, shoving it into its skull and twisting it around, reducing what was left of its brain to pulp.

37

'Have you ever been to Bromwell before?' Amir asked Lorna and Jas as they drove deeper into the dead town. He didn't actually care one way or another; he was just trying to calm himself, and distract himself from the hellish, almost unrecognisable world they were now travelling through.

'Doesn't look like we missed anything,' Jas said briefly, not in the mood for conversation.

'I think my dad brought me here once when I was little,' Lorna answered. 'I wouldn't recognise anything now though.'

'Damn right.' Amir smiled sadly. 'Bloody hell, I drove down this road to work every day for more than twelve years and now I don't recognise anything!'

'If you're a local,' Harte said, eavesdropping from the front of the bus, 'come up here and tell us where to go.'

Wishing he'd kept his mouth shut, Amir reluctantly got up and walked along the aisle, holding onto the passenger rail as the bus lurched over the bumpy road. He looked out through the windscreen, trying to make sense of the carnage flashing past.

'Any suggestions?' Hollis asked.

'Give me a second,' Amir said, quietly wiping a tear away from the corner of his eye. He hoped no one had noticed. He hadn't realised how much coming home would hurt. In spite of the fact that everything looked so very different this morning, he knew exactly where they were – he had done from the moment they'd set off. It was hard to concentrate, to think about where to go next, when everywhere he looked he saw the crumbling ruins of places he used to know, now just fading shadows dissolving away to nothing. His whole world had been ruined beyond repair.

'Well?' Harte pressed impatiently.

'Take a right here, then go straight up the High Street.'

'Think we'll be able to get through?'

'Should do – it was partially pedestrianised. There wasn't a lot of traffic around when it all kicked off.'

'How do you know?' Hollis asked, holding on as Driver swung the bus around the right-hand corner.

Amir wiped away another teardrop, unable to tear his eyes away from the disintegrating world outside. 'Because,' he explained, his voice full of emotion, 'This is where I used to live and work. I was here when it happened.' The bus took a gentle turn and began rumbling up the High Street. He pointed out of the window at the row of shops on the right-hand side of the road. 'Until all this happened, the Bromwell Jewel was the best place to eat for miles around here.'

'Was that where you used to work?' Harte asked.

'That was my business,' Amir answered as they passed the blue-fronted building, its unlit signage dull and its windows dirty. 'That place was my life.'

What remained of the people of Bromwell were beginning to emerge from the shadows, drawn by the sound of the engine. They slowly spilled out from dark corners, but surprisingly, there weren't many of them.

'Why so few?' Harte asked as a grey-suited cadaver dragged itself out in front of the bus. He winced as the powerful vehicle slammed into it with barely a pause, its head smacking against the bottom of the windscreen and popping open like a blood-filled balloon. 'It can't all be down to Martin's music, can it?'

'What else could it be?' Amir wondered. 'That's got to have something to do with it – but look out there. Some of them are holding back.'

He pointed further up the street. Harte and Hollis obediently peered ahead, but the fact that the colour had been drained from everything, the bodies included, made it difficult to make out detail until one of the cadavers moved. Amir was right, though, it did look just like some of the creatures were deliberately keeping their distance, as if they were staying out of the way until the bus had almost reached them and they had no option but to move. Harte turned and looked out of the rear window. Behind them, the scene was disappointingly familiar: the High Street was full of corpses, all dragging themselves after the bus.

'What's all that about?' Amir wondered, his eyes wide, sounding nervous.

'We've seen it before,' Hollis replied. 'They're not as dumb as you'd think. Sometimes they keep out of the way if they think they're in danger.'

'Seriously?'

'You just watch them,' he continued. 'When they're isolated, or if there are just a few of them, they'll stay hidden. Now look behind the bus. The immediate threat's gone, so they come out into the open and follow us.'

'So is Martin making things better or worse? If they're easier to deal with on their own, shouldn't we be trying to keep them apart?'

'I honestly don't know. There's no right answer. Even if you're only up against one or two of them, if they can't see a way out, they'll fight you whatever.'

'Now where?' asked Driver. The end of the street was looming. Amir turned his attention back to their destination. The far end of town had been redeveloped eighteen months ago, with several large buildings built on reclaimed wasteland on the other side of a recently restored canal. There was a big supermarket there, as well as the usual entertainment and fast food joints. He'd spent the last six months cursing the place, blaming it for draining the life from the town and dragging his customers away. Now he couldn't get there fast enough.

'Keep going to the end of the road, then take the bridge over the canal,' he directed Driver.

The bus clipped the back corner of a burned-out car and sent the wreck spinning towards the buildings on their left. It crashed into the bronzed-glass frontage of a large office, releasing a previously trapped gang of bodies which immediately began to pick their way through the rubble and glass into the rubbish-strewn road. Harte walked the length of the bus, pressed his face against the back window and watched them as they joined the pack. Looking around, he could see cadavers coming in from all directions, streaming out onto the High Street and following the vehicle like a herd. There were still fewer bodies than he'd expected, but more than enough to cause them problems.

Driver forced the bus up over the narrow bridge which separated the redevelopment from the rest of the town, jolting over dead bodies, a couple of prams and a motorbike.

'Jesus,' Hollis cursed, gripping the handrail tighter and struggling to stay on his feet. He looked out of the door and peered down into the canal with disgust. The recently renovated towpath boasted plenty of benches and shelters, but over the last eight weeks vast numbers of the uncoordinated dead had fallen into the water. There were so many of them around the bridge that the canal had become a murky quagmire filled with rotting flesh. Bony, barely recognisable heads, limbs and other body parts jutted out from the greasy green-grey sludge at unnatural angles. Horrible though it was, it occurred to him that the canal might actually help them, in the same way that a moat protected a mediaeval castle. Some of the cadavers following the bus would no doubt manage to cross the bridge purely by chance, but many more would join the packed masses below already wallowing in their watery graves.

Harte was reassured by what he saw as he returned to the front of the bus, for there were hardly any bodies on the other side of the canal. He could see a large toy store, an electrical superstore, a furniture and household goods outlet, a bowling alley and the promised supermarket.

'Look for the loading bay,' he suggested, working on their usual tactics, but Driver was one step ahead of the game.

'Good idea,' Amir said quietly.

'We've done this before,' Harte said briefly.

Weeds had sprung up in the previously manicured flower-beds around the once-white supermarket building, their surprisingly aggressive growth no doubt bolstered by the plentiful nutrients supplied by the remains of the dead shoppers lying nearby.

'Great – fuel,' Hollis said, sounding pleased, as they passed the supermarket filling station on one edge of the car park. This was an excellent find. There was a tanker standing on the forecourt; with any luck it would still be full. Even if had already delivered its load, the fuel would be in the tanks beneath the pumps. Maybe they could even drive the tanker back if it was still loaded up – not today, perhaps, but later in the week? They'd concentrate on getting the maximum amount of supplies today; that was why they were here. They could make plans for their next trip tonight as they rested in comfort back at the hotel while they ate decent food and drank themselves stupid.

'The doors are closed,' Harte said as they drove past the main entrance, wiping out another trio of curious cadavers en route.

'Is that good?' Amir asked. He thought it was a strange thing to say.

'Absolutely!' he replied. 'You want to try going into one of those places when the doors have been left open – they're swarming with those fucking things, they are. They're drawn to shops even after they're dead!'

'Are you serious?'

Harte laughed. 'No, but it is easier when they're closed up. The thing is, they can get into buildings easier than they can get out.'

'Like the golf course?'

'Exactly, and the longer you leave it, the more you'll find stuck inside. It just adds to the fun!'

'Fun?' he grumbled nervously. He was sweating profusely, but trying hard to remain calm. The bitter sadness he'd felt since returning to Bromwell had now been replaced by absolute fear and he was wishing most devoutly that he'd stayed at the hotel. He couldn't believe he'd actually volunteered to come – at the time it had looked like a long-overdue opportunity to break the monotony of his prison-like surroundings, but now all he wanted was to be back in his nice, safe, dead-free 'cell'.

Driver skilfully coaxed the bus around a tight corner and into the loading bay, knocking down the 'maximum height' warning sign which hung from a barrier overhead as he reversed into position. This place obviously hadn't been designed with double-decker passenger buses in mind.

'Bingo!' Jas said excitedly. 'Look at that: delivery!'

Hollis couldn't believe what he was seeing. The morning was getting better by the minute. Straddled across the far end of the loading bay was a huge delivery lorry, decked out in the supermarket's distinctive orange and white livery. The doors at the back of it were hanging open and they could see that it was still more than three-quarters full. It looked like they might be able to get what they needed without even having to risk going inside the store. Perfect.

'Going to have to stop here,' Driver announced. 'Won't get out if I go in much further.'

'Okay,' Hollis agreed, grabbing onto the nearest rail again as the bus lurched to a sudden stop. The doors hissed open, letting in a blast of cold air from outside, accompanied by the foetid stench of dead flesh and rotten food. Sean and Webb thundered down the stairs from the top floor, weapons in hand, ready to get rid of the first few bodies which were already inching closer.

'I'll keep these two in check,' said Jas, picking up the chainsaw and squeezing out between Hollis and Harte. He

234

ran after the others, quickly catching up with Sean. Webb was already level with the first of the advancing cadavers, wielding his baseball bat with typical blundering force, making short work of any corpses unfortunate enough to stagger within range.

'Do we try and block them off from the bus?' Sean started to ask, suddenly feeling incredibly nervous again, despite what he'd learnt yesterday.

Jas shook his head. 'No, it's not worth it,' he replied. 'We might as well just get rid of them – it makes it easier in the long run. Look, we can cut them off if we get closer to the bridge. Most of them are going to end up the canal, so we'll just be left with the ones that manage to get across. Dumb bastards.'

He started the chainsaw and marched forward purposefully. Machete in hand, Sean followed close behind, figuring that he'd stay back and deal with those few corpses which managed to evade both Webb and Jas.

Lorna had been subdued since leaving the hotel, but now she quickly sprang into action. Hollis, Harte and Amir were standing at the back of the lorry, discussing how best to organise themselves.

'Couldn't we just drive it back?' Amir suggested.

'Good luck with that,' she said, gesturing towards the other end of the vehicle, where a forklift had become wedged into the front of the lorry after its dying driver had lost control. Frustrated by the men's inactivity, she shouted, 'Come on! It won't empty itself.'

She barged past them and climbed up into the back of the lorry, then grabbed the first thing she could lay her hands on – a tray of tins of beans – and slid it across the floor towards Hollis, who picked it up and carried it over to Harte, who had returned to the steps of the bus. He took the beans down to the front of the bus and stored it carefully in the footwell just in front of the front seat. *We need to stack this stuff carefully*, he thought to himself. *The better we pack it, the more we'll get in. The more we take now, the longer before we have to come out here again.*

It took less time than they'd expected to transfer the useful contents of the lorry to the bus. Hollis went off to explore the darker corners of the loading bay, keen to make sure they'd taken everything of value before leaving. He shifted a pile of traffic cones, shovels and other bits of maintenance equipment, then walked over to the other side of the bay to investigate some wooden pallets which had been stacked up against a wall. He glanced back at the bus as he worked. The others were sitting on the steps, drinking, eating and catching their breath before they headed home.

The pallets were of little interest. Some were broken, others had just been piled up awaiting collection by the next—

—a single cadaver suddenly threw itself at Hollis, grabbing hold of him and sending him tumbling over. His heart thumping, he struggled to right himself and get a grip on the rancid figure which had rushed him. Where the hell had it come from? He forced his hand up, thanking God he hadn't removed his thick leather gloves, gripped the stinking creature's neck and squeezed. His fingers dug deep into its rotting flesh, ripping open its disintegrating trachea and allowing all manner of disgusting decay to squeeze out and run down his arm. After a moment he gradually managed to shuffle himself around and roll right over so that the corpse lay beneath him and he could use his full weight to good advantage. He stared into its revolting face – a mass of pus, dried blood, ripped skin and an infuriatingly vacant expression which seemed to scream 'so what?' at him – and wondered how something so inadequate could catch him off-guard like that. Was it just the fact that he still couldn't hear properly, or was he losing his touch? His confidence wavering, he angrily grabbed the long-shanked screwdriver he'd tucked into his belt and plunged it into the monster's left temple, in one side and out the other. He pulled it out again, stood up and gave the suddenly limp figure an angry kick to the gut to make sure it wouldn't get up.

'You okay, Hollis?' Jas shouted. 'Having trouble?'

'I'm fine,' he answered quickly, determined not let the others know what had just happened. He must have released the cadaver when he'd been scavenging around just now. He'd acted like a fucking amateur, and he felt angry and scared – angry because he'd been stupid and put himself at risk unnecessarily, scared because he hadn't heard the body until it had been too late. He'd got away with it today, but the outcome could have been much worse. He'd hoped his hearing would have improved by now, but if anything, it was deteriorating. How the hell was he supposed to survive if he couldn't hear? Hollis felt more exposed and vulnerable today than he had done when the rest of the world had first fallen dead at his feet. He wiped the gore off his screwdriver and put it back in his pocket as Lorna approached.

'We should be heading off,' she said. 'Are you ready?'

Hollis nodded and walked back towards the bus. She watched him leave, concerned. He was losing his confidence. The others were too self-obsessed to pick up on it, or even to care come to that, but she could see that he was struggling. And like the rest of them, he was too pig-headed to admit it.

The lower floor and half of the top floor of the huge vehicle had been filled. Lorna wearily climbed the narrow stairs and flopped heavily into a chair right at the front, well away from everyone else. The bus began to rumble and shake as Driver started the engine, then it slowly trundled forwards. She could already hear the crashing of badly packed supplies and excited laughter and conversation coming from her fellow looters who were standing in the aisle downstairs. By the sounds of things they'd be lucky if there was any booze left by the time they made it back to the hotel. She closed her eyes, leant back in her seat and tried to shut it all out for a while.

The bus turned around and powered back across the bridge over the canal, jolting back over the debris in the roadway. The movement threw her forward and she opened her eyes again. She gazed down over the dead streets of Bromwell. Even now, almost two months since it had first happened, it was hard to comprehend the full scale of the inexplicable devastation which surrounded her. She could see many bodies scurrying around in the shadows down below, dragging themselves around, ceaselessly and tirelessly, like busy worker ants but without purpose or direction. She couldn't imagine a worse existence: condemned to haunt this dead world until such time that their physical form finally failed them. What had any of these people done to deserve this?

Half an hour earlier, Lorna had watched Webb and Sean taunting a corpse. The pathetic creature had been sliced in half by Jas' chainsaw but it had still been moving. She'd watched it pull itself along the ground, the stump of its spinal cord dragging behind, leaving a crimson snail-trail on the grey paving stones. Like kids teasing a stray dog, Webb and Sean had taken turns to lie down directly in its path, taunting it and playing chicken; waiting until the last possible moment before rolling away, then tricking the corpse into crawling after them in another direction. Stupid idiots. Didn't they care that that used to be a person? Maybe they did. Maybe it just didn't matter any more. Maybe she was the one who'd got it all wrong?

38

Webb, Sean, Amir and Harte were drunk. Their successful
excursion into Bromwell, coupled with the news that
the helicopter had been heard flying nearby again, left them
feeling temporarily invincible. They were fully in control.
Hollis and Jas watched them from the other side of the
Steelbrooke Suite. Their noise was beginning to make Hollis
nervous. The rest of the group had gone to bed, but he wasn't
going anywhere until these stupid, selfish fuckers had settled
down. He didn't want to think about what they might do if
they were left unsupervised – although the hotel grounds and
surrounding area were currently corpse-free, he wasn't prepared to take any chances. Webb and Sean were acting more
volatile than usual tonight, buoyed up by the events of the
day – Sean in particular had been unexpectedly aggressive
when, less than an hour ago, he'd suggested that maybe
they'd all had enough to drink.

After that Hollis decided that rather than antagonise them,
the best approach would be to give them what they wanted:
enough booze to help them lose consciousness. It was the
only way he could guarantee keeping them quiet.

He heard footsteps in the corridor outside. He picked up
his torch and went out to investigate and found Martin. He
looked tired and preoccupied.

'Come to complain about the noise again?' Hollis asked.

'Would it do any good?'

'Probably not. What's up?'

'Just been down by the pool.'

'And . . . ? Got a problem with your pet?'

'Don't take the piss.' He sighed. 'She's acting strangely.'

'Stranger than usual?'

'It's the noise this lot are making,' he explained, cringing as Webb threw another beer bottle onto a pile of empties. 'She's not used to it and it's freaking her out. We've survived here for as long as we have by keeping quiet and staying out of sight. What you're doing now is going to undo all of that.'

'Don't be overdramatic. They're just letting off steam; they're not doing any harm. Listen, I'll talk to them in the morning and—'

'You don't understand,' Martin snapped, his voice angrier, but the volume still restrained.

'What don't I understand?' Hollis snapped back. 'As far as I can see you've spent all your time locked in here keeping your head down. You haven't actually seen what's happening to the rest of the world. I have, and I know that we'll be safe here.'

'Come with me,' he interrupted, turning and walking away, leaving Hollis with little option but to follow. He knew exactly where Martin was taking him, back to the body he kept trapped in the office so he could prove his point. But what point was he trying to make? Sure enough, they turned down the corridor which led to the swimming pool.

'Look, Martin,' Hollis protested, 'I promise you I'll speak to them tomorrow. I won't let this happen again. I'll make them see that—'

He shut up immediately when they reached the window through which they usually watched the corpse. The Swimmer was slamming against the glass. Its dead eyes followed his every move and its numb, unresponsive fingers clawed pointlessly at the window, leaving a crisscross hatching of bloody smears. It slid along as he approached, keeping as close to him as it could.

'Why's she doing that?' he asked, suddenly understanding Martin's concern. 'She's never done that before, has she? She's always tried to get out of the way, not followed like that.'

'You see what I mean? She's scared,' Martin hissed, and turned again, almost as if he didn't want the corpse to hear. He led Hollis down the west wing corridor, stopping only when he reached the foot of the staircase which led to the rooms on the first and second floors.

'Thing is, Greg,' he whispered, 'I know you've managed to stay alive by doing things your way, and that's worked for you. Christ, the very fact that we're both standing here now is proof that we've all succeeded.'

'What are you trying to say?'

Martin thought for a moment, as if choosing his words carefully. 'What I'm saying,' he began, 'is that our methods of survival have to be adapted to our surroundings. Where you were before, it suited you to make a bloody huge noise and to fight and destroy them.'

'And what about here?'

'Here things are different,' he immediately replied.

'How?'

'We're relying on the fact that they don't know where we are.' He began to climb the stairs and beckoned Hollis to follow. He sprinted up each flight to the top floor. Halfway down the corridor was room West 37 – his room. He opened the door and ushered Hollis into his remarkably clean, comfortable and well-ordered living space. Martin walked over to the window which overlooked the car park and the countryside below. Hollis moved closer. He couldn't see anything but the usual never-ending blackness.

'What exactly am I supposed to be looking at?' he asked.

'Down there,' Martin replied, opening the window slightly and pointing. The air outside was cold.

Hollis shivered as a blustery gust hit his face. 'What?' he asked again.

'Look down there on the other side of the road. What can you see?'

As Hollis stared, his eyes slowly became used to the outside gloom. He could see the thick hedgerow which enclosed the hotel grounds, and the gap where the narrow road ran around its perimeter. Beyond that was the hedge on the other side of the road which bordered the golf course and surrounding fields. There was some movement in the field immediately opposite – corpses. He couldn't see how many.

'There are a few bodies. Nothing out of the ordinary. Why?'

'Because that *is* out of the ordinary.'

Hollis leant forward again. He could see the tops of as many as fifteen, maybe twenty bobbing heads moving in the field on the other side of the road. He couldn't see what the problem was. A noise from downstairs – a sudden torrent of drunken, shouted abuse from Harte – distracted him. It affected the bodies too. As soon as they heard it they shuffled closer to the hedge.

'But there are still only a handful of them,' Hollis protested, 'and they'll probably be gone in the morning.' He was tired and cold, and he was beginning to get annoyed with Martin.

'You're not listening to me,' Martin sighed. He shut the window and sat down on the corner of his bed.

'I am listening – I just don't see what the problem is.'

'Christ, Greg, I thought you of all people would understand. *You* might be used to having that many bodies around – *you* might be used to having hundreds more, thousands even. *We* are not.'

'But we can sort them out. They're not a real concern, believe me.'

'The thing is,' he continued, 'we did have that many here to start with, but we dealt with them: we distracted them and we tricked them into moving away with the music. We lit a couple of fires on the golf course, then we locked ourselves down and kept quiet and out of sight. From what I've heard, you did exactly the opposite: you just carried on like nothing had happened.'

'Well, not quite, but—'

'You did! You kept going out to get your food and your fuel and your booze and whatever else you wanted—'

'What's wrong with that?'

'I'm not criticising what you've done . . .'

'You sound like you are.'

'Well, I'm not. I'm just saying that in your situation, back where you were based, that approach might have worked, but you can't do that here. You can't keep going outside, and you can't keep making the kind of noise that those bloody drunks downstairs have been making all evening.'

Hollis was struggling to understand. 'I don't know why you're getting so upset,' he began to say before Martin interrupted.

'I'm not *upset*,' he protested, 'I'm *concerned*.'

'What about? Come on, you have to spell it out for me, because whatever you're hinting at, I'm not getting it. What is it that's bothering you tonight? We knew we were going to attract a few of them.'

'I understood that, but I've been watching the bodies out there for a couple of hours now, Greg, and their behaviour is changing. We've had them this close before, but they've always disappeared by now. Those things out there tonight aren't going anywhere. The music's still playing, and there's still a big enough crowd to keep them on the golf course, but it doesn't seem to be working like it usually does. Christ, man, they're moving in the *opposite* direction!'

Hollis looked out again, carefully considering the frightened man's words. 'What about the helicopter?' he asked. 'It flew over again today, didn't it?'

'Yes. What about it?'

'So we need to do something to make them see us.'

'Is this relevant?'

'I think so – how are we going to attract their attention without attracting the bodies too?'

'I don't know. I was thinking about marking a message on the lawns or something like that.'

'Might work; some kind of beacon would be better though. They won't see your message unless they fly right over us and they happen to be looking down right at that moment.'

'I know—'

'The point I'm trying to make is that we're going to have to risk making our presence known at some point. And we can *deal* with the dead, Martin. We've done it before. Bloody hell, Webb alone has torched *hundreds* of them.'

'He might well have, but there are thousands more waiting out there.'

'Waiting?'

'Yes, waiting – waiting to find out where we are. Driving around in bloody lorries and buses, lighting beacons and making a bloody noise like you lot have done today is just going to lead them straight back to us. You're going to start a chain-reaction: once a few of them know where we are, the whole bloody lot will follow.'

39

At first light, at Martin's request, Hollis walked with him up to the clubhouse to help refuel the generators and set the music playing again. It was the first time in weeks that Martin had walked rather than cycled along the track which ran around the western edge of the hotel grounds. Without his bike he felt as if he'd travelled much further than usual, and that made him feel even more vulnerable and exposed. If he hadn't had Hollis with him he doubted he'd have dared make the trip on foot. Hollis was keen to get a better sense of their location, and he had insisted they initially continue down the narrow lane to get closer to the bodies they'd seen last night.

Martin pointed through a gap in the hedge to help Hollis get his bearings, and Hollis glanced back over the wall of tall laurel bushes at the hotel. He could just about see Martin's window, and it looked like they were roughly level with the area they'd observed last night. Crouching down, he peered through the mass of tangled branches in front of him. On the other side of the hedgerow was a large open field.

'Is this still the golf course?' he asked, his whispered voice barely audible. 'I couldn't really see last night.'

'No,' said Martin, 'this field's part of a farm. The golf course starts another couple of hundred yards further up the road.'

Hollis could see numerous bodies staggering around – there appeared to be at least as many as there had been last night, maybe even a few more.

'I've never seen this many here before,' Martin hissed.

'There's only ever been a handful here at a time, and they've always been moving *towards* the music, not away from it.'

Hollis continued to watch the dead. Although some were clearly still trying to move towards the source of the distant sound, and some were just standing in the same place, constantly shuffling, but never straying more than a few yards in any direction, others were definitely travelling in the opposite direction. He could only assume they were gravitating towards the hotel, or towards the crowd which had been gathered in this area last night. Whatever the reason, their actions added weight to Martin's argument.

Hollis began to wonder whether he had badly underestimated the effect of their arrival and the noise of the bus – not to mention the drunks – yesterday. More to the point, maybe he'd underestimated the steadily increasing levels of intelligence and control which the dead seemed to be exhibiting here.

'There still aren't that many,' he mumbled, taking care to keep his voice low, but struggling to find the right volume because of the muffled sound in his damaged ear. He shifted position again, still not able to see as much as he wanted. 'A few more hours of silence and I'm sure they'll disappear – it's not been that long. Once we explain to the others what's happening they'll—'

He stopped speaking immediately as a corpse rushed towards him. It crashed into the other side of the hedgerow and tried to stretch its gnarled hand out through the tangled undergrowth. He tripped back in surprise, and then moved closer again when the initial shock had faded.

'What is it?' Martin asked anxiously, keeping a safe distance.

'Got a lively one, that's all,' Hollis replied. Once he was satisfied that it couldn't reach him he looked into the dead monster's face through a gap in the branches. He couldn't tell if it had been male or female. Its skin was heavily pockmarked and decayed and its top lip had been torn away, exposing its yellowed teeth. A large flap of skin hung down from the side of its head, covering its ear. Its eyes looked relatively undamaged – and after a moment Hollis realised that the damn thing was staring straight at him. Its sight may well have been limited, but the creature in the field was watching his every move.

As if to prove his point it suddenly threw itself into the hedge again, reaching out as far as it could, and as he watched, the savage thorns and spiky branches stripped the rotting flesh from its bones. Another corpse, alerted by the sudden movements of the first, rushed forward, and then another, then another, and within seconds at least five of the dead were clamouring at the hedge where Hollis was standing. Surprised and unnerved by their unexpected ferocity, he turned back and silently ushered Martin along the road towards the clubhouse.

Hollis only relaxed slightly when they reached the enclosed passageway which led up to the back entrance of the clubhouse. Martin led him inside, moving quickly through the pitch-black ground floor and up the stairs to the balconied landing. Both of the CD players were still working and the combined noise from the music and the generators was appalling, loud enough for Hollis to almost be glad that one of his ears had stopped working. He followed Martin into the meeting room, watched his well-rehearsed refuelling routine, then crossed the landing to the office. He noticed that Martin was keeping his head down, looking at the floor as much as possible.

'What's the matter?' he asked, concerned.

'Nothing,' Martin replied. 'I don't like to look at them, that's all.'

He replaced the CD player and moved to one side. Hollis immediately stepped forward, his curiosity getting the better of him. He leant out of the window, hanging onto the frame for support.

'Fuck me,' he said, forgetting himself, but the music drowned out his words. He glanced back at Martin, who looked away from him, not wanting to share the horror of what he'd just seen. Hollis turned back to face outside.

The sun was rising on the horizon. Incandescent yellow light was slowly seeping across the world, burning away the shadows. Below Hollis, stretching out for as far as he could see in every direction, stood the largest crowd of bodies he'd ever seen. Thousands of them – hundreds of thousands even – filled every inch of the golf course. The size of the crowd was incomprehensible and terrifying. He couldn't compare it to the gathering outside the flats; there the dead had been free to wander, but here they were confined. In an instant, he completely understood why Martin had reacted so badly to the little noise they'd made over the last two days. If this crowd turned on them, he realised, there'd be no escape. *If this number of bodies get any closer to the hotel*, he thought, *they'll either tear us apart or crush us. There will be no way out. And if they don't kill us, with that many of them so close it would surely only be a matter of time before the deadly germs which killed Ellie and Anita started to spread.*

40

With the rest of the group still indoors, Jas slipped out and crept over to the bus which had been abandoned right outside the hotel entrance yesterday. In the sudden euphoria which had followed their successful looting expedition, they had unloaded just enough food and drink to get them through the night, with the intention of finishing the job in the morning. It was still early and nothing had so far been done: lethargy, hangovers and general tiredness had affected everyone – everyone except Jas.

Feeling guilty and uneasy, he crept onto the bus and began to pick up boxes of food. He carried them back through the hotel and up to the middle room on the first floor of the east wing of the building; Room 24 East. Hardly anyone slept on that side of the hotel, and 24 East was one of the largest rooms. The first floor felt safer than the ground floor. He'd done a recce earlier that morning, studying the main part of the hotel and both wings, as well as the enclosed grassy courtyard below, and he'd decided that if anything happened and he ended up trapped in the room he'd just chosen, he'd have the security of being off the ground floor but he would still be low enough to get out of a window without breaking every bone in his body, should he need to make a sudden escape.

His plan this morning was simple: to fill the room with an emergency stockpile, just in case. The others could use it too – well, some of them, anyway. It made sense not to store everything they'd managed to scavenge in one place.

He was getting off the bus for the seventh time when he got caught.

'What the hell are you doing?' Webb asked, stepping out from around a corner, early morning cigarette and beer in hand. Jas jumped back with surprise. The panic on his face was clear and Webb chuckled to himself as he swigged from his can of lager.

'Nothing,' Jas answered quickly.

'Like hell. Doesn't look like nothing.'

'Just piss off, Webb,' he said, 'it's none of your business.'

'Yes it is. That's my stuff you're taking.'

'It's *our* stuff,' he corrected him.

'Whatever. Point is, it's not *your* stuff, you thieving bastard. I've been watching you for the last half hour. I know where you're stashing it.'

Jas sighed dejectedly. How could he explain what he was doing to this stupid little shit without him thinking he was simply creaming off the best of their supplies for himself (which, if he was completely honest with himself, he was). Did he need to explain himself at all?

'Look,' he began, deciding he should give it a shot and see how Webb reacted, 'at the moment everything we've got is scattered around this place. Most of it's up by the restaurant and the conference room, lots more still out in the bus.'

'So you thought you'd help yourself?'

'All I'm doing,' he interrupted, determined not to give Webb an opportunity to argue, 'is putting some of it somewhere else. What if there's a fire and half the building goes up in smoke? What if someone gets sick, like Anita and Ellie did, and we have to shut ourselves away from them? What if the bodies get in here?'

'Bullshit,' Webb spat, full of animosity. 'You're a liar. You're not going to tell anyone else where you're putting this stuff. You're taking it for yourself, you fucker.'

'Oh shut up,' Jas said, struggling to remain calm and not overreact. *He's not worth it*, he silently told himself, but unable to suppress his anger, he dropped the box he'd been carrying and moved threateningly towards Webb, who was still mouthing off furiously.

'You're a fucking thieving bastard,' he continued, his anger unabated and his confidence buoyed up by booze. 'Wait till I tell the others what you're up to.'

Jas lunged for Webb and grabbed him by the neck. After checking that no one else was around, he pushed him up against the nearest wall, knocking his head back with a satisfying thump. 'Do yourself a favour and shut up,' he said, his voice disarmingly calm. 'You're not going to tell anyone anything.'

'Why shouldn't I?'

'Because if you do,' he whispered, moving even closer so that his face was now just inches from Webb's, 'I'll tell them what you did to Stokes.'

Webb immediately stopped struggling. He mouthed a few silent words but, for a second, he was unable to respond. At last he mumbled, 'I didn't do anything. I didn't *do* anything.'

'Yes, you did,' Jas said ominously. 'I saw you.' Not bothering to wait for a response, he picked up his box and disappeared back into the building.

41

'If there's one thing we've got plenty of here,' Ginnie said, her arms fully loaded, 'it's white sheets.'

Hollis moved to let her through and watched as she disappeared outside to find Martin and Caron. Gordon followed close behind. *Those two are attached at the hip these days*, he thought. Finally Lorna came through, her hair tied up in a long ponytail, struggling with yet more linen.

'Here, let me,' he said, holding the door open. She smiled briefly, but didn't say anything. Hollis ducked into the kitchen to pick up a pile of sheets himself, then followed the rest of them out.

The early morning cloud had remained, but it had steadily lightened from dark grey to a brighter white as the sun tried to break through. It wasn't much after eight but it felt much later. *Funny how our body clocks seem to have synchronised themselves with the sun and the moon*, he thought as he walked across the lawn towards the others. In the old days he'd have got up when it was time to go to work and gone to bed when he'd finished watching TV or come in from the pub. Now the only thing which happened with any regularity was the steady progress of the sun across the sky, and they'd all matched their daily routines to the light: up at dawn, ready to sleep by dusk.

Martin was flapping like an over-protective mother hen.

Caron seemed to have a better grasp of the task at hand. 'No, Martin,' she protested, 'we need to start over here and put the letters the other way up to how you're suggesting. Down the lawn, not across it, see? H – E – L – P . . .' As she spoke she pointed to where she thought each letter should go.

'She's right,' Gordon agreed, 'we can make the letters bigger if we do it that way.'

'Doesn't really matter which way up they go, does it?' added Ginnie enthusiastically, pleased to have finally found something useful to occupy her time.

'Keep your voices down,' Hollis nervously warned. They were almost at the boundary fence, near the gap he'd gone through with Martin earlier. They could hear music in the distance, and he felt uncomfortably close to the dead. If only they knew just how many bodies he'd seen gathered on the golf course . . .

Ignoring the others as they fussed and argued, Lorna began opening up the first sheet and laying it out. Using soil, stones and whatever else he could find, Hollis followed her around and weighed down the edges of the material.

'Think this is going to do it?' he asked as she unfolded the second sheet.

'We've got nothing to lose by trying, have we?'

Following her lead, Gordon and Ginnie also started to work. Ginnie laid two sheets down to form the cross of the H, and Gordon secured them. Hollis was coming back from fetching more linen when a football bounced up off the grass and hit him in the face, knocking him to the ground. As searing pain coursed through his injured ear he looked up angrily to see Sean approaching, Webb not far behind.

'Sorry,' Sean began, jogging towards him, but Hollis barged past him.

'What the *fuck* do you think you're doing?' he yelled at Webb, the blinding pain and anger making him temporarily forget the volume of his voice. 'Are you fucking *stupid*?'

'No, are you?' Webb goaded.

Hollis ran at him, but the younger man was too fast and sidestepped his clumsy attack.

'Come here you little bastard,' he seethed, 'I'm going to kill you.'

'No you're not – you can't even catch me!'

'Leave it out,' Lorna pleaded, running after them both. 'Come on, Hollis, this is pointless. He's just a little idiot – he's not worth wasting your time on.'

'You can fuck off too,' Webb spat at her.

Hollis sprinted forward again, but this time he lost his footing and slid in the dew-soaked grass, much to Webb's amusement. He picked himself up, breathing hard and glared at Webb.

Lorna held him back. 'Please,' she pleaded with him, 'just ignore him. He's only doing it to wind you up. Come back and help us get this finished.'

'Fucking idiot,' Hollis shouted, forgetting himself again. 'Why can't you do something useful instead of screwing around all the time?'

'You call that useful?' he shouted back, pointing at the sheets on the grass. 'How is that useful? How's that going to help? Who's going to see it?'

'What's going on?' Jas asked, drawn from the hotel by the raised voices. 'Have you lot got any idea how much noise you're making?'

'It's okay, Jas,' Lorna told him as she tried again to pull Hollis away. 'There's no problem. It's nothing.'

'Come on, mate,' Sean said to Webb, passing the football to him. 'Let's go. No point standing here arguing about fuck-all.'

Lorna looked into Hollis' face. He didn't seem himself. He'd been quiet since he'd been caught off-guard by that body in Bromwell yesterday. 'Is something wrong? Is it your ear again—?' She stopped and looked up at the sky.

The others were staring too as they realised they were listening to the helicopter engine approaching. Webb was the first to spot it: a small black silhouette crawling across the off-white sky several miles north of where they were standing.

'There it is,' he said, pointing up at the aircraft, 'and that's why what you're doing is stupid. How are they supposed to see your letters on the ground when they're not even flying overhead? They're fucking miles away. They'll *never* see it.'

He was right, and Hollis knew it.

'So what do you suggest?' he asked, sounding uncharacteristically desperate. 'What else are we supposed to do? What we're doing is better than doing nothing at all.'

'You need a fucking fire or something,' Webb answered. 'A great big fucking fire in the middle of nowhere. At least then they'll—'

'Shut up!' Jas interrupted. 'Listen!'

It was another engine, loud enough for them all to hear.

'There!' Lorna said excitedly. 'Look at that! It's a bloody plane!'

'Christ,' Sean said under his breath as they stood and stared at the second, much larger aircraft, 'there must be *loads* of them. It's a bloody mass evacuation.'

'That's not good,' Jas warned.

'Not good?' he protested, 'how can it not be good?'

'Because you might be right, and if you are, then they're probably clearing out. And if they're doing that, then they're not going to be flying over here many more times, are they?'

42

'They're a bunch of fucking wasters,' Webb cursed, finishing another can of beer (he'd lost count of how many he'd already had today) and throwing it onto the growing pile of empties in the corner of Sean's room at the back of the hotel. 'They're going to sit in here and fucking rot, I tell you. Just fucking look at them.'

He pulled back a corner of the curtain, letting a little light into the otherwise dark room, to reveal the rest of the survivors, all still outside, writing their pointless message on the grass with dirty sheets.

'Don't let them get to you,' Sean said. 'You just have to ignore them. I've had weeks of that kind of bullshit since I've been here. They're always telling me "you can't do this" and "you can't do that". Honestly, mate, it's been worse than living with my bloody parents!'

'What happens if that helicopter does see us and lands? Where are we going to end up? We'll still have them with us: same shit, different place. I don't know how you've put up with it for as long as you have, mate.'

'What else could I do?'

'You could have stood up for yourself – told them how pissed off you were.'

'And what good would that have done?'

'You could have left them. I would have if I was stuck here. At least back at the flats I could get out when I wanted to.'

'But I didn't want to go out. They told me how bad it was, and how we had to keep our heads down, and I believed them.'

'That was all bullshit! You saw it for yourself yesterday. All right, so it's not exactly a fucking walk in the park out there, but we did okay, didn't we?'

'I was scared because *they* were scared, I can see it now. Until yesterday I was fucking terrified of going outside, but you were right, it was an absolute fucking breeze.'

'Thing is,' Webb continued, the alcohol increasing his ire, 'they don't actually want us here. We're just a pain in the backside to them. They wouldn't miss us if we went.'

'So let's go then.'

'How?'

Sean opened the curtain fully. 'See the road between here and the golf course?'

'What about it?'

'Follow it back towards the front of the hotel.'

Webb did as he was instructed, tracing the curve of the road right around the outer edge of the hotel grounds. All he could see was a field on the other side of the road, empty save for a few hundred bodies staggering around aimlessly. An unruly mob – he couldn't see how many – appeared to be hanging around close to the hedge. 'What am I supposed to be looking at?' he said at last.

'See there,' Sean said, pointing down towards the front of the hotel complex, 'there's a Yaris parked in the road.'

'Yeah, so?'

'Martin and Howard put that there to block a gate.'

'Into that field? So what? Are you thinking of going for a bloody picnic?'

'The point is: there's another gate on the opposite side of the field. We can get out that way without moving any of their bloody lorries and buses. If we go the other way at the fork in the road we can take the brakes off and shift the Yaris, and we're out.'

'But what about the bodies? I can see plenty, but aren't there supposed to be thousands of them round here?'

'I didn't think that bothered you.'

'It doesn't bother me,' Webb replied arrogantly, 'but I'm not about to stick my bare arse out in the middle of a massive crowd of corpses unless I've got no choice.'

'They're all on the golf course up there, well out of the way. Those are just the stragglers. Come on, you've told me you've dealt with bigger crowds than that before.'

Webb didn't answer at first; instead he continued to stare out of the window into the field Sean had pointed out. There really weren't that many bodies there – even the unexplained mass clumped around the hedge wasn't huge. Could they try running for it? Maybe that was too risky. There had to be another way of getting out.

'How did you say you got here?' he asked, a plan beginning to form in his head.

'Scooter,' Sean replied, 'but it's fucked. I've got a flat tyre and hardly any fuel.'

'Can you ride a motorbike?'

43

It was almost eleven o'clock, and Gordon, Ginnie, Lorna and Caron were still unloading and sorting supplies from the bus. They were working slowly, in a bid to keep themselves occupied, making the most of having something to fill their normally empty day.

'Was there really any point in bringing back this much pickle?' Ginnie asked, looking down her nose through her half-moon glasses at the three trays of Branston Pickle Lorna had just carried inside. 'Horrible stuff.'

'One day,' Lorna replied, sweating and breathless with effort, 'you might be grateful for that. And like I keep saying, love, if there was something special you wanted bringing back, you should have got off your backside and gone out there with us, shouldn't you?'

'I'll eat it,' Gordon said unhelpfully, ripping open the packaging, picking up a jar and studying the label. 'I love this stuff. I could live on it.'

'You might have to,' Lorna grumbled.

'Just the smell of it makes me feel sick.' Ginnie was still complaining. 'It really does: just a whiff makes me want to throw up. You know, I used to have a friend who—'

'We should all be thankful for what we've got, and for the fact we're here at all,' Caron interrupted. 'It's funny how perspectives change, isn't it? A couple of days ago, Ginnie, you'd probably have killed to get your hands on a jar of pickle, no matter how ill it made you feel. We need to remember that we—'

She stopped talking. The others looked at her expectantly.

'Remember what?' Lorna asked.

'Shh,' she hissed, 'listen. *They're back.*'

In the distance they could hear an engine, and in an instant all their petty disagreements and pointless arguments over pickle were forgotten as they all dropped their supplies and ran across the central courtyard and through to reception. They burst out of the front door and out onto the car park, to find Hollis and Martin already there, scanning the skies. Amir ran towards them from the other side of the building.

'It's no use looking up there,' he panted, 'that's no helicopter—'

'What?' grunted Hollis. His re-damaged ear hurt so badly that he was having trouble hearing anything at all now.

'It's on the ground,' Amir explained, 'and it's moving *away* from us.'

The entire group turned around as Jas came thundering out of the hotel. 'They've taken my bike,' he shouted. 'Those little bastards have taken my Honda!'

Sean weaved through the staggering corpses hurling themselves at him from all directions. The grassy ground beneath his wheels was dry but uneven, and a deceptively steep slope away from the hotel made it even harder for him to keep control of the powerful motorbike. He didn't dare do anything but aim for the gate in the furthest corner of the field and keep on accelerating. Webb, holding on tight behind him with one arm wrapped around Sean's waist and one hand holding onto his cap, was feeling dangerously exposed. He peered round Sean's back and saw through the confusion that they were almost there, and the gate was open, just as Sean said it would be. Martin had left it like that to make it as easy as possible for the dead to find their way through this field and onto the golf course. He tightened his grip on Sean as the Honda thundered through the opening, leaving the ground momentarily then thumping back down onto the tarmac. Almost immediately a sharp left turn loomed and Sean dipped the bike over to such a sickening extent that Webb thought they'd never recover from the turn. He screwed his eyes shut, held on and waited for the impact which never came. To his amazement they were still moving forwards. So perhaps Sean hadn't just been boasting.

Sean rode in a large loop, bypassing the blocked-off road junction and eventually re-joining the route to Bromwell which they'd taken yesterday. They'd already decided on today's destination: the bowling alley next to the supermarket they'd looted. The journey was faster this morning; though there were many more bodies around than there had been yesterday, it was far easier to steer the bike around the carnage than it had been for Driver's bus. The dead had no doubt been attracted by the noise they'd made the day before, Sean decided, but whatever the reason, it didn't matter. He knew how to deal with them now. They were no longer the massive threat he'd allowed himself to believe they were. The lamentable bastards were just barely coordinated, germ-infested bags of flesh and bone.

They raced down Bromwell High Street, passing Amir's restaurant and the various other insignificant sights which had been pointed out yesterday. Webb, finally feeling brave enough to lift his head and look around, actually found himself silently thanking the others for once. Their day-trip in their lumbering, beaten-up double-decker bus had cleared the way for him and Sean today. The bus had blundered through scores of bodies, forcing masses of wreckage out of the way and leaving a relatively clear – if still treacherous with gore – path through the mayhem. They made their way up and over the bridge spanning the flesh-filled canal (which seemed to be full of even more corpses than it had been before), past the front of the supermarket and then they were there.

Sean pulled up outside the glass-fronted bowling complex.

'What now?' he asked, anxiously watching a group of seven bodies. They had just turned around and were moving towards them. He glanced over his shoulder and saw at least double that number coming up from behind. *The damn things must have dragged themselves up here to check out the supermarket after we left yesterday*, he thought. He suddenly felt uneasy, but he didn't dare let Webb see.

'Go around the back,' Webb answered, his experience of both dealing with the dead and breaking and entering again proving invaluable. 'There probably won't be as many of them there. It'll make it easier when we leave too.'

Sean did as he was instructed, sticking out a foot to trip up the nearest of the corpses as he swerved around the closest group. He turned right down the side of the building, focusing on avoiding more cadavers which were hauling themselves out from behind the building next door. They were *everywhere* – surely they couldn't all be here as a result of the noise they'd made yesterday, could they? Momentarily preoccupied with the dead, he jumped with surprise when Webb shook his shoulder.

'Stop!' he yelled over the noise of the engine, 'turn around – there's a fire door.'

Sean did as he was ordered and Webb slid off the back of the bike and ran towards a dark-blue fire exit halfway down the side of the red-brick building. The door was wedged open by a single skeletal arm which jutted up from the ground, almost as if its dead owner was wanting to have a question answered. The insects that were gorging themselves on its rotting fingertips buzzed away as he yanked the door open and the arm flopped down. Sean immediately drove into the darkness and abandoned the bike, then ran back to shove the body out of the way. Once they were both inside Webb pulled the door shut with a reassuring thump, plunging the entire building into darkness.

'Get a light on!' he screamed, hearing sounds of movement somewhere near.

'What light?' Sean cried, panicked.

'The bike! Use the fucking bike!'

Sean ran back towards the motorbike, but he was knocked

off his feet by a corpse which, more through luck than judgement, smacked into him head-on. He recoiled at the appalling stench which immediately filled his nostrils, then tripped over as the creature's unsteady head rocked back with the impact, then fell forward again, butting him in the eye. The sudden dagger-sharp pain was intense and he collapsed, dragging the body down with him.

'You all right, mate?' Webb yelled. 'Where are you?'

'I'm okay,' Sean hissed through clenched teeth, the sudden shock and pain now beginning to fade. 'I'm dealing with it.' Lying on his back, he reached up and wrapped his gloved hand around the body's throat, squeezing as hard as he could, feeling the decaying skin and gristle giving way as the pressure he exerted increased. Tighter and tighter he squeezed, putrefied flesh dribbling out through the gaps between his fingers, until the body stopped thrashing and slumped motionless on top of him.

Webb had managed to pick up the bike and turn on the headlamp, filling their corner of the building with light.

'Nice one!' he laughed as he watched Sean pick himself back up and kick the cadaver away to one side. 'You're starting to get the hang of this!'

Sean didn't say anything, but he brushed himself down as he looked around, shaking his head to clear the numbness which remained from his assailant's vicious head-butt. His eyes were slowly becoming accustomed to the low light levels indoors. Some sunlight was seeping inside through the glazed front of the building, but most of the bowling alley remained disappointingly dark. He hadn't been expecting anything different, not really, but as they'd driven up he'd been remembering this place as it had been when he'd last visited, on a team-building event with the design company he'd worked for. It was the Friday night before everyone had died, and the whole place had been full of noise, light and people back then. It was so hard to believe that everyone he'd been there with was now dead . . . *Get a grip*, he ordered himself, feeling uncomfortable, long-suppressed emotions beginning to rise.

'Looks like the place was empty,' Webb shouted to him from the other side of the bowling lanes. 'I can only find this one.'

Sean moved forward to get a better view. Webb was dragging the body of a female cleaner behind him by its hair. The poor cow didn't look like she'd been any older than twenty when she'd died. The corpse's light-blue pinafore, grey T-shirt and jeans were stained with blood, pus and Christ alone knew what else. Its arms and legs thrashed about furiously and as Webb bumped it down the three low steps towards Sean a clump of scalp came away from its skull, leaving him holding just a handful of greasy hair and skin.

The body tried to get up, but he was having none of it. 'Sorry, darling,' he said as he put his arms around its emaciated waist, 'your cleaning days are over.' With that he swung the corpse around, clouting its head hard against a concrete pillar, shattering its skull and showering the ground with what was left of its brain. No longer interested, he dropped it like it was an empty beer can and walked away, looking for food and other distractions. For a moment Sean stood and stared into the dead girl's face. At this angle and in this light, it looked surprisingly untroubled by all that had happened to her. *Poor bitch*, he thought to himself sadly. *It wasn't her fault. She didn't deserve that.* He looked back over his shoulder at the carcase which had attacked him just minutes earlier, then looked down at the girl at his feet again. He nudged her chin with his boot, hard enough to make her head roll and reveal the other side of her face, a bloody mass of foetid skin. *Get a grip*, he said to himself again, angry that he'd allowed himself to feel something for the corpse. *I can't afford to think like that any more – it doesn't matter who or what any of these things used to be, they're not human now.*

The hours which followed were unexpectedly surreal. Sean continued to feel a bizarre mix of emotions; nervous, desperate and scared one minute, elated and free the next. After collecting food and drink by smashing open the vending machines (and disturbing a nest of squealing, overfed rats in the process), Webb had suggested they try bowling, but that didn't last long. The electronic scoreboards remained blank, and when the pins and the bowling balls disappeared over the precipice at the end of the lanes they never returned. But for the first few moments, Sean was able to close his eyes and recall how everything used to feel and sound: the reassuringly familiar rumble of the heavy balls rolling down the alley filling the vast room, followed by the clatter and bang of the pins being knocked down.

They gave up on bowling when all the balls had disappeared, neither man relishing the prospect of disappearing down into the labyrinthine bowels of the alley to retrieve them. Instead they cleared a space in the carpeted area where rows of blank-faced arcade machines stood and then, between the two of them, dragged a pool table nearer to the tall windows at the front of the building. As the sun began to sink towards the horizon, and under the vacant but watchful gaze of several hundred dead faces pressed hard against the glass, they played for as long as they were able. Only when the light had all but completely gone did they finally accept that it was time to return to the hotel.

'We could stay here, you know,' Sean suggested as they prepared themselves to leave. 'We don't have to go back.'

'Nah,' Webb quickly replied, 'I want my bed and my beer. We can come back tomorrow.'

'We can go anywhere we bloody well want to tomorrow,' Sean said as he climbed onto the motorbike, already planning his next escape. He wasn't much looking forward to facing the bunch of miserable fuckers waiting for them back at the hotel – in many ways they worried him more than the crowds of cadavers swarming across the countryside. *It doesn't matter*, he decided. *If they give me any trouble, I'll just turn around and leave.*

After all, what was left of the world was his for the taking.

44

Sean drove back across the field, the bike's headlamp slicing through the darkness and illuminating the crisscrossing corpses which continually staggered out in front of him. Halfway across he switched off the light, then turned off the engine just short of reaching the hedge. Largely invisible, they coasted towards the gate in the corner. He was off-course slightly, reaching the other side of the field a little low.

'Go and get the gate open,' he hissed at Webb who was still clinging on tightly behind him.

'What, me?'

'Get the fucking gate open!'

Webb reluctantly jumped off the bike, and using the hedgerow as cover he ran blindly forwards along the furthest edge of the field, anxiously shoving corpses out of the way. He was panting with effort by the time he reached the gate. His hands numb with cold, he undid the latch and pulled the metal barrier open, aware that a mass of shadows were already closing in on him.

'Done,' he shouted quietly, hoping his voice was loud enough for Sean to hear, but the starting of the Honda's engine and the immediate flood of light across the field was welcome confirmation. The bike roared towards him and burst through the open gate onto the road, collecting a single corpse along the way and sending it flying through the air like a rag doll. Webb shut the gate as soon as he was through, struggling with the awkward latch and fighting to ignore the countless dark figures which were swarming ever closer. Two of them clattered against the gate, the force of their uncoordinated impact jolting him back and showering him with droplets of decay.

Sean was already off the bike. He grabbed the cadaver in the road and snapped its neck, surprising himself with his brutality, then climbed into the Yaris which had previously blocked the full width of the gate. He released the handbrake, then jumped out and, with Webb's help, pushed it forward the few feet so that the barrier was secure again.

'You all right?' he asked, looking into Webb's face which was partially illuminated by a ray of early moonlight.

'Fine,' Webb said, glancing back at the two dozen corpses which were now smashing themselves relentlessly against the metal gate. He wished they'd stop; the noise was making him nervous. He climbed back on the Honda and held on tightly as they rode down to the fork in the road, then sharply turned back on themselves and roared up towards the hotel. The building loomed large up ahead, silhouetted against the darkening sky. Sean could already see movement.

'Shit!' he cursed as the light from the bike illuminated a crowd of figures moving towards them across the car park: three – no, *four* – bodies were heading their way. How the hell did they get through? Had they left the gate open earlier? Had they somehow got in through—? No, wait, they were moving too quickly, and their movements were controlled. It was Hollis and the others.

Sean drove up to the front of the building and got off the bike, relieved. 'It's all right,' he said to Webb, calmer now. 'It's okay. It's just Jas and—'

Jas silenced him with a savage right hook which sent him spinning around and crashing down to the ground. He lay there, stunned, as Jas moved towards Webb, who cowered pathetically, covering his face with his hands.

'Don't hit me,' he pleaded as Jas grabbed his collar and pulled him closer. 'Please, I—'

'Leave it,' Hollis warned, forcing himself between the two of them. 'Not out here.'

'The fuckers took *my* Honda,' Jas seethed.

'Not out here,' Hollis repeated.

'Never mind your damn bike,' Harte said anxiously, 'just get them inside before they do any more damage.'

'What are you talking about?' Webb stammered, trying to hide the fear in his voice and failing miserably. 'We blocked the gate – we didn't let any of them through.'

'Just shut up and get inside,' Jas hissed, shoving him back towards the hotel.

'But we didn't—'

'Just get inside,' he shouted, running forward and grabbing Webb again.

Webb found himself looking deep into Jas' eyes, but it wasn't anger he was seeing; it was pure fear. He wrestled himself away and ran towards the safety of the hotel's shadows.

45

'I really can't believe you'd be so damn stupid,' Jas ranted as Sean and Webb were frogmarched into the Steelbrooke Suite. 'What the *hell* did you think you were doing? Are you out of your fucking minds?'

'Fuck you,' Sean mumbled, his jaw still stinging and his head spinning with pain. One of his teeth felt loose and he could taste blood in his mouth. He cowered back as Jas lunged for him again.

'Stop it!' Caron screamed, lowering her voice immediately when she realised how unintentionally loud she'd been. 'For Christ's sake, please stop – we've got quite enough to worry about without you beating each other senseless.'

'What's she talking about?' Sean asked, confused. 'What's happened?'

'What do you think's happened?' Gordon said unhelpfully from the table where he sat with Ginnie. 'It's the bodies,'

'What about them?'

'They're smarter than we've given them credit for,' Martin began to explain.

'How can they be?' Webb started, shutting up when Jas glared at him.

'The noise you lot made coming here a couple of days back started it, and when you went out for supplies yesterday it just made matters worse. What you two did today might just have been the straw that broke the camel's back.'

'I still don't understand,' Sean said as Martin sat down in the nearest chair and dropped his head into his hands.

Howard said, 'They're coming back: there's a load of them gathered over the road.'

'What about the music?'

'It's not working any more.'

'That's not exactly true,' Hollis corrected him. 'It is still working, but like Martin says, they're getting wise to it. It fooled them before, because they didn't know anyone was here. And now, well, it's still drawing them in, from miles around; the problem is, when they get close enough and hear us moving about, or arguing, or driving around on stolen fucking motorbikes, they understandably get more interested in us than anything else. They're starting to work out that the music is just a decoy; that we're the ones actually making the noise.'

'Can't be—' Sean said.

'*Can* be,' Harte quickly replied. 'It's instinctive. It's exactly what started happening back at the flats. The more noise we made, the worse they got. A handful of them broke through our defences, and within a few hours, hundreds had followed. They *learn*.'

'So what are we supposed to do?' Ginnie asked, shuffling a little closer to Gordon. 'Is there anything we can do?'

'What we should do now,' Martin announced, unsuccessfully attempting to exert some authority, 'is exactly what we were doing in the first place before you clowns arrived. We keep our heads down, stay absolutely silent and wait for those creatures out there to disintegrate down to nothing. If we run out of food, then we go hungry. If we start to—'

'No way,' Sean yelled, furious, the fuzziness in his head replaced with anger, 'no fucking way! If you think I'm sitting here in fucking silence with you lot just waiting for the bodies to rot, then you can think again. You can stick your fucking—'

'That's exactly what you're going to do,' Jas said, moving towards him again, 'because if you don't, I'll break your fucking neck.'

Sean recoiled, but Webb, regaining his usual cockiness, laughed. 'Is that right?' he said, goading Jas.

'Don't you start. I'll kill you now if you want me to, you little piece of shit.'

'Come on then!' he yelled, jumping to his feet and squaring up against Jas. The others cringed, willing them both to shut up as the volume of their pointless argument continued to increase.

'Leave it, Jas,' Harte said. 'He's not worth it.'

Webb stood his ground as Jas moved forward again. Their faces almost touching, Jas whispered loud enough for Webb alone to hear, 'So you want me to tell them about Stokes?'

Webb pushed him away and slunk back into the shadows.

'Let's just keep things in perspective,' Lorna said. She'd been watching the discussion deteriorate with disappointment. 'There's no need to panic. They still can't get to us. Every access point is blocked. Like Hollis says, we just need them to forget we're over here.'

'But what about the helicopter?' Caron wondered. 'And the plane? How are we supposed to attract their attention if we're keeping our heads down? We don't know how many more times they're going to fly over.'

'Have they been here again?' Sean wondered.

'Twice more,' Gordon replied.

'*Twice?*'

'They flew over late afternoon,' he said, 'then again just about an hour later.'

'They're clearing out, aren't they? It's like you said this morning, Jas, they're evacuating.'

'I think he's right,' Gordon said.

'Then that's all the more reason for us not to lock ourselves down, isn't it?' Sean nervously continued. 'If we don't let them know we're here now, then they'll never find us. And I'm not just talking about writing love letters on the grass with sheets or playing music. We have to do something big, something that they're going to see – and we have to do it now!'

'Sean,' Martin warned. His own voice was getting louder again.

'Oh just shut up, Martin, and get off my fucking case. You haven't even—'

'Just calm down and be quiet.'

'What if I don't *want* to? I know exactly what we have to do to get that helicopter or the plane to see us, and I'll do it if none of you have got the nerve to.'

At the side of the room, unnoticed by anyone but Ginnie, Gordon stood up and cleared his throat. Hesitant, but feeling a definite need to act, he moved forward into the middle of the argument, placing himself directly between Hollis, Martin and Jas on one side, Sean and Webb on the other. He looked Sean straight in the eye. 'Listen,' he began, captivating the others with his unexpected and uncharacteristically positive involvement, 'you have to listen. I know you're angry, and you're probably just as scared as I am right now, but you've *got* to listen. Please don't do anything stupid. We've sat in here today, and we've watched those things work out where we are. It's only a fraction of them at the moment, but if the rest of them catch on and end up down here, we're going to have a real problem on our hands. I know you don't want to stay here, but I really don't think you've got any choice right now – none of us have.'

Sean stared deep into Gordon's face and carefully considered his words. He knew Gordon wasn't overstating the threat from outside, but were they really only limited to one option? He didn't think so. Being outside today had been such an unexpectedly uplifting experience. Could he turn his back on that freedom and everything he'd seen now? He couldn't stand the thought of being shut away in this hellhole with these people any longer.

The silence in the room was deafening.

'I don't know,' he said eventually. 'I don't know if I can—'

'You have to,' Caron said from the shadows to his left. Christ, he reminded her of her son so much: he was just like

Matthew, so volatile and opinionated, and yet vulnerable too . . .

'I don't *have* to do anything,' he answered, glaring at her, 'none of us do. You can all stay here if you want to, but I think I'll take my chances out there.'

'Just give it some time,' she pleaded.

'I'd give anything for another day like today,' he said, his voice suddenly wavering with emotion. 'Do you know what I did today?' he asked, looking around at the few faces he could see. When no one answered he continued. 'I *lived*,' he said, tears welling up in his eyes, 'for the first time in weeks I actually felt like I was alive and it didn't matter what I did. And I come back here and everything feels wrong again, and it's not because of the bodies out there, it's you lot.'

'What are you talking about?' Gordon asked.

'From where I'm standing there's no difference between the bodies on one side of the fence and the other. There's no difference between any of you and those things out there. You're all dead: you're all just sitting here rotting, waiting for the end to come. I don't really care if I've got one day left or fifty years. I don't care if I don't get through tomorrow. I just don't want to spend the rest of my time trapped in here with us all watching each other decay.'

46

'How many?'

Startled, Martin spun around and saw Harte standing in the doorway of his second-floor bedroom. Hollis, who was standing next to him, hadn't heard a thing, but he looked around when he saw that Martin had been distracted, then turned back to face the window.

'Maybe as many as five hundred or so,' Martin replied, 'it's difficult to tell.'

'Are more still coming?'

It was difficult to make out much detail in the late evening gloom, but there was plenty of movement in the field across the road. The dark mass of inquisitive corpses had grown steadily through the course of the day just gone, and the influx showed no signs of slowing.

'Plenty more,' Martin answered, his low voice sounding tired.

'So what do we do now?' Harte asked, joining the other two at the window.

'Depends,' Hollis grunted. He could hear him now that he'd moved closer.

'On what?'

'On them, mainly,' he replied, nodding in the direction of the throng of constantly shifting figures. 'It depends how responsive they are. If all they're going to do is just stand on the other side of the fence, then there's not much of a problem. If they decide they want to attack us, then—'

'They won't,' Martin immediately interrupted. 'Why would they?'

'If they're threatened they will,' Harte said quietly. 'We've seen it happen loads of times.'

'But who's going to threaten them?'

'What you see as a threat and what they do are very different things,' Hollis explained. 'Take those fucking jokers out on the bike, for example. We just see a couple of idiots escaping for a while. The dead react like animals would: they see the speed and hear the noise and sense the danger—'

'—and then they try and attack before whatever it is can get them,' Harte continued.

'So we stay here and wait for them to rot,' Martin sighed, 'just like we were doing before you lot turned up here and screwed everything up.'

'For God's sake stop saying that! We haven't *screwed everything up*,' Hollis corrected him. 'Be honest, Martin, you were starving, and if we'd not arrived when we did, you wouldn't have lasted much longer. Sean would have cracked eventually and you'd have ended up in this exact same mess.'

'We've just fucked things up a little quicker than you would have on your own,' Harte said, his attempt at humour falling flat.

'But we've got supplies now, and Sean's had his moment. We can let him and Webb leave if they really want to.'

'They won't go,' Hollis said. 'They haven't got the balls to do it. If they had they wouldn't have come running back tonight.'

'Then somehow we've got to keep them under control, Greg,' Martin added, 'stop them getting so wound up – we need to find a way to get them to let off steam.'

'That might be difficult,' Harte announced ominously. 'We have another problem.'

'What?'

'It's why I came looking for you two.'

'What?' Hollis demanded impatiently.

'Driver's sick.'

'Sick? What, like—'

'Yes, sick like Anita and Ellie,' Harte said quickly, anticipating his question.

'The girls who died?' Martin asked anxiously.

'Yep,' he answered, 'so I for one don't actually fancy sitting in here for another couple of months any more.'

'Where is he now?'

'I packed him off to bed with his paper and enough food and drink to keep him happy for a couple of days. I told him we'd keep checking on him.'

'And will you?'

'No fucking way. I might go back up there in a few days and see how he's doing. If he's still alive then he hasn't got what Ellie and Anita had and we're safe.'

'Where's his room?'

'Luckily he's always been an antisocial bastard. He's up on his own on the top floor of east wing.'

'Good,' Martin muttered.

'We've also got the plane and helicopter to think about,' Harte continued, subdued. 'I think Jas is right, and if they are evacuating from somewhere, then they'll probably have completed it soon – the fact they flew over so many times today makes me think they must be close to being done now. We need to get them to see us.'

'But we can't risk giving away our location,' Martin sighed. 'We've already been through this. That might be all it takes to tip the bodies over the edge.'

'Well, we might just have to take that risk,' Hollis said.

'We can't.'

'We might have to.'

'But—'

'He's right,' Harte said, 'we could torch this whole fucking place if we had to. Imagine that! There's the distraction you need. Every single one of those fucking things outside would drag their sorry backsides straight over here, and we could just walk away.'

'No, that'd be suicidal. No way.'

'I'm not suggesting we do it, but it's an option.'

'It's a stupid option,' Martin protested, his voice getting louder.

'Let's wait until morning,' said Hollis. 'We can't make any decisions tonight. I think we should try and work out how the bodies are likely to react, then work out how to attract the attention of the plane, if it comes back.'

'But how are we supposed to do that?'

'Isn't this is exactly the kind of reason you've kept the body by the swimming pool?'

'I suppose,' Martin said, sounding more subdued.

'Well, we need to see how your corpse reacts when we get up close.'

47

The morning came too soon. Hollis' stomach was grumbling, but he was too nervous to even think about eating. He waited for Martin at the end of the corridor which led to the swimming pool. Lorna, Harte, Howard and Gordon waited with him.

'You okay?' Lorna asked, picking up on his obvious unease.

He nodded, but didn't say anything; he didn't want to talk.

Some of the others didn't want to shut up. 'Remind me what we're supposed to be doing again?' Gordon mumbled nervously.

'Stop being such a fucking drip,' Harte said. 'You know exactly what we're doing.'

He was right, Gordon did understand completely, but like the rest of them he wasn't relishing the prospect of being face-to-face with one of the dead, even if they did outnumber it six (and a dog) to one. He wished there was an alternative, but none of them had managed to come up with a safer way of being able to properly gauge the strength of the creature's reactions. Late last night it had sounded like a sensible idea; now they were actually here, they were all having serious doubts.

Martin appeared from the direction of the Steelbrooke Suite. He tried to hang back, but the others made it abundantly clear that he should go first.

'She's your baby,' Howard whispered, pushing him to the front of the crowd.

The group walked down the curved corridor, stopping just before the window into the office. Martin peered in, but it was difficult to see anything through the layer of grease and rotten flesh which was now smeared across the glass – and that alone showed how much The Swimmer's behaviour had changed. Had it been looking for them?

Howard's dog stood beneath the window looking up, her sharp white teeth bared in a silent, sneering growl.

'So how are we going to do this?' Howard asked. He jumped back as the corpse's rot-eaten face appeared at the window. Its dulled eyes looked around at the six people staring back at it. Perhaps realising it was outnumbered, it took a few awkward steps back into the darkness.

'There's not enough room here,' Martin answered. 'We should get her out onto the side of the pool.'

After a few seconds of nervous inactivity, Lorna pushed past the others and followed the corridor around to the entrance to the pool. She shoved the heavy door open, wincing when the smell of the stagnant water hit her. The air was icy-cold, and a sudden clattering noise made her catch her breath – until she spotted the door on the other side of the pool, which was blowing open and shut in the strong wind; Jas and Harte had left it ajar some days before in a bid to air the room a little.

She hadn't actually been in here before, just glanced in from outside. *It would have been lovely*, she thought sadly to herself, *just the kind of place I could've imagined spending my pre-Armageddon time, if I'd ever been able to afford to stay in a place like this*. On one side of the pool were the various items of gym equipment Jas and Harte had been talking about fixing up, and over in the far corner was a pile of sun-loungers, draped with a shroud-like layer of dust. The large open windows and the glass ceiling would allow the whole room to flood with sunlight . . .

Her daydreams were interrupted by the noise of Hollis yanking open the changing room door. He disappeared into the darkness momentarily to prop open the door to the office, giving the corpse a clear passage out to the pool.

'Come on,' he yelled, 'you've been in there too long, sweetheart. It's time you came out to see us . . .'

The rest of the group stood a safe distance back and waited. For a moment nothing happened, but then, very suddenly and very definitely, they could hear the sound of shuffling movement from inside the office. A loud clatter sent Hollis scampering back to the others.

'Can you see her?' Lorna asked quietly. Howard's dog padded forward, then stopped and bared her teeth again. She was normally completely silent, but this time Dog emitted the faintest low growl as more noises came from the darkness.

'Nothing yet,' Hollis replied, shuffling tentatively forward again. 'Hold on, here she comes . . .'

The corpse dragged itself out into the light. It was truly an abhorrent sight. This was the first time he'd seen her in her full glory, Martin realised, and her appearance fascinated him. He felt a strange mixture of revulsion and genuine pity as she lumbered forward. She'd been a guest at the hotel on the day that she and almost everyone else had died. He remembered seeing her, just before the infection had struck; now he was finding it hard to believe that the thing he was looking at now was the same woman he'd seen then. Her figure (and she'd had a great figure, he recalled that *very* clearly) was all gone. Where she had been pert before, now she sagged. Gravity had steadily drained the contents of her bowels down into her lower body. Her feet were swollen and blue, her belly and buttocks distended with gas and other noxious substances, stretching her heavily stained swimming costume completely out of shape. The straps wore deep grooves into the skin on top of her shoulders, where they'd been continually rubbing against her deteriorating flesh.

'Careful,' Lorna whispered, noticing that both Hollis and Martin had continued to move closer to the corpse.

'It's okay,' Hollis said, keeping his eyes firmly fixed on the body. The cadaver, in turn, kept what was left of its eyes trained on the figures which surrounded it. Although its movements were laboured, it was definitely looking around the group: it slowly moved its head from left to right, quickly turning back again when Gordon slipped in a puddle and lost his footing for a moment. Howard's dog growled again, an ominous low rumble of warning, and the body immediately reacted, dropping its head and looking down at the animal standing its ground just yards in front of it.

Then it stopped.

It began to move backwards.

With even less control than before the body slowly began to retreat, leaving behind it a trail of smudged footprints as it shuffled backwards across the tiled floor. It bumped into the frame of the door, shuffled left and slipped back into the darkness of the room where it had spent the last sixty days.

'Fuck me,' Hollis whispered.

'Where's it going?' Gordon asked, unnerved by the creature's unexpected behaviour and hoping that someone else would have a plausible explanation.

'She's trying to get away from us,' Lorna suggested.

'This is great,' Harte said from his position a little further back. 'The damn thing knows it hasn't got a hope in hell—'

'Did you see her checking us out, though?' Howard said, standing next to him. 'I reckon she saw there were too many of us and decided it wasn't a fair fight.'

'I think you're right,' Hollis agreed. 'If it's got any sense left in its head, it's got to know that it's got no chance on its own against six of us.'

'And a dog,' Howard added.

'It knows it's safer back in there than out here,' he continued.

'So what do we do now?' Martin asked nervously. 'Have we actually proved anything? If we go outside, do you think all those bodies are going to start backing off when they see us?'

'They haven't so far,' Lorna said, moving slightly and trying to peer deeper into the changing rooms.

Hollis did the same. 'The difference is that it's still got a choice at the moment,' he said. 'Most of the bodies out in the open don't have anywhere to hide. I think we need to see what happens when we take away its options.'

'Force it out into the open?' Lorna wondered.

Hollis nodded. 'Martin, why don't you go through to the corridor and try to force her back out here – then close the door behind her so she can't get away again.'

'I don't know,' he stammered anxiously. 'Do you really think we should be doing this?'

'Oh, for Christ's sake,' Lorna sighed, 'stop being so pathetic. I'll do it.'

'Be careful,' Hollis warned.

'It's no big deal,' she said flippantly as she walked away. 'It's just a half-rotted sack of shit.'

Hollis watched her leave, then returned his attention to the corpse lurking in the shadows. He could see it hiding just behind the door. It was trying to stand still, but the uneasy swaying of its body gave the game away: an arm would swing out into the light momentarily, or its head would droop down lazily before it managed to pull itself back out of sight again.

Lorna stood in the corridor outside the office and composed herself before going in. The handle was stiff and she needed to shove the door hard with her full weight to get it open. She paused again before going any further to let the stench of the captive corpse's decay dissipate. She felt unexpectedly nervous, but she shook herself. *Christ*, she thought, *what am I worried about?* She'd dealt with hundreds of these creatures before now, and this one wasn't any more of a threat than any other. *And besides*, she reminded herself, *this is one corpse against the rest of us – the damn thing doesn't stand a chance.*

She entered the dark room, trying not to slip in the dark puddles of gunk which had seeped out of the decaying cadaver. She moved quietly towards the light coming from the pool; the corpse in the doorway was so preoccupied with the men outside that it hadn't yet noticed her approaching. Lorna had never been this close to one of the dead before and not been about to destroy it. It was a morbidly fascinating sight, and the nearer she got, the more unpleasant detail she could make out. The open wounds on its torso and legs were filled with teeming movement: thousands of maggots gorging on its decaying skin. A chunk of flesh hung loose from the side of its right calf and she could make out the bones and what was left of its muscles underneath.

For a moment her nerves threatened to get the better of her, but she forced herself to stay focused. 'Get ready,' she shouted, and at the sound of her voice, the cadaver began to turn itself around, but it was far too slow and clumsy. Lorna lifted her hands and shoved it firmly in the small of its back, taking care to touch its swimming costume, not make contact with naked flesh – or what was left of it.

The corpse was knocked off-balance and tripped back out into the open again.

Lorna followed it through to the poolside room, slamming the door behind her and sealing off its escape route, as the cadaver instinctively lurched towards Hollis and Martin, the closest of its aggressors. Howard's dog bolted forward, and he just managed to grab her collar as she leapt up at the Swimmer. Her claws squeaked along the tiles at the side of the pool as she scrambled to break free and attack.

'Watch it!' Gordon yelled as the dead woman heaved its disfigured bulk towards Martin. He instinctively put his arms up to protect himself, but as Hollis shoved him out of the way, the body acted with remarkable speed, immediately turning its full attention towards him instead. It crashed into him with unexpected momentum, shoving him back and over.

'See,' he said as he picked himself up and struggled to grab hold of the hideous figure, 'it has no choice now. We've made it fight. All it can do is attack.'

The monster's greasy skin seemed to slip and slide around its bones as it squirmed relentlessly in his grip. It managed to free itself from Hollis' grasp and immediately lurched towards Harte, the next closest. Harte could see that it had already been damaged as a result of its brief skirmish: the flesh at the top of its right shoulder had been torn away and was now falling down its arm, rather like a loose-fitting sleeve. He looked deep into its vile face: eight weeks ago this had been a vital, attractive young woman – a mother. A sister. A daughter. Now it bore virtually no resemblance to the young woman it used to be, and it fulfilled none of those roles; today it was nothing more than a disgusting heap of barely coordinated flesh and bone, a horrific aberration.

Harte knew nothing of the creature's past; he knew only that it was time to end its pitiful existence. He jumped towards it, grabbed a fistful of hair and slammed its face down onto the tiles at the edge of the stagnant swimming pool. Still it continued to fight, hopelessly overpowered, but relentless to the end.

'Fucking thing won't give up,' he said anxiously as he fought to keep hold of it, but no one else moved.

Howard in particular had seen far fewer corpses than the others; he was overwhelmed by the full extent of this cadaver's grotesque appearance. With every movement it caused more damage to itself – but still it didn't stop, even though he could see rotten flesh literally peeling away from its bones the more it fought. But what else could it do?

The enormity of what they were witnessing was not lost on Lorna. She was far more used to being this close to the dead, so she could ignore the shocking visage and concentrate on the implications of the creature's actions.

'So those bodies outside,' she started as Harte dragged the Swimmer back onto its unsteady feet, 'they're all going to react like this?'

'We've got to assume so,' Hollis answered.

'Dear God,' mumbled Martin, covering his mouth in disbelief.

'Get rid of it,' Gordon said, backing off. 'Please—'

Harte let go of the corpse and it staggered away from him for a few steps, then, as he watched, it turned back and started moving towards him again. He barged it into the pool, and the Swimmer waved its arms furiously, its frantic movements keeping it afloat for a few seconds before it sank below the surface. Martin watched it until it was just a dark shape on the bottom of the pool.

The damn thing was still moving. Even down there, the damn thing was still moving . . .

48

'**H**elicopter,' Sean said suddenly, pointing out of Jas' bedroom window before turning and running for the door.

Jas looked up at the machine crawling across a dull sky peppered with grey and white clouds. He was sure it was the same one they'd seen previously. He scanned the skies behind it, trying to spot the plane which had been following it yesterday, hoping to disprove his own evacuation theory, but though he stared up into the sky for what felt like for ever, it wasn't there. His heart sank. He was certain that meant they were running out of time.

'Aren't you coming down?' Harte asked, but Jas shook his head and remained sitting on the end of his bed, cradling a drink in his hands.

'No point,' he replied sadly. 'I can watch them fly away from here well enough; no need to waste energy running downstairs to do it. Anyway,' he said, taking another swig of his drink, 'they'll be back later.'

'How do you know?'

'I've been thinking about it.'

'And?'

'And,' he began, wearily getting up and walking over to the window just in time to see the helicopter bank left before completely disappearing from view, 'the fact that the plane isn't behind the helicopter this time tells me I'm probably right. The first time it flew over yesterday it went from east to west, then it came back, then it did the same again. I said from the start I thought these people were packing up and moving out, and the fact they made so many trips so quickly yesterday kind of proves my point. It looks like two plane journeys were enough to get them all away. I think the helicopter's back to mop up anyone – or anything – they left behind.'

'So what are you saying?'

'What I'm saying is I think this might be the last time they'll pass over us – maybe another couple of flights at most – but I think this is it. They'll fly back when they've done what they need to do and we won't see them again.'

Harte paused to consider Jas' logic. There was no doubt about it; his scenario sounded completely plausible. After a moment he asked, 'So do you think it was the military or the government?'

'No idea,' Jas admitted, 'probably neither. I doubt there's anything like that left anywhere. No, I just think it's a bunch of lucky bastards who've struck gold. They've got someone who can fly, and they've either found somewhere where there are no bodies, no germs, and no arseholes like Webb and Martin, or they're off looking for a place like that.'

He finished his can of beer and leant up against the window. Martin, Ginnie and the others were outside now, standing around their pathetic message on the lawn, trying not to feel completely useless. He turned his attention to the ever-growing crowd of bodies in the field over the road. Even though they'd all done as they'd agreed and kept quiet ever since Sean and Webb had returned yesterday evening, the dead were still continuing to drag themselves back from the golf course. There had to be a thousand of them there now – maybe even double – and they showed no signs of stopping. *Mind you*, he thought, *who's to say the whole damn lot won't about-turn and start moving away from the music in some kind of bizarre slow-motion stampede? A few hundred breaking away wouldn't be a massive concern, but a few thousand? That's a different matter entirely . . .*

'We need to do something,' he announced, suddenly sounding more positive. 'Sitting here doing nothing isn't an option any more: we've tried that and it hasn't worked.

We've got to get that helicopter to see us next time because it might be our last chance.'

'Let's be realistic about this for a second,' Harte said. 'Even if they do spot us, are they going to risk landing here?'

'Who knows? There's enough space – but you're right, maybe we need to think about getting away altogether, no matter what happens with the helicopter. We're no better off here than we were at the flats – in fact, we've got exactly the same bloody problems: the crowds of bodies are getting closer, and one of us is sick.'

'But we've isolated Driver—'

'Good! That lazy bastard did nothing for me while he was fit and well; I'll be damned if he's going to kill me with his bloody germs now he's sick.'

'We don't know if he's got the same thing yet. It might not be—'

'Come on,' Jas sighed, 'don't be soft. Of course it's the same thing.'

Harte leant back against the wall so he didn't have to look out at the dead. 'So now we've got all the usual questions to answer: how do we do it? How do we get away, and where would we go?'

'Well, if it comes to it we could just drive out of here the same way we came in,' Jas suggested. 'And what about that exhibition centre everyone was banging on about before we got here? That sounded to me like a pretty good place to aim for.'

'I still don't know how you reckon you'll get the helicopter to see us.'

'Fire!' he answered with a grin.

'What – you're thinking of setting fire to the hotel?'

'You idiot! What's the point of doing that? No, I think we need to get out there and cause a bit of carnage in the fields – we need to start a few fires, maybe an explosion or two. Think about it: it'll take the pressure off this place again because those dumb dead fuckers will head for the fire, and if the helicopter pilot does come back, when he sees three or four decent-sized fires near each other but out in the middle of nowhere he'll have to realise that there are people down here, won't he? If he looks hard enough, he'll be able to spot their message on the lawn.'

'And if he doesn't?'

'Then we get in the bus and the van and we take advantage of the fact that the bodies are distracted to get the fuck out of here.'

49

Hollis had fallen asleep on a bench in the courtyard in the middle of the hotel. He'd only planned to sit down for a minute, but that had been a couple of hours ago. He was having trouble sleeping at night, so he was glad that he'd managed a few hours' unexpected relaxation, even though he was now feeling cold and a little nauseous. He shook his head to clear it as he sat up and looked up into the cloud-filled sky above him.

He got up and went inside to look for something to eat.

Hollis found the long, empty hours like this worse than the frantic, desperate times, when they were running or fighting for their lives. At least dealing with crisis after crisis kept him feeling alive. Sean's words yesterday evening had kept rattling around his head: '*You're all dead,*' he'd said. Was he right? Was the gap between the living on one side and the dead on the other really narrowing as much as Sean'd suggested? *If this is the quality of life we've got to look forward to*, he thought sadly, *then maybe he's got a point. At least the dead can move around freely and without fear. Is it better to feel and think nothing than to have your head filled constantly with all these desperate, nightmarish thoughts which are constantly plaguing me?*

'I said, are you okay?' Lorna said, tapping his arm. She'd walked right up behind him and he hadn't even noticed. He tried to convince himself that he'd been preoccupied, his thoughts elsewhere, although the reality was that now he could hardly hear anything through his damaged ear. And that terrified him – in a world where the slightest sound could be the difference between remaining undetected or being surrounded by corpses, how would he survive?

'I'm fine,' he replied, trying unsuccessfully to hide his depression. Lorna was getting to know him too well.

'I'm just going to steal a couple of bottles of wine and some food,' she told him, very matter-of-factly. 'Come up to my room if you feel like a chat.'

'Okay,' he mumbled, watching as she turned and disappeared into the kitchens. For half a second he stupidly allowed his mind to wander. She looked beautiful today, fresh-faced and full of life. Why was she inviting him up to her room? Was it just to share a bottle, as she's suggested, or was there more to it? He'd fancied her for ages, almost since they'd first met, but he'd never got the impression that she felt the same way. *Don't be such a bloody idiot*, he thought to himself, angry that he'd allowed his mind to wander, *you're old enough to be her father! She's only interested in you as a friend – that's the only kind of positive relationship that exists now. There's no room in this fucked-up ruin of a world for love and lust and—*

—and that was the sound of car engines, coming from outside!

Hollis immediately sprinted to the front of the hotel, bursting through the main reception doors and running down the steps into the car park, and almost immediately had to jump to one side as a silver Vauxhall Omega estate car careered towards him. He spotted Harte behind the wheel as he accelerated and swerved past, followed closely by a blue Audi A7, driven by Amir with Webb in the passenger seat beside him, and at the end, a beaten-up dark green Polo, driven by Sean. Where the hell were they going? What a bloody racket they were making!

Hollis turned around and as he saw Jas moving towards the van he ran to stop him. 'What the fuck are you doing?' he cried, slamming the driver's door shut before Jas could climb in.

'Just leave it, Hollis,' he replied, barging him out of the way.

'You're not taking the Transit,' he yelled, throwing himself forward again, but Jas, though a good eight inches shorter, was much stronger, and he'd wrapped his arms around Hollis' waist and swung him around, throwing him to the ground before Hollis had quite realised what had happened. Before he could pick himself up Jas had climbed into the van, locked the door and started the engine.

'Just get inside and keep out of the way,' he shouted through the half-open window.

'You fucking cowards!' Hollis screamed, hammering on the side of the vehicle as it started to move. 'Why are you running away? All you're going to do is let them in here.'

'We're not running away,' Jas hollered back, 'not yet anyway. We're taking control.' He put his foot down on the accelerator and drove away from the hotel.

Hollis ran a few yards after him, but it was pointless. As the Transit van disappeared around the curve in the drive he ran back inside to warn the others.

Jas stopped at the fork in the road and waited anxiously for the other cars to negotiate the hairpin bend to get onto the branch of the road that led up to the golf course. Despite the length of the estate, Harte had managed the tight manoeuvre with the minimum of effort, but Amir was struggling, shunting his Audi backwards and forwards in what was looking suspiciously like a thirty-seven point turn.

Jas tried not to think what effect the sound of his over-revving engine would be having on the crowds of dead bodies gathered nearby. As he waited for his turn to move he reached into his jacket pocket and took out his wallet. He unfolded the photo of his wife Harj and his children, long-dead but still a huge part of him, and kissed it. He hadn't looked at them for a couple of days, and that made him feel guilty – but he'd thought about them, he reassured himself.

He thought about Prisha, Seti and Annia and their mother almost every waking hour since he'd lost them.

'Have I got this right, Harj?' he asked, looking into the last remaining image of his wife's deep brown eyes, 'or are we just about to fuck everything up?'

Sudden movement caused him to quickly put the picture away again. Amir had finally made it around the corner. Sean wasn't far behind. He executed a textbook three-point-turn in the Polo and disappeared behind the fence. Jas put his foot down again and followed, roughly yanking the Transit around the tight bend, crashing into the hedge on either side, no longer concerned about the noise. The other three cars had stopped a short distance ahead and Harte was already running to the Yaris Sean and Webb had moved yesterday to get into the field. With Webb's help he managed to shunt it far enough out of the way to leave the gate clear.

Even from his position at the back of the queue Jas could see the huge mass of bodies that had almost immediately gathered on the other side of the gate. They were pushing forwards angrily, rattling the low metal barrier as Webb sprinted for the safety of the Audi.

Harte flicked the latch and shoved the gate open, knocking the cadavers at the front of the group backwards. They immediately surged forward again, but it didn't matter; Harte was back behind the wheel of the Omega and now he accelerated into the field and sent them flying. Amir and Sean followed in the Audi and the Polo, crunching over the gravel, then pounding over the uneven mud.

Jas brought up the rear, glancing in his rear-view mirror to see the gate swinging shut again. It wasn't locked, but it would have to do for now. Hopefully the sudden arrival of the four vehicles in the field would be enough to distract the slothful crowds. Judging by the vast numbers of them already stumbling towards him, that certainly seemed to be the case.

As they'd arranged, Harte veered off to the left, ploughing into a wave of corpses and driving down the slope of the field towards the bottom right-hand corner, diagonally opposite the gate they'd just entered through. Harte looked back over his shoulder to see Jas was following.

The Transit van was cruising through the sea of figures, but though he was wiping out many of them, it was just a fraction of the hundreds of the fucking things that'd congregated here – many more than he'd expected, and far more than had been visible from their vantage point back at the hotel. Jas accelerated again, following the curving blood-soaked scar Harte had left across the field.

'That's got to be far enough,' Harte said to himself, anxiously trying to work out exactly where he was. His brief had been to drive as far as he could across the full width and length of the field – but he'd not been prepared for just how little he'd be able to see from behind the Omega's wheel. It wasn't like the Transit; his driving position was quite low and all he could see around him now was a relentless forest of constantly shifting corpses. *Better stop and do it here*, he decided, *rather than to end up driving into the bloody hedge and killing myself*. He hit the brakes and as he skidded to a juddering halt, the rear end of the Omega spun out and smashed into a handful of ragdoll cadavers.

Jas pulled up alongside and watched as Harte frantically scrambled out of his seat. He leant over into the back and emptied out his half-full can of fuel, then looked around to make sure that Jas was ready for him. As he tried to shove the door open, almost immediately a mass of emaciated, clawing hands thrust back at him.

Jas reversed a bit, then accelerated forward, driving alongside the estate and scraping a layer of bodies away. In the short-lived moment which followed Harte threw himself out of the driver's door, lit a match and dropped it into the back, then ran over to the Transit. He hauled himself up into the passenger seat just as the inside of the Vauxhall was filled with a scorching whoosh of billowing flame.

Job done.

'Nice one,' Jas said, turning the Transit around and forcing it back up the incline, the engine groaning in effort. The bodies around them temporarily reduced in number as the fire in the car proved to be a more interesting distraction.

Harte twisted around and hung over his seat to watch as the ragged figures surged towards the light. The boot of the Omega – packed with several plastic canisters full of fuel – exploded, showering the dead with flames and red-hot shrapnel. The car itself flipped over on its end and landed in the middle of the hordes, crushing untold numbers of them. Despite being steadily consumed by the flames, those which were alight but still able to move continued to stagger around until their already weakened muscles had burned away to nothing and they collapsed where they stood, setting light to more of the stupid creatures who blindly stumbled into them.

'Can you see the others?' Harte asked, panting with a heady mix of nerves, effort and exhilaration.

'We'll find them,' Jas replied, trying to sound more confident than he felt. Not only were they still surrounded by an unending mass of rancid flesh, but the gradient of the hill was proving difficult for the old Transit; they were slowly getting up it, but they couldn't yet see what was happening at the top, where the ground levelled out closer to the golf course.

Less than a hundred yards away, but out of sight of the Transit van, Amir and Webb were also struggling. The sheer number of bodies which had surrounded their Audi had completely disorientated them. The throngs of disintegrating cadavers filling every available inch of space were making it difficult to see in any direction, and impossible to navigate. Amir was managing to keep the A7 moving forward, but he had no real idea where he was heading, and he wasn't travelling at anywhere near a fast enough speed. His inexperience with the dead was painfully apparent now; rather than accelerate into them, he frequently swerved, or just ground to a halt and tried to nudge them out of the way.

Webb was beginning to get desperate. 'Hit the fucking things!' he screamed. 'Speed up, for Christ's sake!'

'But I don't know where we're going,' Amir protested, wrenching the steering wheel hard around to the right, their wheels skidding in the decay, as he tried to turn them.

'Neither do they!'

'But we might end up in the fence, or too close to the gate—'

'It doesn't fucking matter,' Webb shouted, his voice hoarse with panic and exacerbation, 'we're about to blow the bloody car up!'

'Why don't you drive then?' Amir suggested.

Webb just glared at him, until he suddenly shouted, 'There!' and pointed to the far left, where he'd just spotted the roof of the Transit van, whipping past above the heads of the corpses.

Amir turned around in the direction the Transit had been going and accelerated.

'Keep moving,' Webb moaned, terrified that they were about to come to a sudden stop and get stranded and surrounded, but they burst onto a muddy track of open, gore-soaked space, a sure sign that the van or one of the other cars had been there just a few seconds earlier. Amir followed the bloody route through the crowd until it disappeared again, swallowed up by another mass of lurching figures.

'Where now?'

'Let's just do it here.'

'But the van's not here,' Amir said nervously, 'we can't do it until the van's here to pick us up.'

'You bloody idiot,' Webb seethed, holding onto the side of his seats as the car bounced over a particularly uneven stretch of ground and clattered into another swell of rotting flesh. 'Look, it doesn't matter where the Transit is, does it? Once we set fire to this thing they'll see us quickly enough.'

Amir couldn't think straight. What should he do – keep driving? Or was Webb right, should they just stop now? He winced as the front of the car sliced the legs out from under a ragged body, cutting it in two and sending its head and torso spinning into the windscreen directly in front of him, leaving a large crack and a slimy smear of black blood. There were more bodies than ever up ahead of them now, so many that they looked like a solid black mass, no longer recognisable as individual cadavers. Behind them he could see trees rising up on either side.

Webb realised what was happening before Amir could react.

'You're going to drive us into the fucking fence!' he screamed, covering his head.

Amir finally recognised where he was, but it was too late to do anything about it. He'd been here with Martin and the others, way, way back, when the nightmare had first begun. They'd all spent hours out here channelling the unresponsive bodies away from the hotel. There was a gap in the trees which marked the position of a break in the fence he and the others had made, and on the other side of the fence was the golf course.

He had to make a snap decision. With so many corpses coming towards him he knew he either had to hit them at full speed, or stop and turn back again. *I'm too close to the fence*, he thought as the trees loomed up above them. *There's only one option left now.*

He jammed his foot down on the accelerator pedal. 'Hold on,' he shouted pointlessly as he struggled to keep hold of the steering wheel. As Webb braced himself for the impact he felt sure would come at any second the Audi clattered through the hole Amir, Howard and Martin had hacked in the fence and the wheels thumped back down onto the hard ground and they burst out of the rough and onto the fairway.

Too terrified to make any rational decisions, Amir kept the Audi moving forward as best as he could, driving head-first into the largest crowd of dead flesh that either of them had ever seen. A relentless storm of decayed and dismembered body parts was thrown up into the air as the blood-soaked vehicle blasted through the lifeless masses.

'Where the hell are you going?' Webb yelled, terrified, but Amir didn't answer – he didn't know; he no longer had any idea what he was doing. The plan that Jas and Harte had come up with was ruined . . . maybe if he could find a way of turning around they could get back—

The Audi veered off course as it dipped down a sudden steep incline that'd been hidden from view by the dense swarm. Amir tried to compensate by steering straight back up into the climb but the angle was too sharp and the tyres lost all traction. The Audi began to slide back down the bank again and though Amir tried frantically to regain control, it was no good; the car levelled off. With the engine screaming with effort he managed to keep it moving forward for a few more yards, until the front driver's-side wheel thumped into a low tree stump, forcing it up into the air and then sending the battered blue Audi A7 head over heels until it came to rest on its crumpled roof in the middle of a meandering stream.

Sean had spotted a way to do what he'd agreed with the others and then to get the hell away from this godforsaken place and the fools and cowards he'd been trapped here with. He'd driven around haphazardly for a bit while waiting for Harte and Amir, enjoying the welcome opportunity to obliterate as many corpses as he was able. He'd been keeping an eye on the Transit up ahead as Jas tried – not particularly successfully – to track Amir and Webb. The majority of the bodies in the field were still stumbling towards the burning wreck of Harte's Omega, attracted by the ferocity of the flames and unaware of the danger as the blaze continued to spread through scores of tinder-dry corpses.

But he also noticed a sizeable number of cadavers had somehow managed to open the gate at the top of the field and now they were working their way along the road in both directions. He wasn't unduly worried; the Transit would wipe them out on its way back to the hotel.

Through the crowd he caught sight of Jas again and decided it was time. He didn't know what the delay was, why Amir's A7 hadn't been set alight, but whatever the reason, there was no point in him waiting any longer. He stopped the Polo just short of halfway up the field, almost parallel with Harte's burning Omega, and gave a loud blast on the horn. Many cadavers immediately turned and shuffled towards him, the nearest beginning to thump their decaying fists against the windows and doors. More importantly, the van also turned in his direction. The Transit itself was a pretty terrifying sight. It was almost completely covered in gore; scraps of skin and bone had wedged themselves into every available crevice and putrid flesh dripped off its head-lamps and down the grille of its bonnet.

When it was close enough that he could see Jas and Harte inside, Sean scrambled around and soaked the back seats with fuel. As the van pulled level, he could see Harte making 'hurry up' gestures. Sean opened the sunroof and hauled himself up onto the top of the Polo.

Jas wound down his window and yelled, 'What are you doing?'

'Go,' Sean shouted back, 'just go! I'm not coming back with you!'

'What do you mean?' Jas cried, 'come on, get over here!'

'What do you think I mean?' he shouted. 'I'm sick of that fucking hotel – I'm getting out of here!'

'Are you *stupid*?' Jas couldn't believe what he was hearing.

'Might be,' Sean answered. 'Anyway, when you find Webb, tell him I'll wait down at the road junction for an hour, then I'm going.'

'Going where?'

'Back into town.'

'You *are* stupid—'

'I just don't want to go back inside,' he said, 'that's all. Now piss off so I can torch this bloody car.'

Before Jas could say anything else Sean lit a match and dropped it through the sun roof. As the vapours ignited he slid down onto the bonnet, then jumped off and sprinted into the crowd. He was out of sight almost instantly, swallowed up by the swaying figures which were surging towards the new source of light and noise.

Jas shoved the Transit into gear and motored away, almost willing the vehicle to move quickly through the swarming hordes. Just a few seconds later the stockpile of fuel in the back of Sean's Polo exploded behind them, turning it into a deadly weapon in an instant.

'You going after him?' Harte asked, craning his neck to look for Sean in the carnage.

'Fuck him,' Jas grunted angrily.

'What now, then? Do we look for Amir and Webb?'

As with the Omega, the sudden ball of flame and smoke that had engulfed the Polo and belched up into the sky was more of a draw than the van. The dead converged on the remains of Sean's car like a hunting pack.

'Five minutes,' Jas announced. 'That's all we can give them.' He wasn't interested in what might have happened to Amir and Webb; he just wanted to know why they hadn't done the job they'd been sent to do. They were a pair of useless fools. He cursed himself for leaving the two of them together.

50

'**S**hit,' Howard cursed as the second car exploded in the distance. As he stood dumbstruck in the courtyard in the middle of the hotel Hollis ran back outside, sprinted down the steps and into the car park. He could see a dark cloud of smoke engulfing the sky above the top of the tall hedgerow. Some distance to the left – several hundred yards, he estimated – the dirty pall from the first blast they'd heard continued to climb into the air.

Back in the courtyard, Caron sat down at the edge of the overgrown lawn and poured herself a large glass of wine.

'Idiots,' Martin muttered nervously. 'What in Christ's name do they think they're doing?'

'Helping,' Lorna insisted.

'Helping? How the hell is this helping? Did you know about this?'

'It was partly my idea.'

'What? Why?'

'Because with the best will in the world, the sheets on the lawn thing wasn't ever going to be enough. Jas and I got talking and—'

'And you decided you'd go out there and undo everything we've done here?'

'Well, not me personally,' she smirked. 'But there was no shortage of testosterone-filled blokes ready to do it.'

'At least they're doing something,' Gordon said from the opposite side of the courtyard.

'Doing *nothing* is better than something,' Martin protested. 'Doing nothing is exactly what we all should be doing – all this is going to do is bring the bodies back here to us.'

'They might bring that helicopter as well,' Caron mumbled, knocking back her wine. She was already half-drunk.

'Just give them a chance,' said Lorna as Martin started pacing up and down.

'Think about it, Martin,' Gordon continued, desperately trying to diffuse his increasing panic. 'Lorna's right: this might actually help. The dead, well, they're drawn to fire. We know that they're getting used to the music, so maybe this will keep them occupied for a while longer – and it'll get rid of a few hundred of them at the same time.'

'A few *hundred*?' Martin barked furiously, 'a few *hundred*? Do you have any conceivable idea how many of them are out there? There are *thousands and thousands* of them, all crammed onto that bloody golf course—'

'And you've said yourself that they can't get off it,' Lorna said calmly.

'No, I *haven't*,' Martin snapped. 'I said we'd made it *difficult* for them, not *impossible*. Until now the music's been drawing them in, and it's the fact there have been so many of them all moving in the same direction that has kept them penned in. If they start turning back in large numbers, then we're screwed.'

'But they're still on the other side of the road, behind two fences that they'll never manage to get through—'

'If enough of them have caught alight, they could burn their way through,' he snarled.

'That's hardly likely,' Caron murmured, sniggering into her wine glass.

'Okay, so if it comes to it I'll stand on a ladder chucking buckets of water over them,' Gordon said, beginning to get irritated. The conversation was getting ridiculous.

'We haven't got enough water,' Martin immediately replied. 'Let's face—'

Howard's dog, which had been sitting at Lorna's feet, stood and pricked up its ears.

'What's the matter?'

The dog sniffed the air, and as Lorna leant down to stroke its head it suddenly bolted, running at full speed across the courtyard, weaving through the furniture in the marble-floored reception area and jumping down the steps and straight past Hollis.

He spun around and watched as it hurtled towards the track leading away from the hotel. The little animal finally stopped, just short of the mouth of the road, and started barking. Hollis ran over to her and grabbed her collar. 'Hey, girl,' he said in a soothing tone, trying to shut her up, 'what's the matter with you? All this noise freaking you out—?' As the dog twisted frantically under his hand he looked up to see what had upset her so much.

There were bodies, coming up the track.

From where he was standing Hollis could see at least four of them, but he knew that would be just the start. Many more would doubtless be following close behind. He had let go of Dog's collar in his shock and now she hurtled forward, jumping up at the first cadaver and knocking it flat onto its back. She stood with her front legs on the creature's torso, pinning it down as she savaged it with her sharp teeth. The body on the ground, quite unable to understand what was happening to it, attempted to push the animal away, but the dog was too strong for it.

Four other corpses stumbled past, heedless of the frantic mêlée near their feet.

'Bodies!' Hollis yelled, immediately running back into the building to find a weapon. He swerved to avoid Gordon and Lorna coming the other way, alerted by Dog's strange behaviour.

'Many?' Lorna asked as they passed.

'Enough,' Hollis replied, grabbing a fire-axe. As he turned back again he saw Howard disappearing up the stairs beside the reception desk. *Fucking coward*, he thought, but he didn't have time to sort that out right now.

By the time he'd made it back into the car park Lorna was

on the verge of attacking the closest body with a machete. The corpse, the lopsided husk of a schoolgirl, was advancing towards her imperiously. Lorna, gripping the machete tight, grunted with satisfaction as it connected with the underside of the creature's chin and sliced through its diseased face. A second strike, and its head exploded like a watermelon, showering the ground and the other corpses nearby with blood.

Gordon sprinted forward with big screwdrivers held high in either hand, all talk of dodgy hips and excuses long forgotten. With a guttural yell of savage rage he launched himself at the dead shell of a jogger, still dressed in full running kit, and plunged the screwdrivers into the creature's temples, feeling them hit each other as they crossed in the middle of what was left of its brain. He yanked them free and moved straight onto the next kill, narrowly missing Hollis, who had just swung his axe up into the groin of a horribly decayed vicar.

Howard, who'd not been running for cover after all, came pounding back down the stairs, struggling to catch his breath and tell them what he'd seen. Caron, Ginnie and Martin were gathered anxiously at the bottom of the staircase.

'It's not that bad,' he began.

'Not that bad!' Martin immediately interrupted, pointing outside, 'there are bodies out there! How can it not be that bad?'

'Shut up, Martin,' he gasped, leaning up against the wall. 'Jas and the others have gone into the field through the gate we blocked with the Yaris,' he continued, gesturing back over his shoulder. 'They've left it open so they can get out again.'

'But they're letting them through!'

'Not that many,' he answered quickly, still panting. 'Believe me, there's enough going on out in that field to keep most of them occupied – I only saw about twenty of them on the road, thirty at the most.'

'Thirty!' Martin screamed, 'there are only six of us left here now!'

'It'll be fine,' Caron assured him, the wine she'd had filling her with false confidence. She put her hand on his shoulder, but he recoiled and pulled away. 'Thirty is nothing,' she continued, unperturbed. 'Trust me, I've seen Greg deal with more than that on his own before now.'

Fighting close alongside each other Hollis, Gordon and Lorna had managed to inch their way slowly down the track, leaving the ground littered with dismembered bodies, some still twitching. But the dead were being pushed back. Hollis was quietly praying to himself that they could keep this progress up without being seen or heard by too many more cadavers. He could deal with this number, but he'd seen just how many more of them were amassed on the golf course less than a quarter of a mile away. It wouldn't take much to open the flood-gates and bring thousands of them trudging back here, and there was no way the three of them could succeed against that many.

Howard jogged down from the hotel, meat-cleaver in hand. He stopped by Dog and pulled her away from the corpse, which she was still attacking. Though she had eviscerated the creature's innards, still its arms and legs were moving.

'Out of the way, girl,' he said as he dropped to his knees. Screwing his eyes shut (he really didn't want to see what he was about to do) he slammed the cleaver down, chopping through the cadaver's neck. His arm jarred when the blade hit the tarmac, but the body on the ground immediately stopped thrashing. He let go of Dog and as he scrambled to his feet she had already bounded forward again and leapt up at another corpse. Howard remained where he was, feeling sick. He'd just decapitated someone – no, some*thing*, he forced himself to remember, not some*one* . . . It was some*thing*, and it wanted him dead. He stood up and looked for the others.

'Greg,' he yelled as Hollis neared the bend in the track, close to where the road forked.

Hollis stepped back when he heard his name being called. 'What?' he shouted back, eyeing up his next victim, sporting a blood-encrusted shirt and tie, as it stumbled dangerously close.

'There are only about thirty or so of them. They're coming in through the gate.'

'What did he say?' Lorna asked, stamping on the upturned face which was staring up at her with cold, sunken eyes.

'Don't know,' Hollis grunted as he returned to the fight, 'something about the gate.'

'There's a gate,' Gordon explained breathlessly between kills. 'Ginnie showed it to me earlier. That's how they got the cars through.'

'So if we can beat them back far enough,' Hollis began.

'Then we can get the gate blocked up again and stop them getting out,' he finished the sentence.

Standing at his side, Lorna cracked the skull of another cadaver with her machete, then shoved what was left of the corpse into the hedge. She nodded to show that she'd heard and understood him, and began to swipe at the dead with renewed energy.

'It's no fucking good,' Jas said angrily as Harte continued to scan the area, desperately looking for Amir's car.

'I'll bet they've gone back,' Harte said at last. 'The no-good fuckers have lost their bottle and run away.'

Jas accelerated back up the incline and onto level ground again. For the first time since they'd entered the field he stopped and looked around. There was total carnage all around them now. An unprecedented number of bodies had been destroyed by the rampaging vehicles, the explosions and the fires, and even now, after the initial effects of the explosions had died down, countless more were still hauling their twisted frames towards the two burning wrecks. All around them the charred remains of the dead had been churned into the ground, mixing with the mud to form a single unidentifiable mire covering the entire area.

Bodies began to slam against the sides of the van and Jas put the Transit in gear and drove away towards the gate.

'Screw it,' he said as he accelerated onto the road and began running down the oblivious cadavers which had escaped the field and were now staggering down the track, their backs to the Transit. 'We can't just sit here waiting for them.'

'The gate,' Harte reminded him. Annoyed by his oversight, Jas stopped and reversed back, destroying another bunch of corpses which had stumbled out into the road after them. As he braked, Harte jumped out, pulled the gate shut and locked it. Out in the open, the acrid stench of burning cars and burning flesh stung his throat and made his eyes water. He started coughing as he stepped back from the barrier, ignoring the bodies which immediately started crashing against it and reaching out for him with grabbing hands.

'What about the Yaris?' Jas asked as Harte got back into the van, still coughing.

'Webb and Amir'll need to get out,' he replied. 'The gate will be enough to hold the bodies back for now.'

'We can't just abandon them. Amir's a decent bloke.'

'I know, but we can't see where they are from here, and I can't hear them either.'

'We'll come back,' Jas said. 'We'll get back to the hotel and look out from the top floor, then we'll be able to get an idea of where they are. I'm not just going to drive back out into the crowds again. Anyway, chances are they've both fucked off with Sean.'

'Fair enough Webb, but Amir—'

'We'll come back,' Jas repeated. Harte continued to protest, but Jas wasn't in the mood to argue. He needed to get back to the others and start planning their next move. *Once we're all back inside it's either up or out,* he thought. *If we can't attract the attention of the helicopter pilot this time (and if all this doesn't, what will?) then it's probably time to say goodbye to this hellhole hotel and get away.*

His mind was made up. It was down to the rest of them to decide if they wanted to go with him.

Howard's inexperience was showing. The other three were way down the track, but he was still at the mouth of the road, attacking already incapacitated corpses which were no longer a threat. He didn't want to go down and fight with the others, but he knew he had to – Christ, even the dog was doing more than him. He watched her jump up at yet another cadaver and sink her razor-sharp teeth into its arm, dragging it down to the ground. He tightened his grip on his meat-cleaver and began to run forward again—

—what was that? He could hear another engine – was it the van coming back? At first he couldn't locate the source of the sound; was it coming from the road running between the hotel and golf course, or from the road junction at the end of the track, or even the field? It sounded like it was behind him . . .

He spun around just in time to see Driver's bus careening around the front of the hotel building. Martin was at the wheel. He hurtled down the track towards Howard, who ran for cover as fast as his tired legs would carry him.

'Move!' he screamed at the top of his voice to anyone who could hear him.

Further down the track Gordon looked up. 'Christ,' he cried, grabbing hold of Lorna by the waist and pulling her away from the corpse she was chopping at with her machete. For a moment she struggled to release herself from his grip, terrified that one of the dead had her, until she realised it was Gordon and relaxed. A little further ahead they could see Hollis, still fighting as if he hadn't heard anything.

'Greg!' she screamed, quickly realising what was happening, 'Greg, get out of the way!'

Howard's dog raced back towards him at full pelt,

carrying half an arm in her mouth. Gordon pulled Lorna behind him, holding her upright as she tripped over a headless torso then pushing her into the hedgerow as the bus thundered past. It missed them both by the slenderest of margins, temporarily filling the world with deafening noise and a sudden hot blast of choking exhaust fumes.

'Hollis!' she screamed again as the back of the bus filled the width of the road and he disappeared from view. She stood in the middle of the tarmac strip with Gordon and watched helplessly as the bus raced away, wiping out the last few cadavers which had made it this far along the road. Wrestling herself free from Gordon's well-meaning grip she ran down the road after Martin, until she reached the place where Hollis had been standing.

'*Greg!*' she screamed, and fell to her knees.

'Fuck me, that was close!' came a voice from somewhere on the left.

Lorna looked around, almost dizzy with relief, and ran to help him disentangle himself from the undergrowth.

'Who the hell was that?' he asked as he brushed the last of the twigs from his hair.

'Martin, I think,' she answered.

'What does he think he's doing?'

'Trying to block the road?' she suggested, 'or maybe get rid of the bodies – or both, perhaps.'

The Transit van blasted down the other side of the track at breakneck speed. Jas was looking for the sharp three hundred and sixty degree turn that he needed, but at this pace it was difficult to see much. The hedgerows merged together to look like a single, uninterrupted border around the hotel. Wait, there it was – he could see the back of the hotel sign now, and the sign to the golf club, pointing up the stretch of road they'd just come down.

He slammed his foot on the brake and as the Transit slowed almost to a stop he yanked the wheel around to the left, starting his three-point turn in the narrow space. He crunched into reverse gear and turned his head to start the manoeuvre when Harte screamed, 'Shit!' and dived over towards Jas, who looked back to see, for the briefest of moments, the front of the bus thundering towards them—

The massive vehicle and its makeshift blood-covered snowplough punched into the side of the van and the force of the impact sent it crashing into the hedgerow, showering the road with shattered glass and broken branches. The bus itself continued forwards until its front wheels rammed into the muddy bank at the bottom of the hedge.

Harte, very visibly shaking like a leaf, started checking himself for injuries, but Jas, who could already see that they were both unharmed, shoved him off and called, 'Come on!' as he wrenched open the driver's door and jumped out onto the road. He rubbed his aching neck and turned back to help Harte, who was struggling to open his badly buckled door. 'This way,' he shouted.

Disorientated by the jolting shock and the speed of the crash, Harte continued to try and get the passenger door to open for a second or two longer, unable to comprehend why he couldn't do it. He looked up when he caught movement out of the corner of his eye: the front of the bus was just a couple of yards away from where he was sitting, and it looked like someone was trying to escape from inside – Martin? What the hell was he doing driving the bus? And what had he done—? Blood was pouring down his face and he was banging on the glass.

'Come on,' Jas yelled again, reaching back into the van and dragging Harte out through the driver's door onto the road. Harte picked himself up and ran around to join Jas at the front of the bus. Martin was hammering frantically on the windscreen now, desperately trying to free himself.

'Keep still,' Harte shouted. 'Shut up and keep still!'

But Martin was panicking, kicking and screaming and trying to get himself out of the driver's seat. He obviously had no idea how precariously balanced the bus was – Jas and Harte could see that all the wheels on one side had been forced up the bank, tilting the bus at a dangerous angle.

Harte shouted at Martin again, trying to stop him moving, but his words had no effect. Martin had finally freed himself from the buckled seat and now he stood up and started scrambling up the steeply inclined floor – and though he wasn't a big man, his desperate movements were enough to upset the delicate balance and Jas yanked Harte back out of the way just in time as the huge vehicle crashed down into the road. Martin was thrown across the cab, thumping his head again as he went down. This time he didn't get up.

'Do you think he's—?' Harte began, and stopped.

'Probably,' Jas said, his voice devoid of emotion. 'Stupid bastard – what the *hell* was he doing?'

Harte hauled himself onto what was now the top of the bus and moved carefully along to the door at his feet. He dropped to his knees and pushed against it, actually managing to force it half-open.

'Martin,' he shouted, 'Martin—'

Six feet below them, Martin began to groan.

'We'll come back for him,' Jas said as he pulled himself to his feet. 'Stupid, *bloody*, fool.' He glanced down at Martin's slowly stirring body, then turned and jogged slowly along the side of the bus.

'Looks like he was trying to clear the road,' Harte said, looking down at the track, which was completely awash with the foetid remains of the dead.

'Fucking idiot,' Jas said. 'All he's done is block it.'

'Come on, now – he didn't know we were coming around the corner, did he?'

'That's not the point, is it? The fact is, he's blocked our way out. How are we supposed to shift this thing now?'

'I've got no idea. Come on, we'll sort it out later. We should get back to the others.' He was about to climb off the bus when he heard the distant whine of another engine.

Where was it? *Who* was it? It had to be Webb and Amir; where the hell had they been?

But Jas knew exactly what the sound was. 'it's the helicopter,' he said, pointing up at the aircraft he'd just spotted. His heart began to thump in his chest and his legs felt heavy with nerves. *Come on*, he thought, *this is it*. On his left two huge black columns of smoke were still rising high into the sky – surely they had to see them? Surely the pilot would fly over here to investigate? There was hardly any wind, and the smoke was rising straight up like hundred-storey-high arrows pointing down at the hotel. He willed the helicopter to change course and fly closer.

'They'll see it,' Harte said under his breath, 'they have to . . .'

Jas stared unblinking at the speck of black crawling across the white clouds. He watched it until it disappeared, fervently praying it would bank around and come back.

Minutes passed before he stopped looking.

'That's it then,' he said dejectedly, his voice weak with emotion. 'I don't think they'll be back again. We're completely fucked now.'

51

Webb was upside down, and he could taste blood in his mouth. The light was low and he was struggling to make sense of his surroundings. Was it night already? Had he really lain here unconscious for hours, wherever here was? He could hear running water. What the hell had happened? He tried to move, but a sudden sharp, jabbing pain in his gut made him stop. With swollen hands he reached out and disentangled himself from his baseball bat. One of the nails was sticking into him – fortunately, his several thick layers of clothing had prevented the point from piercing his skin. The pain immediately stopped and he let the bat fall from his hands. It landed with a thump on what was, he now realised, the upturned roof of the car, landing right between Amir and himself.

'Amir,' he said, managing to tilt his head slightly so that he could see the other man's face, 'are you okay?'

Amir didn't respond. Webb looked around again, his eyes gradually becoming accustomed to the gloom. Amir was also upside down, still anchored in his seat by his safety belt. *What kind of an idiot wears a seatbelt these days*, he wondered, *and why am I lying on my back on the roof?* The car, he slowly deduced, had rolled over in the middle of a stream. He began to remember a bit, a few fleeting flashes – ploughing into the bodies on the golf course, Amir panicking and steering the wrong way, the sudden stomach-churning drop – but little else. Still not yet daring to move, he worked his way back through events, trying to make more sense of his predicament. Now he remembered why they'd been away from the hotel. The others would probably have made it back by now; they'd have given him and Amir up for dead. But wait – maybe it wasn't as late as he'd first thought? He angled his head around again so that he could look out of the window on his side. The glass was almost completely obscured by mud and by a corpse which had its legs trapped under the car and was trying unsuccessfully to get away. Whenever the corpse moved its arms he caught glimpses of daylight.

I've got to get out of here.

'Amir,' he said out loud, and managed to reach across and shake Amir's shoulder. He felt cold to the touch – was he dead? Webb shook him lightly again, but still there was no reaction. So what did he do now? Webb tried moving his legs, and after a few scary moments he found that he was able to work them around the edge of the back of the seat he'd been sitting in when Amir had lost control of the Audi. The car had come to rest at a slight angle, the front propped up on the bank, whilst the back end was submerged in the stream. If he could smash his way through the windshield he'd be able to crawl out under the upturned bonnet and get out. What he'd do after that was anyone's guess – the most vivid of the snatched memories he had of the moments just before the crash was the incredible size of the crowd they'd managed to drive into. It was fucking huge.

'Amir,' he whispered for the third time, 'come on, mate.' Still no response. Webb manoeuvred himself into a position where he could reach out and touch Amir's neck; maybe he could find a pulse. After a few moments he thought he could feel a faint *boom boom* and Amir's skin felt warm, if clammy. So not dead yet, not quite. Now he could see better, Webb could make out the puddle of blood on the roof below Amir's upside-down head, and when he carefully turned Amir's suspended head to face him there was a deep gash across his forehead, which corresponded to the bloody smudge in the middle of the cracked windscreen. *How ironic*, he thought, *that Amir was the one strapped in. Poor bastard.*

As he moved again his outstretched foot kicked the fuel can, which had also dropped onto the roof. Burn the car and distract the corpses: that had been the plan, he remembered. It might still work. He had no idea where he was in relation to the hotel, but anywhere on the golf course would be far enough away from the others not to matter – not that he cared about them and their plans, anyway, never mind getting that helicopter Jas had been constantly banging on about to see them: setting fire to the car would cause enough of a distraction to give *him* a chance to get away.

'Oi, Amir,' he said, a little louder this time. He shook his shoulder again but there was no response other than a sudden sickening spurt of blood where before there had been only drips. No good; it was time to move. Even if he managed to get Amir out of the car, he'd never be able to get him back to the hotel – he was going to have enough trouble getting himself off the golf course as it was.

Struggling in the confined space, Webb spun himself around on his back through a slow one hundred and eighty degrees and booted the windscreen. Three good, strong kicks to the already weakened glass was enough to shatter it and kick it through. He turned back and grabbed the can of fuel and his baseball bat, then set about crawling out of the car. The appalling sight which greeted him was almost enough to send him scuttling back under cover but he forced himself to keep going. For as far as he could see the stream was a sickening stew where an incalculable number of corpses had fallen in and been unable to get out again – but they'd been strangely protected in the stream bed, and they continued to move constantly, never stopping, but never getting anywhere either. There was little more than a trickle of moving water, filled with unidentifiable lumps of bodies and the whole thing was a disgusting putrid brown-green hue reminding him of vomit.

The nearest bodies were trapped, either by each other or by the upturned car, and he found that he was able to move around them with surprising freedom. Working quickly he opened the fuel can and set it down under the bonnet. He tore a strip of rag from the back of a corpse which was stuck facing away from him, soaked it with fuel and jammed it into the mouth of the can. Taking out his lighter he lit the rag and started to scramble away.

'Webb—'

What the fuck was that? He spun around anxiously. It sounded like Amir, but he was dead, wasn't he? Jesus Christ, what if he was wrong – what if Amir was still alive; if he'd just passed out because of the blood? He could see him through the cracked windscreen; he didn't look like he'd moved. He must have imagined the noise. Amir's eyes were still closed and the blood was still dripping and—

—and the rag was still burning. Webb jumped to his feet and hauled himself up the steep bank, grabbing at random corpses and using them as leverage, stamping his feet down onto flesh and bone and whatever else he could get a grip on, until he'd managed to throw himself over the top of the bank, straight into a solid mass of bodies the number of which he couldn't even begin to appreciate.

He dropped to his knees as the car behind him exploded—

—flattening hundreds of cadavers in a rough circle around the epicentre . . .

Webb found himself buried under a mass of dark figures. *Keep moving. No time to think.* He knew he had to make the most of the delay before the rest of them started moving towards the blast, but as he clambered back to his feet and began to trip through a quagmire of body parts he glanced back over his shoulder. The car – or parts of it, at least – had been blown back out of the ditch. He could see twisted chunks of its blackened frame burning fiercely. *If Amir wasn't dead*, he thought callously, *then he is now.*

All around Webb, hordes of bodies were turning and advancing towards him, staggering unsteadily through the noisome slime coating the once-pristine golf course. Thousands upon thousands of continually moving feet had churned the remains of countless fallen creatures into the cloying mud until everything was covered with a thick layer of foul-smelling sludge. *Keep moving*, he told himself; *it's the fire they're heading for, not me.*

He instinctively dropped to his knees and began to crawl through the slurry between the emaciated feet of the nearest corpses, hoping that keeping low would be enough to stop the dead from reacting to him. *The stupid things never look down*, he tried to reassure himself. *If they looked where they were going*, he smirked, *there wouldn't be so many of them stuck in the bloody stream, would there?* He lowered his head and held onto his baseball bat as he began to move through the forest of spindly legs.

Which way now?

Time to make another decision – he couldn't keep crawling like this indefinitely. Lifting his head momentarily, he glimpsed the trunk of a large tree to the right ahead and he altered his course, intending to use it as cover as the crowd continued to gravitate towards the burning A7. If he stayed on the blind side of the trunk, they probably wouldn't see him . . .

In less than a minute he was there, and he cautiously raised himself up behind it, holding onto its rough bark to pull himself back onto his feet. Down at ground level the sheer bulk of the bodies above were so tightly packed that they'd acted like a canopy, muffling the rest of the world; now that he was standing straight again he could see over the heads of the dead, for almost all of them were walking with their heads bowed, as if the physical weight of their skulls were too much for their weakened bodies to support. He hadn't appreciated that before, but he'd never been this deep into the crowd of corpses and dared to stay still before now either.

Music? No, he had to be imagining it. Could he really hear Martin's music? He'd imagined hearing Amir's voice just a few minutes earlier; was this another cruel trick of his tired mind? His ears suddenly locked onto the frequency of the tune playing in the distance and it became clear: some godawful screechy country and western number was echoing around the golf course. *Thank God for Martin Priest*, he thought.

He cautiously peered out around the side of the tree, quickly pulling his head back in again when a particularly grotesque figure raised its arms and lunged towards him. *Christ, for a second in the confusion it looked like Stokes, but that's impossible . . .* It was just the low light, and his nerves playing games with him. Webb looked again, carefully, forcing himself to concentrate – and then he saw the clubhouse, just a couple of hundred yards away. *Reachable.*

I'm going to get out of here.

Webb dropped back down to his hands and knees and began to crawl.

52

Hollis and Gordon lifted Martin out of the bus, passing him up through the door they'd managed to force open.

'You stupid bugger,' Gordon muttered as he struggled with Martin's legs.

He groaned, but didn't otherwise respond.

'He just panicked,' Hollis whispered, 'that's all. He was just trying to protect this place.'

'Just trying to protect himself, more like.'

'It really doesn't matter now, does it?'

As they reached the end of the bus Hollis called Howard over to help lift Martin down. Between them they lowered him awkwardly to the ground. All around them Harte, Lorna and Ginnie were cleaning the drive, scraping up what was left of the dead with shovels and transporting it in wheelbarrows and buckets away from the hotel.

'Mind out,' Hollis said, almost knocking Harte into a waist-high pile of dismembered limbs.

'Watch what you're doing,' Harte grumbled. 'You going to chuck him on this pile? Stupid bastard nearly got us killed just now.'

'No, he didn't,' Hollis said quickly, '*you* nearly got yourselves killed – you were the ones who drove into a field full of dead bodies and started blowing cars up. That was nothing to do with Martin.'

'And I suppose it was our fault he crashed into us as well?' Harte said grimly.

'Whatever,' Hollis replied, refusing to be drawn into yet another pointless argument.

The road now clear, Harte turned and walked back

towards the hotel. Howard, Hollis and Gordon followed carrying Martin, who continued to moan. Ginnie and Lorna were close behind. They found Caron sitting on the steps outside the main entrance. She looked up as Harte stomped past her, then moved to the side to let the others through. It had started to rain – just a light mist – but it was refreshing, and Caron decided she'd rather sit out and get wet than go back indoors, no matter how dirty the rainwater. Lorna stopped and sat down next to her.

'You all right out here?' she asked.

'Fine.'

'Aren't you cold?'

'I'm fine,' she snapped.

'Sorry,' Lorna said, taken aback by her reaction.

'It's all right,' Caron replied, 'I just don't want anyone fussing, that's all.'

'That's your job, isn't it?' Lorna said sarcastically.

'I've given all that up,' she said quietly, taking a swig from her bottle of wine. She offered it to Lorna, who took it gratefully.

'Shame,' she said, wiping her mouth. 'You were good at it.'

Caron shook her head and stared out towards the edge of the hotel grounds. 'I don't think so.'

'What makes you say that?'

'Because all the people I've tried looking after recently are dead.'

'In case you haven't noticed, love,' Lorna whispered, 'pretty much *everyone*'s dead, and it had nothing to do with anything you did or didn't do for them. This is what happens when you have too many men – too many egos – stuck in one place together.'

Caron was silent for a moment, then she shivered. 'I suppose,' she said, and lifted the bottle again. 'Do you know what we need to do now?'

'What?'

'Absolutely bloody nothing.'

'Nothing?'

'I might be pissed,' Caron blathered, 'but I know what I'm talking about: the more you try these days, the less you get. Those boys went outside today and tried too hard, and now we've lost Amir, Sean and Webb.'

'Webb's no great loss,' Lorna muttered.

'No, but the others were,' Caron interrupted angrily, slurring her words slightly as she became more emotional, 'and we didn't have to lose them. If we all just sit still, be quiet and do nothing, we'll be okay.'

The rain began to fall with more persistence and Lorna stood up, then reached back down and held out a hand to Caron. 'Come on,' she said, hauling her up onto unsteady feet. Together they walked along the glass-fronted corridor beside the courtyard until the silence was broken by the sound of running feet.

Howard was pounding back down the staircase at the end of the opposite wing with Gordon following close behind.

'More trouble,' Caron said dejectedly. 'It's always trouble when people like Gordon and Howard start moving quickly.'

'You don't know that,' Lorna sighed as they walked towards the restaurant, 'but you're probably right.' She braced herself for bad news, but was surprised by the self-congratulatory smiles which greeted her.

'It worked,' Hollis said as she walked over to him and took the proffered can of beer.

'What worked?'

'Jas' little stunt outside today!'

At the mention of his name Jas turned around and grinned. 'You should see it!' he enthused. 'We've just been watching from upstairs – we shifted *thousands* of them today, and the rest are more interested in the fires we started than anything we're doing here.'

'Congratulations,' she said with a smile, though she was not exactly sure how she felt. Was it even worth reminding him of the pointless sacrifices which had been made? Perhaps it was better just to shut up and not burst his bubble.

'I don't think we should do anything else today,' Harte continued, picking up where Jas had left off, 'but maybe we should think about getting out of here tomorrow or the day after that. We could take one of the lorries from the road junction.'

'Are we going to gain anything from that?' Lorna asked cautiously, remembering Caron's earlier words.

'You can just stay here if you want to,' he snapped, and she sighed, not interested in hearing the familiar arguments all over again.

'Well, I'm not going anywhere,' Caron announced, her drunken voice louder than intended.

'Shut up, Caron,' Jas laughed, 'you're pissed.'

'I might well be,' she replied, 'but I'm not stupid.'

53

Webb's progress over the final few yards of the once perfectly manicured golf course had been painfully slow, but he had almost reached the clubhouse. The dead were walking over him, oblivious to his presence, sometimes even standing right on top of him and not realising; the damn things had no idea he was there. He was pretty sure the number of cadavers around him was increasing, as was the depth of the repugnant sludge through which he was forcing himself. The sickly morass was almost a foot deep in places now, thanks to the many hundreds of corpses that had gravitated here, then been dragged down and trampled underfoot. Webb was covered in the damn stuff; it was in his hair and his eyes, in his nose; he could even taste it at the back of his throat. It had permeated his many layers of protective clothing and he could feel it, cold and repellent, on his skin. He tried to convince himself that it was just mud, despite the occasional eye, or ear, or other equally distinguishable shape that floated by.

How far now? Even though the music was muffled down at ground level, it was getting uncomfortably loud. He allowed himself to glance up momentarily, and through the tripping, sliding legs saw the front of the building was now only a couple of yards ahead.

It was impossible to be certain, but the congestion around the door up ahead didn't look as bad as he'd expected – there were a huge number of corpses around the building, but some kind of decorative low wall or fence on either side of the door seemed to be channelling many of them away. But regardless of how many there were, he was going to have to get up to get inside. He lay still for a moment longer, collecting himself and trying to steady his nerves. He'd kept close hold of his baseball bat, and his only option, as far as he could see, was to get up, smash his way through the crowd and then batter the door (and any corpses that got in his way) with all the strength he could muster. Hopefully the speed and surprise of his attack would be enough to confuse the cadavers for long enough; by the time they realised what was happening, he hoped, he should be safe inside.

And what after that? He wished he'd listened more closely to Martin when he'd been talking about the layout of the building, but he had a vague memory of a back entrance which was connected to the road, which he could use to get back to the hotel – back to safety, and food and drink, and his room, and then . . .

Another decaying foot pressed down on the small of his back, pushing his face closer to the foul stench beneath him. He closed his eyes and tried to focus on what he was about to do, though his guts were churning with nausea and fear. *Try and get a little closer*, he decided, *then just go for it.*

He slithered on until the ground dropped away slightly and he realised he'd reached the top of a gradual low slope which had been disguised by the number of bodies tightly packed around the building. The slope led directly to the building's wide double door. Taking a final noxious breath, Webb heaved himself back up to his feet, knocking several cadavers down into the mud as he did so. Dripping with the odious slime he lifted his baseball bat high and swung it around his head, hacking down a wide circle of corpses disorientated by his sudden appearance, and before any others could react he ran to the door, slipping precariously down the slope. For the moment it looked like it was working – and it was immediately apparent why: in the fading light the dead could hardly see him. He was rendered virtually invisible, camouflaged by the thick layer of decomposed human remains that made him look just like them.

He had only a few seconds of freedom to get into the building. *Do it now*, he told himself, his mind racing, *before they realise.*

He hammered the baseball bat down on the clubhouse door, and it immediately began to splinter, but still it held tight. He swung the bat again, bringing it right over his head and crashing it down on the door, and this time the nails sank deep into the wood and he had to yank hard to release the bat before he could strike for a third time. As he swung the bat back and then heaved it forward again with all the remaining strength he could summon, it hit the door with a dull thud, and he saw that a chunk of flesh had been torn off a body behind him. He glanced behind him: the nearest cadavers were moving forward again, attracted by the noise he was making. It was impossible to see exactly how many there were, but that didn't matter – it was like a chain-reaction: one group inevitably attracted the next, and on and on . . .

Webb shook the rotting flesh off the nails and swung it again, grunting loudly with effort, and this time there was a satisfying crack as the top panel of the right-hand door gave way, leaving a hole large enough for him to get his hand inside and force more of the wood away. He could feel the first clawing fingers on his back now, then the deceptively soft impact of the first body crashing into him. Now working with desperate, breathless speed he threw his bat down and pulled more of the wood away until the hole was big enough for him to shove his head and one arm through. It was virtually pitch-black inside the building and he could see nothing, but with his outstretched fingers he could feel the wooden bar which had been carefully secured across the door, typical of Martin's pedantic workmanship. Webb yanked it out of the brackets which held it in place and dropped it to the ground.

Another corpse grabbed Webb's shoulders, pulling him back, and he allowed himself to be moved away for a fraction of a second, then he shook himself free and ran back at the door, building up enough velocity to hit the middle with sufficient force to throw both sides of it open. He ran into the darkness without stopping, arms outstretched, feeling his way through the shadowy building with no idea where he was going.

Fighting each other to get through the narrow gap, the first of hundreds of bodies followed Webb, the force of so many more behind keeping them moving at a speed which almost matched his.

54

'**Y**ou don't have a clue what you're talking about,' Harte protested, shoving a handful of food into his mouth. 'You've never seen so many of them as there were out there today.'

Gordon shook his head and took a plate from Ginnie. 'And I don't want to know either,' he said, sniffing appreciatively at his food. 'I saw more than enough, thank you. What's this?'

'Stew,' Ginnie replied.

He stabbed his fork into a lump of something, shoved it into his mouth and chewed as Ginnie watched him expectantly. 'Not bad,' he said with a grin, and he took another mouthful.

'Remember that night back at the flats when you did the cooking, Gord?' Harte asked, laughing. 'Fuck me, what was it again?'

'Some vegetarian rubbish,' Lorna laughed.

'When was this?' Howard asked, struggling to see the others in the semi-darkness. He was sitting just outside the main circle so that he could feed Dog without anyone complaining. After the way she'd fought today he thought she deserved a treat.

'We'd only been there a couple of weeks,' Lorna explained. 'Most of us went out looking for food, but Gordon pulled the old "dodgy hip" routine and decided we'd all be better off if he stayed behind.'

'I *have* got a dodgy hip,' he protested.

'When it suits you,' Caron mumbled.

'*Any*way,' Laura broke in, 'he said he was going to cook a

meal while we were all out, trying to make up for the fact that he was too scared to go out—'

'That's not true,' he interrupted. 'Honestly, Ginnie, it didn't happen like that. We were just—'

'So we left him cooking dinner while we were all outside risking our necks, and the silly bugger only went and fell asleep! Then he tried to convince us all that he hadn't – but he'd burned the whole bloody meal – you should have smelled it! We had to chuck those pans out. I swear you could smell it over the bodies, it was that bad!'

'And we made you eat it, remember?' Harte chipped in.

'Stokes loved it,' Gordon answered back. 'He wasn't bothered – bit of carbon never hurt anyone, he used to say.'

'It wasn't the food that finished him off though, was it?' Jas said quietly. The mention of Stokes and his sudden demise brought the conversation to an abrupt halt.

'You're a bundle of laughs, you are,' Harte sighed, annoyed that the mood had been spoiled unnecessarily. 'Why did you have to say that?'

For an awkward moment no one spoke, choosing instead to concentrate on their food and their own thoughts.

Harte was glad of the increasing early evening darkness; it made it easier to avoid eye-contact. He was happy that they'd gone outside today – it had been for the right reasons – and they'd achieved far more than they'd ever expected, but he'd be lying if he'd said he didn't regret the way things had turned out. They should have thought it through more carefully, and involved the others from the start – maybe Amir and Webb would still be alive if they'd planned things better. Mind you, he didn't feel any sympathy whatsoever for Martin, who sat groaning a short distance away. His head had been bandaged up – maybe they should have bandaged up his mouth too, Harte thought. That bloody man was becoming a liability.

Until Jas had mentioned Stokes, the mood in the hotel had been more positive and upbeat than any of them would have expected. *Look at what we've achieved,* Gordon had told them all a short while earlier: *hundreds, possibly even thousands of bodies destroyed – and the hotel's defences have been unexpectedly strengthened by Martin's total inability to drive the bus!*

'Anybody want another drink?' Hollis asked, suddenly feeling uncomfortable and looking for a distraction.

'Get me another can please, Hollis,' Jas replied, his voice low as he thought about the helicopter and their missed opportunity today.

'And me,' Harte added.

'Wine,' Caron ordered.

'How much have you drunk today, Caron?' Lorna wondered.

'Have we got any wine left?'

'I think so – why?'

'Because if there's any left, I haven't drunk enough.'

Hollis got up and walked towards the bar, leaving the others laughing at the state the normally prim and proper Caron had allowed herself to get into. He'd only been gone a couple of seconds when the fragile silence in the rest of the hotel was broken by a loud crashing noise.

'What the hell was that?' Jas cried, jumping up from his seat. 'Was that you, Hollis?'

'It wasn't me,' he shouted from the next room, 'it was something out back.' He put the bottle down on the bar and ran through to the kitchen. The noise had emanated from the back of the building. Though it wasn't yet completely dark outside, it was difficult to see details inside. He weaved his way around the equipment and supplies stacked up in the cluttered room, but stopped short, just by the back door—

—there was something moving towards him, dragging itself slowly along, and the stench of dead flesh filled the air.

Hollis picked up a carving knife from the rack on the wall and raised it high, ready to slice the foul thing's fucking head right off.

'Don't—' it mumbled, breathing hard.

'Fuck me,' he shouted with surprise, dropping the knife. 'Christ almighty, it's Webb! Everyone, quick, get some light in here!'

Harte, Gordon and Lorna were there in seconds, Harte carrying one of their battery-operated lamps, which he switched on to reveal the survivor in his full gory glory.

Webb was covered from top to toe in the stinking grey mire through which he'd crawled for hours. He was struggling to breathe, and could barely move his limbs, which were heavy with exhaustion. He managed a single lurching step forward, then fell against an oven, knocking over a pile of pots and metal trays and filling the room with an echoing cacophony of noise.

Hollis grabbed his slime-covered arm to steady him, then led him slowly back into the restaurant.

'Is he okay?' Ginnie asked.

Howard's dog jumped up and began to sniff at Webb, who had collapsed heavily onto the nearest chair. The dog cowered back and began to snarl. She let out a sudden bark, and Howard immediately wrestled her away. 'It's just Webb, girl,' he said, trying to calm her down. 'It's just Webb, okay . . .'

Webb looked at the faces gathered around him with wide, relieved eyes. He felt as if he'd had to run many times the actual distance he'd covered to get here. He never thought the time would come when he'd actually be pleased to see these people again – even Lorna, Jas and Hollis, whom he'd grown to hate with a passion, suddenly felt like long-lost friends. Gordon passed him a bottle of water and he drank thirstily as the inevitable questioning began.

'What happened?' Jas asked first. 'We lost you—'

'Amir took a wrong turn,' he replied.

'You were supposed to drive around a field – for God's sake, how can you *possibly* take a wrong turn in a bloody empty space?' Harte jumped in.

Lorna nudged him to be quiet.

'He got confused by the bodies,' Webb explained, 'ended up on the golf course.'

'So why didn't you turn back?'

'We couldn't – there were too many of them.'

'Where is Amir?' Lorna asked softly, and Webb shook his head.

A brief moment of silence followed.

'How come you were gone for so long?' Jas asked at last.

'The car got stuck in a ditch,' he mumbled. 'I couldn't get Amir out – I think the crash killed him anyway. I did what you asked me to, though.'

'You blew the car up?'

He nodded.

'Where?'

'On the golf course.'

'With Amir in it?'

'He was already dead.'

'And you made sure of that,' Jas muttered.

Hollis glared at him. 'Give him a break,' he said angrily, 'you're not helping.'

'Webb,' Howard asked, getting a little closer now that his dog had calmed down, 'how exactly did you get back?'

Webb swigged more water and dropped the empty bottle on the floor. 'I ran,' he answered, still struggling to think straight.

'We know that,' Howard continued, his stomach suddenly twisting with nerves, 'but which way did you run? Did you come back through the field and over the gate, or did you find another way through?'

He was shaking his head. 'No,' he replied, 'I came back across the golf course.'

'And how exactly did you get off the golf course and back into the grounds of the hotel?'

'I followed the music.'

'So you managed to reach the clubhouse?'

'I came through it – broke in, and got out the back way.'

Howard looked around. Had no one else realised what Webb was saying?

'What's wrong, Howard?' Hollis asked.

Howard was speechless with fear, unable to say anything for a second or two. At last he started, 'If he came through the clubhouse—'

The penny dropped.

'Shit!' Hollis said. He turned and ran out of the room and back through the kitchens, Lorna and Harte, who'd both realised what was happening, hot on his heels. Hollis was the first to reach the back door and as he flung it open and ran out onto the lawns behind the hotel complex, he saw them:

Bodies.

Hundreds, *thousands* of bodies, steadily advancing through the gap in the fence that Martin had showed him days earlier: a huge, unstoppable wave of cold, dead flesh was now rolling relentlessly forward in their direction, enough decay to surround and swallow the entire hotel and everything in it. And it was too late to stop it. There was no way they could hold back a crowd as big as the one he'd seen out on the golf course yesterday morning.

'Oh God,' Lorna said with her hand over her mouth.

'What the hell are we going to do?' Harte demanded.

Hollis looked at him, but he couldn't answer. He couldn't think straight. None of them could possibly appreciate the scale of what was suddenly unfolding around them.

'Fuck!' Jas cursed as he rushed out into the open and pushed past the others. 'We've got to get out of here.'

'Where are you going to go?' Hollis asked, still staring unblinking at the advancing dead.

'Anywhere,' he answered, already sprinting back indoors.

'There's no point running,' he shouted after him. 'There's no way out.'

'Leave him,' Lorna pleaded, grabbing hold of Hollis' arm and dragging him back inside. 'Come on!'

Hollis pulled himself free and ran a short distance further away from the building, trying to gauge the true size of the crowd which was surging closer by the second. He was distracted by a sudden engine roar and a flash of light as Jas came powering around the side of the building on his Honda, desperately looking for an escape route. Their options were terrifyingly limited: bodies were still stumbling through the gap in the hedge, making it impossible to even consider trying to get out that way, and the wreckage at the front of the building had rendered the road away from the hotel useless too.

Jas accelerated forward, driving in a wide arc as close as he dared to the nearest cadavers. It looked scarily like they were speeding up as he approached, as if they were moving towards him, trying to cut him off. These bodies were definitely different: they showed none of the reluctance and caution that some of the corpses had exhibited before now. *Did they now understand the huge advantage they had over us living*, he wondered? They were marching forward like an unstoppable invading army.

For a second Jas rode parallel with them as they stormed relentlessly ahead. They were hugely outnumbered – there were thousands of corpses for every single survivor.

At last Jas turned and rode back towards the hotel, his muddy wheels leaving a dirty brown mark across the letter 'P' from Hollis and Martin's now redundant cry for help.

'Block the doors,' Lorna shouted as Hollis pushed his way back inside.

'What with?' someone's frightened voice shouted back from the shadows.

'Anything!' she screamed as she began to drag whatever she could find in front of the door. Hollis helped her, the two of them pulling on the top of a tall freezer unit and bringing it crashing down. The doors fell open, sending loose metal shelves and racks flying, filling the building with even more noise.

'We've got to block off every entrance down here,' Hollis said breathlessly, the clattering still ringing painfully in his ears.

'If we're not getting out of here,' Harte asked, moving to one side so that Gordon and Ginnie could get past, 'where are we going to go?'

'We need to stay by the supplies,' Lorna answered quickly. 'We could try and fortify the restaurant, perhaps? Or maybe the Steelbrooke Suite?'

Lorna and Harte disappeared into the shadows, followed by Hollis, ushering Howard and Caron out of the way. They sprinted towards the Steelbrooke Suite, pausing only to glance into the restaurant. Webb was still sitting exactly where they'd left him, staring into space. Martin sat two tables away, slumped forward with his bandaged head in his hands.

'Come on,' he yelled, 'shift yourselves!'

Webb looked up, but he didn't move.

Jas ran back from the front of the hotel and bustled into Hollis, distracting him. 'Leave them,' he grunted, pushing his way towards the large conference room in the far corner of the building. 'It's all their fault.'

'You couldn't find a way out then?' Hollis shouted after him. Jas disappeared into the darkness without responding.

Inside the Steelbrooke Suite, Lorna had already begun to pile tables and chairs against the doors and glass walls to strengthen them. Ginnie and Gordon were bringing in all the food they could find and stacking it in the corner. Howard's dog rushed across the room at a ferocious speed, skidding on the parquet flooring, then she began to bark furiously at the windows, pacing up and down the two glazed walls. Hollis looked up just in time to see the first corpses slamming against the tall windows, hammering at them with their fists, trying desperately to beat their way inside. In a matter of a few seconds what looked like hundreds of them had appeared across the full width of the back wall, spreading out in either direction, blocking out what little light remained.

Then when the size of the crowd along the back wall was enough to cover almost every square inch of glass, the bodies began to spill down the side of the building, moving slowly but with unstoppable intent and determination, pouring themselves around the outside of the hotel like rancid molasses.

'We can't stay here,' Gordon shouted.

'We can't get out of here!' Jas screamed, already on his way back to the other end of the building. 'Get the front secured – *now!*'

Everyone in the Steelbrooke Suite stopped what they were doing and ran through to the other end of the building. Some took the east corridor, others the west. Harte, who could outrun just about all of them, cut straight across the courtyard, throwing the glass doors open and barging through. He arrived in reception to find Jas struggling to push the wooden desk over to the door. He shoulder-charged the other end of the huge piece of furniture and it began to judder awkwardly across the floor tiles.

'Get anything you can find to help block it up,' Gordon ordered as he added his weight behind the desk, and Ginnie, Lorna and Howard did as he said, disappearing into anterooms and store cupboards, bringing out everything they could find to help seal the entrance. A final coordinated shove of the desk and it slammed up against the door, completely blocking it. The three men had just moved out of the way when Hollis dragged a tall-backed leather sofa up onto its end and pushed it over so that it dropped down against the desk at an angle, wedging it hard against the door frame.

'Shut that bloody animal up!' Ginnie screamed.

Howard reached down for Dog's collar and tried to pull her away, but she stood her ground and refused to move, barking furiously, her eyes fixed forward. The bodies had advanced all the way along the side of the hotel and now they had begun to spread across the front. Through the gaps between the piled furniture he could see them moving continually, steadily surrounding the entire building. The steps leading up to the main entrance held them back temporarily until the weight of flesh surging forward forced the leading cadavers to climb.

Howard let go of Dog and turned back to helping barricade the doors, trying to ignore the rotting faces that stared back at him as they slammed their bony hands against the glass. For a moment he thought he saw one of them grab the handle and try to pull the door open.

'Is that going to hold them?' Harte asked, wiping sweat from his eyes.

'It's going to have to, isn't it?' Lorna answered pragmatically. Her voice echoed around the now almost pitch-black reception area. As well as shutting out the final shards of fading light, the haphazard blockade had also changed the acoustics of the room, muffling the sounds outside and amplifying the noise indoors. 'What now?'

Gordon and Hollis moved closer. 'Where will we be safest?' Gordon wondered.

'Right in the middle of the building?' Lorna suggested. 'Either that or we should head up?'

'There's no way out if we go up,' Harte said ominously.

'I don't think we have a lot of choice at this stage.'

'We need to get out of sight,' Hollis said, 'find a room big enough for all of us where they won't see us.'

'We could try—' Harte began to say before being interrupted by a horrific scream from the other end of the hotel. It was Caron. For a second he froze in terror, not wanting to know what she'd found, but even from that distance knowing what was happening. The others began to run towards the source of the sound.

'They're inside,' Caron cried, running down the west wing corridor.

'How?' Hollis demanded.

'The swimming pool,' Jas said, his voice full of desperation and disappointment. 'The fucking things must have got in through the doors into the pool.'

'Then block off the bloody corridor off!' Gordon yelled, pushing past Caron and hurtling towards the pool and gym, but it was too late: by the time he got there the creatures were already swarming out into the open, steadily filling the marble-floored area in front of the restaurant, bar and the Steelbrooke Suite. They were moving with renewed speed, their progress helped by the pressure of those behind, and within seconds they had burst through the doors into the courtyard and begun to spill down the glass-fronted corridors on either side. In places the decorative glazing began to crack and give way under the pressure. The noise of the shattering glass seemed to excite the dead still further as they spread through the building.

'Up!' Jas shouted, loud enough for all of them to hear, 'first floor, middle room. Trust me!'

With no other option, Lorna, Ginnie and Howard began to climb the staircase at the reception end of the west wing corridor. Caron and Gordon ran back down the hallway towards them, glancing back over their shoulders at the steadily advancing tide of corpses which washed after them. Hollis shoved them up the staircase, then turned to face Harte and Jas.

'What about Webb and Martin?' he asked. The nearest bodies were now less than thirty yards away.

'Fuck them,' Jas said, 'we left them in the restaurant – with a bit of luck they'll have managed to block the door before they got in.'

'All of this is Webb's fault,' Harte seethed. 'He doesn't deserve to survive.'

'What about Driver?' Hollis demanded, the nearest bodies now close enough for them to be able to see the horrific detail in their dead faces. 'We can't just leave him, can we?'

'He's probably dead already,' Jas snapped. 'If you want any chance of living, get upstairs – now!'

For a moment Hollis didn't move, struggling with his conscience. 'Which room was he in?'

Harte was struggling too. 'East wing, top floor,' he replied, 'though I can't remember which number . . .'

'Leave him,' Jas said again, grabbing both men's arms and trying to drag them up.

'Oh, fuck it,' Harte snapped, squirming free from Jas' grip and running down to reception then back across and up the corridor on the other side. 'There's food over there.'

'What the hell are you doing?' Hollis gasped as he disappeared.

Jas shoved him again and they began to climb the stairs, stopping on the first landing where they could still see down to reception and over to the staircase on the other side of the building.

'Fucking idiot,' Jas muttered. 'What a waste of fucking time.'

Harte threw himself up the staircase at the end of the east wing, tripping on the final step and stumbling into the wall. Oblivious to the pain he picked himself up and ran along the top-floor corridor, opening every door he passed, unable to remember where he'd left Driver, and equally unsure why he'd bothered coming back for him – it was a stupid, spur-of-the-moment decision . . . but it was too late now. This was it; Room 39. He recognised a patch of torn wallpaper and a scratch just to the left of the door.

He grabbed the handle, pulled it open and burst inside. 'Come on,' he gasped, fighting for air, 'we need to get out before—'

The room was empty. It was definitely the right one – there were trays of dirty crockery and half-eaten food, and empty bottles of water, and the bed had definitely been slept in – but there was no Driver. Harte, shocked, almost forgot the mayhem which was engulfing the rest of the hotel. He looked in the bathroom, under the bed, in the wardrobe . . . but Driver definitely wasn't there.

The sound of more glass shattering elsewhere brought Harte crashing back to reality. He raced back along the corridor and down the staircase again. He could see the courtyard below, jammed full of corpses, with still more trying to force their way in. They were at the bottom of the staircase too, and they were beginning to climb. With no other option open to him he closed his eyes and accelerated, wincing with disgust as he crashed into the first cadavers. He lowered his head and kept battering his way through the surging crowd until he reached the reception area. He had a momentary respite, then he was deep amongst the dead again, this time racing towards the foot of the stairs leading up to the west wing rooms. Soaked with gore and gagging on the overpowering stench of decay, he began to force his way up, step by step. A hand grabbed his shoulder and fired full of adrenalin he clenched his fist and pulled it back to strike.

'Don't hit me, you fucking idiot,' Jas cursed as he pulled him up by the scruff of his neck. 'No good?'

'Not there,' he wheezed breathlessly as they climbed to the first floor.

Hollis and Lorna were standing on the landing waiting for them. 'What do you mean, not there?' Lorna demanded.

'He's cleared out,' Harte answered. 'The clever bastard's pulled a fast one on us – I bet there was never anything wrong with him.'

'Clever bugger,' Hollis muttered. 'He had more brains than we gave him credit for. Just because someone's not talking all the time, it doesn't mean they're not thinking, does it?'

He peered down the staircase. The bodies were definitely climbing.

'What now?' Harte asked.

'Block it up,' Jas replied. 'Gordon and Howard are already doing the stairs at the other end. Just get what you can out of the bedrooms and throw it down. We'll make sure those fuckers will never be able to get up here.'

55

Webb had heard Harte moving around. The sudden surge of bodies dragging themselves into the main part of the hotel from the swimming pool had snapped him out of his catatonic exhaustion, and with the rest of the survivors running around like headless chickens, he seized his chance. As the first corpses appeared in the door of the restaurant he pushed past them, smashing them away before they'd even realised he was there. He left Martin behind, pathetically sobbing for help, and when he looked back he'd already disappeared, swallowed up by an unstoppable mass of decaying flesh.

Pursued by a surging stream of deadly corpses, Webb fought his way to the nearest east-wing staircase. For a few anxious seconds he'd stopped at the top of the first flight and watched the courtyard outside fill with an incalculable mass of rancid skin and bone, then the bodies began to drag themselves up after him. He knew they'd make it all the way upstairs eventually; it was inevitable. He breathlessly scrambled up the next flight to the first floor and peered out of a small window overlooking the back of the hotel. The sun had disappeared, but there was just enough light for him to be able to see the massive scale of what was happening outside. Every inch of space around the hotel was filling with corpses, from the walls of the building right the way back to the boundary fence. And still they came! He craned his neck and saw that the tireless grotesques were continuing to force their way into the hotel grounds, ripping and tearing at others around them, desperate to keep moving towards the living.

Which room was it? Webb ran down the corridor, peeling off layers of stinking clothing as he moved: east wing, first floor . . . it had to be one of these. *Something must have happened to stop Jas bringing the others up here,* he thought as he yanked door after door open. Empty. Empty. *Empty—*

He began to doubt himself. Was it definitely on this floor? Jas wouldn't have used the ground floor, would he?

Jesus Christ, they were already here! The corpses at the front of the crowd had managed to drag themselves up onto the first floor – had the racket he'd made yanking doors open and slamming them shut made them move even faster? Struggling to contain his panic, soaked through with cold sweat, Webb watched as the first cadaver slowly hauled itself off the last step and began to move down the corridor towards him. It was followed by an incalculable number of creatures. *Were these things ever human?* he asked himself.

In the disappearing light the creature in front looked like little more than a skeleton covered with the most meagre layer of dripping flesh. It was naked, save for a few remaining scraps of cloth which hung around its neck and waist, and every step it took caused it more damage. And yet it stared at him with cold, black eyes, and it moved towards him with unquestionable intent.

Room 18 – empty.

Room 19 – empty.

Webb looked up again: the dead were coming along the corridor from both directions now. That meant that both staircases were blocked solid with bodies. That meant there was no way out.

Room 20 – empty.

Room 21 – empty.

A sudden increase in the speed of the corpse to his right distracted him: the cadaver leading the pack had fallen, and though it had immediately tried to get up again, it had been crushed by the feet of the many others following close behind.

Room 24 – found it!

With huge relief he pulled the door open to reveal a stack of boxes at the far end of the room: Jas' secret store. Incredibly, he was the only one there. He waited out in the corridor for a few more seconds, knowing that it might be weeks before he emerged from this cramped little hotel bedroom again, then, with the nearest bodies just a few yards away on either side, he took a deep breath and went in to Jas' sanctuary, immediately shutting, locking and dead-bolting the door behind him. He'd not even managed to get the chain on before they were banging and hammering on the wall and door, baying for his blood.

His heart racing, he looked around and eye eyes alighted on one more extra precaution: he dragged the heavy wardrobe over to the door to wedge it shut. That would be enough to stop the dead – or anyone else – from getting in.

Webb leant back against the wall and began to weep with relief. *Thank God no one else can see me*, he thought as he wiped the tears away. He started to sob, but then he put his hand over his mouth to stop the noise. He sank to the ground.

I can't let them hear me. I have to be completely silent. If I sit here and wait in silence, they'll start to disappear. I can't let them hear me . . .

Webb finally lifted his head and looked around the L-shaped hotel room. So where was the rest of the food? He got up and tiptoed over to the pile of three boxes he'd seen from the door: it turned out to be the only pile. But Jas had stashed loads of stuff up here, hadn't he? So where was it? He'd seen him carrying several loads, and when he'd crept inside to check it out, there'd been loads more than this . . . He opened the top box (trying to be quiet, cringing at the noise of rustling cardboard) and looked inside: some food, some drink, some clothing . . .

He wished the dead out in the corridor would shut up so he could concentrate; it was doing his head in, all their relentless banging on the door and the muffled sounds of fighting as even more of them filled the first floor and tried to force their way closer to him. There was maybe two week's worth of food here, perhaps a little more if he was careful. What the hell was going on?

Confused, disorientated and scared, Webb tried to make sense of what he'd found. Was this the wrong room? Should he have looked in Room 25? He went back to the top box and this time he spotted a piece of paper, stuck to the front. He picked it up and carried it over to the window, struggling to make out the writing in the twilight gloom. At last he managed to decipher Jas' scrawled handwriting:

Webb, the stuff in the boxes is your share. I put the rest somewhere else.

He sank to the floor under the window and covered his head with his hands. The damn banging outside was getting louder . . .

'I don't think we can get anything else down there,' Gordon announced breathlessly. Jas peered down the stairwell, which had been almost completely filled with furniture.

'Good,' he said, satisfied that they were about as safe as they could be, for now at least. 'We'll keep checking, just to be sure they can't get through.'

'Nothing's going to get through that lot,' Lorna added. 'It's the same at the other end. I don't know how we're ever going to get down either.'

'We'll worry about that later,' Gordon replied. 'I'm in no hurry to leave.'

Jas turned around and walked back down the corridor, meeting Harte and Hollis halfway. As Hollis went in to help Ginnie and Caron, who were busy shifting boxes of supplies, trying to work out exactly what they had and where to store it all, Harte pulled Jas back.

'What's the matter?' he asked, looking around for the new threat.

'Nothing,' Harte answered quickly, his voice quiet, 'I just wanted to say, good idea, you clever bastard.'

Jas shrugged. 'No problem. I could see this coming; that was why I wanted to get away. I did it for myself, really.'

Harte looked at him. 'Thanks, anyway,' he said. 'You might just have saved our lives.'

Jas nodded and walked back into the room. He edged around the bed, stepping over the boxes and bags of food and other supplies to get to the window. He surveyed the devastation outside. He'd never seen so many bodies packed so tightly into a single space. *Maybe the helicopter will come back tomorrow*, he thought. *Maybe I'll try and find a way to get up onto the roof so they can see me. Then again, maybe I just won't bother . . . the harder I try, the more chance there is that everything will get screwed up again.*

He turned around and looked at the people he now found himself trapped with: Harte, Hollis, Lorna, Caron, Gordon, Ginnie, Howard and his dog.

I can't afford to let anyone make any more mistakes. We've got nowhere left to run now.

One month, three weeks, six days and eighteen hours later

Sean walked back towards the hotel, his feet crunching through the late December frost. He felt slightly sick – he had that same sickening feeling in the pit of his stomach that he used to get when he went back to work after a holiday. It had been a long time since he'd felt anything like this. Come to think of it, it had been a long time since he'd felt anything.

Why am I here? He kept asking himself the same question, over and over. It wasn't because he liked the people he'd left behind – all right, some of them were decent enough, but most of them he'd never even have given the time of day to if he'd met them before all of this had happened. So – what? Was he doing this out of some misplaced sense of duty? Maybe he was, or maybe the truth was he just wanted some company. It had been more than seven weeks since he'd last spoken to anyone else. He was lonely. No one should be alone at Christmas.

The streets were relatively clear now, and he was able to move without fear of attack, now the bodies had deteriorated to such an extent that they no longer posed much of a threat. It was hard to think that the remnants of people littering the ground had caused such panic and fear. He looked at them today with pity, but still with some contempt.

For the most part the dead were unable to move now; very few could support their own weight, and the majority had decayed to such a degree that they could do little more than lie there, helpless on the ground, and watch him. The only things that moved were their heads and their clouded eyes. Sean forced himself not to look back at them. Even after all this time it hurt to think that just about everyone he'd ever known and cared about was like this now.

When he'd left the hotel Sean had headed for the canal-side penthouse apartment overlooking the centre of Bromwell that had belonged to his former boss. After disposing of his dead ex-employer and her husband he'd found himself with a relatively safe and secure vantage point eight storeys above the devastation. He'd sat up there and watched the dead. From up there it looked as if the bodies were dragging themselves along the otherwise empty streets looking for help, or maybe a shelter of some kind. Sometimes it disturbed him to think that these pitiful, abhorrent creatures might have retained some thought-processing capacity, perhaps even some level of memory or a degree of self-awareness – what if they'd understood what had happened to them? Were they lying there in the gutters, knowing what they used to be, feeling the constant, gnawing pain of their gradual decay and waiting for the end to finally come?

Sean had parked his car a short distance away from the junction that he, Martin, Howard and Ginnie had blocked with lorries so many weeks ago – that same junction where Webb had made him practise killing the dead; the same junction where he'd sat in a lorry and waited for hours for Webb the day he'd left the hotel, struggling with his conscience and his nerves, wondering whether he should go back to the others or take his chances on his own. He'd been so unsure back then, but his time on his own out in the open had changed him. He was ten times the frightened schoolboy he'd been when he'd first arrived here, terrified of every shadow as he drove up on his scooter in the middle of the night.

He climbed over the bonnet of the first lorry. The vehicles blocking the roads were all still in place, he noticed. That was a good sign. He slid down to the other side, crossed the junction, then forced himself through the narrowest of gaps past the front end of the coach. He began to walk towards the hotel, wondering what kind of reception he'd get when they saw him. Would they be happy to see that he was still alive, or would they turn on him because he'd walked out on them? He hoped they'd understand. He paused for a moment and listened, hoping he'd be able to hear Martin's music, but there was nothing. That didn't mean anything, he decided, not now there was no need to control the dead any longer.

He jogged around the corner and immediately found himself face-to-face with the wreck of the Transit van and, behind it, Driver's bus, which was lying tipped over on one side like a beached whale. His heart sank. What had happened – had anyone been hurt? He climbed up onto the side of the bus and ran along its length. The hotel was visible in the distance, wrapped in a light mist. All around it the ground was covered in a deep grey slush: the remains of thousands of cadavers. The foul mire stretched all the way from the building to the road, but that didn't necessarily mean the people in the hotel hadn't survived, did it?

He wanted to shout out, but he couldn't bring himself to do it. Even after all this time he didn't feel comfortable making any noise out in the open like this.

Though he'd got used to dressing like a human being again, sourcing a large wardrobe from the shops in Bromwell, whenever he spent time out in the open, he reverted to the strong boots and waterproof gear preferred by Webb, Hollis and the others. He was thankful for the protection now as he jumped down onto the road and stepped into the partially-frozen once-human sludge. A paper mask over his mouth and nose did little to diffuse the horrendous smell and his uncertainty increased as his feet sank into almost eighteen inches of liquid decay. He hated walking through this stuff. He knew it was stupid, but he couldn't help thinking there might be something lurking deep under the surface which might somehow have survived and which might be about to grab him and drag him down – a hand attached to a perfectly preserved cadaver, perhaps, buried by chance deep under the foetid remains of hundreds more. Other than the crunching of the thin layer of ice on the surface of the slush, and the sucking and sliding of his boots, the rest of the world was unnaturally silent. He focused on getting to the building up ahead.

'Anyone here?' Sean's voice echoed uncomfortably loudly around the interior of the hotel. He'd reached the main entrance and had managed to force his way in past the barricade of furniture which had been piled up against the front door. His already low expectations sank still further still as he walked through the silent building. The sludge in here was shallower than outside, but it was no easier to navigate – more to the point, it was immediately clear that the corpses had had the run of the hotel. But had the others managed to get away before their shelter had been compromised?

The staircase at the reception end of the west wing was impassable. It had clearly been blocked from above. With suddenly renewed optimism Sean ran the length of the corridor and found that the staircase at the far end of the wing had also been blocked in a similar way. Could someone still be upstairs? He continued through the hotel, working his way through the slime-filled corridor which led to the swimming pool. The glass doors and some of the windows surrounding the pool had been smashed, no doubt by the pressure of the immense invading army of the dead, which had obviously run riot here. The pool itself formed a bizarre and noxious centrepiece, piled high with bodies which had stumbled into the water and been unable to get back out.

Sean worked his way around the side of the building, looking up at the many bedroom windows.

'Hello!' he shouted. 'Hello! Is anyone there?'

One first-floor window was open and he moved towards it as quickly as he could, not daring to run and risk slipping over into the germ-ridden tide of liquefied flesh around him. When he was almost directly underneath the window he risked shouting again, 'Can you hear me? Is anyone there?'

There was no response, and he was about to continue further around when he noticed a pile of mattresses on the ground. Whoever had survived the taking of the hotel by the dead, he decided, had managed to get away. He stared up at the window again and wondered who'd been trapped up there: Webb, Gordon, Caron or Martin Priest, maybe? Howard or Hollis? Lorna? Jas? What about Howard's dog?

I guess it doesn't matter now. They're probably long gone.

He headed back inside, to continue searching, just in case, and discovered that unlike the west side, the east staircases were relatively clear: though it was still soaked with the putrefied remains of hundreds of bodies, it was passable. The entire east wing was ghostly-silent, save for the steady dripping of decayed flesh as it trickled down the stairs. He started at the top floor, not expecting to find anything, but determined to check all the same, but if anyone had been trapped up here, he thought logically, surely they'd have tried barricading the access points too? He opened a couple of doors, but the rooms were empty – then he stopped when he remembered that Driver and his germs had been quarantined up here. He walked back down the stairs to the floor below and shouted out again, listening to the way his voice eerily echoed across the empty first-floor landing, wishing that someone – *anyone* – would answer back. Christ, he suddenly felt desperately lonely; he'd expected to find the others here, and the fact that they'd gone hit him hard. If he'd stayed, he could have gone with them. He hadn't realised how much he'd been craving company until it was clear that he was on his own and it was going to stay that way. He continued back down to the ground floor.

Sean readied himself to leave. He called out a few more times, but he knew it was pointless. There was nothing to stay here for.

In Room 24 East, emaciated, dehydrated and sitting half-dressed in his own waste, Webb leant back against the wall under the window and covered his head with his hands. He wanted the voice outside to go away. Only silence was safe.

Stop! he screamed to himself, too afraid to say the words out loud, *Please stop! You'll bring the bodies back again . . .*

He curled himself into a ball and lay sobbing on the soiled carpet, waiting for the noise outside to disappear, terrified that the banging on the door was about to start again.

The story continues in:

AVTVMN

AFTERMATH

Acknowledgements

This book was originally announced back in 2006, and written shortly thereafter. At the time the previously released *Autumn* books – some published independently, others given away for free – were doing well, a low-budget film adaptation of the first novel had been announced, and everything was moving along nicely. Then things went a little crazy . . . My novel *Hater* was released, Guillermo del Toro became attached to a movie version, and the *Autumn* and *Hater* books were subsequently acquired by Thomas Dunne Books in the US and Gollancz in the UK.

Sounds like a dream come true, doesn't it? It was. It still is.

The only downside was that there were a lot of people waiting expectantly to read this book five years ago, only to have it snatched from them before they'd even seen the cover. So I'd like to publicly apologise and thank them all for waiting. Sorry for the unintentional but unavoidable delay. I hope you (finally) enjoy *Disintegration*.

I also want to thank my family and friends for their continued love and support. Thanks also to Brendan Deneen and all at Thomas Dunne Books, Jo Fletcher and all at Gollancz, John Schoenfelder and Scott Miller.

Finally, thanks to the close-knit community of zombie authors of which I'm proud to be a part, particularly Wayne Simmons and Iain McKinnon, and also to Richard Grundy, Craig Paton, Antony White, Michael Dick, Jack O'Hare, David Naughton-Shires, David Joseph, Daniel Boucher and all the other artists and designers who've contributed to the on-going www.lastoftheliving.net project.